TRUTH OR WOLF

WOLF BROTHERS BOOK #1

ANNE MARSH

WWW.SMARTYPANTSROMANCE.COM

COPYRIGHT

CHAPTER
ONE

~ALICE~

Nudity was an inconvenient but unavoidable part of pack life.

— STEPHENIE MEYER

I hadn't planned on the wolf.

Big and shaggy, with Yeti-worthy fur and paws the size of dinner plates, it rubbed up against the beech tree where I hid an insufficient ten feet above the ground in a deer blind. Unfortunately for my citizen scientist self, the June firefly count was turning out to be more dangerous than anticipated.

Then again, nothing had gone to plan this year, which was why I'd slunk back to Moonlight Valley, Tennessee, a month ago.

There was no hiding my failures in a place as small as Moonlight Valley. Everyone knew Sally Aymes's niece, even if I'd spent eight years away.

I'd imagined returning in a blaze of glory, with a great job and a polished-up image. Instead, I was a scientist-turned-pet-hairdresser, broke, and cleaning out Aunt Sally's ancient trailer.

After losing my scientist job, I had nowhere else to be, and she'd left me her place, her possessions, and her four geriatric cats in her will. I would have preferred to inherit a romantic inn on a beach or vintage jewelry, but I was

1

grateful. Oedipuss, Barack Obameow, Genghis Khat, and Emperor Meowpatine were welcome—if demanding—company.

"Get. Shoo." I pelted the wolf with beech leaves.

Unimpressed, the wolf butted the trunk with its head. My tree refuge shuddered.

I jumped, almost dropping my phone. I had only one bar of service and I was resisting using it. There was, after all, just one option for a critter problem in this small town.

The Boone brothers owned All-Purpose Animal Services and were the local animal whisperers. If you had a problem dog, a problem horse—any kind of four-legged trouble, pest, or roadkill—you hauled it to them or you called them. Sometimes, they'd even pick up the phone and talk to you. Despite their animal-handling talents (or perhaps because of them), they were beastly themselves.

All but Atticus, the older Boone twin and the subject of my secret crush, were named after trucks. After their daddy had picked out his new truck from *Consumer Reports*, he'd bestowed the leftover names on his offspring. Maverick, Knox, Ranger, Mack, Ford, and Rebel had gotten the short end of that naming stick, while Atticus had inherited the family name.

It suited him. Where his brothers were gorgeous, rough, and mostly feral, Atticus looked like the red-haired, ginger-bearded love child of an astrophysicist and a Calvin Klein underwear model. He was a forensic accountant who did math for fun and who had successfully run for county tax assessor in the last election.

Constant and semi-stalkerish observation in high school had confirmed that Atticus was cheerful, smiling, and pleasant—the kind of man who not only held the door for you at the Piggly Wiggly but carried your bags to your car and put the eggs on the back seat. He had the same broad shoulders and muscled build as his cranky, evil twin, but he packaged his goodies in business suits. Atticus was *nice*.

He was also my first crush (and my second, third, and only crush other than a brief but memorable week when I'd binge-watched the animated *Hercules* movie and fallen in lust with a long-haired, cheerful, muscled Hercules singing and leaping around a historically inaccurate wooden ship). Like my animated crush, Atticus Boone was one-hundred-percent hero. He probably slept on a pedestal, the ivory marble kind that museums plopped antique busts of Homer and Odysseus on.

2

I'd been thinking about him for ten years, although I'd planned on at least five additional years of daydreaming and had therefore avoided all things Boone since my return to town a month ago. My crush was safe, it was fun, and it made me happy.

Atticus's identical twin, Ford, looked exactly like him (which was the definition of "identical" after all), except he was perpetually grumpy, with a broody glint in his icy blue eyes. His default expression was stuck on scowl, and he did not like me. The feeling was mutual.

Still in my tree, I ran through my options. I could call my coworker and boss at Vanity Fur Pet Salon, but Sanye and I were both more qualified to wash and curl the wolf than run it off. I could leave a message for county animal control, but it was a department of one, staffed by my third cousin twice removed, Alessandro Aymes, and he was out of town overnight.

Giving in, I called the number. Miraculously, someone picked right up, greeting me with an irritated sigh. This identified the Boone on the other end of the line as Ford.

He was pushy, rude, and arrogant. Being in his company was like biting into an M&M only to discover there'd been a factory malfunction and all you got was a bright candy shell and no chocolate. Pretty on the outside, but entirely disappointing on the inside.

I got straight to business before he could irritate me further. "I have a critter problem."

"I am sure you have a plan to deal with that, Alice." He sounded awfully laconic for my taste, seeing as how I was facing down death-by-hungry-wolf. "A multipoint checklist. A strategy."

"Yeah." I glared at the trees. They were unimpressed by my badass eyeballs. "By calling you. Do you have caller ID? ESP? Is Ranger flying his spy drones again?"

I had no idea how Ford had correctly identified me as his caller, but I did check overhead for a hovering drone. Ford's brother Ranger was notorious for both his love of flying gadgets and his weird boundaries.

Ford sighed gustily. "How do you want me to help you, *Alice*?"

"I'm trapped up a tree. By a wolf. Did you know that there are wolves in the woods between my trailer and your family place? Because I did not, and it's put a serious crimp in my plans for the evening."

Muffled cursing ensued. Part of me suggested that hanging up in outrage was a suitable next step, but mostly I wanted someone to fix this problem

3

fast, and I'd empty my depleted checking account to acquire Ford Boone's help.

He finally ran out of swear words. "A wolf? What color?"

"Does knowing the color change your strategy?" I leaned over the edge of the blind and double-checked that my lupine nemesis was still down there. Spoiler: it was. "Brown. Black muzzle. Can you please help me? And I'd like the local discount, please."

While I strongly believed in paying my way, I was also a fan of coupons and secret discount codes. This correlated strongly with my broke state.

Ford digested, then asked, "Are you cheaping out on this rescue?"

"You know what? If I'm paying, send Atticus. I think I should get to pick my white knight."

This demand bought me additional silence. Ford's business skills were terrible.

"Sit tight," he said gruffly before hanging up without pleasantries.

I alternated between staring at the wolf—which showed no signs of leaving —and the bushes where the fireflies were coming out in cheerful swarms. Each time they flashed into view, I made a mark in my journal with my orange pen. I might as well do what I'd come out here to do while I waited. After all, science was important.

Firefly Watch was a citizen science project, monitoring firefly populations in North America. Since I firmly believed the world needed more fireflies rather than fewer, I participated whenever I was in Moonlight Valley.

Less interested in science and firefly counts, the wolf hung out at the base of the tree. Periodically, it cocked an ear in my direction. Once, it peed on the tree trunk.

An eternity and two hundred fourteen distinct firefly flashes later, a diesel pickup truck rumbled up the road. It stopped out of sight and then a big, burly man strode through the trees toward my blind. I didn't know what the proper wolf-scaring equipment looked like, but he was disturbingly empty-handed.

He wore steel-toed work boots and faded blue jeans that clung to powerful thighs and an impressive bulge in a place I had no business staring at. I'd hired him to do a job, a critter-scaring job. Nevertheless, the way he filled out his company T-shirt was hard not to notice.

Atticus usually wore suits, but this more casual look was surprisingly attractive. I shamelessly ogled as he stopped near my tree, hands on his hips. The wolf yawned, less impressed.

The wolf's teeth were far more scary than Atticus's.

Atticus sighed and herded the wolf toward the bushes. I couldn't catch what he said, but it involved some impressive male growling sounds.

An unexpected heat spread through my body, a delicious prickle of sexual awareness that I had experienced in exactly never. Where some people went zero to sixty on the attraction-o-meter, it took me the better part of a millennium. I took my time when it came to sex.

Wet cracking sounds filled the clearing.

This was when I realized I didn't want the wolf dead. Merely away. Possibly exiled to Siberia or Timbuktu. "Don't you dare kill it, Atticus Boone!"

"Are you sure?" he yelled back.

"Yes!" I bellowed. Alive but gone was a simple but elegant plan, one the wolf shouldn't resist too hard. Plus, weren't wolves an endangered species? Singlehandedly destroying an ecosystem wasn't part of my master plan.

"I will take that under advisement," he snapped. "But this particular wolf is asking for it."

The wolf yipped and then there was a whole lot of commotion. Was Atticus wrestling with the animal like the Tennessee version of Crocodile Dundee?

I leaned out of the blind, trying to see Atticus past the blind, the tree, and the bushes, and I spotted not one but two Boone brothers staring up at me.

Only one of them was wearing clothes.

"Rebel Boone, put some pants on," I hollered down because the youngest Boone was pure trouble and I already had my hands full with my crush on his brother. Seeing Rebel naked as a blue jay was disconcerting.

Rebel caroled out an apology. He sounded mighty happy about his undressed state, a happiness surely fueled by the whiskey fumes wafting up to me. Atticus pointed in the direction of the truck and barked out an order.

As Rebel loped away, I realized we were missing more than his pants.

"Where is the wolf?"

"Gone," my rescuer said.

I would have appreciated additional details—for instance, was the wolf *gone* gone or was he lurking nearby, tucked behind a beech tree and making plans for a scientist snack the minute Atticus left? I leaned farther out to look for it, putting all of my weight on the edge of the blind.

The wood was old and damp. Termites had taken up residence, causing serious structural damage. My elbows sank into the wood, I lost my balance, and then I was hurtling toward the forest floor.

Atticus caught me.

Holy moly, he *caught me.*

He snatched me out of the air and cradled me against his broad chest like I was the heroine in a movie. I was touching *Atticus.* His gaze trapped mine, blue eyes glowing with inexplicable emotion as he kept me from crash-landing on the hard, unforgiving ground. My imagination rioted.

He looked like a muscled, horse-riding English duke with powerful biceps. Or a lumberjack! Big and broad, muscled from all that ax-swinging. Being held by him was amazing, better than anything I'd ever imagined. Perhaps avoiding him for the last month had been a mistake.

He frowned down at me, clearly less affected. "Alice."

Deep and strong, confident and authoritative, his voice washed over me. My heart banged around inside my rib cage as if my insides had turned into a gigantic bouncy house—up, down, knocked sideways on my butt.

Steely eyes examined my face, likely assessing my lopsided bun and the tree sap decorating my cheek, and his frown deepened. I should have said something, but my face felt like it was on fire. Plus, my bun picked that moment to mostly unravel and flop over my face.

God, I was hopeless at dating.

I wanted to insist he put me down, but who was I to demand he not act the white knight? I felt like I could burrow inside him, lose myself in his heat and strength.

This was silly. Atticus was a person, not some celestial god (despite my adolescent conclusions). He had two arms and two legs like everyone I knew, plus that amazing beard.

He also has a penis, a naughty voice in my head whispered; it'd been a *really* long time since I'd seen one firsthand.

Atticus muttered something and set my feet on the ground. What he said, I had no idea, because one of my favorite fantasies was playing in my head—the one where the Duke of Boone came striding through the heather, cloak billowing around him, a man whose mission was to find me and offer himself (his penis, his heart, and his centuries-old estate) up on a silver platter—and therefore my focusing skills were poor.

"I'm okay," I said-guessed.

That must have been the correct response because, sadly, he slid his arm away and stepped backward. I swayed toward him in an embarrassing moment of weakness.

His gaze swept down my body, his blue eyes intense, full of an interest I hadn't spotted there before. Was he checking for injuries? Wolf damage? His motive seemed more personal than our previous interactions, and that had me regretting tonight's sartorial choices.

When I'd headed out earlier to count fireflies, I'd thrown on my favorite citizen scientist T-shirt. Embroidered fireflies spotted my chest, charmingly cute but hopelessly unsophisticated and unsexy. If I'd allowed for encountering the object of my high school crush out here in the Tennessee woods, I would have chosen better than ancient jeans, a baggy T-shirt large enough for two, and eau de bug spray.

"Why are you out here in the woods, Alice? Are you officially becoming a hermit? Giving up on us in Moonlight Valley to play house in the woods?" The growly, concerned note in his voice made something quiver—*quiver*—inside me.

This wasn't the vague crush I'd felt whenever I'd spotted him passing through my life before. This wasn't me crushing on the captain of the high school math team.

This was far more specific.

It was lusty and fiery and I itched to bullet journal the parts of him that I wanted to explore.

"Science," I blurted out, waving an arm toward the creek that meandered through the woods and provided all the standing water a firefly could want. "I'm out here doing science. Counting fireflies."

His deep chuckle plucked on my stomach and parts lower. And then big, calloused fingers gently closed around my arm as he steadied me. "So you are a big fan of citizen science?"

Warmth spread through me. This was awesome. We had something in common—a shared love of fireflies and public participation in scientific research. We could find other things in common, like my appreciation for his fine form or the way his fingers loosely braceleted my upper arm and brushed my skin.

"The program is really important," I babbled. "It's tough to find a mate when you're a firefly: you're literally shooting in the dark."

He nodded solemnly. "No pickup lines, just flashing."

That sounded…dirty. And also scientifically accurate. We contemplated the mating habits of fireflies for a moment in silence.

"Who would've thought the woods was one big pickup scene, right?"

He looked at me.

Yep, I officially had zero cool.

I wanted to say something funny or interesting, but I would have needed to draft out that speech in my journal. This was why I hadn't anticipated approaching the object of my crush for another five years. It would take me that long to come up with a good plan.

He was annoyingly attractive, standing there in his All-Purpose Animal Services T-shirt, plain white letters on navy-blue cotton, with nary an embroidered critter in sight. I couldn't stop looking at him, and it made me want to… do *things*.

I hadn't dated much, hadn't ever quite understood why two people would meet and then move right to ripping each other's clothes off, but it suddenly made sense. I imagined peeling his boring T-shirt off his body like the candy wrapper on a delicious Ferrero Rocher confection, and heat flooded my body.

His gaze dropped to my mouth.

That was… That was… I was pretty sure he was signaling that he was having kissing thoughts. Or maybe I had leftover dinner or tree sap stuck to my lower lip.

This wasn't like me. I'd worshipped Atticus Boone from afar with a chaste if passionate devotion. My sudden intense attraction to his muscly biceps in that ridiculously plain T-shirt made no sense!

Fireflies emitted pheromones to attract appropriate mates to make baby fireflies. Perhaps I was similarly affected. Or maybe the Boone brothers emitted their own brand of chemical attraction? The majority of Moonlight Valley's single women had remarked on their good looks and stalked them through the Piggly Wiggly's produce section.

I mustered my remaining dignity (which wasn't much). "Let me know how much I owe you. I'll write you a check. Or Venmo you."

A brief head shake. "We are all good."

"That seems like a bad business proposition for you." Not that I wasn't reluctantly grateful—the upside to being broke was that I had gratitude on tap —but I didn't want to take advantage of him. Not like that.

Another, more disapproving head shake. "Where is your car? How did you get here?"

"I walked." Gas wasn't cheap, and the exercise was good for me.

"I'll drive you home." He reached over and took my hand, pulling me away from the tree in a smooth move. "You can catch me up on what you've been doing since you returned to town."

"I'm not here for long," I babbled. "I'm relocating to Nashville."

Atticus grunted. Spoiler: it was not a sound of shock and dismay.

I was vaguely disappointed. I'd seen various Boone bachelors at a distance, including him, around town in the two weeks I'd been back. I'd also heard the gossip about their doings.

All six brothers remained single, which ranked up there as one of the Wonders of the World. Since Moonlight Valley was a small town, many details about their comings and goings (and sexual shenanigans) had been shared with me.

It was therefore safe to say I knew a lot about the Boones.

Possibly (probably) someone had shared my future plans with him. Did he think they were foolish? Whimsical? Deeply disappointing on a personal level?

Oblivious to my social overthinking, Atticus tugged me toward a big, beat-up black Ford, liberally coated in mud. That poor truck had been places.

The sensation of his hand wrapped around mine, however, made it hard to focus on modes of transportation. My body lit up where our fingers touched, flashing urgent, lust-filled messages to my brain.

I loved his casual possession of my hand. He didn't have to stop with a mere palm, fingers, and thumb. He could have the wrist, too. The entire arm. Me.

He didn't pause when we reached his truck. Instead he opened the passenger-side door, a door that was substantially farther from the ground than seemed safe because his truck was lifted on an enormous set of tires. The vehicle looked rugged, ready to run over anything and everything in its path.

I set a foot on the running board, preparing to hoist myself up. My butt brushed Atticus's front, which was closer than I'd realized. He gave a husky groan, then his hands closed on my hips and lifted me effortlessly up into the cab.

Before I had time to really appreciate his strength (or to feel like a professional dancer or an Olympic figure skater), Atticus leaned into me, broad shoulders blocking out the trees and any lurking wildlife. Heated blue eyes with swirls of amber burned into mine. I hadn't realized his eyes weren't pure blue.

Was I supposed to do something? I'd appreciated Atticus's gentlemanly side before. He was the only Boone brother with noticeable manners, which I attributed to God having used up all the charm on this one. Still, if his good manners were the cause of his restraint, this seemed like the right moment to indicate that if he was attracted, I was exponentially more attracted, and we should get on with kissing.

Should I touch him? Keep my hands to myself? Where would they go? My hitherto vague fantasies had not prepared me for this moment.

Atticus braced one big hand on top of the open door. His other hand claimed a spot on the seat beside me. He rubbed a tiny, embroidered firefly on my shoulder. Heat spiked through my body.

He dipped his head toward me. "I like your shirt."

"Me too," I agreed breathlessly.

I'd known Atticus for years, watching him from afar as my peripatetic childhood had taken me to and from Moonlight Valley. In all that time, however, my imagination had never suggested this moment.

In fact, my head had never gone further than coffee or a cold beer at the local bar. Not that I liked beer, but I sure was willing to order one if I ever worked up the courage to ask Atticus out for a drink.

I'd also daydreamed about calm, rational, well-planned dates—like a picnic or paint-your-own pottery. As Atticus was steady and sure, quietly confident without feeling the need to put others down or get angry when they screwed up, we'd have awesome, mature conversations.

About…something. Probably the best way to file our taxes or double-entry bookkeeping. Possibly Atticus's upcoming reelection campaign.

Now, I realized, my fantasies had been safe.

There was nothing *safe* about the man in front of me, his eyes heated and warm, like being this close to me turned him on. He was deliciously danger-ous, and I only hoped the danger was all to my nonexistent virtue.

"Alice Aymes, you keep looking at me." He growled this, sounding more like his evil, grumpy twin than calm, in-control Atticus, leaning into me.

What could I say? I had eyes; I looked. He looked right back. It must have been a trick of the light that made his eyes seem all amber now rather than sapphire-blue as they stared at me, hot and focused. On *me*.

He's looking at me.

This really worked for me, although I wasn't sure what my next step should be.

A ten-minute encounter in the front seat of a borrowed sports car my freshman year of college, some dorm room groping and football game kisses, and then a handful of first dates that had gone nowhere and made me wonder why people hooked up when there were more relaxing options. Long baths, sofa naps, and cleaning out my fridge came to mind. Front seat shenanigans were terra incognita for me.

Fortunately, Atticus had the map.

He leaned all the way into me, and instinct suggested I wrap myself around him and hold on tight in case he had second thoughts about debauching me in his truck. One big hand slid around my waist, warm and heavy. *Yes, please.*

I almost whimpered.

I wanted something, and I was absolutely going to get it.

I'd waited years for this kiss, and now Atticus was finally delivering, inches from my mouth. I wasn't leaving this truck unkissed, that was for sure.

He tugged and I helped, all but throwing myself against his chest, tilting my face up. No fireworks had ever gone off in my body before, but today was clearly my Fourth of July.

Atticus twisted his fingers gently in my hair, fisting the messy length, and went in for a searing kiss. He slammed his mouth down over mine, not holding back. I wriggled against him, trying to fit all of my body against his.

Heat sparked where I pressed against him, cursing the blue jeans and T-shirts that kept us apart, the layers of sensible cotton and the thin barrier of my underwear. He licked and bit and sucked, his lips owning mine in a ruthlessly sensual assault. It felt so good that I opened up and moaned.

His tongue swept inside my mouth and then I learned what a kiss could be.

Because Atticus Boone was kissing the daylights out of me and I loved it.

I was nowhere near done with him when he let go of my mouth, cradling my head between his palms. "Yes?" he asked.

I loved me a good plan, but right now I was living in the moment as much as someone like me could, and my only plan was to emulate Shonda Rimes and say *yes* to everything.

I'd take everything Atticus had to offer—kisses, touches, sex. This would be our baseline sex, the first time, the orgasm by which all others would be judged.

"Yes." My hands grabbed at his shirt. "Take your shirt off now. Now."

11

He gave me a fierce smile and then leaned away, stripping his T-shirt over his head smoothly. It sailed away and I took him in. There was a lot to take in, thank God, baby Jesus, and all the saints of sex.

He was all strong shoulders, sun-kissed skin, and thick slabs of muscles. I couldn't decide whether I wanted to look first or touch first. Or taste. I definitely added *tasting* to my *yes, please* plan.

He, however, was clearly of the *touch, don't look* mindset, because he covered me, caging me with his body, and it felt so perfect I'd have liked to freeze-frame the moment, keep it to take out and remember when life dealt more crap cards my way.

Atticus wasn't taking things slow at all. He kissed me again, shoving my T-shirt up with one hand and releasing my bra. God bless front clasps.

He palmed my breasts, rubbing and pinching the nipples, and that felt even better. Heat tore through me, lust mixing with some other emotion. God, I couldn't believe we were finally, really doing this.

"You are so pretty, sweetheart," he whispered roughly, somehow managing to sound both grumpy and turned on, and I didn't even mind that his hot eyes were focused south of my face. He was finally looking at me, and I was desperately trying to figure out how to speed this up and go straight to the happy ending. "But this isn't our best idea."

He was wrong, and I was happy to prove it. This time, *I* grabbed *him*, dragging his face down to mine and kissing him senseless. Equal opportunity was important.

Plus, I didn't want to stop now that we'd finally gotten going, and from Atticus's hot looks, he shared my sentiments. His big hand went down the back of my panties, cupping my butt, and I about expired on the spot.

The blissful feeling stopped abruptly when he pulled himself away, bracing a big hand on the top of the truck door as he glared at me.

I returned his look, unsure. This detour formed no part of my *yes* plan. Based on the obvious evidence pressed against the front of his blue jeans, he wanted me. Also, he was an amazing kisser.

I was undoubtedly broadcasting these conclusions on my face. His face, on the other hand, broadcast lust mixed with frustration. His breath came hard and fast, more proof that I wasn't alone in these lusty feelings of mine.

He groaned but didn't close the unfortunate distance between us, words tumbling from his mouth as if he had to get them out fast or not at all.

"Alice, I'm not who you think I am, and damn it, I want you—that hasn't changed, and I've felt like that for a long time—but you need to know something—"

This was when my attention abruptly switched from his beautiful, glowering face to a spot over his shoulder. A spot previously filled only by trees and bushes, harmless nature, and fireflies putting out in the hopes of finding a mate.

Now there was a wolf standing there.

No. Not a wolf.

Horrible, wet sounds filled the air, like bones crunching and being origamied into a new and uncomfortable shape. And then, in the place of the wolf, stood a man.

A big, naked man who was the twin of the man who'd kissed me.

My brain froze.

This was scientifically impossible.

There could not be a wolf one moment and a person the next. Science in general—and biology in particular—did not work that way.

"Ford, you son of a biscuit," the naked newcomer growled. "Did you find Rebel and send him home?"

"Goddammit," the man I'd kissed snapped. "Did you shift in front of her, Atticus?"

Revelation was an icy shock. My stomach quivered, sexy feelings fleeing faster than deer stampeded by a predator. I looked carefully at the face of the man who'd kissed me.

Except maybe he *wasn't*. A man, that is.

Because if one brother could change into a wolf, then perhaps the others could. And worse, I seemed to be kissing the wrong twin.

The wrong twin who'd made me feel amazing things.

CHAPTER
TWO
~ALICE~

Werewolves? Oh please, just plain stupid. Who wants to get it on with a man ruled by his inner dog?

— KAREN MARIE MONING

"Y ou're—"

I got the first half of my accusation out, but the direct object stumped me. *A werewolf. Not Atticus.*

One of those conditions was more important than the other, but which?

Ford met my eyes, I'd give him that. But then, none of the Boone brothers were the kind of men who backed down.

He was... He was... I got lost in eyes the warm amber-brown of Toblerone. The feeling was sweet and delicious right now, but, like any candy bar in my possession, I was sure it would be a short-lived kind of pleasure.

I was certain my own eyes were billboards for my emotions. Frustrated lust, horror, and—last, but absolutely not least—incredulity as my scientist brain slowly took over from lust brain and began processing the existence of wolfmen despite all biological evidence and scientific facts to the contrary.

Naked Boone brothers seemed almost as unlikely as werewolves to make an appearance in my life, and yet I'd seen not one but two and a half Boones without so much as a stitch of clothing on them.

Ford frowned and then winced—almost as if he felt my mental withdrawal —and moved away. The muscles in his back flexed and bunched as he reached for the T-shirt he'd discarded at my command and pulled it on.

Atticus strode toward us, and I ducked down to hide. The truck's open door blocked my view of him from the waist down, but I resolutely kept my eyes on his face anyhow. I'd be a gentlelady even if my curiosity killed me.

"Who are you kissing in the truck? Is it Deelie Sue?" Atticus's smooth voice, deep and comforting, flowed over me. A hint of Southern seasoned each syllable, and my heart ached hearing him.

Atticus was the man I wanted. The one I'd dreamed about and yearned for. My rib cage tightened on my internal organs, heralding either a heart attack or a panic attack.

I'd kissed the wrong brother.

While this was not the most humiliating thing that had happened to me, it ranked top three, so I allowed myself ninety seconds to wallow. I squeezed my eyes shut, letting my head sink into the headrest. My stomach lurched.

I did not make mistakes like this. It was like misclassifying a firefly as a crocodile rather than a beetle.

For a brief moment, I fantasized about stealing Ford's truck and driving south. Through Texas, over the border, down Mexico, and along Argentina until I reached the tip of the continent where it was just me and the very treacherous Cape Horn.

If I ran out of gas, I'd detour and take up residence in the Galapagos. Be an island hermit with my ignominy.

Because not only had I kissed the wrong brother, I'd kissed *Deelie Sue's* man. Ford's on-again/off-again girlfriend. She was his hookup buddy and the person who'd dated Ford the most in our small town.

I wasn't sure what the current state of their relationship was, although to give Ford credit, he'd never seemed like the kind of man who'd run around behind a woman's back.

He was blunt, so he knew how to use his words. If he'd wanted to move on, he'd tell you. So almost certainly he and Deelie Sue were broken up (again), but I still hated thinking about it.

Kissing Ford was like impulsively choosing that weird ice cream flavor in the frozen aisle of the grocery store because why not switch things up, getting home, and realizing it would be a week of avocado banana when you could have had chocolate.

I could screw my eyes shut, but there was nothing I could do about my ears, which meant I heard Ford's next words clearly.

"It doesn't matter who I'm kissing, blockhead. Go away." Ford's voice was husky and rough, and his last few words got louder. He must have turned back around to look at me. I did not open my eyes to check.

"Does too matter." The sound Atticus made was neither snort nor growl. More of a polished cluck, I decided. The kind of elegant, concerned noise I'd have expected him to make when he discovered a math error in someone's income taxes.

"Go away," Ford suggested again to his brother.

"Why are you angry about me shifting in front of Deelie Sue? She's one of us."

My citizen scientist brain suggested I should add wolf counting to my firefly tracking. Newsflash: I was up to three. Possibly, four.

"It's not Deelie Sue in the truck," Ford snapped.

Atticus muttered a word I'd never heard him say before. He did not sound happy.

I leaned around the man mountain that was Ford. "Hi."

Atticus's eyes narrowed. "You're kissing Alice Aymes?"

Unfortunately for my lifetime of Atticus fantasies, he did not sound jealous. This was the kind of voice you used when your younger brother reversed your pickup truck into a fire hydrant, leaving visible paint damage.

Mortified heat prickled my face. Gritting my teeth, I acknowledged that Atticus had not been fantasizing about me, but that that didn't mean I was a romantic failure. It was a marketing failure.

Feeling incrementally better, I glared at the two Boone brothers in front of me, my gaze swinging between them. "What is wrong with you?"

They're werewolves, my brain hypothesized again.

Which was impossible.

Wasn't it?

Werewolves were an unknown species. Did it involve the full moon? Did they get hormonal on certain calendar dates? Was I about to become a human-flavored Lunchable for a wolf pack?

Ford made a less smooth, rougher sound. It was so remarkably similar to the other wolfish growls I'd been subjected to tonight that I updated my hypothesis. Because if I was almost certain sure my first wolf of the night had turned into the pantsless Rebel Boone, I knew for certain that Atticus Boone had arrived on four furry legs and shifted into a naked man.

Anger spread through me. I didn't like being made a game of, and someone hadn't been entirely truthful tonight. I glared at Ford Boone.

"Ford Boone, you are a liar."

The man in question swung around and braced one strong arm on the open door of his truck. This produced a stab of heat that I ignored to the best of my abilities. He might have had pretty forearms, but he was an asshole. I'd hated him for years, and one good kiss wouldn't change that.

"Am I?" He sounded pissed.

"I answered that question. Why didn't you tell me you weren't Atticus?"

Where Atticus was smooth and deliberate, Ford was all rough edges and sharp bits. Hateful, rude Ford.

"You assumed I was Atticus. You never asked. Not when I showed up, not when I caught you, not when I put you in my truck, not when I had your mouth underneath mine. Now you want to say I'm not who you wanted."

I hated him. So much.

"You are a *liar*!" I repeated, louder and more emphatically as I tried to drown out the liquid heat swirling in my belly. He didn't get to receive that desire. He didn't *deserve* that desire.

"Welcome home, Alice. You may have learned to kiss while you were gone, but you're as uptight as ever."

I hopped down from his monster truck and slapped a hand against his chest. "You knew I thought you were Atticus."

Atticus sidled off. Negative-thought balloons dive-bombed toward me.

Ford caught my wrists, pulling them over my head as if we were posing for one of those old-school romance covers. All I needed was the big ballgown with an unlaced bodice. Mentally, I might have dressed him in a pirate shirt and a pair of skintight breeches.

His big hands wrapped around mine, making his point clear. He was in charge here, not me. I wriggled anyhow, because manhandling was not actually on my list of sexual fantasies, but he held me firmly in place.

"Things not go according to plan, darling?"

I wriggled more pointedly, but Ford stepped into me, and since he was at least twice as large as me, this meant that his massive trouser snake pressed against my stomach and my breasts rubbed up against him. The pleasant heat swirling around in my belly exploded into an inferno, and I swallowed a moan.

I was not making sexy sounds for Ford Boone. No way, no how. I tilted my head back so I could stare him in the eye.

The effect was less angry than I'd have liked because the man was built like a lumberjack. Or an orc. A big, ugly, rampaging monster who had trampled all over my boundaries. He stared at me, the heat in his eyes less desirous and more contemptuous.

"Why would I kiss you if I could kiss **Atticus**?"

That particular Boone brother emitted a muffled sound. If he'd been one hundred percent the gentleman I'd mentally imagined him to be, he'd have made himself scarce.

"I've got a secret for you, baby girl." The drawled words made me see red. A sea of anger drowned my flutter of sexy desire. I wasn't a get-mad kind of person, but for Ford I'd make an exception. He'd *lied*. About two things, now that I thought about it.

"Are you a werewolf?"

"Why?"

"Because it matters?!" I'd had a long night where nothing had gone right. I had no plan to regroup. I might never regroup. I might spend the rest of my life fulminating about the ways the last hour had gone wrong. Mentally I drew a thick, black line through today's entry in my bullet journal.

Ford dropped a match on the gas can of my wrath. "It doesn't matter."

"ARE YOU A WEREWOLF?" I shouted up at him.

"YES!" he shouted down.

I'd read about people shooting daggers at other people with their eyes. Tonight it made sense. I hated Ford, and if I could have eviscerated him with my eyeballs, I would have. Ford Boone was a werewolf.

Atticus was a werewolf. My brain could not wrap itself around that.

Ford was easier to comprehend. Ford had never been a gentleman or made me daydream about romantic dates with lattes and a shared plate of cinnamon buns. Ford growled and glared. He wasn't a romantic hero—he was an asshole. I'd never once idealized *him*.

Sure, he was objectively as handsome as his suave twin, but all those good looks were eclipsed by his personality. A moon's worth of rudeness blocked any sexy thoughts his rugged face and muscled form might beam my way.

Mostly blocked. Okay, so my whole lunar eclipse analogy was as scientifically unsound as tonight's firefly count was turning out to be.

Because I was under the influence of sex pheromones or something, and I really wanted him to kiss me again. Push me up against his truck, devour my mouth and touch me, and magic away our clothes so that we could get a whole lot closer. I wanted his fingers and penis inside me.

I wanted him.

His blue eyes, now fully amber, glared down at me. They might have glowed in the rapidly gathering dark, focused on me with an almost predatory intensity. Which I guess made sense if he were really a part-time wolf. Or maybe he was a part-time man?

I wondered whether sex between a human girl and a werewolf man was even possible. I wondered whether he had an extra-special expandable penis like I'd read about in an article on wolves and weird animal penises. Plus, I might have fallen down one or two interesting (and sexy) wormholes on Aunt Sally's Kindle where supernatural heroes came with bonus penis accessories.

A girl could hope.

Ford might be an asshole, but his assholery was accessorized by those gorgeous eyes and a pair of shoulders a girl could hang on to. Those shoulders promised he'd block out all the bad things the world tossed my way…and I was horribly tempted to discover whether it was just another empty promise.

"I hate you." I hoped I was as sure as I sounded. It certainly had been a night for challenging my beliefs. "How long have you been a werewolf? Is this a bitten or a born kind of thing?"

My inner scientist was as interested in this man as my inner hussy.

His grip gentled on my wrists. His fingers brushed against mine, his thumb stroking over my palm. I imagined other places he could touch me like that.

He rested his forehead against mine, his eyes staring into mine, and whispered, "Always. I was born this way, and I hate you too, Alice. I hate you most."

His mouth was much closer in this new position. When he exhaled roughly, I felt it; it made me think unfortunately romantic things about how that air had been a piece of him mere seconds before and now I was inhaling him, making him a part of me. Simple respiration and a lack of personal boundaries became sexy times.

I blew out a breath. He could take it back. Ford's eyes might be devastatingly gorgeous, but I didn't need them. Or him. Or anything.

Then he stepped away. His hands let go of mine, and his monster dick no longer made its presence felt against my belly. This was good. I even remembered to bring my arms down and shake them out, as if I hadn't liked being stretched out like a virginal sacrifice. He watched me intently, his mouth twisting into a mocking sneer.

"Do you want to discuss all the ways I'm not like Atticus, or do you want to focus on the one thing we have in common?"

I needed my planner. And my colored pens. This merited a new list. "Obviously, all you two have in common is a last name and werewolfism. He doesn't have to trick me into kissing him."

Ford frowned, a tiny flinch in his facial muscles that was there and gone faster than a firefly flicker. His mouth tightened, his forehead wrinkling with angry lines.

I figured he wasn't about to compliment me on my interest in citizen science, so I marched back to the tree where the blind was, prepared to climb up the ladder and retrieve my bookbag. I'd get my things and leave in a righteous huff.

Except that apparently Atticus had already done that for me while I'd been pressed up against his brother. He held out my bookbag to me. I took it silently. What was there to say?

Atticus must have disagreed because what he said was, "We need to talk."

This was not *Alice, I've made a mistake in not noticing you heretofore* or *Alice, you kissed the wrong brother and the right brother would be me.*

I couldn't help but notice that *talk* really meant *tell Alice what to do*.

There was a beat while we all considered Atticus's words and came to that conclusion.

Ford huffed, a sound better suited to an angry hippopotamus than to a wolf-man. "People can't know about werewolves, Alice. We're a secret."

Did he not consider himself human? Was he part of a whole different species?

"And?" I studied them. It made sense that the Boone brothers had those thick, lush beards. It wasn't a great hair-care routine or a secret fascination with lumberjacks—they were wolves and they had pelts. I hypothesized that the color of a Boone beard matched the color of the wolf's fur. I needed more data points. "Are there other werewolves in Moonlight Valley? Am I living in a town full of werewolves?"

Atticus sighed. "There are a few werewolves in Moonlight Valley."

I couldn't help but notice that last bit: *in Moonlight Valley.* So, were there other werewolves in the state? The country? Was there a werewolf *planet*?

21

"Shifting is a secret," Ford told me pointedly. "And we vowed to keep it that way."

Atticus nodded. There was a gentle sternness in the way his gaze held mine, although the dominant emotion seemed to be disappointment. He hadn't wanted me to find out his big werewolf secret, and now I wasn't handling the great reveal in the way he wanted.

I hesitated, but I had questions. "Is this like a werewolf cult? I'm really good at keeping secrets and my middle name is tolerance. You don't have to worry. I won't tell anyone."

I mean, obviously I *wanted* to. Counting fireflies was important, but proving the existence of werewolves and shape-changing humans was game changing. It unlocked a whole new bonus level in the game of science. I could write a paper. Run studies. I had so many questions that could be answered by a well-designed experiment or six.

And yet... secrecy. *Shoot.* I mean I could understand why the Boone brothers didn't want the whole world to know about their wolfish abilities. They'd have every trophy hunter and government agency banging on their door even if they could also be cover stars for *National Geographic.*

For one weak moment, I let myself fall into old habits and fantasize. Maybe Atticus would offer to marry me in exchange for my silence or, better yet, he'd fall madly in love with me thanks to my gold-medal-level discretion and super team loyalty. We'd exchange vows, have amazing sex, and live happily ever after.

Except...

Except that story felt off. It was like I'd found the pages from a sci-fi romance stuck inside a book about a sexy duke. All I could see was Ford's face. And his mouth. His shoulders. Some parts more south of those amazing cheekbones and collarbones. It was Ford Central inside my brain.

"I won't tell anyone," I assured them both. And then to Ford, because fair was fair: "Send me your bill for taking care of my wolf problem tonight."

And with that I marched off into the woods. I was going to my auntie's trailer, I was going to bed (sadly, alone), and I was going to *embrace* the thought that tomorrow was another day.

* * *

The universe had other plans for me. My first clue was the enormous tree on top of the trailer. It was nice that the air was full of delicious pine tree scent, but there was so much tree everywhere that I could barely make out the algae-stained metal sides of my temporary abode. There did not appear to be a functional roof beneath all that wood.

Think positive, Alice.

For example, *Even though there's a tree on top of my trailer, I accept myself and my anxiety deeply and completely. The cats have miraculously survived.*

Perhaps it was a hallucination. Or I'd taken a wrong turn on my self-righteous march through the Boone brothers' woods and reached the wrong trailer. I liked this theory, but the familiar piles of junk dotting the yard disproved it. Plus, I recognized my car.

"Here, kitty, kitty, kitty." I made the obligatory psps psps noises.

No fabulously evil and dictatorial cat horde appeared.

Please GOD let them not be cat pancakes.

I moved closer as fast as I could. The enormous pine seemed stuck firm to the trailer, but I knew how gravity worked. Plus, shit always rolled downhill. A delicate branch tiara decorated my yellow Beetle. On the other side of my car, I identified the root cause of my problem. *Literal* tree roots fanned out above a gaping hole in the ground where the tree had uprooted itself and fallen over.

Last week's rain loosened the soil, my brain suggested, because there sure hadn't been any tornadoes today. I'd once fallen down the Yahoo black hole and read about a guy who vindictively chainsawed trees so they landed on new construction, but this didn't fit what I saw here, either.

"Saturated soil," announced a voice behind me.

I shrieked and whirled around. Rebel Boone's big, capable hands steadied me then let go as quickly as they'd arrived. He'd discovered his pants since I'd last seen him, which was a silver lining. There had been enough naked Boone brothers in my life already.

"Saturated soil. You have a tree problem."

"I have a cat problem."

"And a roof problem." Rebel had sobered up miraculously fast. I wondered if that was attributable to his werewolf metabolism.

"Grade-A problems all around." I started a mental list of things to do. It was long and I was only halfway through when I swallowed a jaw-cracking yawn. With the sun finally fully down, the welcome chill of a Southern summer night promised that at least I wouldn't spend the next eight hours sweating profusely.

I made more frantic kissy noises, wishing I had the bag of cat treats to shake. The cats required more bribes than a biker gang. Eventually, Emperor Meowpatine popped out from nowhere and wreathed himself around my ankles. The volume and enthusiasm of his greeting confirmed that his food dish had been one of tonight's casualties.

Rebel bent over and said something to Emperor Meowpatine. I'd swear the cat nodded before flouncing off to disappear into the mess of branches.

"Can you talk to them?" I tried not to cry. Tonight had been a series of disasters.

Rebel shrugged, assessing my tree house once more before he disappeared into the woods. Like all the men in my life, he wasn't interested enough to stick around.

I sat down on one of the twenty toilets that decorated the yard. I'd counted fireflies, I'd put Ford in his place, and I'd almost completely forgotten his kiss. *Liar*.

Rather than speculate how my belly went hot and molten from the memories of Ford's mouth devouring mine, I pulled my planner out of my book bag. I'd need to find a tree service and make alternative living arrangements.

Aunt Sally hadn't carried insurance, which was something I was sad/glad about. Sad because I would have welcomed a tree-sized check and glad because that meant one less phone call I had to make.

Recover from natural disaster, I wrote. *Step One: Do not cry hysterically. You cannot afford the tissues.*

Emperor Meowpatine trotted out of the carnage, followed by his posse. I did a quick head count and was relieved to learn that all four cats had survived.

The header on my planner page mocked me. Recovery was the plan, but how? I added a second bullet and waited for inspiration to strike.

I was tired and I wanted nothing more than to crawl into bed, but that bed was under a tree. Maybe I could buy a tent? But where would I pitch it? The small clearing was chock full of Aunt Sally's stuff, and the tree had only spread the mess around.

It was summer, so it was just starting to get on for pitch black, but I liked to be inside and locked up tight before it got dark. I carefully redirected my thoughts away from the reasons why I disliked the dark so much.

I removed the branch and reversed my car, as far as I could get it from the treetastrophe. The Beetle seemed unscathed, if full of pine needles. It smelled better than it ever had, to be honest, like Christmas or a really amazing candle.

On the downside, my fuel-efficient car was small. If I'd known I'd end up sleeping in it, I would've bought a monster SUV.

I debated the tiny backseat versus putting the front passenger seat down. This was a case where inches mattered, and I felt too much like the last piece of pie under a cloche. Car-sleeping was an invitation to be visited by the local wildlife.

Which, apparently, included werewolves.

Engine sounds returned me to my present dilemma and I looked over to see Ranger driving his ATV around Aunt Sally's toilet decorations. The third Boone brother had hazel eyes that regarded me seriously from beneath his mop of shaggy brown hair.

He jerked a thumb at the trailer attached to the ATV. It held a cooler, an empty dog kennel, and a bag of dried cat kibble. "We'll use this."

He got busy removing the kennel and the cat food, setting it all up in a sheltered corner of the yard as an impromptu kitty condo with in-house restaurant. Emperor Meowpatine would approve.

"What?" This was not on my list.

"We'll put the stuff you want to take with you on the trailer. You can't stay here. There's a tree on your bed," he said patiently, as if maybe I hadn't figured out that I had a tree emergency.

I looked around the yard, not sure where to start. I had no front door, thanks to the tree, so I couldn't pop inside and fill up an overnight bag.

Plus, it was high-handed of Ranger to assume he got to make my plans. I'd spent the last few years being independent, and while I might fantasize occasionally about a billionaire sweeping into my life, I understood the value of that independence.

"You don't need to take me anywhere." My anxiety levels rose. "I've got this. I just need a minute."

Ranger grunted, neither confirming nor denying my ambitious statement. Instead, he walked past me with a polite "Excuse me" and confidently inserted himself under the branches. Shifting sounds ensued.

"Is your third cousin twice removed out of town?" he yelled.

"Alessandro is away for the night."

"Aunt Sally's family? Your momma?" Ranger was clearly taking the roll call of my family connections. He expected there to be someone to help me. It was no secret that the Boone brothers were close.

My family, on the other hand, did better apart. We were loners, independent. Asking for help was a sign of terminal weakness. My parents both worked hundred-hour work weeks, and I hadn't even known that Aunt Sally was sick until I'd received a call from the hospital.

I missed Aunt Sally, even though we'd had a minimal relationship. She'd been soft and tall, with long hair that was half gray, half brown, and she'd worn lots of floral cardigans.

These were superficial details to know about a person, but Aunt Sally had preferred to live alone. She did better with cats than people. I was ashamed I hadn't tried harder to get to know her, although she certainly liked her space.

She and my momma had texted almost daily, mostly cat photos and Minion memes. During the summers I'd spent with her (and my parents upgraded to 120-hour work weeks), we'd been two ships passing in the night, our communication limited to brief nods and smiles like warning lights flashing on the bow.

Ranger grunted again and pulled himself out of the tree. He held out a handful of underwear. A pink flush crawled up his cheeks. "That's all I can reach. Might need to go to Walmart, or you can borrow something up at the house. Do you have a bag?"

"There's no way I can impose like that."

Ranger's pretty face hardened. He'd made up his mind to rescue me and that was that.

Sure enough, he reached around me to tuck my underwear into my book bag. He'd folded it into origami squares.

"It's not imposing. It's neighborly. Plus, we've got plenty of space and you need a roof." He examined the mess that was my trailer. "And four walls and a new door."

I tried not to panic at the mental arithmetic that list sparked. I couldn't afford even the door.

I'd been broke and unemployed before slinking back to Moonlight Valley, and even though I was now gainfully employed, I was still mostly broke. Starting over again would delay my plans to move to Nashville and open my own business.

The tree might have knocked the stuffing out of my trailer, but it hadn't done anything helpful like push my suitcase out into the yard.

I looked halfheartedly through the debris in the yard while Ranger held an animated *pspspsps* conversation with Oedipuss, Barack Obameow, Genghis Khat, and Emperor Meowpatine. I could see how the Boone brothers had earned their reputation as animal whisperers.

Eventually, Ranger slung a denim-covered leg over the ATV, tapping the seat behind him. "You climb on now."

"I can figure something out." I clutched my bookbag closer. "I'll camp. Get a motel."

Ranger stared at me. I could practically hear his thoughts: *But that's impractical. Why would you waste good money when we have an empty bed? Plus, you don't have any money, good or bad. And there's no motel in Moonlight Valley anyhow, only that closed-up B&B. I guess you could camp on the porch there?*

Eventually, he settled for changing the topic. "Aunt Sally was good people."

He said that as if she'd been more than one person. On the one hand, I liked the idea of a plethora of Aunt Sallys, a mysterious, older woman with a hidden side. On the other hand, I wasn't sure how I felt that he'd known her better than I had.

"I don't want to be a bother."

This time his seat pat was downright irritated. "It's not a problem."

When he put it that way... Oh, who was I kidding? My options were car camping, spending the money I'd saved to start my business on an overpriced hotel, or staying with the Boones. Awkwardness ensued as I fit myself into the tiny space behind Ranger. He'd definitely misjudged the size of my behind relative to his own. Eventually, though, I was on.

"You hold tight now."

Ranger Boone was a bossy one, that was for sure. I wanted to ask him if he was an alpha wolf, or if that honor went to Maverick because he was the oldest Boone. Or maybe they took turns?

Were American wolves more democratic than the admittedly fictional wolves I'd read about in books? Maybe they voted or got along and nobody bossed anybody about. I slid my arms around Ranger's stocky frame, examining the possibilities in my head.

Ranger took off more sedately than he'd arrived.

"Wait." I glanced over my shoulder at my feline entourage, who had gathered to see us off. "You think they're okay?"

They'd already had a shock, what with the tree coming down on them. Leaving them seemed wrong, even if they were indoor/outdoor cats and I no longer had an indoors to offer them.

Ranger nodded. "Cats have a righting reflex."

"What?"

"Righting reflex. Means they'll turn in the air if they fall. Land on their feet."

Not for the first time, I wished I were a cat.

* * *

It was a good thing that I knew for a fact that the Boone brothers weren't serial killers or criminals.

Ranger took us down yet another tree-lined, dirt trail that was seriously lacking in natural light. The ATV was too loud for easy conversation, plus I was talked out for the night. I wanted to lie down on clean sheets, with a good pillow and a roof.

Ranger's solicitude for my cat clan was surprising. Here was a guy who changed into a wolf (presumably) and who dealt with other people's animal problems for a living. A surprising number of people paid them well to run off a raccoon that had moved into their attic or to relocate moles and mice from their yards.

According to Alessandro, the Boone brothers got called to deal with whatever local animal control couldn't get to. He'd made it sound like the Boones got his leftover business, but I wondered.

I spent the first ninety seconds of the ride failing to solve my housing dilemma. The rest of the time, I wasted on trying and failing to forget what it had felt like to kiss Ford Boone.

Unlike the men I had kissed before—an admittedly small sample set—he not only knew what to do with his mouth and his tongue, but he was into it in the best of ways. I almost felt bad that I'd compared him to his brother.

I had not yet succeeded in forgetting Ford when we pulled up in front of the Boone place. The sheer size of the Gothic-looking Southern mansion always surprised me. The number of Boone brothers seemed directly proportional to its immensity, and I wouldn't have put it past their daddy, Darrell Boone, to keep making boys until he'd had enough for a landscaping crew.

Ranger turned the ATV off and I stared up at the house. Each of the three floors had a covered balcony or veranda, outlined with fancy white railings. Baskets of pink begonias and green ferns hung from the porch ceilings. The Boone brothers did not shy from high maintenance.

Outbuildings for All-Purpose Animal Services clustered behind the main house, along with a number of small cottages and cabins. A live oak alley stretched away from the front of the main house, forming a tunnel of silvery leaves in the moonlight.

"I thought you might like the guesthouse." Ranger nodded his head in the direction of one of the small cabins tucked into the trees.

There was really only one thing to say. "Okay."

I thought of a second thing, an awkward moment later, although Ranger had already hopped off the ATV, grabbed my things, and started toward the nearest cabin. "Thank you."

I followed close on his heels because it was really, *really* dark now. I had hated the dark ever since an unfortunate incident when I'd been five, when my parents had miscommunicated about who was on childcare duty and left me alone overnight. It was not a childhood memory I cared to recall, although it had made an impact on me.

Therefore, I accidentally trod on Ranger's heels when he came to a sudden stop in front of one of the cottages. He grunted.

"I use this when I need some space, but you can have it. I'll let my brothers know you're staying with us. There's a party down at the lake."

He set my things on the cottage's tiny porch and strode off downhill toward the aforementioned lake, leaving me alone in the dark.

My heartbeat promptly escalated like popcorn popping in a pan. This was graduate-level social skills, but I needed the remedial class. If I followed Ranger down there, would it seem like stalking? Or trying to crash their party?

And was I worried about Atticus's good opinion...or Ford's?

An animal howled nearby, followed by rustling sounds. It might have been a wolf. Or a rabid opossum. That bear I'd been so worried about running into while camping in my car.

An unpleasant sound jumped out of my mouth, half curse, half fright. A screech owl yodeled overhead, dipping low enough that the wings stirred the air near my head.

It was at this point that I remembered that no one had answered my questions yet about werewolves. I was pretty sure wolves were carnivorous, so was I even safe?

29

I did *not* want to be alone in the dark in the woods in the middle of nowhere. Were there other werewolves running around Moonlight Valley? What if I was the only human here?

I tried to remember what Ford had told me about his lycanthropy problem, but I'd been shocked and he'd been stingy with the details. He'd been born this way, but he hadn't explicitly said that one good bite (or bad, depending on your point of view) could transform you into a wolf. What if the woods were full of hungry, bitey werewolves?

Somehow the fear in my head transmitted its panicked feeling to my feet and then I was launching myself down the grassy slope toward the waiting lake. Those traitorous chicken feet picked up speed, ignoring my brain's commands to *stop it, right now*. No. No no nooooo.

That scream ricocheting off the dark trees was mine, but I had no time to be embarrassed about that undignified loss of control because if I missed my footing now I'd slide downhill on my face. The lake rose up to meet me, or possibly it was the bowels of hell.

I could actually see flames dancing on the black surface, and a second scream built in me. But right before I launched into the watery depths, something hard snaked out and wrapped around my middle.

I bucked like a wild thing, trying to smash my head backward. My head was hard; it would do as a weapon. I clawed at the steel band squeezing my waist and realized my captor was human.

"Stop it." I half recognized that husky, male voice. It belonged to a Boone all right, although I wasn't sure if the speaker was Atticus or Ford. This did not reflect well on me. When I ignored his order in favor of continued wriggling, he hoisted me off my feet.

I hung there in the air, back pressed to his front, his arm squeezing my middle gently. It was not a dignified position, which helped enormously with my Boone identification—

"Ford?"

My captor froze, and then he lowered his arm, carefully setting me on my feet. His big hands found my shoulders, turning me around to face him. He was a dark shadow in the moonlight, shaggy hair spilling around the hard planes of his face.

"Alice?" His thumb brushed over my skin where my T-shirt had slipped to the side. "Alice Aymes?"

"We meet again." Relief rushed through my body. Ford might be a wolf, but he was the wolf I knew, and despite his tricking me into kissing him earlier, I somehow knew he was safe. He wouldn't hurt me. The only thing I was in danger of was dying from unrequited lust.

"Are you okay? Did someone scare you?" Concern flooded his voice.

His sympathy melted the stubborn plug I was keeping on my emotions and I panic-freaked, lunging forward to bury my face against his throat.

Huffing the man like a perfume sample in Macy's was poor manners, but my prior plan to avoid him was scuttled now anyhow. I'd been thinking about him since we'd parted ways earlier and now I needed him to hold me. Did I care if he wasn't really into me or if I'd been merely a convenient mouth to kiss? No, no, I did not.

"There's a tree on top of Aunt Sally's trailer and now I have so much to do that I'm not sure where to start." Fall-running down his stupid hill was an excellent analogy for everything else I was feeling. My life was out of control and the odds of a catastrophic landing were high.

Ford gave good comfort. He rubbed my T-shirt–covered spine with one big hand, while the other threaded through my hair and cupped the back of my head. He made the best human-sized anchor ever. "You're gonna be okay, Alice. I promise."

I sagged against him. My muscles had done enough work for today and they deserved a break. "Thank you, Ford."

The hand rubbing me stopped. "Alice, I'm not Ford, darling girl. I'm Atticus."

I didn't know if I was disappointed or relieved.

CHAPTER

THREE

~ FORD ~

The wolf stands on its hind legs, places its forelegs on the scientist's shoulders, and places its jaws around the scientist's head. This is just the wolf's way of being friendly. If you're an animal who doesn't know how to talk, a very clear signal is communicated: "See my teeth? Feel them? I could hurt you, I really could. But I won't. I like you."

— CARL SAGAN

The day I'd fallen for Alice Aymes had stuck with me.

Even though her presence in Moonlight Valley had been transitory over the years, like a comet that made an appearance only every ten years (or summers), she'd made an impression that no amount of time could dull. I'd always had feelings for Alice, feelings that made me desperate to hold onto her, to convince her to stay here with me.

I'd been seventeen, a whole year older than her. She'd been sitting under a tree, so intent on writing something with a strawberry-scented pen that she hadn't heard me coming.

The focusing had given her forehead a cute little pucker and tiny curls of her brown hair were busy escaping from a complicated knot. She smelled like body lotion and peonies, sweet and soft.

I never had liked being ignored, so I'd reached down over her shoulder, snagged the pen, and written my name into her…journal. Notebook. Thing.

There'd been no fathoming those grid-covered pages with their overabundance of boxes and circles, checks, and X marks. Lists? Maybe. A collection of lists that was in serious danger of disappearing underneath an avalanche of stickers.

I'd planned on asking her out for a date, maybe after pointing out that now I was atop her list. Number one. Someone she should make time for. Instead of smiling up at me, however, she glared, her dislike for my presence clear.

She'd pressed her lips together. "You just added yourself to my grocery list, Ford Boone."

I'd squinted. Sure enough, my name had topped a list of salad fixings and paper towels.

"That won't do."

I'd twitched the notebook out of her hand, flipped the page, and written myself into a blank space. To make my intentions perfectly clear, I'd added myself as number one on that list—and then numbers two, three, four, and five because I'd been making a point.

Then I'd returned the notebook because even at seventeen, I'd figured out that being a gentleman trumped being a villain. Look at Atticus.

"No," she'd snapped. Reaching into a strawberry-covered box by her side, she'd peeled a sticker off a sheet and slapped it over my name. Then she'd flipped the page and done the same to my name on her grocery list.

My knees had bumped her shoulder. "I'm gonna have to do it again."

"No way." She'd jumped up, hugging her notebook to her chest, and bolted. My wolf had whined with excitement: **CHASE HER!**

Of course I'd listened and of course I'd gone after her—and of course it hadn't taken me much more than seconds to catch her. My legs were longer, and I was more determined.

Wrapping an arm around her middle, I'd scooped her up in my arms. It'd felt so good holding her like that that I'd swung her in a circle. I'd never wanted to put her down.

Then don't. Let's keep her.

Alice had not shared my wolf's opinion. "You put me down, Ford Boone! This is not *Clan of the Cave Bear*!"

I'd had no idea what she was on about. Nevertheless, I hadn't been able to stop the smile that tugged at my mouth as I did what she'd ordered. "Yeah? You think you can make me?"

She could, of course. I'd never do anything that upset or scared her, so I'd set her down carefully.

That was my first mistake.

Screwing up already, my wolf had opined.

Turned out, he was right.

She'd poked me in the chest with an accusing finger. "You are a Neanderthal, Ford Boone! This is not some movie where you can cart me around like a barbarian without consequences!"

"No?" To prove my point (and also because I'd hold her any way I could), I scooped her up in my arms again and twirled us both in a lazy circle.

Alice had flailed her arms, torn between holding onto me and pushing me away. It had been cute. Eventually, she'd wrapped her arms around her own chest, making a visible effort to regain her dignity. I preferred her undone and honest, open and giving me hell.

"Down!" she'd ordered again.

I put her down. Again.

She would've made an excellent alpha wolf, except that she wasn't a wolf at all. I knew it, my wolf knew it, even Alice knew it, although to be fair it probably had never crossed her mind that people could shift into furry forms.

Girl is missing out.

I'd ignored my inner wolf. "You gonna go out with me?"

"When hell freezes over." She'd hugged her notebook closer. The laughter on her face said she thought I was teasing, not serious. "We don't like each other. Plus, you're way too bossy."

"Alice, you're the one telling me what to do. Guess that makes you the bossy pants in this relationship."

Disapproval had rolled off her. "You think being bossy is enough. Being bossy *and* having a plan works better."

She's got you there.

She had. I'd told her what to do, what I wanted, and it sure hadn't worked for me. I'd chalked this up to not having a whole lot of practice in the fine art of asking.

Asking made you vulnerable, plus I was a werewolf. We were all about the telling.

Hell, yeah.

35

I'd considered asking her how she would have gone about getting a date with me, but she was already walking away.

It was then that I'd made mistake number two.

I hadn't chased her.

I'd let her walk away, straight out of my life.

It had seemed smart. She hadn't liked me much (or at all), plus she'd been head over heels for my brother. Atticus hadn't wanted to date her, either. He didn't feel the tug that I did when I saw her.

Still, tonight, after riding to Alice's rescue in the deer blind and then catching and kissing her after she fell out of said deer blind, I kept returning to our teenage encounters. Trying to figure out what had changed—or not—between us.

Ordinarily, the lake would have been a good place for quiet contemplation and self-reflection. Right now, however, it was loud. My brothers had built a giant waterslide out of foam pool noodles, tarps, and random odds and ends from our barn. It was an engineering masterpiece, and tonight was its inaugural run.

The event should have been downright exciting, but I was in a bad mood after losing Alice yet again to Atticus, and in a contest he wasn't even actively participating in.

As a result, I was stress-eating barbecue-flavored potato chips from a family-sized bag. It was that or drink, and I was not a drinker. Not after growing up with Darrell Boone for a daddy. My cup wasn't even half full—I'd drunk all the Cheerwine an hour ago.

Usually I'd shift into my wolf and go for a run to clear my head; I loved racing through the Tennessee woods while one-hundred-percent animal. Right now, though, shifting would only remind me of all the reasons I wasn't the right man for Alice Aymes, so I stayed in my human skin.

Ranger showed up with a cooler of his state-famous barbecue before I finished my pity party. The delicious aroma was almost enough to tease me out of my mood. Ranger grilled competitively, and he'd alerted us that he was trying out a new recipe tonight. Mostly I think he wanted to see if he could trick our guests into believing his tofu was chicken.

I was contemplating fetching a plate when I heard a commotion on the hillside between our house and the lake. There was lots of hollering coming from the girls we'd invited over. Only a few of them were shifters, but they screamed right along with whoever was shrieking her way down my hill.

It was annoying. We were apex predators, so unless there was a polar bear or a Siberian tiger shooting toward us, there was no need to fuss.

Deelie Sue was the worst offender, but I'd have bet every dollar in my wallet that she was playing to the crowd because that was what Deelie Sue did and it worked a treat. First she made you like her, then she sold you a vehicle you didn't know you lusted after.

Two years after she'd started at the local used car emporium, she'd bought the place and rebranded it as Wheels of Good Fortune, selling both used and new vehicles. She made excellent money, although she kept that truth on the down low.

People looked at her and saw a smoking-hot blonde who'd been a Miss Tennessee Teen and then Miss Tennessee. Every Moonlight Valley boy plus a few girls had a picture of her sprawled on the hood of a car in a star-spangled bikini. The bikini itself was framed and hung behind her desk.

Underestimating Deelie Sue was costly, but people looked at Deelie Sue in that bikini and decided she was dumb as a brick. Sexy, but dumb. Only later, after she'd sold them an overpriced car they didn't need did they wonder what had happened.

Giving up on my barbecued tofu fantasies, I strode over to Deelie Sue and wrapped her up in a bear hug.

"Knock it off," I whispered into her ear.

She leaned away, her tiara-winning boobs about popping out of her bikini top. She wore a pair of Daisy Duke shorts and suntan oil even though it was dark. Moisturizing was her religion.

"You boys know how to party," she said. I was betting she'd be passing out business cards before long, making new friends and working the room. Beach. Whatever.

Deelie Sue curled up against my chest, laughing. She'd joined me on the Cheerwine wagon as she'd driven a new sports car to the party and she was too practical to risk both her driver's license and her expensive vehicle by engaging in some drunk driving.

I suspected that not hurting other people and obeying the law were a distant third and fourth in the Deelie Sue-verse, but that was not a problem for tonight.

We could take her for a ride, my wolf opined.

Come to think of it, even though my wolf usually suggested banging anyone and everyone, not being terribly discriminate, he did not sound serious.

We're getting old.

I snorted. As if.

It'll be Viagra next. Stories of our glory days. We need to do something we'll be able to remember when our brain cells are failing us faster than our dick.

Deelie Sue would have been amenable. She liked flirting, and we'd been friends with benefits for years. Plus we were both wolves, which meant we loved being skin to skin. Loved that feeling of connection. Nothing said *you're not alone* like having someone else pressed up against you.

Hot damn, YES.

Deelie Sue leaned into me, I leaned back, and then I had an awkward revelation that all this casual leaning might have sent the wrong message. I was not up for sex with Deelie Sue.

I was, in fact, decidedly *down*.

Old.

Old news, rather. Deelie Sue and I had hooked up a number of times over the last five years. I'd told her that I wasn't doing that anymore four months ago. As she'd been busy expanding her used car empire to a second site, I hadn't seen her again until tonight.

I realized I wasn't interested in seeing her tonight, at least not this close up. Accordingly, I tried to remove her gently from my person.

Deelie Sue burrowed into me closer than a tick on a deer.

This was a problem.

Got faith in you.

The lack of interest exhibited by my penis was concerning. It was usually one-hundred-percent go when it came to sex—particularly hot, creative sex. And truth was, I loved sex and I really, really wanted to have more of it.

But sex without feelings wasn't enough, which five years of hooking up with Deelie Sue had proved.

Seeing as how she was also a wolf shifter, it would have been downright convenient if my wolf and I could have fallen for her, but as I'd discovered, there was nothing convenient about feelings at all. Still, I'd kept on hoping I'd fall, so I'd kept on seeing her.

Until this summer.

Until I learned from Alessandro Aymes that his third cousin twice removed had returned to town.

Eventually, I managed to pry Deelie Sue off my person and made my way over to Ranger, who was setting out his barbecue on a folding table. It smelled amazing, despite its being one-hundred-percent vegetarian. Soy grilled up shockingly well.

Ranger gave Deelie Sue side-eye. "Are you all back together?"

No, thank you. We're otherwise engaged, said both my penis and my wolf.

"Nope." My stomach twisted as if I'd gone airborne off the end of the waterslide. "That was wishful thinking."

Ranger nodded. "Good, 'cause you two are not supplementary angles."

Ranger was taking an online geometry class from an Ivy League university and it had colored his thinking. Usually, I had no idea what he was talking about most of the time, but tonight I got it. Deelie Sue and I didn't fit together, not in any of the ways that mattered.

I was about to share that revelation with him when Atticus popped out of the shadows near the bonfire, a woman tucked up against his side.

My wolf started growling because that was Alice Aymes he had his arm wrapped around. I could feel the telltale amber sheen rolling over my eyes as I got madder and madder.

"Headlights," Ranger warned beside me.

"What is she doing?" I'd thought that even though she'd picked out my brother as her fantasy mate, it had been merely a fantasy. Instead, a mighty unpleasant fact stared me in the face.

"She's sleeping in my bed tonight." Ranger tipped his head toward Alice. "She's coming home with me."

My wolf redirected our anger to Ranger. "What do you mean she's coming home with you?"

Ranger stared at me. I hated when he did this because with his big, mathematical brain he saw straight inside me. He added two and two together and accurately deduced that I was jealous.

Alice was gorgeous. She'd been gorgeous as long as I'd known her, which had been for some time, but tonight something had clicked when I'd spotted her up in the blind.

If not now, then when? I'd thought. If I waited any longer, something could happen, and not the kind of something that had her moving to Nashville while I stayed here. I knew from local gossip that she'd recently earned a business degree and had aspirations to open up some kind of boutique in the city.

It wasn't that Alice was the most attractive woman I'd ever laid eyes on.

(She was.) I didn't want to be feeling any of these emotions, but she was inescapable, from her melting brown eyes to the distracting spray of freckles that decorated her cheek, her throat, and the slope of her bosom.

And that was only the outside, the gift wrapping on the important part of Alice. Her insides were even more beautiful.

I hadn't intended to escalate things earlier tonight. I'd planned to fix her wolf problem and then maybe get a kiss. Ask her out on a date. Letting her think that I was Atticus, putting my hands on her, that had all been an impulse.

Usually, I was a big planner. I hated surprises, hated the vulnerability of not knowing how someone would respond to me.

But I'd taken a chance on Alice. Her kiss made me burn. There had been so much heat, a frenzied buzzing of desire that got under my skin and had all my body parts standing to attention. If I'd done a roll call, my heart would have been first in line.

When she'd thought I was Atticus, she'd looked up at me with all the trust in the world. Her Atticus was a hero, someone she outright adored. *It was amazing*.

I wanted her to look at me that way for real, but I'd screwed up big time by not correcting her mistake. I should have stopped her long before the kissing and told her who I was.

I'd planned to have a mature, sensible conversation with her, take care of her wolf problem, and sometime in the not-so-distant future, ask her if she wanted to get a coffee—the fancy kind with a thousand grams of sugar and whipped cream—with me.

Sweeten her up. Make our move.

Uh-huh. That plan was now shot to hell, but I'd gotten my kiss—and I couldn't regret it.

I agree.

The kiss had been amazing, although I sure hadn't enjoyed the way it had ended in her outright rejection of me. She'd *hated* the possibility of kissing me again and even acknowledging I existed. I was not Atticus, she did not want me, and that was *before* she'd discovered that I was a werewolf.

Poor taste in men, my wolf clucked in my head.

I wasn't so sure about that. Sure, Atticus was my brother and I'd always give him what-for, but he was a good guy. The ladies liked him, he had courtly manners, and his ability to add, subtract, and do their taxes won them over.

I was rougher, ruder, and not at all nice, hamburger to Atticus's filet

40

mignon. It was no surprise that she wanted to be a player on Team Atticus, and therefore I should not be thinking about her naked.

I slid another look her way. Atticus had a steadying arm wrapped around her shoulder as she pointedly ignored me.

We should pop him. We can take him.

We're not assaulting my brother. Shut up. My wolf sulked and retreated. I moseyed up to the bonfire and set about ignoring both Alice and Atticus while giving them sidelong glances.

At some point in the evening, one of our lady guests suggested that we play a game and ride doubles down the waterslide. It was like Spin the Bottle, but without the bottle and with a lap dance instead of a kiss. As game premises went, it was compelling enough that we all tromped up the hill and gathered around the top of the waterslide.

It looked a long way down in the dark. I bet I'd feel like a rocket ship heading into the stars when I hit the bottom.

Deelie Sue nudged my arm. "You wanna be my ride, Ford?"

She'd always liked to go fast, and I'd always liked this about her.

I had never been big on going slow. I'd been known to argue that you should always skip to the good part when you could. Alice, however, made me want to go slow, slow, slow because I did not want my shot at her to be over and done with forever.

Deelie Sue ran over and climbed into the starting chute of the waterslide. It was, in fact, a repurposed cattle chute that had come from the rodeo where they'd used it to shoot angry cows into the arena for roping. We were using it to launch ourselves downhill.

"Come on over here, big boy!" Deelie Sue lounged against the top of the slide like a game show model.

News flash: I did not want to go over there.

My gaze shifted to Alice. She'd made her disinterest clear, and yet I wanted to see her reaction.

Surprisingly, she'd peeled her gaze off Atticus and was now glaring at Deelie Sue as if she wanted to push her down the slide. Suddenly, I had a plan.

"I'm all yours," I drawled and started over.

Alice's gaze bounced between me and Deelie Sue. Something flickered in her eyes. Possession, possibly. Jealousy, if I was a lucky wolf. Whatever it was, she hated the idea of me wrapping myself around Deelie Sue like the tortilla on a burrito. Maybe she did care a little about me.

I chewed on that while I toed off my work boots and stripped down to my boxer briefs. Wet jeans were no fun and would make me go slow. My T-shirt came off to the hooting and hollering of the crowd.

Show her what she's missing!

Most of the crowd seemed to be enjoying my show. The ladies—and a couple of the gents—had plenty to say. It ran along the following lines. *Damn, that man is fine* and *Can we look AND touch?* and *Sign me up for that pony ride.*

When I was down to my boxer briefs, I jumped onto the slide, patted my lap, and snuck a peek at Alice.

Her face was Barbie pink, her forehead puckered like she was doing a whole lot of thinking and didn't like her hypothesis. Her eyes were the best part, though, shooting me a hot look that made me glad the night was losing its heat fast and that the slide was clammy wet beneath my backside.

I got Deelie Sue settled between my legs after a brief argument about whether she should straddle my hips and ride me like a cowgirl. I did not think that would be good for her knees, my secret hopes with Alice, or my personal boundaries, so we agreed that I would wrap myself around her and steer us both, while she would keep her body parts off my goodies.

Someone turned on the hose to lube up the slide, and Deelie Sue squealed at the cold. I gritted my teeth and wrapped an arm around her to keep her safe because, sure enough, my brothers' hands shoved at my back and then we were flying down the slide, twisting and turning, the woods a breathtaking blur on either side.

When we hit the bottom of the slide, we flew up into the air, Deelie Sue laughing hard, before gravity took over and we came down, down, down into the lake. The shock of all that cold water pushed us apart, but when I surfaced, Deelie Sue was already swimming for the dock. She hadn't bothered to wait for me.

She pelted up the hill in her wet bikini and I followed almost as fast. It might be summer, but the lake never warmed up much.

"Your turn to pick who you want to ride down with," Ranger announced when I reached the top. Normally he sounded dour and uncheerful. Now, though, he sounded almost happy. It was confusing. Ranger was not someone who was easy to read. "You pick whoever you want to go with, anyone at all."

I knew who my first choice was. My eyes met Alice's, and I readied myself for her rejection. It was a risk, asking her like this.

My wolf perked up. **No pain, no gain**.

"Alice." Her name came out like a growl, soft and rough, as if the distance between us didn't matter at all. "You want to go with me?"

Her eyes narrowed, her pretty lips parting. She was still wearing her cute, if oversized, citizen scientist T-shirt from earlier. I deliberately looked from her to Atticus. I hoped she'd understand that I was demanding she pick between us.

For the record, I would never force her. My brother was a good man, even if he could be an uptight jackass most days of the week. I loved him and I'd respect her choice. I wanted the chance to change her mind. To prove to her that I wasn't the bad brother.

"You come on now." She stabbed a finger at the slide commandingly, as if she were inviting me and not the other way round. Alice liked being in charge as much as I did.

I didn't even try to restrain my smirk. "You got it."

So many sex jokes, my wolf moaned. **Where to begin?**

Again I sauntered over to the slide, and again I got on; this time it was better because it was with her. She was adorably flushed as she followed, unable to hide her anger with me or her embarrassment about the state of my boxer briefs.

I patted my thighs. "Strip and climb on."

Alice gave me a look that said *in your dreams, buddy*. Or maybe that was someone in the crowd. A wolf could dream about naked sliding, right?

Less dreaming, more reality.

"What you see is what you get." Alice waved a hand at herself.

"Fine," I agreed, hiding my enthusiasm for getting Alice in any way, shape, or form. "All aboard."

Her forehead wrinkled as she assessed my lap, and I was deeply grateful for the cold clamminess of my boxer briefs. Then she toed off her hiking boots, climbed gingerly over the side of the chute and knelt between my thighs. I had a moment to be deeply grateful that she'd shed her boots as her feet came perilously close to unmanning me as she tried to find a spot to sit.

Losing patience, I finally set my hands on her waist and flipped her around, planting her butt on top of my boxer-briefs-covered crotch. I didn't want her getting torn up any by the slide.

Atticus slapped me on the shoulder. "You two have fun. Here's to a happy ending."

On top of me, Alice muttered something about this not being *that* type of movie.

I stared up at him and he gave me a slow tip of his head. An amber sheen rolled over his eyes and I realized he was excited for me.

I'd been oblivious not to realize it before. Atticus wasn't interested in Alice, not romantically. Even though she was smart and gorgeous, funny and frighteningly well organized, he wasn't interested in her because he'd understood my feelings before I did.

It made sense. We were twins.

I grinned at him, and he shoved my shoulder. "Ride 'em, cowboy."

His wish, our command.

I wrapped my arms around Alice and held on tight. Atticus shoved us down the slide.

I was never letting go of her.

CHAPTER

FOUR

~ ALICE ~

I don't care for werewolves. They're all right, I guess, if you go for the shedding, savaging the country-side thing. But they're not very scary nor very sexy and so what's the point?

— MAGGIE STIEFVATER

T'd never been a risk taker. Plans were best as I hated unknowns. I was not bold, I loathed being first in line, and I would have totally remained onboard if I'd been part of an explorer's crew. That had to be why my sympathetic nervous system was in overdrive, urging me to run away as I stared at the enormous waterslide and the Boone brother who expected me to climb onto his lap and ride him like a sexy toboggan.

Wanting Ford Boone was not part of my plan, but he was a force of nature. He'd sauntered into my life, introducing previously unknown sexual stimuli, and I'd responded.

And it wasn't only the delicious effects of his touch, his kisses, his body taking up my space, or even the sexy alpha male smirk he deployed my way. No, his sexy stimuli only accounted for a fraction of what consumed me. Forty percent. Maybe twenty. The rest of it was me remembering how we'd never gotten along on any of my previous visits to Moonlight Valley.

Thoughts of Ford so consumed my brain that I had no room for Atticus.

My neural system had removed my romantic (if one-sided) memories of Ford's twin. He'd been erased along with other useless, outdated memories like how to fix a music cassette stuck in a Walkman or to replace the batteries in a pager.

Maybe I'd make new Atticus memories. Maybe this could be a good thing. On the one hand, I'd always known that my feelings for Atticus were one-sided, not fact-based, and of the fantasy sort.

On the other hand, Atticus had always been nice to me. He didn't smirk or argue—he was all smiles with a side of reserve, honest, solid, and as reliable as math or my beloved science. He was Grade-A hero material, and we all knew how love stories ended when a hero got involved. I secretly wanted the fairytale wedding, the castle, and the prince.

But now when I daydreamed, my prince didn't come. Instead, I'd switched to fantasizing about the ogre. When Atticus had caught me, halting my down-hill plummet, and had told me who he was, I'd been *disappointed*. The romantic scene I'd been directing in my head—fate had *literally* cast me into his manly arms!—had cut to black. I hadn't been attracted to him at all.

He hadn't been Ford.

Which was disappointing.

I'd fantasized about Atticus for years, so this sudden switch in my romantic focus should have been cause for concern. Was I shallow? Incapable of committing to one fantasy man? Would this cause problems when it was time to fantasy-commit in my dream fantasy wedding?

Right now, there was no room in my head for fantasy because I was surrounded by a lumberjack-sized, flesh-and-blood man. Half man. I wasn't sure whether werewolves qualified as Homo sapiens. Did they share DNA with us?

I'd read once that the average wolf penis was seven to ten inches long, and from what I could feel, Ford was superhuman in that department. The lake water that had rapidly and unpleasantly transferred from his boxer briefs to my shorts did nothing to dampen our enthusiasm for each other.

Ford had also given Deelie Sue the first ride tonight and, frankly, that was both upsetting and gross. My fantasy men were monogamous and fiercely loyal, so the reality of Ford did not make me happy.

Did I want to be a jealous, angry, petty person because Ford had spent time with a gorgeous and smart woman I admired, who also happened to be his on-again/off-again girlfriend and a terrifying business success?

No, I did not. I firmly believed women should build each other up, not tear each other down. Plus, Ford hadn't made me any promises and I didn't want to have feelings for him. But I did. True, those feelings were mostly unpleasant, akin to having cracked open my ribs and performed open heart surgery on myself. I also wanted to shove Deelie Sue down the slide again.

He'd held her. He'd wrapped his arms around her like he was doing now to me. Obviously Ford was an expert and prolific dater. He'd had lots of practice at it, while I was paddling around in the kiddie pool.

I'd probably overestimated his kissing ability, especially since I'd believed I'd been kissing Atticus. I'd likely projected all of Atticus's wonderful personal qualities onto Ford's mouth. I snuck a peek at his mouth now, to refresh my memory. It was beautiful, in a sensuous, masculine kind of way.

Prior to tonight, I'd never been a big fan of kissing. Kissing required the kind of preparation I put into my dental cleanings with not much more reward. But Ford's mouth had felt right. Hard and gentle at the same time, and I'd leaned into that oxymoron. I'd wanted to eat him up and then have seconds.

I'd thought our audience on the waterslide was bad, but the worst part was yet to come. While I'd been lost in my thoughts, Atticus had stepped up to the side of the slide-chute-deathtrap that Ford and I were sitting in. I half expected him to demand I sign a waiver, but instead he said something to Ford and they shared a moment of twin ESP, secret messages bouncing between them.

Then Ford's arms tightened around me and his mouth brushed my ear. My insides tightened and stood at attention.

"Hold on, baby."

"Wait—"

Staking a claim on my not-man and rising to a challenge were fine, bold acts, but I was also a big fan of living, and I definitely wanted said living to take place outside of the emergency room at the hospital. But Atticus gave Ford an enormous shove and sent us hurtling down the slide.

I screamed like a mashed cat, and Ford chuckled behind me. I had enough oxygen feeding my brain cells to note that if I'd been falling to my death with Atticus, he would have checked in on my mental health and offered statistically based reassurances that all would be well.

As my fantasy Atticus was a superhero, he could have managed all that on our rapid descent down the Waterslide of Death. Ford was simply irritating, even if his arms did pull me closer.

I appreciated that because, oh my GOD, we were flying, shooting off the end of the slide, and for one unforgettable moment we were up in the sky, like E.T. riding his bike or a spaceship hurtling out of a docking bay right as the massive, metal doors closed. It was me, Ford, and the stars. It was magical.

The next moment, of course, gravity took over, and we were plummeting toward the lake, which was going to be full of mud and fish, that slimy weed that always seemed to grow in overabundance, and aquatic salamanders. I yelled louder, wishing there was a way to yell *CUT!* to stop this particular scene. Unladylike cursing might have been involved.

"Hold your breath," Ford ordered.

I wanted to argue with him, but there was no time. Ford hit the water first, pulling me into his body, and then we were under and sinking fast. The world went topsy-turvy, and I had two seconds to regret my poor life choices before Ford propelled us toward the surface.

He hollered happily when we broke through and into wonderful, breathable air. I wrapped myself around him like a baby monkey, my legs crossed behind his back, my arms strangling his neck.

My arms had the right idea.

"We're not dead," I babbled. "This *is* like in the movies."

"Alice…"

Ford rested his forehead against mine. We were so close that I had no problem hearing his whisper despite the hooting and hollering coming from the bonfire. He treaded water effortlessly. His powerful, bare thighs brushed my legs and my backside as he kept us afloat. His boxer briefs were not enough fabric to keep my hotter thoughts at bay.

"What?" I whispered, then shot a wary glance at the slide. "Are we in the landing zone?"

Instead of answering, he backstroked us toward the edge of the lake with lazy, coordinated grace. I cursed myself for the husky moan that came out of my mouth, even though who could blame me? There was a whole lot of wet, muscled Ford stretched out beneath me, and I wanted to explore his big body with my hands.

He stopped short of the shore, though, his feet bumping against the muddy, weed-slick bottom as he stood up. When I tried to wriggle free, his hands caught me gently by the waist.

He blurted, "Alice, can we… I'd like to…?"

He always seemed so together, so sure of himself and his next move. This discombobulated version sounded frustrated and possibly as off-balance as I was.

Or maybe that was the aftereffects of launching ourselves into midair off a homemade waterslide. I couldn't be sure with a sample set of one, but I had no plan to repeat the experiment. I waited for him to add a verb or two to his questions.

Another gleeful pair of adventurers hurtled down the slide, their hollers filling up the silence. They landed with an enormous splash and then swam for the other side of the little beach.

The ripples were still washing against us when Ford shifted beneath me. A moment later I felt him gather me closer. As much as I'd enjoyed using him as my own personal saddle and transportation device, this was also a fine position.

The muscled planes of his stomach were a fingertip away, the delicious warmth of his lake-wet skin warming me up. The heat in me only grew when the hard, beautiful, red-bearded lines of his face bent over mine like we were the stars in a romantic cinematic closeup. It was almost too much, and I flinched away.

Ford let go of me, his hand steadying me as I floundered for a moment, trying to find my footing. I'd forgotten how much I hated the slimy, rock-pitted bottom of a Tennessee lake.

I shrieked, pulling my feet up. My face burned. Partly, I didn't want to be seen as someone who couldn't handle a little alligator weed or milfoil. Mostly, though, I wanted to wrap myself around Ford again and hang onto him.

This was stupid. Doomed to failure. A romantic apocalypse. I wasn't the first girl he'd taken for a ride tonight, and I likely wouldn't be the last. We'd kissed, we'd touched, and he'd put his hand inside my panties, bless my heart.

He'd also made it clear that I argued too much for him, and because I was feeling like a brat, I gave myself permission to *be* one. Temporarily. Before I returned to my responsible, mature adult life.

I smacked the surface of the lake with the flat of my hand, sending a tidal wave of water over Ford's beautiful, arrogant face. It served him right.

"Come here," he growled.

I shivered, mostly because I was cold. The lakes in this part of Tennessee never had gotten the memo that it was summer.

"Get lost." I shoved away, trying not to let my feet touch the bottom. There was pond scum and bacteria invading my body. *Gross.* Worse, it was so dark that I couldn't see below the surface of the lake. Even my hands were almost invisible shadows beneath the water.

"This was a terrible idea," I told him, swallowing lake water.

"I know. You don't like lakes. I'll get you right out, but stop talking for a minute because I need to tell you something."

This was one of the many problems with Ford. He liked to give orders. "Don't tell me what to do."

"Sorry—I shouldn't. It's a habit. I do it too much."

If I hadn't been trying to stay afloat in a disgusting pool of weeds and water, I'd have given some thought to who he ordered around on a regular basis. Was this a boyfriend/girlfriend/*Fifty Shades of Grey* kind of ordering? Or was he alluding to his business practices? Or maybe he had a secret dog-training business that I was unaware of and his commands were all of the canine variety.

"Alice." He caught me firmly around the waist, tucking my back against his front. "Deelie Sue and I aren't seeing each other. We haven't seen each other for months."

I nodded awkwardly, refusing to admit how much his words pleased my inner cavegirl.

He continued, "You and I, we've known each other since we were teenagers."

"This isn't a scene from a reunion movie," I informed him, rather suspiciously.

"What?"

"Sometimes, I like to pretend that I'm on a movie set. That all this"—I waved a hand, accidentally splashing Ford in the process—"is a scene."

"What's your favorite scene?" He sounded genuinely interested.

"It changes." I shrugged. "Tonight, when we went flying off the end of the waterslide, I had myself an E.T. moment—you know the scene where he's riding that bicycle across the night sky? It felt like that. But that's not usually my favorite."

Should I tell him? Confess? I wasn't sure what I wanted to do.

"And when you're not airborne? What's your favorite then?"

Reluctantly, I admitted, "I'm a sucker for that Mr. Darcy scene where he comes tramping over the field, his coat billowing all around him. He's so big and stern and kinda grumpy."

"You're not Team Bingley?" His voice tickled my ear and warmed up parts of me that hadn't finished cooling down from our first encounter today.

I shrugged. "He's a sweetheart, and I'm sure Jane will be very happy."

He inhaled. "Alice—"

Resting against him seemed like a weakness, but he felt so good that I decided I'd tolerate it until he'd finished his speech.

His next words came out fast, as if he'd decided to say everything quickly before he lost his chance. "You didn't like me much when we first met, and I get that I was an ass. But I've grown up. We both have.

"You left Moonlight Valley and you got a college degree. I know you've got a business plan, that you're on your way to doing amazing things. And you're not the same person you were then, any more than I am. I don't want to fight with you."

I blinked lake water from my eyes, trying to discern where he was going with this speech, and noticing—now that we weren't plummeting through the air—how the water reflected the sky overhead. It was dark and beautiful, tiny sparks of ancient starlight dotting the lake's surface. With Ford holding me up, I could see it all.

He kept on doing it, his arms wrapped around me securely, not making a joke out of this or threatening to dunk me. When I didn't say anything, he settled his face against mine. His beard tickled my cheek.

"I'm gonna take your silence as agreement," he whispered, apparently interpreting my stationary, non-swimming status as a sign that I was onboard with his plan to stop fighting. His lips moved against my cheek as he spoke, his beard brushing my skin. The warm sensations that evoked in me made me want to happy laugh—and squirm.

Here I was, treading water in a Tennessee lake with Ford Boone, and we weren't arguing.

I didn't understand what had changed for him. Why he seemed to be choosing...me. Not that there was anything wrong with me, of course, but where I'd always opted for a satisfying fantasy life over dating real people, he'd gone for quantity over quality.

"Ford, you remember our high school days? We disagreed about everything. If I said it was Monday, you insisted it was Tuesday. You didn't pay any attention to facts. You always have to be right, and I don't know if we can get along. We always argue."

"Arguing's not such a bad thing."

See? He was arguing with me. I forbore to point that out, although I really wanted to.

"It absolutely is. You argue about every little thing, even the boring things like what I ate for breakfast and what I read in an online fan forum for Tulum."

"Alice," he whispered, "when we argue, that's me listening to you and you listening right back. I'd never not pay attention to you. I like to know about your day, about what's going on in your head. There's nothing you could think about that I'm not interested in. *You're* the most interesting person I've ever met and I *love* the way *you* think."

If I'd been a firefly, I'd have been flashing a million times a minute. It wasn't so much his insistence that I was a deeply interesting person as the utter sincerity in his voice. Ford didn't seem to mind that I wasn't funny or a good storyteller.

In fact, he seemed to like me—geeky, awkward, argumentative science nerd—exactly as I was. An embarrassing moisture that had nothing to do with the lake water all around us collected in my eyes.

"You love to *argue* with me? You mean like telling me I'm wrong all the time? Why would I think that was a positive?"

His beard brushed my cheek again, the corners of his mouth tugging up with his grin. "You like telling me how wrong I am. Admit it."

The man had a point. I contemplated it while Ford floated us in a lazy circle. Somehow my head had found its way to his shoulder. He was harder than my favorite bath pillow, but also sexier. Warmer.

It occurred to me that while I'd never be convinced that arguing was a relationship feature, it didn't mean that Ford had hated me. Maybe he *had* been respecting my opinions.

"They weren't all bad," I blurted out.

"What weren't?"

"Our fights. You stuck around. You didn't storm away or give me the silent treatment." And now that I realized he hadn't been mad—that his arguing with me had been respect and a weird version of romantic foreplay—I didn't know what to think. "The werewolf thing was unexpected, though."

"I bet it was." The smirk in his voice came through loud and clear.

"How does it work?"

He shrugged. "I can shift when I want, although if I don't shift at full moon, I'll be itchy, break out in hives. My wolf likes to talk my ear off, too."

"He talks to you?"

"All the time."

"What's he saying now?"

"Nothing polite. He likes the way you smell."

I decided not to explore that idea any further. "So you don't eat people."

"Nope."

"Or turn into an inhuman beast that rampages about the countryside?"

"Not yet. Are you disappointed?"

"Can I see?"

He laughed. "Not in the middle of a lake with witnesses, baby girl."

"So it is a secret." I frowned. He'd yelled at Atticus for public shifting earlier today, so it made sense that not all of their party guests were in on it. "Do you have to kill me now that I know?"

His arms tightened. "You're safe. The Wolf Council will never know unless you go making T-shirts or talking to Oprah. It's just something I am."

"Okay, then."

"So we're good?"

"I'm not sure I'm ready to forgive you yet for pretending to be Atticus."

"I'm not sorry." His voice was deep and rich—and apparently connected to my vagina. "I'm not sorry we kissed. I'm not sorry we're here."

"But you *are* sorry for pretending to be your twin brother?"

Ford snorted and strode for the shore. Water sheeted off him like he was a medieval Viking warrior coming ashore to plunder. And while I fully recognized that the historical reality of that scenario was not okay, a small part of me enjoyed the fantasy and directed a brief movie in my head where he strode and plundered and I more than met him halfway.

I was so caught up in this fantasy that it took me longer than it should have to realize that Ford hadn't answered my question. "Ford?"

His feet hit the shore and he tossed me gently over his big shoulder, butt up, hanging down over his back with absolutely no dignity at all. His arms curved around my legs, and my wet hair flopped over my face. The spectacular view of his butt almost but not quite made up for the indignity of his patting my backside with his big palm.

"Brat," he growled.

I pinched his butt. He'd started it.

"You assumed I was Atticus. You didn't ask and I never said."

"You *knew*," I insisted. "I can't believe you."

He sighed and strode toward the hill. "Alice, I need you to listen me."

"Why should I?"

"I want a chance."

"For what?"

"To start over," he growled. "To see you. To see what we could be together."

Was I surprised? Yes.

But it was a chemical reaction, surprise priming me to pay extra attention by releasing norepinephrine in my brain.

It would pass.

I'd stop being surprised and move on to blasé.

Then I realized Ford had paused and set me down.

Then I realized he was waiting for me to give him an answer.

Not that he'd actually *asked* a question. He'd done that alpha wolf thing of barking out a command-slash-desire. Presumably I was supposed to agree.

My gaze bounced down his legs, which were wet and muscled. He had an intriguing dusting of hair that merited exploring. "I'm sorry, you what?"

"I want for us to start over. We're suited for each other."

"You think we're suited?"

"I promise that we're *suited*." He made it sound dirty. "We can do whatever you want. Talk about whatever you want. But I'm taking you out on a date."

"A date."

Awesome. I'd turned into a parrot.

"Friday night football and barbecue, hunting for fireflies along the creek, watch a movie cozied up in the bed of my truck—a date."

"You cuddle?" I needed details about this alleged cuddling agenda.

When he frowned and nodded, I had my first inkling that this could work. Not that I could honestly imagine cuddling with Ford—my imagination was great, but not *that* great.

Okay, so us dating didn't sound *entirely* unpleasant. A tingle of excitement built in me. Or maybe that was the blood rushing into my lower extremities after being submerged in the lake?

Regardless, I did not know how to answer his demand (because it had not been a request). I definitely wanted to make Ford work for it. And I needed to think.

Far too many things had happened to me tonight. I'd kissed Atticus, discovered he was Ford, discovered my trailer squashed beneath a massive tree, rescued the cats, and been rescued in turn by Ranger. Then I'd gone for a near-naked waterslide ride in Ford's lap—and I'd liked it.

I needed time to process these new data points. I wasn't planning on staying in Moonlight Valley, not longer than it took to sort out the trailer and save up the money I needed to launch my pet emporium business.

Suiting with Ford Boone wasn't going to move any part of my master plan forward. It would keep me stuck here because there would be one more reason not to go.

"We need to go back," I said, focusing on the practical next step instead of answering him. I stumbled on the rocky shore. This was no Maldivian beach with soft, silky sand.

Ford caught me effortlessly, mostly because I crash-landed against his bare, wet chest. His muscles held me up and I let them. His thumb caressed the corner of my mouth.

I liked it far too much.

"I'm not kissing you." My breathless delivery left the accuracy of that statement open to debate.

He regarded me steadily. "Why not?"

"Because you lied to me. You pretended to be Atticus."

"And you want my twin," he snapped. From the iceberg in his voice, he didn't like that thought at all. He looked frustrated.

I grabbed his muscled bicep and tugged him to a stop. "I don't want Atticus. But I don't like that you lied to me, or that you were giving rides to the Queen of Used Cars. We kissed each other and then—"

My feelings were not logical. Ford and I were not a couple. We were not dating. Until tonight, I hadn't known that he'd had thoughts of kissing me. We were both commitment free. Yet my brain kept replaying the scene where Deelie Sue had straddled Ford's lap in her itty-bitty bikini and ridden him. I didn't like that memory.

It wasn't a logic thing, I realized with no small degree of horror. It was a *feelings* thing.

Feelings were the worst.

I shifted uncomfortably. There were sharp, stabby rocks underfoot. The staircase built into the side of the hill felt like it was a million rocky miles away.

Ford picked me up. *Again.* It was becoming a most unfortunate habit. I snuck a peek at his face. Was it…hopeful?

A boyfriend had once tried to pick me up. He'd been two inches shorter than me, and I'd worried that I was too heavy. My being taller had made us off-balance and he'd quickly aborted. The ease with which Ford did the heavy lifting for us was seductive, and it needed to stop.

Us dating was as useless as tits on a bull because Ford would never leave Moonlight Valley. He was a Boone and a werewolf. That was two strikes right there. The third was that I had to leave.

I was headed to Nashville, to open my pet business. I had plans, and I would execute those plans. If I stayed here, I wouldn't be a small business owner—I'd be a microscopic business owner. Cell-sized, minuscule, and impossibly limited. Vanity Fur Salon had already cornered my market.

Ford broke our silence first. "There's nothing between me and Deelie Sue. Our ride was a joke, a friends thing."

I didn't sit on my friends' laps.

"I don't know if I can believe that," I admitted.

"I'm asking you to trust me, Alice. She and I, we don't suit. The only thing we have in common is being a werewolf. I wish you had known it was me in the woods, because..." His voice lost its roughness, the growl softening to a sweet burr. "Go out with me, Alice. Please. I'd like that second chance with you."

CHAPTER
FIVE
~ALICE~

*Wolves were big and scary and so fluffy, how could anyone resist hugging one
just to feel all that fur?*

*"Ignore the fluffy," she muttered. "Remember the part about big and
scary."*

— ANNE BISHOP

I was Vanity Fur Salon's least productive employee.

Not even Deelie Sue's surprise text inviting me for coffee after I
finished my shift of washing and clipping could make me focus. She'd
offered to be my business mentor and share lessons learned from running her
used car emporium.

On the one hand, Deelie Sue was a successful businesswoman who was
respected by a great many people, myself included. On the other hand, I felt
weird about my waterslide shenanigans where I'd gone for a hot ride with her
ex-boyfriend mere minutes after she had. He'd asked me to step out with him
and added his contact information to my phone.

On a third (and purely hypothetical) hand: werewolves. Werewolves
existed, and both Ford and Deelie Sue were werewolves. If I'd correctly read
between the lines during Ford's explanation about his semi-seeing Deelie Sue
for all those years, there was some kind of expectation that werewolves hung

out with other werewolves and made werewolf babies, presumably to ensure the continuation of the species.

And on a fourth hand (I had octopus aspirations): I'd spent way too much time thinking about Ford and his broad shoulders and narrow waist, his sexy growling and the way he'd literally stepped in to be my rock. It was his fault that I was thinking about sex instead of the poodle I was clipping or my to-do list.

My to-do list couldn't compete with his kisses, that was for sure.

Nor could the goldendoodle on my table, adorable as he was.

I'd conducted a retrospective on that last Fateful Encounter (and yes, since that Friday night had been epic in all ways, I thought it merited capital letters) and had concluded that Ford was an amazing kisser. I hadn't gotten a firsthand look at his penis, which was an oversight, all puns intended. What I'd felt, though, had been impressive. It was safe to say he'd only gotten better with age.

I'd never expected to get stuck on Ford's big hands or to be making a mental list of all the places I'd like to feel those hands. Yet here I was, standing in Vanity Fur Salon, grooming an increasingly grumpy goldendoodle, trying to remember what Ford's hair had felt like when I'd run my fingers through it...

Great. I was having sexy fantasies in my place of employment.

I didn't know how to categorize my intrusive sexual thoughts about Ford. His outer packaging was hot and lust-worthy, but his admission—that our kiss in his truck had been the culmination of a longtime dream for him and that he wanted to kiss me again—was overwhelming.

This was *Ford*. I hated him, or thought I did.

His admission to liking me was even stranger than discovering he could change into a wolf. Which I had questions about. So many questions. Perhaps I'd mistaken an understandable scientific interest in lycanthropy for lust?

Five days had passed since Aunt Sally's trailer had suffered its fatal demise and kicked off my Boone-filled bizarre night. I'd slipped out of their guest cottage the next morning before anyone else was up and had avoided Ford ever since.

Fortunately, Alessandro had been out of town for only that one night, and on returning he'd immediately swished his fantastic hair and declared that since he would absolutely need a house sitter in the future, I should move in now so that I could learn the ropes. I'd been at his place for a few days, and since he didn't have any plants and took Pom-Pom with him, I knew he was lying. I appreciated it.

What would I even say if Ford and I met? *Hi, Ford. I'm not big on bars or eating in public, but maybe you'd like to go to a pottery class with me on a date? We can put our arms around each other and get dirty.*

No. That would work only if he was also a fan of the movie *Ghosts*.

Or how about this?

Dear Ford, I obviously lack any sense of self-preservation or feminism because—even though you let Deelie Sue give you a sexy lap dance at the waterslide in front of me—I'm okay with it. We could go hang out with the puppies at the local animal shelter and get our oxytocin up! Unless dogs don't like werewolves?

No. That was potentially awkward.

"You haven't told me what happened Friday night."

Sanye Jansen-Webster's voice from the workstation next to mine startled me. I'd been hyper-focused on Ford and not the poodle I was clipping.

Sanye was tall and redheaded and looked like a Fae queen. She'd married her high school sweetheart, Evan Webster, the day after they'd graduated and three days before he'd joined the military.

Local gossip claimed the speed of their nuptials had been because her daddy, Lucky Jansen, was a horrible piece of work. He didn't even merit a *bless his heart*—most people in Moonlight Valley outright said *damn him*. He was awful, and even after Evan's tragic death in a training exercise, Sanye had never gone back home.

"And don't tell me it was nothing," Sanye continued, "because your cheeks are the color pink called *I Got Me Some*."

I clipped another lock of poodle fur. "Three naked Boone brothers."

Sanye choked.

"Three naked Boone brothers," I repeated. "That's what happened. Plus hot looks, a kiss, and practically skinny-dipping. Did you know Ford wears boxer briefs?"

"Stop." She clutched the pug she was grooming against her hot pink smock. "We can't talk about this at work."

"HR policy? Sexual harassment?"

"Time constraints," she said dryly. "I need to be able to give the mental image my undivided attention."

I clipped away. The goldendoodle would be bald, but hey, distraction! "You know Knox and Ranger, right? You went to school with them?"

Although her gaze was fixed on the pug, I knew she was seeing something —some*one*—else entirely. "Yes, but I was closest to Maverick. He was best friends with Evan."

Evan had been amazing, and I couldn't begin to understand her loss. Sanye glanced away and blinked her eyes rapidly, looking part resigned and part mad. She hated crying. We both did, but in her case it was because she'd grown up hearing her father claim it was a character flaw.

In addition to being a motorcycle aficionado who spent all his free time riding around Moonlight Valley with his friends, Mr. Jansen was a businessman who owned a massive design company that decorated exotic hunting lodges. The one time I'd been to his house, there had been fur rugs on the floors and a ton of creepy stuffed animal heads hanging on the walls.

He'd done lodges for some famous people, which got him mentioned in various design magazines, and then he'd done a luxury boutique hotel that had received dubious press for its rosewood.

The semi-scandal had been a popular topic of conversation in Moonlight Valley for a summer, although that had partly been due to the way Mr. Jansen had stormed around, yelling that he'd used only *reclaimed* wood.

Alessandro had confided to me once that he wasn't convinced and was *keeping an eye on him*. It might have been the beer talking, or maybe my cousin really was staking out the local rich guy looking for signs of illegal lumber usage.

Sanye likely would have moved away from Moonlight Valley and put multiple states—if not an entire continent—between herself and her father, but Evan's family lived nearby. She spent time with them at their church and hung out with them on weekends.

Sanye could have given Deelie Sue a run for her money in the Miss Tennessee department. God had given her one of those beautiful faces that were all cheekbones and looked even better in a picture than in real life.

Most important of all, however, she was just plain nice. She had a smile for everyone and never refused when asked to do something. She was an amazing baker, and someone was always asking her to whip up a cake for their event. She'd made Jonah inside the whale for our church and a multi-layer cake shaped like a beehive containing frosting bees when you cut into it for the county fair.

Meanwhile, I could barely open a box of Duncan Hines without spilling it.

Objectively speaking, I should have been a mistress of baking. Baking was science, and I excelled at science. Perhaps I should have hidden myself in a university lab or gone to work for a big corporation in their research lab, but I'd decided science was my passion and not the kind of thing I wanted to do on a daily basis for a paycheck.

This might have had something to do with the chemistry prerequisites I'd failed twice in college. Nevertheless, when I'd returned to Moonlight Valley unemployed and broke this summer, I'd been labeled the science nerd and resident STEMinist. It was a responsibility I took seriously.

Sanye slid me a glance. "Come over to my place tonight and tell me which brother's better-looking naked, all right?"

"I can't." I had another ten minutes on my shift and was nearly done with the goldendoodle. "I have to go out to Aunt Sally's trailer and clean things up. Get a dumpster out there and some contractors. That tree isn't going to move itself."

It would have been handy if that tree had been an Ent and therefore able to get up and walk away.

Sanye frowned at me. "There's no tree on your trailer."

"What?"

"I mean, clearly there *was*, but it's not there now. You have a really large stack of firewood and a lot of sawdust, though. And the yard's been cleaned up." She thought for a moment. "And the trailer's gone. There's only the pad and the hookups left."

This was—

I was—

The goldendoodle yelped, and I eased up on my grip. "I haven't signed anything yet with the contractors. What if they try to charge me a fortune? I'll have to sell a kidney or trade sexual favors.

"Maybe they went to the wrong site and now there's some other home-owner who's wondering where his workmen went and meanwhile all of Aunt Sally's things are headed toward the dump."

"It wasn't a mistaken cleanup, Alice. I saw the Boone brothers there. You can calm down now."

None of this made any sense. "Why would they do that? They specialize in animal removal, not tree removal."

Sanye laughed. "Probably has something to do with you seeing them naked."

* * *

I needed to eat my feelings. I planned on stopping at the Piggly Wiggly for the family-sized bag of Cheetos and a bar of Cadbury's. But first, I needed to discover what had been done to my trailer without my permission.

Except, no, I wasn't, because suddenly my phone was blowing up with multiple texts from Ranger explaining that he'd found Emperor Meowpatine wandering in the woods. He'd provided a minute-by-minute log of the cat's voyage and current activities.

Reluctantly, I called All-Purpose Animal Services.

Ranger picked right up. "Got your cat here."

Ranger believed in using words sparingly. In fact, he'd been known to drive across town to leave a note rather than make a phone call, so his heads-up was unexpected.

"What's he doing over there?" I'd picked up my feline wards from the smushed trailer the same morning I snuck away from the Boone place; they should have been in Alessandro's house, scratching his furniture and making themselves at home.

"Cats like to go back after they move," Ranger supplied after a long pause.

"They're homesick?"

"Or stubborn." I could hear him shrug.

"I'll be right there," I told him.

I texted my cousin and let him know I'd be out with Sanye, but then I'd resume my (spurious) house-sitting duties. I did not tell him that Sanye and I were paying the Boone brothers a visit.

Alessandro and the Boone boys did not get along, partly because there had been some brouhaha about who could hunt on Boone property and whether they'd illegally had a wolf as a pet. (In light of my recent encounters with naked Boones, I had some new thoughts about what might have happened there.) Alessandro hadn't been able to prove they'd violated Tennessee's captive wildlife permit regulations, but he was certain they'd done it.

It also had a lot to do with the one and only Boone girl, Mackenzie Boone, and Alessandro mooning after her all through high school.

Mackenzie—who'd been stuck with the nickname Mack because no one could resist the obvious truck joke—was super nice despite having grown up in Darrell Boone's proximity. She was loads of fun and one of the girliest people I'd ever met. People expected her to be a tomboy because of her situation, having all those brothers and no mother, but she wasn't.

The Boones ran their business from a bunch of outbuildings behind the main house on their property, and the drive out to their property gave me time to think. Was Mack a wolf shifter? I hadn't mentioned werewolves to Sanye, but Mack had to know what her brothers could do, and it made sense that she'd be able to do it too. Huh.

I'd partly come back to Moonlight Valley because Tennessee was a pretty place and I loved it. But another reason was that Aunt Sally's passing and will meant I had a free housing option. Living in her trailer saved me money while I worked up my business plan. And I had a guaranteed job working alongside Sanye at Vanity Fur Salon. We were the only pet-grooming business in a twenty-mile radius.

I suppose I could have opened up shop in town, if I hadn't mind being a very, very, VERY small business, but I'd always dreamed of being a business-woman in a place that actually had foot traffic.

I loved Nashville. I'd spent a lot of time walking that city and thinking about what kind of storefront would suit me best. I had a plan, and these last few months in Moonlight Valley felt like the calm before the starter's gun went off on a race. I was ready, I was prepared, and I was going to win. I spent the next mile running through a few scenarios in my head. I'd be polite, get my cat, and...

"Boone central."

Sanye's gleeful words jolted me from my thoughts. I stared out the windshield as she pulled into the parking lot the Boones had put in behind their sprawling farmhouse for All-Purpose Animal Services. A big barn with the business name painted on the side housed the main operations; smaller outbuildings contained animal kennels and offices.

Happy barks announced our arrival as we parked; the Boones didn't have to worry about anyone sneaking up on them with that welcoming crew. A pair of broad shoulders beneath a company polo shirt disappeared into the barn, fast enough that all I caught was a glimpse of faded blue jeans before the shoulders' owner vanished.

The part of me that was full of feelings wondered, *Was that Ford? If so, is he coming back? Should we run after him? Yell something funny or amusing?*

The smarter, more logical part piped right up, however, saying, *We're a science dork with limited human interaction experience—actual face-to-face conversation after a heartfelt confession is not in our skill set.*

"Are you going after him?"

Sanye's skill set apparently included mind reading. I beamed her an urgent need to leave in search of the Moonlight Valley Café's legendary double-decker ice cream brownie, but she turned off the car.

I stared at the barn door through which Mr. Shoulders had disappeared. "This is such a bad idea."

For starters, I hadn't achieved one-hundred-percent success in telling the Boone brothers apart when they were fully dressed.

Sanye grinned. "Go. Get your cat. Get you a cute Boone. Easy-peasy. If you've seen him naked, he's interested."

She made a naughty finger waggle. Her pointer finger seriously underrepresented the mighty fineness of Ford's penis.

The barn door opened and two redheaded, bearded men of heroic proportions sauntered out. One of them cuddled a fluffy cat. After carefully setting the cat down, they proceeded to flatten themselves on the ground and peer under the barn. Sweet baby Jesus. The skies opened up, the clouds parted, and a lightning beam of lust shot down and lit up my southern regions.

The twins wore faded blue jeans, incongruously preppy white polo shirts that read *All-Purpose Animal Services*, and work boots.

God bless those work boots. They were big, heavy, and perilously close to motorcycle boots without any of the illegality or trouble that came with bikers. They shouted confidence and demanded a girl look up, and then up some more.

The brothers' hair was roughly the same length, the same lush, well-tended beards framing their mouths. See? I wasn't a bad person for having mixed them up.

They looked exactly the same on the outside, and I hadn't been a town regular for years.

Sanye honked the horn and waved vigorously when the two redheads popped out from under the barn.

The one on the left was Atticus. He was more laid-back with people, reserving his uptightness for numbers. He didn't have anything to prove, and people liked him. No. They loved him. He'd won every contest he'd ever entered, up to and including his race for county tax assessor. I wasn't sure the election board had even bothered to count the votes.

Ford, on the other hand, was the master of gruffness. He was taciturn and cranky, the kind of man who invested in a *Keep Off the Grass!* Sign.

He held himself in check, his eyes scanning the open space in front of the barn. His eyes promised that, if there was a threat, he'd take care of it. His frown made him look stern even as Atticus waved at us warmly. I'd noticed Ford's reserve on Friday. He didn't bend, didn't open up easily. Few people were on his access list.

I glanced between the two brothers, forming a new hypothesis. I wasn't attracted to Atticus at all. My obsession with him was over and done with. My loyalty had been transferred.

To Ford.

To double-check, I gave Atticus a look. Objectively speaking, since he was Ford's twin, he was a Moonlight Valley hottie. He had great shoulders, a nice smile, and an excellent work history.

I looked at Ford...and *BAM*. I was a lust-filled fool.

It had been five days since he'd taken me for a ride down his waterslide, and despite what had seemed like a heartfelt plea for dating opportunities, he hadn't made any effort to reach out to me. No texts or phone calls, no casual stopping by my place of employment or accidental run-ins in the freezer aisle of the Piggly Wiggly. To be fair, I hadn't reached out either, unless you counted some fevered dreams.

"Which twin, Alice?"

Sanye nudged me, asking me to choose, pushing me to make the decision I'd been agonizing over. It was remarkably easy. "Despite years of obsessing over Atticus, I'm going to go with...Ford. That makes me fickle. Easily persuaded. Possibly opportunistic."

I made my attraction sound like a joke, but if it was, it was the most profound and complicated joke ever. These feelings I had for Ford weren't arbitrary at all. They were fact-based, fueled by years of knowing him and sparked by our kiss and his confession.

We might've had a history of animosity and arguments, but I'd also spent the last five days dreaming about him and imagining all the ways he could fit into my life.

Temporarily, sure.

Until I moved to Nashville and opened my store, sure.

Until the feelings blew over and we both moved on, sure.

"I don't hate him." I tried to find the words to explain exactly what Ford made me feel. "I mean, I certainly disliked him plenty when we were growing up. He wasn't nice to me, although he hung out with me plenty."

"The bully likes you." Sanye's grin grew bigger. "This is the stuff of romance."

"Or a really unhealthy relationship." What worked on the pages of a book was not always a good life plan.

"You know who he is."

"Not the important stuff," I argued. "I know that he can't sit still, that he's got a weakness for cold cherry soda on a hot day, that he's a sucker for kitten memes but won't admit it. I know he stole Mr. Trimbull's tractor and drove it into a pond doing laps when he was fourteen, then came and pulled it out the next day with his brothers and apologized."

I paused and thought for a moment. "And also that he's a morning person —deal-breaker—who whistles when he walks the dogs and puffs out his cheeks when he's deep in thought. Oh, and he still wears the same brand of black boxer briefs he wore in high school."

Sanye cackled gleefully. I was glad one of us found this funny. "You know him well."

"Not really. That's stuff you learn when you live near someone and spend all summer with them."

"Do you know what Atticus wears under his jeans?"

I made a face. "I don't have a clue."

Sanye gave me a long look. "Did you really have a crush on Atticus, or was he a safe thing because he and you were never really going to have a relationship?" I opened my mouth, but Sanye rolled over me. "Did you maybe like Ford all along but it was easier to pick Atticus?"

Nope. That had *not* occurred to me. "No." I turned to glare at her. "Absolutely not. No."

"Ford is an overplanner who doesn't take chances. He's all gruff and stoic, unless it involves animals and then he's a big marshmallow. He blew up at Dean Worthy when he found out that Dean left his dog home alone for a week while he went to Vegas.

"So?" I'd have had something to say to Dean.

"He went right down to Dean's place, broke in, and took that poor dog home with him. Gave Dean the finger on his Ring doorbell."

"So he impulsively commits felonies."

"He heard what Dean had done and did something. He doesn't worry about the consequences of doing the right thing or maybe being inconvenienced. He acts. He doesn't sit around planning out every last step of his day. Atticus is the safer choice, especially for someone like you."

"Nope," I said, hoping it was true.

"Ford and Atticus are *twins*."

"On the outside. Not the inside. They're not clones in some kind of space romance."

"Yeah, but you told me that Ford was no stranger growing up. You know all kinds of things about him. You spent entire summers with him, seems like. But your fantasy man was Atticus?"

"Atticus is a hero," I grumbled. "He's nice."

Sanye laughed, poking me in the arm. "Sure. Or maybe he was the safe choice."

Ford had disappeared under the barn. His legs, plus his amazing, bitable butt, were sticking out. Atticus put his hands on his legs, pulling, and Ford popped out with an armful of kittens.

I realized that while dream Atticus was a real good time, it was Ford who gave me that certain zing. Even if Atticus was the safer choice, I wouldn't be making it. Ford was unpredictable and rough, explosive in a chemistry sort of way—and I wanted him.

He wasn't a grumpy, hot stranger. The first two words were true, sure as shooting, but he was no stranger—and not because I'd had my tongue in his mouth and my butt planted on top of his mighty fine penis.

All righty, then. I had the basics of a working plan: a) get out of the car and yell at Ford and then b) kiss him senseless.

Simple.

Memorable.

Actionable.

That was good enough for me. I got my backside out of the car and marched over to the twins.

CHAPTER
SIX
~FORD~

Another werewolf thing. Like most animals, we spent a large part of our lives engaged in the three F's of basic survival. Feeding, fighting and...reproduction.

— KELLEY ARMSTRONG

"Coming in hot," Atticus muttered, plucking the kittens from my arms. "Best of luck with that."

I sat up, brushing off dried mud and cat fur. Alice was stomping toward me, ponytail swinging with her wrath. She was covered in dog fur and looked adorably hot.

My lizard brain promptly arrived at the only sensible conclusion: I was going to make Alice mine.

Hot damn!

But first I was going to lay down a few rules.

This is where you lose the girl. Unless she's into *Fifty Shades* stuff?

"Ford..." The way Alice said my name was a challenge, one that made my balls tighten and my heart squeeze.

Alice was looking at me as if she were waiting for something. I was almost certain she was playing one of her movie scenes in her head, and I just wished I knew which one. I had no idea what my lines were supposed to be.

Instead, I handed Atticus the kitten I'd rescued from underneath the porch.

69

I was gonna need both hands to coax Alice into seeing things my way, and the first thing we'd be discussing was why it had taken her five days to search me out. It irritated the heck out me that she'd waited so long. She hadn't texted me. She had, in fact, flat-out ignored me since Friday.

It had been five days. Five days since I'd kissed or held or touched her.

It had felt like an eternity. I was not good at being a gentleman, but for her I was trying. I hadn't wanted to push, so I'd stayed away and let her consider what I was offering. Had I made yet another mistake in giving her space? Perhaps I should have been showing her what I could do for her, proving that my wolf wasn't a bad thing.

"What do you want?" Irritation seeped into my voice. I'd made it clear I wanted her, and I couldn't be anyone other than the wolf I was. She'd have to accept it or I'd have to let her go. I was hoping and praying that acceptance was the way this thing between us was headed, however.

And bed, my wolf interjected. **Let's not forget the bedroom, 'kay?**

My wolf was a horndog.

Alice blinked and gave herself a little shake like she'd been a long distance away, somewhere in her head. Her gaze focused on my midsection.

"So about my tree problem."

"What about the tree?"

"You removed it."

"I did."

She was wearing a hot pink T-shirt with *Vanity Fur Salon* embroidered on the teeny-tiny pocket on her right boob. You couldn't fit more than an SD card or a condom in a pocket that small.

The shirt was tucked into a blue-and-white-striped skirt that belled out around her hips and stopped several inches above her knees. There was a big bow at the base of her spine that I itched to untie. She wore a pair of bright red Dr. Martens, the kind that made no sense at all.

You'd never blend into the woods wearing those. You'd stand out and make a target of yourself. It was good she had me to look after her.

"And then after you removed my tree—*without my permission*—you removed my trailer?" She glared at my belt buckle like it had personally offended her.

I shrugged. "There wasn't much to salvage there, sweetheart."

I'd gone through the debris, though, setting aside anything that looked like it might be of interest to her. Truth was, after six thousand pounds of pine tree had landed on her place, she'd owned a pancake, not a trailer. I'd seen scrap metal compressed less thoroughly. Still, I'd picked up what I could from the yard and organized it into piles. I had plans to put something in the trailer's place.

"You should have asked!"

"Excuse me for helping. But that tree wasn't stable, and there were electrical lines down. I figured you didn't want to accidentally set half of Moonlight Valley on fire."

"If I wanted your help, I would have asked you."

I felt her words like a visceral punch, cutting through my ribs and slicing into my heart. I must have flinched because she paused and looked like she was searching for an explanation. She started to stammer out something about impositions and not having the money and not meaning whatever it was I thought she'd meant.

I didn't want to hear it. Didn't want to hear her say I had no chance at all with her. It was pure torment being near her when I couldn't have her, couldn't touch her, help her, fix what was bothering her.

I lifted my hands up. "It wasn't a big deal. This is the South, sweetheart. Everyone owns a chainsaw."

"It must have taken you hours." She sounded disbelieving, as if she could not imagine a universe in which someone would do this for her.

It had taken me most of yesterday, but I was happy to do it for her. I would have done it for any of our neighbors, although I preferred doing it for her.

"We want to buy your land, and I can offer you cash."

"Can you wait a minute?" Alice's gaze shot up to meet my eyes, stormy and turbulent. I could feel the telltale amber sheen rippling over my own eyes as I got worked up.

"You can get a new place, something with better insulation and more square footage."

Alice ignored my real estate pitch and stepped into me. I wasn't prepared. One second she was trying to kill my belt buckle with her eyes, and the next she was leaning up on tiptoe to press her lips against mine. That was it, I conceded our battle.

My wolf whined. **No!**

But I was a predator at heart, so it took me only another second to respond.

I wrapped an arm around her waist, preventing any retreat, and deepened the kiss. I wanted everything Alice would give me. Surprising me, she was on board with this plan of mine, moaning and opening up to me. Her hot little tongue invaded my own mouth, taking no prisoners. I growled.

I'd done nothing but remember what she'd felt like when I'd had her in the front seat of my truck. Her soft curves, the way her breasts filled my hands just right, and her delicious ass. Five days of imaging her stripped down and welcoming me. Five days of a never-ending hard-on.

I had apparently discovered unknown stores of restraint because I wanted to do more than growl. I wanted to shift, to give her my mating bite, to put my scent all over her, everywhere, so that everyone in Moonlight Valley and the whole world would know she was mine.

Part of me even wanted to attempt the mating bite so she could be with me in every way. I wanted to run by her side, to show her the dark world of the woods, to den with her, to fill her up with my cubs.

Let's go! We can do it right now. Love on her, leave our mark!

No. I doubted her third cousin twice removed, Alessandro the Asshole, would like that, but I didn't care. His feelings on the subject didn't count, and as far as I knew, Alice had no other family close by.

Alice kept right on kissing the heck out of me, oblivious to how close she was to becoming a werewolf's forever mate. Her tongue in my mouth was slick and determined to make me hers, a plan I was wholly onboard with.

Bite, bite, bite!

I needed more. We needed alone time and to not be kissing in a public space in front of my brothers and her girlfriend.

Not breaking our kiss, I lifted her off her feet and carried her past Atticus's boots, now sticking out from underneath the porch where our barn cat had had her kittens, past the kennels where Ranger was feeding a stray skunk, and into the barn.

Alice never said stop. More miraculously, she wasn't issuing directions, orders, or commands either. I guess we'd finally found something we both agreed on. She curled against me, tilting her head to better fit herself into our embrace.

She'd moved on from my mouth, pressing a trail of kisses upward, over my cheek, along my ear. She also had a death grip on my neck, her legs wrapped tight around my waist, her heels digging into my ass. It was easy as pie to waltz her across the floor and into the empty tack room.

As soon as I got her inside, I shut the door because my brothers were too nosy to stay outside for long. They'd be along, offering advice, hooting and hollering and generally trying to make one or both of us blush. Plus, I had a plan for that door. I turned and pressed Alice up against it. Her hands fumbled with the edge of my shirt, shoving it up.

It was not the best moment to realize, surrounded by bridles and saddles, reins and halters, that I didn't want hot, quickie sex with Alice in my family barn.

I mean, I *did*, but I was playing for keeps and shoving her pretty little skirt up and tearing her panties off, putting myself inside her and riding her hard the way we both wanted, wasn't going to win Alice over. Not for keeps. Not the way I needed her.

I thought about giving it to her. I sure did.

But sex wasn't all I wanted with her.

I wanted her to be my mate.

I wanted to marry this girl.

Finally! What have you been waiting for?

Alice. I was all in, and wasn't that the truth? Someday after we'd been married for a day, or a year, or forty years, we'd have hot quickie sex in this tack room. We'd make those kinds of memories together and they would be worth waiting for. We'd have all the spontaneous, dirty, hot sex…when I'd put a ring on it.

But now wasn't that time. It was too soon. I needed her to take me seriously as a suitor and respect me. If I put out now, I'd be nothing but fun and games to Alice Aymes.

But laid, my wolf griped. **You'd be laid.**

I grabbed her hands when they started in on my belt buckle and dragged them over her head. It was hard to focus on the next step in my plan with her hot curvy body pressed up against mine.

It was even harder to think because Alice was a kissing fiend. I needed to distract her fast, or I was going to lose this argument.

I kissed my way down her cheek, trying to cool my engines. I was hoping I had forever. The next ten minutes were a drop in the bucket compared to eternity with this woman, so my dick would have to wait.

She wriggled, her husky little moan doing wicked things to me. We were pressed up against the wall, her riding my thigh. I could feel the heat of her through her panties and my jeans, and it almost undid all my good intentions. Her scent was amazing—musky and sweet. I'd have known her anywhere.

"You're so good at this." Alice's words were flatteringly breathless. I could make her scream and holler my name with a little more time and attention, and I loved that thought.

"At what?" I rested my forehead against hers, letting go of her wrists. I could count each freckle on her nose. Kiss them. I'd mussed her up good: her hair had come down from its cute little twist and her shirt was all untucked.

"Loving on me. Kissing. Making me hot."

Alice was honest to a fault. If I made her unhappy, she'd let me know. And if she was happy, she'd share that, too. She didn't hold a grudge, but she'd push back if I pushed her too hard. I respected that about her.

Her hand fisted my T-shirt. "I think we should kiss again. Consider it an experiment."

"In the name of science?"

"Absolutely." She nodded vigorously. "We should see if we can replicate our results, seeing as how our first attempt went so well."

I could feel the grin stretch my face. I was on top of the fucking world as I pressed one hand against the door beside her face and tightened the other possessively on her butt. Since her skirt was rucked up, there wasn't much between me and her. I hooked a finger in the side of her panties and tugged gently.

"That sounds like a plan."

I dropped a kiss on her forehead where she had the faintest of freckles. You'd have to be close to see them—kissing close—and they felt like a secret she'd been keeping just for me.

"Great." She tugged on my shirt. "Now?"

"Go out with me tonight?" I kissed one freckle, then its friends and neighbors. "You want to go see a movie at the drive-in? Get ice cream or dinner?"

Alice pulled back, frowning. "Go out? No. Not unless you've got a deserted island or a mountain cabin we can hide out in."

"Alice…" I searched her face, looking for signs of humor. She wasn't making a joke. My wolf whined uncertainly. I didn't know where I'd gone wrong, how to salvage this situation. This couldn't be just sex. "Alice, we can do whatever you want. Let me take you out on a date."

Her frowned deepened. I had no idea what she was thinking, but I could feel her pulling away from me even before she shifted in my arms. Reluctantly, I set her down.

We had two different definitions of *mating*. She was thinking sex, but I was thinking something more. No. Not more. I was thinking *everything*.

"Not tonight."

"Then you tell me when."

"Why?" She straightened her clothes, tucking her shirt in. We'd crumpled the bow on her skirt.

"Because I want to take you out. I want us to have time together to talk."

"About what?"

"Anything," I said quickly. "You can read me the weather app. Or tell me about the firefly population in Moonlight Valley and who's getting it on with who. Insect gossip."

A smile tugged the corner of her pretty mouth. "Okay."

"So that's a yes?" I didn't want there to be any doubt.

"Yes, I'll go out on a date with you. You and me—Ford Boone and Alice Aymes. We can put out a press release, let the world know that hell has officially frozen over."

* * *

I grinned at Alice Aymes's backside as she strode away because her bow was all kinds of lopsided and she had creases where she hadn't before. I'd left a mark, palming her ass.

We're awesome, my wolf said. He was a self-satisfied son of a bitch.

She'd laughed when I'd pointed out her rumpled state. She didn't mind that I'd messed up her pretty outfit and shrugged off my offers to make it up to her. I'd have liked to take her shopping and do something nice for her.

I hungrily watched her go, settling into the passenger-side seat of the car she'd come in. She shot me an impish grin and thumbs-upped me. Emperor Meowpatine was perched on her lap.

I thumbs-upped her right back. Let her see how big mine were.

"Do you have dirty inside jokes, Ford?" Ranger sauntered up next to me, a kitten riding his shoulder.

My grin faded and I shot my brother a look. "That's none of your business."

"I'm not thinking lusty thoughts about your girl." Ranger squinted at the departing car. "I'm recalling a piece of unsubstantiated trivia correlating the size of a man's thumb with his penis. Hold your hand up."

Ranger waved his thumb in the air between us. I ignored him in favor of watching Alice's ponytail whip back and forth as her friend's convertible got going. She flashed me a smile that almost had me running after her.

She didn't mind that my brothers and her girlfriend knew we'd been kissing.

"I'm not comparing thumb size with you."

"Come on, I want to see who has the bigger thumb."

"Shut it, Ranger. I'm not thumb wrestling with you."

Was it too soon to text her? Make a reservation at a nice place to eat, one where she could dress up? The car disappeared. I debated shifting and running alongside, but if her friend noticed me, there would be questions.

"I don't want to wrestle; I want to compare our pollices."

"Not a chance."

Fortunately, Atticus came over, although less fortunately, he wanted to know if Ranger had made it out to take care of Mr. Otis's skunk problem.

A mama skunk and six babies were living underneath the Otis porch, which would have been a decent timeshare arrangement except that the entire skunk family had taken issue with Mr. Otis's dog sticking its muzzle in their front door so to speak. Things had got heated and stinky fast.

Ranger groaned. "Listen, I move we discuss the issue before things go any further between Ford and his femme fatale."

I narrowed my eyes at my older brother. "She is not a femme fatale. And also, *what* issue?"

"I meant it in the firefly way." Ranger blinked innocently. "Not the French way."

Uh-huh. I hoped he wasn't about to bring up Alice's infatuation with Atticus. An infatuation, I was certain, that had been cured at the waterslide last Friday.

"We're good." Atticus gave a brisk nod. "There's nothing to discuss."

"I think we should add it to the family agenda." Ranger propped his hands on his hips. "Clear the air. Bring everything out into the open."

My glance slid to Atticus like a car hitting black ice. "You know what he's talking about?"

"I don't rightly know, Ford."

Ranger settled his big paw on my shoulder, nodding like a preacher over a dead body. "The truth is, Ford—and I know you're still in the limerence stage of your true-love agenda, but that doesn't negate an outstanding issue that—"

"Ranger, we don't have until the cows come home."

"Fine. The issue is that none of us likes Alice's third cousin twice removed, Alessandro Aymes."

I exchanged a look with Ranger, then Atticus and I looked at each other. We were twins; we could about read each other's minds. We'd done it before we could talk even, and it had driven our momma nuts. Our unspoken conversation went something like what follows.

Together: *No one likes Alessandro except for some ladies down at the bar. He's a jackass.*

Me: *Didn't he write you up for having a dog off-leash?*

Atticus: *Yep. It was Rebel.*

Me: *Hope y'all peed on his truck.*

Atticus: *You've liked Alice since she first showed up in Moonlight Valley. I'd never get in the middle of you two. I'm planning on being the best man in your wedding* (which was only slightly jumping the gun).

Me: *Thanks for having my back.*

Atticus: *But she's hot and smart, so you owe me.*

Me: *I could see that.*

Atticus: *Good talk.*

"Knock it off." Ranger waved his hand between our faces, snapping our magic twin bond. "Y'all need to use your words so everyone can participate."

Atticus sighed. "Ranger, no one likes Alessandro and not because his name spells *ass*. After the moves he tried on our sister—"

"And the times he arrested Maverick for illegal animal possession," I added.

Alessandro was not only a dark-eyed, fantastically good-haired, handsome bastard, but he actually had the power to arrest, unlike many animal control officers. It was an unfortunate fact that he particularly liked to harass my brothers.

"Although in all fairness, Mav likely did have illegal animals," Ranger observed. "He broke those lizards out of the zoo in Nashville that one time, and then there was that dog-fighting ring he busted up—"

"None of that was ever proved in a court of law," I said.

Someone needed to stick up for our oldest brother.

"Precisely," Atticus said. "But Alessandro brings it up all the time. He's certain we're up to illegal animal shenanigans here. When he was at the Catty-wampus last week, on account of their Friday night two-for-one drinks, he suggested that Mav was likely the person who'd made off with Jennie Dean's Pekinese on account of his being a known pet thief."

I shot him a look. "Mav hasn't liberated an animal in over four years, but Alessandro won't let it go. Plus, Mav can't stand small dogs. Says they yap too much and won't stop growling at his wolf."

We'd had our share of run-ins with Alessandro Aymes over the years. It didn't matter whether we were breaking the law. He was always right there, breathing down our necks and asking questions.

I'd always figured this was because Alessandro hadn't recovered from Mack's teenage rejection of him. We'd all written him off as a self-important windbag with shampoo-commercial hair.

Ranger propped his hands on his hips and nodded thoughtfully. "So we are all in agreement. But that doesn't change the fact that Alessandro Aymes has it in for us and Miss Alice is related to him."

"Is there a point to this story of yours?" I crossed my arms over my chest and frowned at my brother. Ranger usually did have a point—and often an important one—but it took him longer to reach a conclusion than it did to drive from one end of the state to the other.

"My point is Alessandro may feel that, as Miss Alice's third cousin twice removed, he should be standing in place of her father and nonexistent brothers. He won't take kindly to your attempts to date her, and that's even if she doesn't spill the beans about our lycanthropy."

"Alice wouldn't do that," I said. "We can trust her."

Our daddy had worried about Momma telling the world about werewolves. It was one of the many ugly reasons why he'd bitten her, to try to change her over. He'd figured that if she was one of us in every way, her family wouldn't want the truth coming out.

"My intentions are honorable. She's my one and only." When wolves mated, we mated for life—and I'd found mine. I was sure of it.

"I know, Ford." Ranger's mouth tightened. "She's your bald eagle, your Appalachian elktoe. We all know she's rare and you're gonna do everything you can to keep her safe. But don't expect Alessandro to welcome you with open arms."

"I have no desire to hug Alessandro."

"Ranger is right." Atticus tipped his head toward me, his eyes holding mine. "Alessandro will hate this. And since he's a sneaky asshole, you need to watch your back."

"He'll try to make trouble for you," Ranger continued. "Say the word, and I'll make trouble for him."

This shocked me. And by the arrested look on Atticus's face, Ranger's eye-for-an-eye approach toward my dating life and its potential roadblocks was a surprise to my twin as well.

Ranger looked innocent and pleasant—and people underestimated him. Sometimes I forgot he excelled at figuring people out because he was an emotional chameleon himself. Relationships and emotions didn't come easy to him, and he'd gotten real good at mimicking the people around him.

The most important thing, though, was that he had my back.

CHAPTER

SEVEN

~FORD~

Make yourself a sheep and the wolf will eat you.

— GERMAN PROVERB

I was so lost in dirty, happy thoughts about Alice that I did not pay attention to my surroundings.

Wolves were predators, hyper-aware of their habitats and potential opportunities for chasing prey, and I was the wolfiest of the wolfy. But I was also close to our den, in our territory, and distracted by desire to make Alice my forever mate by biting her, so I'd let my guard drop.

I didn't hear the Range Rover pull up behind the kennels or recognize that I had company until the pack was almost inside the barn. Lucky Jansen gave an obnoxious, braying laugh, and the males accompanying him—Big Joe and Carmine—laughed along. It was fortunate Lucky's daughter, Sanye, had already left because they had not spoken in ages. I understood her refusal.

Lucky and my deadbeat daddy had been business partners and Iron Wolves pack members together once upon a time. For a short while, Maverick, as the oldest brother and our daddy's heir apparent, had run with the Iron Wolves, but then he'd got out and cleaned up his act. My brothers and I had made it clear we would have nothing more to do with Lucky ever again.

We didn't even have to defend that decision to the good folks in Moonlight

Valley. Most people knew Lucky as Mr. Jansen, the sleazy but successful politician who'd suspiciously gotten himself elected to state office last year and split his time between the Tennessee State Capitol and doing "business" in Moonlight Valley.

What most people did not know, however, was that he was a werewolf and his "business" consisted of extracting "business taxes" from various wolf-owned businesses in the state. He had ways of forcing his targets to pay up, and I was not okay with that.

Scrappy wriggled in my hand. We'd been listening to country music together, keeping each other company. He was a baby opossum we'd rescued from the compost bin behind the general store. Black eyes twinkled up at me from his gray-and-white face. Scrappy needed to be fed with infant formula six times a day, but eventually he'd grow up and we'd release him into the woods.

For now, though, I tucked his baby blanket around him and set him into his cardboard box. Then I slid him out of sight. I didn't need to corrupt the opossum's morals by exposing him to the likes of Lucky Jansen and his crew.

Big Joe and Carmine were nothing more than jackals and hangers-on. They took orders and didn't possess a single independent thought of their own, although from the scratched-up state of Carmine's face, he'd been on the wrong end of a wolf fight.

I'd known Lucky since I was a pup. He had come by our house more than once for Sunday dinner when Momma had been with us, and he had brought us Christmas presents. Once upon a time, I had believed he was a decent man.

As an adult, I knew better. He was a con man, a liar, and a bad businessman.

"Hey, boy." Lucky tipped his head at me, his eyes scanning the barn.

I reached over and hit Pause on the album playing on my iPhone. Lucky spoke so low and fast it was like listening to a whole other language, one I had to strain to pick familiar words out of.

"Lucky. Big Joe. Carmine. What are y'all doing here?" I shoved my hands into the pockets of my jeans. I had no intention of shaking their hands or of making nice.

"That's no way to speak to your Uncle Lucky." Lucky shot me his slick politician's smile as he straightened his suit jacket. His neatly trimmed beard framed preternaturally white teeth.

That he used a laser tooth-whitening service in Nashville was an open secret in town. The gleaming toothiness made me think *shark*. Worse, though, he had the superficial charm of my daddy, all surface and no substance.

"We're not family," I responded flatly.

Not by blood, and not by choice. Though my daddy had partnered with him, Lucky Jansen meant nothing to me, and I intended for him to know it.

"You must be Ford," Big Joe piped up from behind Lucky's right shoulder. He looked disappointed. "We were hoping to see Atticus. He's a real nice guy, plus he's a businessman who knows how to respect a fellow businessman."

"It's not your lucky night, then. He's not here." I rested my hands on my hips. I wanted the wolves out of the barn and off our property.

"Hold your horses, boy," Lucky rasped. He raised his hands up in front of his shirtfront, as if he thought I should slow my roll or calm down. "We're here on business. I've got a proposal you'll want to consider."

"Hard pass." The manners Momma had worked so hard to instill in me meant I couldn't say *Fuck off, I'd rather be dead than working with you.*

She would have been proud.

"Now, you listen to me."

"No. You all have a nice night now." I pointed to the barn door, then half-turned back to the work bench and the baby formula I'd been measuring.

"You don't turn down free money," Big Joe whined.

"Nothing's free in this life, and I don't want anything to with you all."

I'd stop them if they started anything stupid, and never mind that they were used to dominating anyone they approached. They lived on fear and nerves, but they couldn't hurt me. I knew how to handle myself, no matter how dangerous they were.

"Why not?" Lucky asked neutrally, as if we were discussing what color I wanted him to paint my barn.

"I'm not breaking the law."

"What about to keep your family safe?"

A chill ran down my spine, insistent and damned unpleasant. I turned and glared at them. They were making threats, and no one threatened my brothers and me. Carmine, who'd moved closer to me with Big Joe, winked at me.

"Are you threatening me?"

"Not at all," Lucky said.

"You bet," Carmine chirped. He wasn't one to speak up unless it was with his fists.

Lucky talked over him, getting the words out before I could evict him and

83

his goons. "You hold your horses, boy. Nobody has to get hurt here, but if you want to keep your brother out of jail, then you hear me out."

"Keep my brother out of jail? You're gonna have to explain that to me."

Big Joe grinned. Unlike his boss, he hadn't had a dental cleaning in far too long. "Maverick."

"Mav?" I scowled. "Nope. There is no way. I am utterly unconvinced. He broke up with y'all years ago."

"Sure did, but before that he ran a little illegal import business for us." Carmine sounded sure of his facts. Gleeful, too.

"So now y'all are thinking to turn him in? You do that and you'll be his plus-one in jail."

"Boy, I told you to hear us out." Lucky sounded impatient and more than a little exasperated. The jovial smile had vanished from his face.

"Go on." I braced a hip against the workbench, figuring that I did need to hear it all. Then they could go, and I would figure out my next steps. It had to be bullshit.

"Your daddy and your momma had themselves a real big argument out in the woods about a year ago. I'm not sure what he was doing to the lady." Lucky paused, and I fought to control my temper. This was not the time for my eyes to go amber, not in front of an audience.

"Whatever it was, it was loud and it was messy. That brother of yours, Maverick, he busted in on them, and there were words between your daddy and him. And then he goes for your old man, and there's a fight the likes of which I've never seen."

I hadn't been there that night, but I'd never once stopped wishing that I had been. Maybe I could have stopped our daddy from trying to give Momma the bite and bring her over.

She'd told him more than once that she didn't want to go over wolf, didn't want to try for the change, but in the end he had ignored her as he always did. The only thing that mattered was what Darrell Boone wanted, and he'd wanted to make his wife into a werewolf.

This wasn't the time, however, to think about how much I missed Momma or to wonder if there was some way to bring her back.

Because our daddy had almost succeeded that night. He'd made her into a wolf, but then she hadn't been able to shift back.

She was stuck.

"It's not news to me that they fought, Lucky."

"Seeing as how your brother was there and now the lady's gone, I'd bet there's a body buried out there in your woods."

He was wrong. There wasn't a dead body—Momma was running around in her wolf form—but most people thought she'd run off because she'd up and disappeared, never to be seen again. Lucky had taken it one step further and decided we must have hidden her body.

"Don't be talking about Momma." I shoved off the workbench. This fool needed to shut up now. I was done listening.

Turned out our old man had hedged his bets. He'd married Momma for her money, money that had bought the Boone farm. He'd wanted to turn it into cash, but she'd set it up as a trust for her boys and he couldn't undo that because it had been her own, separate property before the marriage.

He'd insured Momma's life six months before he'd tried to turn her, figuring he'd come out ahead either way. That was how he thought, and I only wished it had come as a surprise to my brothers and me.

After he'd tried to turn Momma and mostly failed, however, he'd had to answer to the Wolf Council. Werewolves in America mostly liked to keep to themselves, but the council dealt with any problems that cropped up and came down hard on wolves who broke our laws.

They'd made our daddy disappear. He was doing hard time now in the remote wildlands of Alaska. Worse, he'd be trapped in his wolf form for the rest of his life because once the mating bite was given, a wolf couldn't be away from his mate for more than a full turn of the moon. He'd shift into his wolf and be stuck.

That was what had happened to our old man shortly after he'd left Moon-light Valley so involuntarily. Ranger had spoken for all of us when he'd said he hoped the old man ran into a hungry polar bear sooner rather than later.

"Your daddy and I were in business together," Lucky pointed out. "He'd joined my pack."

"And?"

"And he owed me money. First he said he'd put the Boone spread up as collateral for the debt, but then your sister's boyfriend, that Oliver Holmes, swept in and charmed your momma into letting him put all her property into a trust."

"Oliver isn't Mack's boyfriend." He had, however, been a friend of Momma's and then later Maverick's adviser at university.

When our daddy's less-than-stellar character had become obvious, Mack had convinced Momma to draw up a trust and put all her assets into it and make her kids the sole beneficiaries. She'd trusted us to take care of her, and we had failed her.

Lucky ignored me and swept on. "Your daddy was understandably upset, but he promised me that he would make good on what he owed, but instead he up and ran away. Rumor says the Wolf Council sent him packing, but for sure he's gone and I've got to do it all on my own. That's where there's room for you and your brother." Lucky surveyed the barn.

"So, you've got an opossum problem? A raccoon that needs relocating?"

"Your daddy *handled* business problems for me..."

I stared at Lucky, not knowing what he was getting at. I was, however, sure he would tell me.

He made an impatient noise. "He worked as the enforcer for my pack."

Lucky Jansen's pack was more of a biker gang that got furry. What they couldn't terrorize with their fists and their bikes, they dominated with their claws and teeth. I'd thought they stuck to their own kind, but maybe I'd been wrong.

"You and Atticus, you two are gonna handle the problem cases for us." Big Joe spelled it out even as I realized what Lucky was driving at. He wanted me to go beat up on anyone who had the guts to stand up to the Iron Wolves.

I made a sound of disgust. "Hell no, I'm not doing that."

"Hell yes, you are. You do what I tell you, boy."

"Hell. No. I am not your boy, either." Punching my visitors in the mouth was growing in appeal by the moment.

Lucky must have cottoned on to my rapidly fading patience because he inserted himself between me and Big Joe before the two of us could get into it. "We got video of your brother going after your daddy. Shot by an unknown source, of course." He winked, pulled out his phone, and pecked at the screen. "I'll send that video to you now.

"The funniest thing happened during their fight. One minute, there's your brother standing there, and then there's some kind of magic, something entirely unnatural, and he's turned into a wolf.

"You and I both know the truth about shifting, but it'll come as a shock to most of the fine people in Tennessee. Imagine something like that running on the local news. Or YouTube. TikTok. It would be one of those viral sensations."

The phone in my back pocket buzzed, and my blood ran cold. This was bad. Beyond bad. Not only would Maverick be in trouble with the council for letting out the big lycanthropy secret, but Lucky would hold it over his head.

"I could sell that video to one of those television shows that hunts unnatural creatures. Or I could drop a word in Alessandro Aymes's ear. Let him know that there are unsanctioned wild wolves running around your property.

"Either way, someone's gonna come hunting for your brother, and I bet they find him." Lucky stared at me. "Or one of you."

"No one will believe you," I said. "They'll say you fabricated the whole thing."

Lucky's teeth gleamed unnaturally. "Or say that I share the first part of that video, boy. No one's seen your old man alive since this fight; it'll look like your brother went after your old man and killed him. It should be more than enough to see him arrested, tried, and convicted by the fine state of Tennessee.

"And if that don't work, there's a little surprise for you at the end of the video. Watch it. Think on it. I'll give you until the full moon to decide.

"You come on out to the Iron Wolves' bonfire that night and you can shift and run with your new pack—or I'll send a copy of this video to the local police chief and his teenage son. It will be all over the internet before you can say *wolf.*"

*   *   *

I reminded myself to think and plan out my next steps, not just growl and snarl at anyone who came my way. Lucky and his goons had told me they had copies of that incriminating video stashed on multiple servers with instructions to upload it to YouTube if anything suspicious happened to one of them.

I thought about texting Maverick, but there was no point. Maverick was now a law-abiding wildlife biologist who taught science courses at our local community college and who was also up in the Smoky Mountains. He was looking for hognose snakes for some paper he was working on and was completely unreachable other than by satellite phone.

As this was not a conversation I wanted to be having in a public space, it would have to keep until Maverick came home.

Given that Lucky Jansen had extended his "invitation" to me and my twin, I had no choice but to bring Atticus in. He had a level head and gave good advice, plus there was the whole secret twin communication thing. I did not keep secrets from him.

I had no intention of including my other brothers in that conversation, however. If it turned out that the only way to keep Maverick out of jail was shaking down local business owners for Lucky, we would do it alone.

Having a copy of the video on my phone made me nervous—Ranger had drilled it into us all that anything that went on our phones also went up into the cloud where it could be accessed by him, the U.S. federal government, a billion hackers, and probably God himself.

Trying to mitigate the exposure, I downloaded the video to my phone, deleted it from my online storage, and turned off all my syncs. I doubted that would be enough if I was hit by a bus and someone went through my phone, but at least I'd tried.

To be on the safe side, I went way up the mountain where there was no internet and my phone got only one sad bar of service. I put it into airplane mode for good measure and opened the video.

Maverick hadn't ever said much about that night when he'd confronted our daddy and Momma hadn't made the shift back to human.

What I saw on my phone made me see red.

CHAPTER
EIGHT
~ALICE~

Where does a werewolf sleep? Anywhere he wants to.

— PATRICIA BRIGGS

I'd expected to find an empty yard when I returned to the spot where Aunt Sally's trailer had stood (or at least, as empty as it could get considering she'd been a bit of a hoarder). I'd told myself that it could be a nice symbol of starting over. A blank slate.

To my surprise, it was *not* empty.

There was a house where there had once been the remains of the trailer and the tree-catastrophe.

A teeny, absolutely darling, tiny house.

The house was pink with white trim and had a white picket fence. There was a tin roof that would sound amazing when it rained and I was tucked up in bed. It was the cutest, most feminine thing I'd ever seen.

But the pretty scene was marred by the big snarly wolf-man lounging in one of the Adirondack chairs that had been set out on the postage stamp-sized front deck. He was glowering anxiously and wearing his usual lumberjack outfit of a black thermal and faded blue jeans that hugged his thighs and hips.

As I walked up—after pinching myself to verify this was not some kind of

89

weird house-porn dream—I realized the shirt's color made his eyes almost gray.

He kept right on glowering, his stern gaze never leaving my face, and I promptly got all hot. Ford's grumpiness bothered me in all sorts of sexy ways, and not because we'd spent yesterday afternoon kissing in his tack room.

"Why are you here? Why is there a *HOUSE* here?" I walked up the steps and waved a hand around Aunt Sally's yard.

It was Thursday afternoon and I'd finished my shift at Vanity Fur Salon. Alessandro had asked me to meet him here because he wanted to choose some things to remember Aunt Sally by.

Instead of answering my question. Ford snagged my hand and pulled me down onto his lap. I landed less than gracefully, provoking an annoying smirk from him, but then he leaned into me and gave me a soft, hot kiss that made me stop being annoyed and start wondering exactly how much time we had before Alessandro showed up.

Once I was breathless from his kissing, he leaned back, his big hands holding my hips as if he wasn't ready to let go of me. I liked that, although his next words had me frowning.

"Welcome home."

My mouth fell open for obvious reasons—if wishful thinking could have transformed a broken-down trailer into a cute little cottage, the real estate market would have been revolutionized—and stared at him.

"Welcome...home?"

"Yeah." A smile-smirk tugged at the corner of his mouth. "Your home. You can move in now, or you can put it on the market and buy something you like better."

"I'm confused." I needed four eyeballs because half of me wanted to memorize Ford's beautiful, grumpy face, but the other half wanted to check out the amazing cottage that had sprouted on Aunt Sally's trailer pad.

It looked like something from Pinterest. I didn't know anything about tiny homes, but this one was a chocolate box of a house.

"While we negotiate a price for the land, you need a place to stay. This one is yours. We can move it later if you want."

I blinked more rapidly than a firefly looking for a mate. Ford was speaking English, but I was not following. "Whose house is this? Where did it come from? Did it fall out of the sky like the house that landed on the Wicked Witch in *The Wizard of Oz*?"

There had been no tornado warnings that I was aware of, but clearly anything was possible.

"I built it. I got a kit." Ford picked up my hand and curled my fingers around a key. The pink ribbon tied to the key matched the paint on the house.

"You built it?"

"Yeah."

"In a few days?"

Ford nodded.

My gaze bounced between the key I was holding and the man who was holding me. This was... I was... "You can't build me a house."

He shrugged. "Sure I can. I know it's a common misconception that men won't follow directions, but I made an exception for you."

"It's an entire house! It's too much. I mean, I'm no expert on dating, but this is not what you bring someone on a first date."

He regarded me intently. "What do you bring?"

"I..." was not sure what part of *not an expert* had failed to register with him. "Flowers. Candy. A scented candle or maybe bug spray if you're going walking in the Tennessee woods."

I waved my hands around as if I could pluck reasonable, coherent words out of the air. He clearly did not understand dating any more than I did. "This is nuts. You're too much."

A slow smile lit up his face, here and then gone like the sun peeking out from behind the clouds. I made a mental note that Ford Boone liked getting me all riled up.

"Go inside. Check it out." He lifted me gently off his lap, then plucked the key from my hand and reached around me to insert it into the lock.

I stood there sandwiched between Ford and the front door, his torso pressed up against my back as he reached an arm over me to push the door gently open. This must be what it felt like to be standing at the pearly gates, watching them swing wide. It was...magical.

"You gonna go in, baby?"

Because I had the curiosity of a cat, I did look inside. My feet crossed the threshold all of a foot, and I looked and then looked some more.

There was a little galley kitchen with maple wood countertops and blue cabinetry. Someone had painted the window frames a matching blue and left them open to catch the night air. White shiplap lined the walls, and the floors were honey-colored hardwood. A fairytale-worthy staircase curved up and up to a sleeping loft. A bathroom, door ajar, sparkled with subway and Moroccan tiles.

And, miracle of miracles, a minuscule mudroom with built-in cat beds and litter boxes had been prepared for Emperor Meowpatine and his entourage. There was even a teeny desk with a notepad and pen already set out for writing lists.

"I can't," I said, more reluctantly than I cared to admit. No one expected a house as a present, not unless they were related to the Queen of England. I could not accept this.

Ford gave me a soft kiss. "Sure you can. Don't you want a house?"

"Of course I do. But that's not the point." I forced myself to look away from the house and faced him. I had to curl my fingers around the doorframe (pink!) because my house lust was sucking me inside. "This doesn't make sense. I should go look at rental lists or get an Airbnb until I've got Aunt Sally's stuff sorted out."

"No." His eyes sheeted amber. I'd noticed that happened when he was frustrated. "This is a perfectly good house. It's small, yes. But it meets all the zoning and permitting laws. I've had a licensed electrician and plumber out to hook things up, and I've done all the rest myself.

"It has four good walls, a ceiling, locks on the doors. I wouldn't ask you to stay anywhere unsafe. You'll be comfortable here, and you won't be wasting money on a rental."

I shook my head and threaded my fingers through his. He'd misunderstood me. "This is a gorgeous house."

"Then what's the problem?"

"The problem is that it's a *house*. It is far too valuable for you to go around lending. Do you think you're Oprah?"

"It's not a loan," he said obstinately. "It's a gift."

My mouth fell open. "Ford."

"You deserve a nice house."

"You can't be serious."

"I am." He frowned at me.

"Why would you give me a house?"

"Because you need one and I could do it. You don't have a place of your own to stay. You'd let me give you a hoodie or a casserole, right?"

"This is a *house*," I gritted out. "It's not the same thing at all. You're comparing a drop of water with an entire ocean! You could rent this out for a fortune!"

He shrugged. "I can't rent it because I gave it to you."

"You can't give me a HOUSE!" I hollered.

"I CAN!" he shouted back, making the windows rattle.

I'd known Ford was stubborn, having experienced it firsthand on more than one occasion. Right now, however, he was reminding me his stubbornness could be both a blessing and a curse.

He'd nominated himself to take care of me, having decided that someone should do it, and I was discovering that kisses were not the only seductive thing in this world. His desire to take care of me was also appealing. He didn't ask; he just went ahead and did it.

He gave me the faintest shadow of a grin, the hard line of his jaw underlining his determination. He'd made up his mind, and that was that.

Ford had to be the most irritating, stubborn man I'd ever met...and he was also the most thoughtful. He wanted to fix things for me, take care of me. That simultaneously made him the nicest and most presumptuous thing ever.

"You want to know something?" He banded his arms around my middle, his mouth brushing my ear. I shivered. The man had an unfair advantage—he could wrap me up in all his sexy. How was I supposed to resist?

"I bet you'll tell me," I grumped.

He snorted. "I'm gonna win this argument for one reason."

I shook my head. "It's not going to be because you're right."

He nipped my ear. "I'm gonna win because there's no way you can move this house on your own."

He made a good point.

Also, he was going to win because I was weak and I coveted his house. And him. And him in what was apparently now my new house.

"All right," I conceded. "Yes. Temporarily. For now. Thank you."

The grin on his face grew like the sun coming up over the horizon or something suitably poetic. Looking out for me made Ford happy. This was very much a win-win situation from my point of view.

Plus, I liked making him laugh and feel good. And it was starting to seem like all I had to do was show up and be myself. It was intoxicating. He didn't want me to be someone different, and he definitely wanted to spoil me. I could live with that.

I let him nudge me all the way inside and then I gave up resisting and bounced around like a bargain shopper on Black Friday, checking everything out. How could any girl resist? He'd built me a *HOUSE*. Even better, I realized as I checked it out, he'd salvaged what he could from Aunt Sally's things.

"I can't believe you built me a little love shack," I told him.

He snorted. "Is that what you're calling it?"

"You think I should name it? Temporarily?" It would be like naming the kitten that followed you home: I would fall in love and never, ever give it back.

"You bet." Ford leaned against the wall, doing that sexy, smoldering slouch that men seemed to know how to perform instinctively. He was the best wall art ever.

"The Little Love Den, it is." I grinned at him. I had no idea how to thank him. Words did not seem sufficient.

Still trying to work it out, I climbed up into the sleeping loft and laid down on the bed. The skylight above my head would offer a view of the stars come nightfall, and Aunt Sally's favorite blue-and-white quilt on the bed. I didn't know how he'd managed to save the bed covering from the wreckage, but there it was, clean and only a little the worse for wear.

I rolled over onto my stomach, resting my chin on my hands. With Ford on the stairs, this made our faces level. It was like a scene from a romance novel where the heroine is up in the hayloft and the hero-stablehand pokes his head through the trapdoor and then everything was lined up for kissing. In other words, it was a sign from the universe. *I'm listening, Universe.*

Ford looked at me stoically. "I know you don't need rescuing. You're strong and smart. You can fix anything. But maybe you could let me help."

"Why?" People, in my experience, did not actually help for no reason at all. Sometimes they did it to feel good at their church or because they were paying back someone else's help that they felt guilty for. Most of the time, however, they wanted something in return. My parents had certainly believed you had to work hard and free lunches did not exist.

Ford rested his corded forearms on top of the stairs. He had all these interesting lines and muscles in his arms that moved and flexed. All I had to do was reach out and I could have my wicked way with him. I liked this closeness, although it made me nervous.

"Because it makes me feel good to be your white knight. You could let me help."

"When did you get to be such a good talker?" The Ford I remembered stomped and snarled. He'd never been one for persuasive argument.

He lifted an eyebrow. "Maybe I'm very motivated."

I decided we needed a new topic of conversation. "So how much does a house like this cost? What strings are attached? No one gives away houses for free."

To give Ford credit, he looked horrified. "This isn't a sex thing."

"Ford Boone, I'm ashamed of you!" The corners of his mouth quirked up, and somehow my fingers were tracing those cute little dents. "So you never, ever want thank-you sex? Or I'm-so-grateful sex?"

He exhaled, sounding put-upon. "It's a gift, Alice."

"So I should feel free to give you gifts?" He frowned, but I kept right on teasing him. "Like, what if I wanted to give you a kiss?"

"That," he said gravely, "would be acceptable."

We were practically kissing now, so it was hardly inconvenient.

I fisted the front of his thermal and tugged him toward me, and I kissed him.

THANK YOU!

That's what my mouth started out saying, anyhow, but then the conversation went off the rails.

Someone (me) was making husky, whimpering noises, and someone else (him) groaned, and then there was a whole lot of *YES* and *MORE PLEASE* and *LIKE THAT?* and *YOU BET* being exchanged between us.

I got to be in charge for only two seconds. Ford took over our kissing, his big hand cupping the back of my head and angling my face toward his. His mouth covered mine, devouring me like he couldn't wait another moment to get inside me.

This worked for me. I melted into his kiss despite the awkward kissing logistics. His mouth moved over mine, his tongue making hot forays inside my mouth as he staked his claim.

I felt worked up and hot, restless and energized, all at once. I also felt safer and more at home than I ever had, which I suspected was going to be a problem. My imagination sprinted off into a future where Ford and I kissed all the time like this.

But then the sharp staccato of a fist hammering on my (MY!) new front door jolted me back into the present. Ford's hand slipped away as he turned to glare at the intruder.

"What the hell is happening here?" Alessandro barged through my front door without waiting for an invitation, glaring angrily at Ford.

I knocked my forehead against my new bed. "Alessandro! Did I say you could come in?"

"What is going on here?" Alessandro didn't sound chastened—he sounded pissed off.

I shook my head and buried my face in the bed. "You can't tell? Did you miss sex ed in high school?"

Ford made a choked noise. I blamed it on my saying *sex* in front of my third cousin twice removed.

"Alice…" Alessandro propped his hands on his hips. He wore his animal control officer uniform, which consisted of sensible khaki pants an olive-green uniform shirt. His shiny gold badge was pinned over his heart and he sported an official patch on his arm. I was supposed to be impressed, I was sure.

But I wasn't a stray dog, and I was tired of the people in my life deciding that they knew best for me. My parents had argued that, after college, I should go work for a big company like Petco or Chewy and learn the pet business ropes from experts. They also thought moving to Nashville at my age was overly ambitious and that instead I should be focused on internships, externships, and listening to them.

I was so tired of it that I gave in to the urge to misbehave.

"Look! The house fairy's come! And left a house under my pillow." And then when Alessandro's eyes narrowed, directing a glare my way, I gave up altogether on being nice. "It's like a Barbie house except that it comes with a Ford doll instead of a plastic boy toy."

Ford made a rough sound. I promptly added it to my catalog of Ford sounds. It was husky and amused with notes of disbelief.

"This is your house?" Alessandro looked stunned. He, too, was surprised to see Aunt Sally's old trailer replaced with a cute cottage.

"Mm-hmm. I came out here and I found this house. If you'll excuse me, I have my Ford to play with." I gave Alessandro another moment (I was feeling generous) to process his disbelief before I stabbed a finger at the door. "Out. Feel free to start going through the stuff outside."

Much to my surprise, Alessandro turned and stormed outside.

* * *

Having my third cousin twice removed stomping around the yard was better than any contraceptive.

I would not be fooling around with Ford where Alessandro could storm in on us. Again.

"We need to go," I told Ford.

He looked at me steadily, a whole lot of heat in his dark eyes. That heat was cohabitating with some very sexy promises along and, for a moment, I was tempted to pull him up into the loft and set about convincing him to christen my new bed.

The sound of Alessandro investigating Aunt Sally's inexplicable collection of toilet lawn ornaments was a deterrent, however.

I settled for landing a quick kiss on his mouth.

"Later," I promised him.

He nodded and retreated down the steps. I followed. I'd never owned a house before, and my new place had won me over. It felt like more than a place to sleep or live in.

I'll take care of you, I mentally told Little Love Den. *I love you* and *I will always, always hire a trained arborist to prune the big, nasty trees in your yard.*

I let Ford tug me outside and then I fussed around with the key. Most folks didn't bother locking their doors in Moonlight Valley, but I wasn't going to take any chances and it would be dark in a few hours. Alessandro shot us a glare-glance as we walked past him, and I decided to ignore him.

It was the perfect temperature for a walk, plus Ford knew these woods. Perhaps he'd run around them in his wolf form?

He set a big, warm hand at the small of my back and gently steered me along a path that was more or less invisible. It took us through a hollow surrounded by hardwood trees and filled with mostly waist-high grasses. As far as hiking trails went, it was easy and pretty, although I had some unwelcome thoughts about deer ticks.

The more dark set in, the more the fireflies came out, blinking and flashing. We were basically walking through a gigantic firefly orgy. No big deal.

Briefly, I wondered whether I should be making conversation, but the silence between us was companionable. I liked that I didn't have to rush to fill it up with words.

I looked at Ford from the corner of my eye and caught him watching me. He had donned his usual inscrutable expression, and I had no idea what he was

97

thinking. He'd done so much for me—I felt like I should have done a better job of thanking him.

He shook his head, as if he could read my mind. "We're good."

We were. We walked in companionable silence, holding hands and enjoying the woods. I didn't have to be interesting or sexy, flirty or Pulitzer-Prize-winning smart. It was enough to enjoy some time together.

Our quiet time did suffer some when I heard Alessandro's truck roaring passive-aggressively away, the rumble of his diesel engine echoing off the trees.

"The coast is clear," I announced, more jubilantly than was polite.

The corners of Ford's mouth quirked up. "Alessandro wants what's best for you. I mean, he's a jackass, but—"

"But he's an affectionate donkey?"

Ford lifted one shoulder. "He's annoying, but he's your family."

"Ford Boone, you do know what year this is, correct?"

He gave me a small head tip.

"Because," I continued, "I don't need my family's approval if, say, I wanted to date someone. I would be free to see them because it was what I chose to do. I'm the only one whose permission is needed and I already gave it!"

Ford threaded his fingers through mine and raised my hand to his mouth. His lips teased my skin. "I should warn you then that we wolves take our mating seriously. We settle down with one person for life."

I nodded thoughtfully. "Do you believe in fated mates? Or some kind of supernatural sign like a blue moon?"

I didn't want to make fun of his traditions or beliefs, but I'd also read romance novels where the hero knew as soon as he met the heroine that she was his one and only. I liked that thought—it was straightforward, sure, and free of the usual dating awkwardness. Instead of going to a bar and hoping to meet your perfect person, the moon or your wolf instincts or whatever pointed him or her out to you.

"No."

"So then what?" Part of me, I had to admit, was disappointed.

He looked thoughtful. "Not fated. That would imply I didn't have a choice."

"And do you? Have a choice, that is?" I was far more invested in his answer than I should have been.

The corners of his mouth twitched upward, his eyes heating. "I would choose you."

I might have flushed. This was the best—and the worst—answer ever, one that filled me with both anticipation and dread. Bottom line: this man was not fooling around. He'd looked at me and he'd decided he wanted his chance. Not that Ford Boone was some kind of Neanderthal who wouldn't take *no* for an answer. He would.

The problem was that I wanted to give him a *yes*.

"When did you decide that you wanted to be a business owner?" Ford asked.

"For as long as I can remember," I admitted. "I used to sit under my daddy's desk at his work in the summers, before they started sending me to Aunt Sally's. School was out, and they never could line up enough childcare because they worked ridiculously long hours.

"One year when I was little, I'd been given a plastic cash register and a hundred-piece grocery set. I decided to go into business, but I was also convinced that it was unethical to sell fakes, so I cleaned out the kitchen and held a sale in front of our house. I sold two hundred dollars' worth of groceries for ten dollars and twenty cents."

Ford laughed. "Is that so?"

"I was real popular with our neighbors.

"Later on, I started reading every business book I could get my hands on. I worked one summer in the pet store two towns over from Moonlight Valley. My parents were fine with it because Aymeses always work.

"You came in once when I was working, do you remember? You made me look up fourteen different kinds of kitten formula and call you sir."

He snorted. "I came in every day for a week to make you do that."

He had and I'd wanted to kill him. "I'd see you in there with your momma and Rebel, sometimes Ranger. He liked to look at the tropical fish."

There was a flash of something large and furry, sleek and almost silver. It was a white wolf, here and then gone on the edge of the clearing.

"Someone you know?"

I couldn't read the expression that flashed over Ford's face. "Not all wolves are people too."

"How do you tell them apart?"

He shrugged. "Scent, mostly."

The path, such as it was, petered out, leaving us standing on the bank of a creek that wound its way through the hardwood trees. The moonlight filtered down through the branches and the creek swept on past, whispering secrets. It was magical.

"This was my momma's favorite spot for a walk."

We both looked around the clearing, as if she might appear.

"I was sorry to hear about her." I wrapped my arms around Ford's middle, squeezing gently. "She was a special person and I know everyone in Moonlight Valley misses her and hopes she'll be back. If there's something I can do, please let me know."

I was sure lots of people had told Ford and his brothers exactly this. But I meant it. I wanted—*needed*—to be here for him, however I could.

He nodded, pressing his lips together as he hugged me. *Offer accepted.*

"It's complicated," he said gruffly, his mouth brushing my hair. "But thank you."

I didn't think running off was all that complicated. It also didn't seem like something that Mrs. Boone would have done. No one had ever doubted that she loved her family. (Well, with the obvious exception of Boone Senior but, as Aunt Sally had said more than once, a woman had to take the bad with the good and we all knew which category *he* fell into.)

After a while, we stopped talking, walked back to my new house, and let the memories be for now.

Sitting on that porch with Ford, time slipped as gently away as if we were watching water bugs skate lazy circles on the creek's surface. You kind of forgot that you had places to be, a to-do list, obligations. It was nice.

I couldn't help but think about future evenings like this and how nice it would be to always have Ford as my porch buddy. How it was both safe and seductively disturbing, this casual intimacy between us.

And how I wouldn't have missed this night for anything.

CHAPTER
NINE
~ALICE~

Bring it on, fur-ass!

— CHARLAINE HARRIS

"So you're dating Ford Boone."

I looked up from my workstation at Vanity Fur Salon and discovered that Alessandro was my next client. Pom-Pom, his hyperactive Pomeranian, pranced around his boots. Unlike my sour, grumpy cousin, Pom-Pom was a darling and had even made friends with my cats.

"We're going out on a date." I did not want to overstate or jinx things. Alessandro had already shared his opinions (uninvited) about the advisability of Boone-Aymes interaction when I had stopped at his house Thursday night after saying goodbye to Ford.

I'd packed up my stuff and my cats and announced my intention of moving into the Little Love Den, so that might've contributed to his pouting. Also, I'd avoided him assiduously since then, so booking a grooming with me might have seemed like a feasible plan to my cousin.

I was not in the mood to listen to his opinions on my love life then, and I was no more in the mood now. My feelings had more ups and downs than a yo-yo. I missed Ford. I worried that I missed him. And I missed more than his grumpy face, stern eyes, and big hands.

I'd accepted the Little Love Den as a temporary landing place, but not as my forever home. Secretly, I planned on working something out with Atticus and Ranger, taking less for the lot as a way to compensate Ford for the time and money he'd spent building the tiny home.

If Ford discovered I was plotting to repay him, he'd be pissed. I normally avoided confrontation. My parents had argued, and then argued some more. Mostly they'd battled about who got to go into work and who had to stay behind with me.

Fighting with Ford was different. I even looked forward to it. When we disagreed, we learned things about each other. It also made me realize he cared about me. Ford did not ignore what I did or thought. I wondered what we would disagree about on our date and mentally started a list of possible argument topics.

This was not what most people did to prepare for a date. I was a little strange.

Since we'd parted ways on Thursday, I'd thought about texting or calling him a billion times for no other reason than to hear his voice, maybe to invite him to count fireflies with me so we could hug in the old deer blind that was my firefly-count headquarters.

I'd always been a big fan of hugging and holding hands. I loved the warm connection and the firm, strong grip of a man who worked with his hands, calloused and rough-gentle. I loved leaning into someone and knowing he was there.

Up until I'd kissed Ford in his truck and he'd kissed me back a week ago, I'd thought the hand-holding and the hugging was the best part of dating. My previous experiences with kissing and sex had been disappointing, to say the least. Ninety-nine percent of the boys I'd gone out with hadn't wanted to spend much time on my favorite part, either.

In high school we'd all been trying to figure the sex thing out and no one had had their own place (or even their own car). Dating had been an imperfect art that had not improved much in college. I'd had to initiate the snuggling and then I'd had to do all the foreplay. It was a lot of work and not much reward. Ford had made me rethink that conclusion.

It had caused me so much rethinking that I wasn't done by the time I'd finished grooming Pom-Pom. Alessandro had made a few attempts to converse, but I ignored him. Now I gave a last brush, adjusted my client's jaunty bow, and kissed his head.

"Done!" I waved a hand toward the cash register at the front of the salon. "Let's go!"

Alessandro reluctantly picked up his dog. "Where are you going on your date? Are you wearing that?"

I narrowed my eyes suspiciously. "Why are you asking?"

I had not gone on many dates, either during or outside of my Moonlight Valley stays. As an employee manual-following Vanity Fur Salon employee, I wore a hot pink T-shirt with the salon name on it. This let our potential customers know they were dealing with a bona fide employee and not some random person who had decided to sneak onto our premises and groom their dogs, although we were allowed to choose what else we wore.

Today I'd paired the shop tee with jeans and a white T-shirt. The outfit was comfortable and went in both the washer and the dryer, which was an important feature given the amount of loose fur that accumulated inside the salon. Whether it was date-worthy was debatable.

I reached for my journal, flipped to a new, blank page, and wrote: *Buy fun date-night clothes*. This was for me, not Ford.

"Do you think I should buy costumes?" I looked at Alessandro out of the corner of my eye as I adjusted the blue-and-white bow on Pom-Pom's head. He (Alessandro, not the dog) had turned bright red. "Naughty school girl? Are there others?"

Alessandro sputtered.

If there were costumes in my dating future, it was the far distant, hundred-years-away future. Ford had said he wanted to take this slow and get it right. *This* being our dating and *it* being...I had no idea. Maybe he'd meant our entire relationship? It was a lot of weight to put on a two-letter pronoun.

Ford had texted to make sure I was in safely on Thursday night, but he had not reached out on Friday. We'd agreed on tonight for our date, but I suspected we would not be christening the bed in my new, temporary home even though he'd said *I would choose you*. He'd make me wait for more than kisses. How long did a courtship take, anyhow?

I was not a patient woman. I liked instant grits, fast-acting carbs, and freezing my soda pop cans to make slushies. Not kissing me because he'd decided to conduct our relationship by medieval courtship rules would only result in us arguing—and him learning a very important thing about me.

"I'm worried about you dating one of the Boone brothers," he said as we headed toward the cash register.

"Oh, really?"

I might have subsequently overcharged him.

"Yes," he growled. "They're renegades and rule-breakers, the whole lot of them. They keep a pack of wild animals on their property. They're dangerous. I don't want you spending your time anywhere near them, let alone on a date with Ford Boone. He is not boyfriend material."

"That's what you think."

"He's not nice." Alessandro glared at me over the cash register. Pom-Pom started barking because, like every male, he also felt the need to weigh in uninvited on my personal life. "He has family here, and you want to relocate to Nashville. So the way I see it, he'll convince you to stay in Moonlight Valley and then you'll never get to leave and have that…"

"Why wouldn't I be able to leave? Does he have a secret dungeon? Handcuffs? A daddy fetish? Is he an orc in disguise who is going to impregnate me and drag me off to his orc mountain?"

Alessandro dragged a hand down his face. "You need to stop reading what's on Aunt Sally's Kindle."

I refrained from pointing out that *Alessandro* knew what was on there. It had been eye-opening. And fun. Alessandro, however, looked scandalized. It must have been the orcs.

"I want you to be happy," he spat out. "And you've always wanted to have your own business in Nashville. Which you can't do if you're settling down with Ford here in Moonlight Valley. Guys like him want to stay near their family homes. Have lots of babies. Drive a big truck and go tubing on the river. He's never going to *leave*, Alice. And you have always, *always* wanted to go."

I hated it when people suggested that my big Nashville plans were about running away, rather than running toward a big success. There was nothing wrong with wanting a career and commercial success.

That does not make me a bitch or a bad person! It does not doom me to lonely unhappiness!

"That'll be forty dollars, please." I held out a hand. "Do you actually like your job?"

Did grownup people *get* to like their jobs?

"I have excellent health insurance and retirement benefits," he said a little stiffly.

I decided not to admit that those were, indeed, an incentive. Part-time groomers at Vanity Fur Salon did not qualify for benefits, and as a self-employed businesswoman, I'd also be on my own.

"Closing time!" I chirped cheerfully, and stabbed a finger at the door.

Alessandro left. There was some snarling at the door, however, which let me know that my wolfish date was there, waiting for me outside.

I barreled out, almost catching Alessandro in the door as I shut and locked it. He and Ford were busy exchanging testosterone-filled man glares while Pom-Pom yapped furiously in solidarity.

"Hey." I grabbed Ford's hand and squeezed it, happiness bubbling up in me.

Much to my enjoyment, he pulled me into his side, and for a moment I enjoyed the boneless feeling of bliss as I cozied up. He was warm and solid, smelling of pine trees and cedarwood. His beard tickled my cheek as he leaned down and dropped a kiss on my forehead. I glowed. *Take that Alessandro!*

"Evening, Alice. You look—"

"Ready!"

I tried to drag him away from Vanity Fur Salon and my cousin, but he dug in his heels (he was wearing *cowboy boots*) and refused to budge.

"We should say hi to your cousin."

"Third cousin. Twice removed." I considered removing him even further, possibly to Antarctica. "Consider him greeted."

Which was the point at which I got my first real good look at my date. Ford had cleaned up for me. I could have told him it wasn't necessary—I found scruffy Ford in his beat-up blue jeans and shoulder-hugging T-shirts absolutely scrumptious. There was no need to repackage what already worked.

I had been wrong.

Date Night Ford wore dark jeans, the aforementioned cowboy boots, and a green button-down shirt that brought out the color of his eyes; his red beard was neatly trimmed. He'd rolled his shirtsleeves up, exposing strong, muscled forearms. Lightly dusted with hair, they promised he had the useful kind of strength—for getting shit done, fixing my car, or plowing me a three-acre flower garden. They also (spoiler alert) made a gal wonder what else he was hiding underneath his clothes aside from the wolf.

Pro tip: All men should roll up their shirtsleeves, all the time.

Ford had asked if I had family here in Moonlight Valley the other night. He'd hoped to ask my daddy's permission to step out with me. Possibly, he'd planned on bringing my momma flowers to get on her good side.

I could have told him the best way to do that was a business merger or a promotion. They were both busy conquering the corporate world in Nashville and did not have time to concern themselves with my dating life.

So I was surprised to see him standing there by his truck, holding a bouquet of flowers. To be specific: extravagant, bright pink and white lilies that were unexpectedly odiferous.

Ford held the flowers out...to Alessandro.

Alessandro gaped.

"For you." Ford jiggled the bouquet and the plastic wrap crinkled. There was a flower-shaped dog toy stuck inside the real flowers; Ford was apparently leaving nothing to chance and courting Pom-Pom as well. "They're pet-safe as long as you don't let Pom-Pom eat them."

Apparently no one had ever given Alessandro flowers before because he seemed at a loss for words.

Ford shoved the flowers into Alessandro's hands, then scritched the top of Pom-Pom's well-groomed head. He had to retrieve his hand quickly because it turned out that Pom-Pom did not like the smell of a wolf-man.

Ford looked at Alessandro. "You don't have to like me as long as Alice does, but you're her family. So I'll tell you: I'm taking her out tonight, and I promise she'll be safe with me."

Alessandro glared. More growling came from both the Pomeranian and the man.

"Oh my God." I threw up my hands. Since I was clutching Ford's hand in mine, I took him with me. "Let's stop with the posturing and go."

Ford nodded at Alessandro. "Are we good?"

Alessandro squint-glared at Ford. The flowers had helped with his mood some, but he was still cranky. "Why?"

"Because I can't talk with Alice's parents before I take her, so you're the next best thing."

Alessandro nodded, responding to some unspoken man-to-man mind question. It was super annoying. "Have her home by midnight."

Ford nodded, tucked my hand into the crook of his elbow like we were in a black-and-white movie, and walked me out to his truck.

I felt like a beauty pageant contestant during the evening gown competition, the kind where they brought out the lady's daddy to parade her across the stage. I even let him open the truck door and help me up into the seat. Fortunately for him, he didn't try to do my seatbelt for me, although he did shut the door.

Greedily, I watched him stride around the truck and get in, recognizing that I looked more than a little silly and eager as I twisted to keep him in view. It was worth it. He was sex on a stick, Ford was. If our date consisted of nothing more than watching him walk, I'd be a happy woman.

Ford fired up the engine and, in an upset and slaphappy giddy fog, I watched as Vanity Fur Salon disappeared in our rearview mirror. The salon, however, was the only thing that turned invisible. We paraded up Moonlight Valley's main street, drawing eyes wherever I looked.

"I'm sorry for how Alessandro acted." I shook my head. "He's living in the previous century, and I haven't been able to train him out of it."

Ford shrugged. "It's good for family to be protective. I look after mine, too."

There was a hint of wolf to his voice; I'd noticed that when he went overall protective, his voice dropped to a growl. His eyes, when they slid to mine, were blue without a hint of gold or amber. He wasn't upset, then—merely making a point. A smile flickered on his face, and I melted a bit.

Ford didn't smile all that often, so I treasured it when he did. In all the summers I'd spent in Moonlight Valley and all the times our paths had crossed (loudly), I'd never once guessed that Ford had a sense of humor. Or was a flirt.

Devious? Yes.

Intelligent? Absolutely.

Serious and stern? Spank me, daddy! (No, really, he was.)

Funny and flirty? Not on my radar.

This man surprised me, and not just with his shapeshifting.

We were such opposites that I'd never once, not ever, imagined Ford Boone would be interested in me. Not because I was unattractive or had a fundamental flaw, but because heretofore I'd been certain I irritated the heck out of him.

And vice versa.

But here we were…

Going on a date.

He slid a hand across the seat to find mine. "Penny for your thoughts?"

"I hope I'm worth more than that."

His slow smile set me on fire. "Absolutely."

107

I considered teasing him, demanding an entire dollar, but then I told him for free.

"It seems weird and highly unlikely, the two of us going out on a date together. On purpose. We practically grew up together. We ran around the woods and swam in the creeks with the other Moonlight Valley kids like a pack of wild animals."

That barely there smile quirked the corners of his mouth. "And?"

"Wait. *Were* they wild animals?"

"Some of us were wilder than others," he muttered. And then, when I stared at him, he added, "No, not all of them were wolves. And the existence of shapeshifters is a secret, Alice. I can't name names."

"Because the wolfie council will come down on you."

He grimaced. "Something like that. Wolves are not supposed to come out to humans."

I was in the *know*.

A werewolf girlfriend.

Special.

Well, sort of. Ford and I had not put any labels on what we were to each other, and the idea that we'd voluntarily spend time together would have seemed laughable as recently as two weeks ago. But here we were, in his truck and going on a *date*.

"My point is we hated each other. Before. We were always fighting. So it's weird now to think we're dating."

"I like weird." He reached over and squeezed my fingers.

"Say that again when I'm licking all the seasoning off your Doritos and you're stuck with a bag of naked chips," I said.

Ford laughed. Now I wanted to stop for a snack, darn it.

"But seriously," I protested. "I'm too comfortable with you. I should be all nervous because we're on a *date* and my dates do not go well. And that's if they happen at all.

"I date once in a blue moon, which means every two years or so. My flirting skills are rustier than the Tinman after a rainstorm, and I don't think I can manage romantic. Or sexy. Dates are supposed to be those things, at least if you want a second one."

He nodded thoughtfully. "Maybe you've got the wrong definition of sexy or romantic then."

I stared at him suspiciously. "Have we moved on to the arguing portion of tonight's agenda?"

He gave a bark of laughter. "Hold your horses. I meant that I don't need you to pretend to be anyone other than who you. I like you. I think you're sexy."

No one had ever called me sexy before. Usually I heard something along the lines of *you'd be sexy if...*followed by a list of sex acts I should perform. Ford's genuine admiration made me feel beautiful.

Nevertheless, it was a bad idea to want things with Ford. I was one of those shallow-rooted plants, like kale or sweet woodruff. I was easy to pull up and transplant.

Ford had deep roots, roots that went down, down, and then down some more. He was a local business owner; he had a huge family that all lived in Moonlight Valley. He would never, ever leave Tennessee, and you'd have to pry him out of Moonlight Valley. He was at home here.

But Moonlight Valley wasn't my home. It was my pit stop.

Somehow, though, I'd stopped counting the hours until I could get out of town. I'd started putting down baby roots, even though Ford hadn't asked me to do so.

We'd barely passed the twenty-minute mark in our first honest-to-God date, for crying out loud.

* * *

Ford had suggested we hike to a waterfall known only to the Boone brothers. Not only was it three miles off the main road, but you practically needed a secret decoder ring to find the path. Despite its hard-to-find status, Ford had shouldered an enormous pack and confidently struck out into the woods, me following close on his heels.

It was the prettiest time of a summer day when the heat had moved on some but the light was golden and warm. Despite it's being suppertime, we had hours yet of daylight.

After years of bad dates, I felt like I'd achieved dating nirvana. Ford led me down the trail, holding branches and plotting the steadiest, driest course. It had rained heavily recently and muddy spots littered the trail.

His attention and chivalry left me feeling awkward and red-faced. I did not know what the etiquette was when the guy you were first-dating helped you over a fallen tree trunk or moved a branch. There were only so many times I could say thank you before it felt weird.

The first time I felt Ford's gaze on my butt, I thought it was wishful thinking on my part (hah). The second time, however, I realized that, thank you baby Jesus, he was not just being a gentleman wolf.

His fingers held mine longer than was strictly necessary and his gaze lingered on my butt after he'd jumped me down from a particularly large tree that had fallen across the path. He seemed to shake himself afterward, frowning at the innocent bushes and trees surrounding us, or up at the sunny sky, or at a ladybug that had meandered into our path.

His clenched jaw, the way his hands tightened on the straps of his pack, his determined stride—these were all signs that he was appreciating me, my butt, and my jeans.

It was almost a disappointment to reach our destination. I'd never been one of those people who twittered on about how the journey was so much more important and fun than the end goal, but now I got it.

Walking side by side with Ford was perfect. Still, the spot he'd picked out for our picnic was beautiful. Twin waterfalls cascaded down the rock face to land in a deep pool lined by trees far below us. If I'd known this place existed, I would have come here to swim every summer. I wished I'd brought a swimsuit.

"Beautiful." His voice was low and gruff, but it held equal parts confidence and sweetness.

He wasn't looking at the waterfall.

He was looking at me.

Ford wasn't a poet. I hadn't ever heard him sing or even hum. But somehow he managed to say so much with that one word, to say everything.

I wasn't his teenage nemesis or his childhood friend. I wasn't awkward, nerdy Alice or future business owner Alice. I wasn't Alessandro's third cousin (two times removed) or the Boones' neighbor and Aunt Sally's frequent guest. Or rather, I wasn't *just* those things—and he liked all of me.

Ford insisted on setting up our dinner. Or was it a linner? Dupper? I wandered away to look over the edge and down at the splashing water. After a dizzying moment, I conceded defeat to my fear of heights and laid down on my stomach. This was a much better position from which to peer over the edge.

"Come sit down." The quiet authority in Ford's voice made me quiver.

Big hands plucked me carefully off the ground. He set me on my feet, his body between me and the edge.

He hesitated.

We were close enough together that he had to feel the pounding of my heart trying to drill its way through my ribs. He bent his face to my throat, pressed his mouth against me, breathing me in. I liked that some invisible, unseen piece of me was traveling through him, taking up space in his lungs.

His eyes opened, lashes gliding up. The heat there about burned me up.

"We should eat," he said hoarsely. His eyes devoured me like I was a six-course meal of delicious pie.

"We could start with dessert." I sounded breathless.

His fingers tightened on my hips.

I slid my hands up his arms, linking them behind his neck and erasing the few inches of space between us so that I could press my body against his. Ford more than met me halfway, stepping into me, wrapping his strong arms around my waist and pulling me into his big body.

It was like a dance. The heat of his body radiated through the soft material of his shirt, his hard chest and stomach pressing against me. His eyes had gone over gold, his wolf rising with his passion.

I raised up on tiptoe and nipped his bottom lip.

"Mine," I whispered against his mouth.

It was a statement of fact, not a challenge. But it seemed to shatter Ford's control, because he covered my mouth with his, a rough growl tearing from his throat as he kissed the heck out of me.

Heat flooded my belly and moved south.

This man could *kiss*.

In the interest of giving him the most accurate performance review possible, I needed to get his shirt off. I needed to find out what the hard, muscled breadth of his shoulders felt like. I wanted to touch all of him.

I wanted to strip off my clothes.

Strip off everything and let him see all of me.

I needed his big, calloused hands cupping my face. Or my boobs. Or lower. *The answer is D! All of the above.*

My fingers got the memo from my brain to shove up his T-shirt and insert themselves beneath the lucky cotton hugging his bare skin. They untucked and undid, slipping beneath the back of his jeans to trace the delicious, hard man dimples at the base of his spine.

Yes! Let's go lower!

There were limitations to how much Ford I could touch while his jeans came between us, but I was highly motivated to try. My fingers teased his backside, pulling him to me, while he groaned something that sounded feral.

Words? Don't care!

All that mattered now was getting Ford naked.

I broke our kiss long enough to pull my own shirt over my head. For one wild moment, I considered tossing it over my shoulder. Letting it blow free in the breeze, hang from the branches.

Then sanity temporarily reasserted itself and I set it down on our packs. There was no point in courting ticks as well as Ford. And because I believed in equality, I unbuttoned his shirt while he unzipped my pants. We were making so much noise we wouldn't have noticed an army of hikers stumbling into our picnic spot. We were in the eye of the lust storm.

Ford steered us toward the picnic blanket he'd set out, sliding his large hands inside my jeans and cupping my butt. This was an excellent incentive to head in the direction he wanted, so I let myself be scooped up and set down on the blanket.

He came down over me, covering me with his body. I finally got his shirt unbuttoned all the way, only to discover a white cotton T-shirt standing between me and the promised land.

Unhappy at the level of effort unwrapping Ford was taking, I growled and attacked the offending cotton. The hot press of his muscular thigh against my core made me feel better (and how!), but I wanted more.

"Off," I demanded, tugging on his shirts.

Ford sat back on his knees and ripped off his button-down. It flew across the clearing, followed by the T-shirt, as his hot gaze moved over me.

But then, gosh darn it, he stopped moving. His eyes narrowed, some of the hot, lusty fog clearing as he inventoried my best black lace bra, sex hair, and unbuttoned jeans.

He frowned as if his wolf had picked *this* moment to chime in, shook his head like a dog coming out of the lake, and exhaled roughly. "Damn it."

We did not need religious sentiments right now. I reached for him, but he shook his head again. Frowned. Mouthed a particularly vicious curse.

These were not the sexy compliments I had been hoping for. Instead, he shot to his feet and paced, giving me an excellent view of his fine ass. Mentally, I added my own heartfelt *damn it*.

Sexy times were over.

Heaving a sigh, I stood up and put myself back together, congratulating myself for having had the foresight to not toss my clothes everywhere. Looking for them like a toddler on an Easter egg hunt would have been awkward.

We needed to talk about what had happened—or not happened. Ford kept pulling back, here and in the barn on All-Purpose Animal Services' business premises, and when we'd been almost skinny-dipping in the lake that Friday night, and on my night of ill-fated citizen science research.

Our kisses and frantic groping, not to mention the full-body hugging and hot looks, all pointed to the fact that Ford Boone wanted me—quite a lot—but was trying to be a gentleman. Or at least restraining his inner wolf.

I pulled on my shirt and sighed dramatically. Yes, I was feeling put-upon. I had not appreciated my previous romantic encounters trying to rush straight into physical intimacies faster than a sailfish bursting out of the water.

But with Ford, I felt like I was the one pushing him, and that was not okay either. I needed for us to be on the same page.

"I don't want to keep my hands to myself. My wolf doesn't either." Frustration saturated his expression—with himself, me, or possibly the lack of bedroom amenities at our secret picnic spot. I had no idea what was going through his head.

"I'm sorry." I had pushed, had disrespected his boundaries. "I should have asked if you were ready to be intimate with me."

Rueful amusement replaced exasperation on his face and he gave a bark of laughter. "Alice, I want to get this right."

I knew that. "My first clue was when you brought flowers for Alessandro."

"He didn't see that coming." A smile tugged at the corners of his mouth. "But he's your family, so he's gonna matter."

"He's so pretty that he deserves all the flowers," I said lightly.

Ford's smile faded. He looked at me cautiously. "I think we're more than suited. We would make good partners. Mates."

That word—*mates*—hung in the air between us. I could see it there, twirling and sparkling, beckoning and promising me things.

Things I could not have for real because I had no intention of staying here in Moonlight Valley for much longer. Things I couldn't have because I was the air plant in this pairing, while Ford was a shepherd's tree with roots that extended downward for hundreds of feet. It scared me.

"We don't know each other," he said, and I nodded vigorously because he was right even if some small, unexpected, overreaching part of me felt hurt by that claim.

"But we could," he continued. "I want to know everything about you."

It was a tall order, knowing everything about another person. Heck, it was a tall order just knowing *something*.

The beginning of a relationship was the fun part, like trying on clothes or sampling something new from a buffet restaurant. It was about *trying* more than it was about liking your choice or returning for more.

The expression on Ford's face, though... His face said he wouldn't try. He would *succeed*; he would come back over and over. He would be there for me if I agreed that was what I wanted.

His face held hope and an unexpected nervousness. This big, gorgeous, self-made man wasn't sure that *he* would be enough for *me*.

I never wanted him to feel less than. That's what did it, made me wake up. I was being self-centered, focused on myself and what I needed and wanted, but there were two of us standing here, face to face.

I would have to trust Ford, at least with my dreams and my hopes for my future. I didn't want to. I wanted to hang onto this handful of sexy, romantic, fun moments with him and not tell him the truth.

That I was leaving Moonlight Valley as soon as I had my business start-up cash socked away.

That I didn't see a future for us, not one that lasted longer than a few months or maybe a year.

I had plans, plans that did not have a line item or checkbox for Ford's honorable intentions or for courting and mating a werewolf.

I must have spent too long looking for words because Ford straightened up, and even though he didn't move, I felt him pulling away. He thought I didn't want him, not that way, not as someone more than a casual hookup.

"I should have shared some things with you on Wednesday." I wanted to reach out, to snag his hand and hold onto that bit of him, but I didn't. "I'm sorry. There's probably a better way to say this, but I'm going to put my cards on the table.

"I came to Moonlight Valley with a plan. I'd stay at Aunt Sally's and work at Vanity Fur Salon, but those were temporary things. I'm here, in Moonlight Valley, for two years max and probably only one. That should be enough time to wrap up Aunt Sally's things and save what I need for my business seed money.

"I'm not here for good, and I don't think I could settle down here. I have plans for a business in Nashville. There are opportunities there, a chance to really make something of myself. If I could, I'd open my store tomorrow and be out of here. But I like spending time with you so much and we..."

I didn't know how to finish that sentence. There were no good choices.

Ford stared at me as I spoke, the heated warmth fading from his eyes as it was replaced by something more reserved and distant. He tipped his head, clearly coming to some conclusion.

Part of me panicked, wishing I wasn't who I was. I wished I wanted to be a small-town girl, content to be Ford's mate and live here in Moonlight Valley forever. But a bigger part of me could feel the walls closing in and felt suffocated imagining that future.

I wanted to be more.

I wanted to put my dreams first.

Ford turned away from me and swiped his shirt from the ground, slipping into it. If I had kept my mouth shut, if I'd kissed him more and talked less, we could have kept on going. We could have dated, could have done this thing for a few weeks or a few months.

But even if he'd wanted to court me, it might not have worked. This wasn't one of those TV shows where you get married in ninety days.

Scaredy cat.

Those words rang out loud and clear in my head. My heart had something to say. Ford was right, and we were suited. I was just scared to take that chance with him.

"We should head back," Ford said. His voice was completely polite, with not a hint of his wolf peeking through. He could have been a trail guide or some random guy in the ice cream aisle at the Piggly Wiggly. He'd closed off that part of him he'd been offering to me; he'd shut me out.

I tried to send him an apology with my eyes, but my mental telepathy skills were poor. Instead, I nodded. "Yeah, we should."

What we both meant, of course, was that we shouldn't.

Shouldn't date.

Shouldn't try this again.

Shouldn't hope for more.

CHAPTER
TEN
~FORD~

...what was the good of being a movie werewolf? You howled at the moon; you couldn't remember what you did, and then somebody shot you.

— ANNE RICE

"How was your date with Firefly Girl? Have you set a wedding date?"

I looked up from the tabby kitten in my hand and found my brothers hovering in the door of the barn and watching me expectantly. The results of my date must have been obvious because Atticus and Ranger shared a concerned glance when I didn't offer an opinion.

"It went south, huh?" Atticus stroked his beard.

"It's not up for discussion." I tucked the tabby kitten into the incubator and picked up Caldenia. She started gnawing on my thumb, living up to her name. Ranger had all but memorized Ilona Andrews's *Innkeeper Chronicles*, and he'd decided christening a kitten after an intergalactic predator was a good idea.

We'd removed Begonia, Caldenia and Chow-Chow from underneath a greenhouse. They'd been underweight and hungry and had more fleas than a leopard did spots, but they were doing better now.

"What did you do?" Ranger asked, stepping forward, hands braced on his hips.

What did I do...?

I didn't much want to think about that. Or, quite honestly, about what I didn't do. Which was kiss Alice, fall into bed with her, and then slide one-hundred-and-ten percent into love with her. My love-meter was stuck at ninety percent, and it was driving me bonkers.

My wolf whined, wanting to shift and burn off our aggression. **We could have had her. You were a fool.**

Last night after Alice had clarified her expectations for our dating life, we'd returned to Moonlight Valley more or less in silence, driven to her place in silence, and then parted ways in silence. There had, in fact, been silence all around, because I wasn't going to accept anything less than total commitment from Alice Aymes.

I'd had fun with other girls, but pulled at me. Both my wolf and I knew she was my mate. If I was ever going to give someone my heart and my bite, it would be her.

Nevertheless, I also knew that if I stuck around after she'd made it clear she would not allow herself to feel anything other than lust for me, I'd be giving up my pride along with my heart. I'd be reduced to tagging along at her heels, begging for whatever scraps she tossed my way.

Sex wasn't enough, not when it came to Alice.

But we could have started with sex, my wolf growled.

Couldn't, I growled right back.

I wanted all of her.

I glowered at my older brother. "I didn't do a damn thing."

Ranger frowned and paused, as if thinking something over, and then asked, "Are you seeing each other again for a second date?"

"Ranger."

"Ford."

"This topic is off-limits."

"Can I date her?"

I answered him with a hair-raising growl. I reckoned that and my bared teeth sufficiently **communicated** my feelings on Ranger's dating Alice. Those feelings included rage, jealousy, and a strong sentiment of *when hell freezes over.*

Ranger raised his hands, tilted his head to expose his throat, and took a healthy step back. He wasn't going to push it.

"Stand down, Wolf Boy. I'm not fixing to ask your Alice out. I simply wanted to confirm a data point. Your feelings for her are not friendly or familial."

I glared at him some more. Ranger could be supremely aggravating.

"So why are the two of you not seeing each other again? Did Alessandro object? Because we, your pack, could pay him a little visit and run him out of town."

"No," I gritted out.

"Did her parents object?"

"They work a lot." For Alice's sake, I wished that weren't true. She clearly worried about pleasing them and living up to their standards, and yet they never seemed to be home.

Ranger clicked his teeth together, his hazel eyes flickering with streaks of wolfish amber. He was as mad as if I'd been accused of having sex in public or trying to change Alice into one of us. "Did you try to change her over? Are you thinking about it?"

"No. Damn it, Ranger! We are done talking about this."

"We are not," he countered. "Because so far this has been a one-way inter-rogation and not a conversation. It would be healthy for us to talk and exchange our ideas, let each other know how we feel about this situation. You and Alice aren't doing this, so clearly I need to be modeling that behavior for you."

I tucked the last kitten into the incubator. It licked my thumb before curling up with its siblings. "You want to know what happened? She's only interested in a summer romance. She's not planning on staying in Moonlight Valley.

"In fact, she's planning on leaving as soon as she can. She doesn't want a forever kind of man. She's got..." I glared at the barn walls, trying to remember exactly what Alice had said. Right. It was burned into my brain.

"She has *business plans*, along with parental issues and poor self-esteem and a deep-seated need to please her family and prove to them that she's a fucking excellent person who can make a fortune selling other people crap for their pets. Which she already is—an excellent person, that is—but apparently it doesn't count if she doesn't do it in Nashville."

Atticus glanced between Ranger and me, his brows drawing together. "She can't have business plans in Moonlight Valley? They're Nashville-specific?"

119

"No." I shrugged. "So that means there won't be a second date."

Now Ranger looked confused. "She can't be a businesswoman and a girl-friend? Not that I think she should mix the two, as there are limited local opportunities for sex work. That biker club over in Green Valley isn't hiring."

"It's not sex work. She wants to sell dog toys." That did not come out right, but I plowed ahead anyhow. "She doesn't have room in her schedule for a serious relationship. I would be her side gig."

Atticus looked confused. "So?"

Ranger huffed impatiently, in agreement with Atticus. "Why can't she? Why can't you two have a temporary romantic interlude? I'm assuming she doesn't mind the whole wolf thing?"

I crossed my arms over my chest and leaned against the workbench. Maybe this way I wouldn't give in to the urge to throttle my brother. "The wolf is not the problem."

At least I didn't think it was.

"She's your Firefly Girl," Ranger said, continuing his thought as if I hadn't spoken. "But she probably speaks a different love language than you. She flashes and you're hearing *temporary*, but she has a shorter definition of *forever*, that's all.

"The mating season of the *Photinus carolinus* lasts two, maybe three weeks a year. They mate, they lay eggs, they die."

"I was hoping for a *happy* love story," I interrupted. Ranger was not helping.

He shrugged. "They are happy, and they are forever. It's just a shorter kind of forever than we wolves are used to. But so what?"

"Ranger has a point." Atticus nodded slowly. "If you have a chance to be her mate, you take it. You don't know what's gonna happen tomorrow or if she'll really leave."

I shook my head, not liking the direction in which the conversation was headed. "You want me to settle? To accept a handful of days from her? That's pathetic."

"You're a wolf." Ranger patted me on the shoulder. It was more of a bone-rattling thump than a reassuring touch, but I gave him credit for the thought. "I want you to go after who you want. You convince her, and convince her good. You make yourself some opportunities."

I liked the idea of going after Alice. I was a wolf of action, so going after her, making my case, making myself a chance? Those were good things to my mind. What if I did use whatever time she allowed me for as long as I could?

Alice didn't want to stay here in Moonlight Valley, and she was no prisoner. I would certainly never do what our old man had done to Momma. So I could lose her. Fine. She was an independent woman and she would make her own choices. *But...*

I wouldn't beg.

Good plan. We're not a pup rolling over for a belly pat. We're hunters! Predators! Top of the food chain!

My wolf was right. So if what she wanted was to give me her leftover time and none of her serious emotion, what was preventing me from dictating some of the terms in this relationship and making some plans of my own? Creating my own timeline and an Alice Aymes plan? Making a mark on *her* pride and heart and mind before she left town?

"You make an opportunity." Ranger thumped my shoulder again for emphasis. "You do that convincing. You dominate all the doubts."

Atticus nodded emphatically. "No doubts."

"And, when or if she leaves town"—Ranger shrugged—"*you* leave first, with happy memories and no regrets, because you defended your territory, you left your mark, you caught your prey."

It looked like I had a plan for tonight's big town barbecue.

Find Alice.

Woo Alice.

Get back together with Alice.

My wolf howled. **Let's go!**

* * *

My nerves were fifty percent because of Alice.

More like a seventy/thirty split.

My wolf was right. That other thirty percent, however, was due to Lucky Jansen and Big Joe's visit and what I'd witnessed on the video he'd shared with me.

But I'd already decided I wasn't pulling in Ranger on this one; I'd wait for him to go before I told Atticus the whole story.

After their combined pep talk, we'd turned to company business. First we'd gone out on a roadkill call and given the remains a respectful burial, then we'd been called out for a bee emergency.

Mr. and Mrs. Twipple had bees in their attic. They'd had bats two months before, so it was apparent Mr. Twipple had not upped his home improvement game. He was pushing ninety, though, and had no business being on a ladder, so I'd made a list of supplies I'd need from the home improvement store to patch the hole in their eaves that had turned their attic into wildlife central.

Ranger had rambled the entire job about how he'd helped district law officers with their speeding enforcement program by launching a drone that identified misbehaving drivers. And how he'd paid calls to all the local police stations to teach them to fly their own drones.

He was proud of his drone work. He'd been doing it pro bono for years and was convinced he'd be reincarnated as a bird so he could fly for real.

"You can see everything. It's like an aerodynamic Eye of Sauron."

Neither Atticus nor I could understand his avian love.

We'd nodded and suggested we go check out the weird noises Mrs. McCreery had been hearing in her attic. Which turned out to be a colony of bats. As well, a raccoon had been living up there and getting into the trunks of old costumes she'd been storing for our regional theater. We'd gotten a two-for-one from that visit.

Bats were good neighbors to have and useful pollinators, so Atticus had spent the better part of an hour sweet-talking Mrs. McCreery out of her determination to poison the entire colony. It wasn't the bats' fault they'd mistaken her attic for a nice, dark cave.

Ranger and I had rehomed the bats into some big plastic tubs and then blocked off their return route to prevent them from staging a reverse move-in. When they'd left her, she'd been complaining about the amount of bat poop she'd have to deal with; she had not appreciated Ranger's pointing out that she'd been gifted with some high-quality fertilizer for her garden.

After we got back to the farm and Ranger finally took off with the enormous tub of bats—he planned to release them on a nearby mountain slope—I put a hand on Atticus's arm to keep him from leaving.

He gave me a questioning look, and I mouthed *hold on a moment*. We waited together, listening to Ranger as he mumbled to himself, laughing quietly at the jokes or whatnot he was relating to his bat buddies.

I counted to three after the barn door closed before turning to Atticus. "We have a problem."

"Alessandro still hunting for wolves?"

"Not that I've heard."

Alessandro Aymes had been a pain in our behinds for many reasons, not least because he'd caught sight of Momma once after our old man had changed her.

We'd set up a camera by her den, and we took turns going out there, but she avoided us. I don't think she recognized us either as wolves or men, but we held onto the hope that she was just freaked out and embarrassed and would come around.

"Then what's up? What's the problem?" Atticus asked.

"I had people drop by on Wednesday. Lucky Jansen and Big Joe. Carmine."

Atticus raised a brow. He was not a member of the Lucky Jansen fan club, either. "Those fools? What did they want?"

"You might want to sit down for this."

Atticus sat down. I stayed on my feet, pacing while I told Atticus about their visit and subsequent demands.

"Shoot," he growled, his wolf making itself felt. He wasn't much more in control than I was. "What was in that video? Or do I not want to know?" His face said he was imagining plenty.

"You should know," I said grimly. "Someone had a camera on Maverick shifting into a wolf and going after our old man. If Lucky publishes even the first half, it'll seem like Mav is responsible for our old man's disappearance, and it's not as if we can produce our old man as counterevidence."

Atticus frowned, clearly turning possibilities over in his head. He understood that this was bad news.

And I wasn't done yet. "It's gonna look like murder. The video's dated, so we can't claim it was an old fight."

"What if we claim the date was doctored and the fight happened years before our old man disappeared? Especially seeing as how werewolves don't exist."

I'd already considered that. "Mav is wearing that weird rose-pink T-shirt the town had made up for the annual fun run that year."

Busted by cotton and altruism. It really sucked.

"Did you call Mav and ask him about this?"

"Nope. He's up in the Smoky Mountains playing biologist."

"You let anyone else in on this?"

Atticus meant had I told our other brothers or, God forbid, our sister.

I shook my head. "The fewer of us involved, the better, in case we do end up having to do Lucky's dirty work for him."

Atticus nodded. "I agree. We'll leave Knox out of this on account of his terrible temper; he and his wolf would go knock Big Joe and Carmine's heads together. And Rebel's got his college finals coming up soon. I don't want to put anything else on his plate."

"I wasn't planning on letting Ranger in on this, either." I had thought about this, and I felt strongly that Ranger shouldn't be getting involved. Ranger was smart, though. Scary smart. If any of us could think our way out of this mess, it would be him. But I didn't want him dragged into a bad business.

Atticus had apparently come to the same conclusion. "We'll limit it to you and me, and—when he comes home—Maverick. But I'm not ready to be Jansen's pet wolf just yet. There has to be something we can do."

"I've been thinking on that. Jansen's video is the problem. If we could erase it somehow, then the Wolf Council wouldn't have any reason to come down on Mav, and there wouldn't be anything for Jansen to take to the police, either. He wouldn't have any proof that Mav went after our old man."

"You want to try to hack into Jansen's phone? And his iCloud thingy? And anywhere else he might have put this?"

"Yeah," I said glumly. "That would require us being omniscient. Maybe an electromagnetic pulse. I'd like to do it, but I don't rate our chances of succeeding. I was more thinking we make a video of our own, catch Jansen shifting or something. Then we hold it over his head and it's like nuclear détente."

"How are we supposed to get him to shift on our schedule?"

"I had some ideas about that…" I could feel my face pinch because I didn't like the best idea that had come to me.

Atticus studied me and, thanks to our twin connection, knew exactly what I was thinking. "Deelie Sue."

"Yeah." I did some more thinking, but I was out of ideas. Jansen wasn't gonna come over, run in my woods, and shift on command. He didn't trust me before, and he certainly wouldn't trust me now that he'd given me an ultimatum.

Atticus kept right on as if I hadn't interjected. "Deelie Sue has access to Lucky. Or she can ask him out for a run in their wolf forms."

Deelie Sue had dated Lucky a couple times, plus she'd had some business dinners and a coaching session with him. I didn't understand why a smart, successful woman like Deelie Sue would want to see an evil bastard like Lucky Jansen who was more than twice her age, but there was no accounting for taste. And maybe he gave excellent business advice, particularly if you were in the business of being evil henchmen.

"You think she would do it?"

"I do." I let out a deep breath, because Deelie Sue's help wasn't a sure thing—and it would come with a price tag. "She likes people owing her favors, that's for sure. And we could buy all our vehicles from her."

I didn't like the idea of using her, or of her using us, but I couldn't come up with any other options.

"Maybe she'd do it if we asked because Lucky's blackmailing us is wrong?"

I shrugged. "Maybe. You make a good point. But then, if we're being fair, we're asking her to take the two-wrongs-make-a-right approach with us."

"How much time do we have?" Atticus looked resigned.

"Lucky gave us until the next full moon. He and his gang have some kind of weird, cult-like party planned for that night, and we're invited."

Atticus winced.

"That gives us about two weeks, and Mav should be here by then," I said. "We can go all wolf on his sorry ass."

Atticus smirked, but he didn't seem amused. "You want the first crack at him? Which skin do you want to wear?"

"We'll take turns—once in our human skins and once as wolves."

"Nicely balanced." Atticus looked pleased.

That was Maverick mostly sorted. Next up: the Moonlight Valley community barbecue and putting my Woo Alice plan into action.

It was turning out to be a very busy night for me.

CHAPTER
ELEVEN
~ALICE~

Sweet. It's time to claim our woman.
  She's not ours. Jesus. Would you settle down? We just met her.
A wolf wants what he wants.

— JULIETTE CROSS

I was in a funk. A Grand Canyon-sized ravine of a funk.

Not even discovering that an extremely uncommon firefly species had decided to take up residence in my woods snapped me out of it. As the fireflies had flashed on and off, looking for love in the usual places, all I could think about was Ford.

I moped. And hosted a pity party in the deer blind from which I'd been counting fireflies. Worse, I moped at work.

When we'd unboxed this month's dog toys this morning, I couldn't even bring myself to comment on what had come in and what I would have chosen differently. Sanye had given me so much side-eye all week that her eyeballs should have been stuck sideways.

Tonight's destination was barbecue night, a monthly Moonlight Valley event held in the town park. It was the first one I'd been to this summer, and ordinarily I would have been looking forward to it.

The food was amazing, thanks to Ranger Boone's competitive barbecue skills, although the park itself was really an ambitiously named acre of grass behind the multipurpose town building. It had parking, though, and a half dozen grills and a nice view of the Tennessee mountains.

Sanye's patience snapped as she parked her ancient Volvo with terrifying speed and imprecision between two rusty pickup trucks. After cutting the ignition, she turned to me and stopped bottling up her feelings. "You're in a slump. You've been a sad sack all day, and I'm pretty sure it's about your date yesterday."

I sighed, my face droopier than a basset hound's. I did not feel like being social tonight. "You're an excellent guesser."

"He's probably here." Sanye gestured at the crowd milling around the barbecue grills.

Moonlight Valley took its barbecue very, very seriously. Our town had won the Tennessee Bar-B-Que Contest at the state livestock show three years in a row, along with the State Championship Barbecue Cooking Contest, the Tennessee Pitmaster Battle, and several other competitions. Our pitmasters were legendary, and Ranger Boone was the best of them all.

"I know." My heart hopped in my rib cage like a bunny startled by a wolf.

"So what's your plan?" Sanye knew me well.

"It's a simple one," I said grimly. "If I can't avoid him, I'll say hello. If Aunt Sally is looking down from heaven, she'll be proud of me."

"Why don't you take advantage of him behind the band gazebo?"

Hot kissing behind the gazebo was a time-honored Moonlight Valley tradition, but Ford's kisses came with strings.

"He wants more than I can give him."

I didn't sound convicted because I was wondering if I could come up with a plan to have my hummingbird cake and eat it too. In other words, have a genuine relationship with Ford, pursue my dreams, and *not* break his heart or my own.

Sanye tapped her fingers on the steering wheel. "I've refrained from adding my two cents' worth about this situation between you and Ford. I understand you have a business plan, and you need to move to Nashville to execute it. But unless you're literally planning on devoting yourself twenty-four-seven to commercial world domination, I don't understand why there's no room for seeing someone. Why can't you have love? And hot sex?"

"Sanye—"

"Shush. I didn't get all that long with Evan, and what time we did have together came at a price. Nothing worth having is free, and we both had to accommodate each other. I had not *planned*"—she nudged me with her elbow as she said this—"on living in military housing in California as the wife of an enlisted man. It was not the glamorous West Coast adventure I'd imagined, and I hated it.

"I had an absolutely terrible job at the Dollar Store, there wasn't a speck of anything green around me, Los Angeles traffic was even worse than in the movies, and every plant on the balcony of our apartment died because of the drought. But you know what? I might have hated California, but I loved Evan, and I wouldn't have wished away a second of that time we got to have together.

"So when you tell me you won't even think about seeing someone because it might mess up your business plan, it makes me angry. Why won't you consider the *possibility* that Ford might fit into your dreams and your plans?"

"I—"

"Ford Boone might not be your Evan. He might not be your one and only. But you have declared it to be an impossibility and closed yourself off from every chance of love.

"I know you want to start your own business. I know you want to show your parents that you have what it takes to be successful. But being successful at love is the biggest deal, where you come out richer than rich. So what is the point of building the world's best pet business if you're alone like Scrooge?"

"I haven't figured that part out yet! Okay?" I considered making a break for it into the barbecue-loving crowd, but I knew she'd catch me. "You're the love expert, not me. I've never been in love, and I don't know what I'm missing.

"Love is scary. It has no boundaries. I hate being vulnerable, I'm a very messy person on the inside, and I need at least a year—probably a decade—to strategize a relationship with Ford.

"I can't stay here, and pretending that I can is doing him a disservice. It's lying. He asked to *court* me. He brought Alessandro flowers. He was thinking forever, and I..." I thunked my head on the headrest.

"And you what? Do you not see yourself with Ford Boone long term?"

"No. That's exactly the problem. I *could* imagine it. My imagination has suggested a house with a white picket fence and an overabundance of cats and dogs. I can see my moving up to be part owner at Vanity Fur Salon, or maybe opening a competitor business.

"We'll go to church on Sundays and Walmart on Saturdays, and we'll have one of those couple routines. We'll finish each other's sentences and order for each other if we're in the bathroom when the wait staff comes."

"And that scares you."

"And that scares me. Because that life is the best life for a lot of people, but not for me. I would hate being stuck here. I would hate knowing I'll never know what I could have done in a place like Nashville even if the alternative is a cozy farmhouse and fur babies…"

We sat there, and I was pretty sure we were both imagining that farmhouse and how Ford would come striding through the front door and all the animal chaos. He'd sweep me off my feet and kiss me hello, even if he'd been gone for only ten minutes.

It was such an amazing daydream that I dreamed it twice.

* * *

Ford was AWOL. I'd expected to find him hanging around Ranger's barbecue pit or to see his shoulders disappearing into the crowd. I'd expected to come face to face with reminder after reminder of him.

It was anticlimactic.

I was tempted to peek underneath one of the plastic-tablecloth-covered tables where people were congregating to devour Ranger's delicious barbecue.

My heart had a palpitation, skipping a beat when I spotted Ranger bent over his pit, frowning fiercely at the coals. His brother Knox worked beside him, dishing up coleslaw and slices of custard pie. I decided to torture myself by hanging out near them and watching them work. Everyone knew that men who could cook were sexy.

Nevertheless, no movie scene played itself out in my head when Knox took a break from the pit and sauntered toward me, flashing me a friendly smile. Objectively, he was a pretty, pretty man, but nothing in me lit up in recognition when he looked my way. We were not compatible fireflies.

As I stood up from my picnic table to prevent him looming over me, I decided that if Atticus had eyes the color of a Bora Bora lagoon, and Ford's shifted between the blue of deep water and a raging storm, Knox Boone's eyes were a cold, frozen blue. Like a blue raspberry slush where the blue was really a PSA so you could tell it from the strawberry flavor. Even his warm smile was not enough to melt the ice in his gaze.

"How you doing?" Knox had a smooth, radio announcer's kind of voice. Somewhere, somehow, he'd learned to speak without the distinctive Southern twang his brothers had.

"Just fine," I lied. "And yourself?"

My manners were impeccable.

"Good." His gaze focused on the near-empty plate next to mine. "Is Sanye with you tonight?"

"She drove me over here, but now she's helping out her father-in-law. He's collecting for something." Sanye's father-in-law was better than any GoFundMe.

Knox nodded, his gaze sharpening as he looked about the crowd, as if maybe he was having thoughts of hunting down Sanye. He looked hungry and a little frustrated. I tried to imagine him shifting into a wolf but got stuck on what color he would be—would his pelt match his beard so he would become a dark brown wolf with icy blue eyes?

And then the crowd parted in an almost biblical way. I would have been entirely willing to believe that the clouds opened up, a beam of light came down, and angels began singing. I turned, following the source of the commotion, and found Ford Boone standing directly behind me. His rich blue eyes glittered.

Those eyes sucked the oxygen straight out of my lungs because, unless I was grievously mistaken, Ford was hot for me.

"Alice, can you spare a moment?" he asked in a rough, husky voice.

I nodded.

My master plan flew out the window.

Without any concern for what his brothers, my friend, or the legendarily nosy residents of Moonlight Valley might think, Ford wrapped his muscled arm around my shoulders and steered me away from the crowd and toward the gazebo.

We were hardly alone. Crowds of picnicking, gossiping, barbecue-eating Moonlight Valley-ers surrounded us. They had a lot to say—calling out greetings, asking questions. I was almost certain someone snapped a picture of us, probably for the town Instagram account.

Ford's arm slid from my shoulder, his hand trailing down my arm to tangle up in my fingers. We were *holding hands*. In *public*. *After* we'd all but broken up last night.

I was half hoping, half dreading he'd kiss me next, but instead he steered us behind the gazebo, brushed off the bottom step, and sat down. Since our hands were attached, I followed him down, my behind landing less than gracefully next to his. I couldn't remember how to sit. I crossed my legs. Uncrossed them.

"I've been thinking." His shoulder brushed mine.

"Uhhhh?" I hoped he hadn't brought me out here for witty conversation. I wondered whether it would be weird if I leaned into his shoulder.

"You said you planned on getting out of town as soon as you had the money saved up. You thought you were looking at, what? A year and change?"

My speedy departure was not the topic of conversation I would have chosen. I'd been sort of hoping to revisit Friday, to apologize some more for inadvertently trampling all over his feelings. I wished fervently that I would grow some conversational skills, but, as always, I failed to manifest my dreams into reality.

"Fifteen months," I blurted out. "Eighteen, tops. Fewer if I can sell a kidney or Aunt Sally turns out to have owned a valuable American Dolls collection."

Ford's eyes narrowed, and he nodded, stroking his beard thoughtfully. We sat like that next to each other on the steps—him studying me as if I were some kind of interesting mathematical problem he intended to solve, me watching him manhandle his beard—for far too long.

Abruptly, he asked, "I'd like to propose something."

What? Propose? He was sitting, not kneeling, I told my heart.

"Let's date for the next twelve months, but only for twelve months."

"You want to go out on a twelve-month-long date? Why?"

He lounged beside me, at his ease. Me, on the other hand? I had an old board splintering into my spine and a whole lot of questions.

"Not an extra-long date," he corrected. "I want us to be in a relationship together, but it'll be one that has an expiration date."

"Ummm," I contributed.

"So we'll agree on twelve months and then everything will be over and done with before you need to go." *Dating* was apparently synonymous with *dread chore* in Ford's mind. "And it's long enough that we can have some fun, get to know each other, but not form a lasting attachment."

It sounded like he'd put a great deal of thought into this. I loved a good plan, but this one made my heart squeeze, and not in a good way. I'd be downgraded. Instead of being the girl he wanted to court and mate, I'd become his booty call and hookup.

I shifted on the step. Sex was wonderful, and it was great when two consenting adults had fun together. It was just...

It was just that he'd agreed to give me exactly what I wanted. A lighthearted, commitment-free summer kind of romance. *Yay... I win?*

No. You lose. *This is* not *what you wanted*, an annoying voice whined inside me. *This is* bad.

But I'd gotten what I wanted, so...good?

"You... We..." Ford might have to wait until tomorrow for me to form a coherent sentence. This was not at all how I'd planned on the evening going. Angry tears pricked my eyes. "We'd hook up? Whenever we felt the urge?"

Ford shook his head, turning so he could look me in the eye. His face was stern and distant, almost angry, but not quite. Amber flashed in his eyes.

"No. I do not want to randomly hook up with you when one of us has room in our schedule. We would have a relationship. We would see each other, go out on dates, text, make up silly nicknames for each other.

"I would open your doors, pull out your chair at the table, and lend you my shirts. I would look out for you, not because I lack respect for you or believe you cannot take care of yourself, but because I would be proud that I could do that for you."

His frown deepened as he thought about this impossible, mythic, beautiful future, a future in which we were together. And then he launched straight into speech, not done rocking my world.

"You would give me shit about being chivalrous, of course. But I would be doing these things because you were my girl and you deserve it. You would come over to mine, spend time with my brothers because they matter to me. I would meet your girlfriends, and I will refrain from killing your third cousin twice removed." There was more fierce frowning. My heart swooned. "Assuming that all this is acceptable to you."

"Oh." My heart launched itself out of the pit of despair it had fallen into and shot up toward the sky. "So the courting thing is still on?"

"It is." He nodded.

"For twelve months."

"Yeah."

The smile splitting my lips was epic. "And we'd be an honest-to-gosh couple, doing all the couple things?"

His face softened, his eyes inventorying my face. "Yeah, with one-week and one-month anniversaries and me making you dinner and buying you little gifts out of the blue."

I sucked in a breath, excited. But then I realized he'd left out a crucial step in this plan. "But what if we don't want to be done after our time is up? Are we allowed to revise and revisit?"

The sternness returned to his face. "Once the twelve months are up, we're over. Even if you're here in Moonlight Valley, our relationship is done. That's my proposal. Yes or no?"

Ford glowered at me, jaw set.

"And one more thing," he added. "There will be absolutely no revisiting. You don't bring up an extension or additional months again. You don't ask. I don't ask. One year and we're done."

I loved a strict plan, but this was a level of dating skill I did not possess. My heart panicked, banging around inside me like a pop can rattling wild and free in a truck bed. "Would you give me the cut direct?"

He frowned. "What?"

"Like a nineteenth-century society matron meeting someone who's blotted her social copybook," I babbled. "And so she looks through her, pretends she doesn't see her when they pass in town. Would you ignore me? Would you *see* me?"

I imagined being ignored by Ford. I did not like that mental picture one bit.

He shrugged. "Yes, I'd see you."

"Would we be friends? Merely friendly? Church acquaintances who pretend they remember each other's names?"

"I don't know."

"Would we talk? After we drop each other like hot potatoes? Will we have a countdown app or a big Doomsday clock?"

"I'd be polite. I have manners—I'm not an animal." He frowned fiercely. And a little sadly too, I thought.

"I know," I said, sounding more than a little sad myself. "But I don't have a whole lot of experience with dating, and I'm not sure I could be your girlfriend for a whole year and then be nothing at all to you. I'll have feelings by then."

"But you could leave me to go to Nashville and that's fine?"

"There is absolutely nothing wrong with having dreams and ambitions. I won't apologize for wanting to pursue my goals." I folded my arms across my chest. My fingers brushed his side, undermining my self-righteousness, but whatever.

"I'm not asking you to apologize for thinking of your future and what you want." He inhaled sharply, his flannel rising and falling over his impressive chest. His eyes darted to mine, then glared out at the woods. "In fact, I want to support you. That's a good reason for the twelve-month limit. I won't be holding you back; you won't feel like you're leaving anyone or anything behind."

I let myself lean against his shoulder. It was flannel-covered, hard and muscled. It was my new happy place. "You've thought about this."

"I know you like plans."

It was more like I needed them. I did not do well when I was asked to ad-lib my life or go off-roading through life's choices. In fact, it was safe to say I'd failed spectacularly whenever I approached a situation without a well-thought-out checklist and a backup plan.

I wasn't going to apologize for that. When you got on a cruise ship, you scoped out the exits and you marked the lifeboats. You made sure you had a life jacket and you practiced safety drills.

Then you got on with sailing and going wherever it was you'd wanted to go. You got on with the fun stuff.

Twelve months with Ford was around-the-world-cruise territory, and I wanted to agree. I wanted to run up the gangplank in this weird analogy and wave goodbye to the shores of sanity and good reason.

"What if we—"

I'd been about to ask *what if we did this for real and I stayed here and we didn't stop at twelve months? What if I put my Nashville business plans on ice indefinitely?*

"What if we..." he prompted.

That was Ford. He listened to me. And then he tried to give me what he thought I wanted.

"Yes," I said, answering his first question rather than the one I'd posed. "Yes."

And then quick as a snake I scooted over onto his lap, threw my arms around his neck, and pressed my mouth against his.

It was our first boyfriend/girlfriend kiss—quick and chaste. It would make an excellent welcome-home kiss or a thanks-for-picking-up-coffee-creamer kiss or a hundred prosaic, everyday kisses. I couldn't wait to try them all out.

I had twelve months to kiss Ford as much as I wanted.

Boy, did I have plans for this man.

CHAPTER

TWELVE

~ALICE~

Some people will tell you werewolves can only shape-change under a full moon, but people also say there's no such things as ghosts.

— PATRICIA BRIGGS

esterday we'd sealed our twelve-month deal by kissing the heck out of each other behind the band gazebo, and this morning the cute howling of baby wolf pups woke me up.

This was the ringtone I'd picked for texts from Ford, and I took a moment to stare up through the skylight (that he'd made! for me!) at the pretty blue of the morning sky and compare it to Ford's eyes in poetry that would never, ever be spoken aloud. Only then, after he'd been properly appreciated, did I read my text.

Ford: We're going out tonight.
  Me: Where?
Ford: Someplace with fireflies where we can run around.
  Me: So this is a Twilight sort of date? Are we going to chase deer? Are you a VAMPIRE too?
Ford: There will be no sparkling. 5 ok?

. . .

It was absolutely okay, and I was ready when Ford's pickup stopped in front of my tiny house. Ford might not have been a sparkly ancient vampire, but his truck gleamed in the early evening sunlight. He'd washed it for our date.

Based on Ford's cryptic description of our date-night activities (which sadly did not specify sex, kissing, or bedroom-adjacent activities), I'd donned soft, high-waisted leggings that made a sexy detour below my belly button. I also wore a matching crop top and an unbuttoned long-sleeved cotton shirt I could deploy if the temperature dropped in the woods.

Most importantly, my workout gear hugged my curves and would, hopefully, draw Ford's attention to key areas of my anatomy. I was advertising discreetly.

Ford was early, which was good as he'd have to make it past Alessandro, who'd taken up residence on my front porch. Alessandro had come over specifically to harass Ford. As this appeared to be their love language, I'd stopped demanding they knock it off.

After much arguing, I had, however, convinced Alessandro that buying a rocking chair solely in order to sit on it holding his shotgun was unnecessary. He could torture Ford about Ford's intentions without investing in props.

Alessandro invited Ford into my house, offered him a diet soda (that Alessandro *had* bought to be mean) and grilled him about his opinions on the local sports team, preferred flavor of barbecue, and belief in God. When he'd acquired enough inside information to write a position paper, he slapped Ford on the back, gave me a quick hug, and glared at both of us as we trooped out of the house.

Even though we'd already gone out together once, that date had not ended well. This time felt easier already. More comfortable.

I wasn't misleading Ford about my intentions, and we'd both been honest with each other. We had a twelve-month deal and a relationship plan. I could relax and enjoy his company because we were on the same page of my planner.

Once he'd helped me into the truck, opening and closing my door for me exactly as he'd threatened-promised, he settled into the driver's seat. We grinned at each other. We'd made it.

"So, what are we doing tonight? Are we really hunting fireflies?"

"I've got a plan," he answered mysteriously, his eyes roving over my body with heated appreciation.

Ford loved looking at me, and I loved that he loved it.

He was all stern intent and focus, as if he were making a plan of all the places he would kiss me next and how. I wondered whether he'd ever considered writing those things down because, boy howdy, would that beat dirty sexting.

We drove for a couple minutes, sneaking peeks at each other from the corners of our eyes. I felt like a teenager again.

I was also bubbling over with questions, because I needed to know everything about this man, but I didn't want to kill the conversation before it started either. I'd written down a list of possible questions earlier, rank ordering them, and now I started at the top.

"Anything surprising happen today?"

The corner of Ford's mouth tilted up. "I got a beautiful, smart woman to go out with me."

His tone was light and flirty. I wanted to fast-forward through the night so I could find out what would happen and then go back and live it all again in slow motion.

Ford told me a funny story about helping a peacock cross the road. He'd also had Elmer Johnson's hog climb into the cab of his truck.

When I looked down—not wanting to be sitting in pig leavings for obvious reasons—Ford chuckled. "I detailed my truck."

That explained the truck sparkle.

"Why would a pig even do that?"

Ford shrugged. "Guess it wanted to get out and see the world some.

"Not as bad as the time I came home to find Momma and two of her church lady friends standing on the furniture. Darrell had put down some rat poison, and this big ole rat had eaten it and come inside to die.

"I cleared up the clutter outside and put some peppermint down, which was a tried-and-true nonlethal way of convincing rats that they would prefer to change directions and go somewhere else. Momma made me check out the living room for a month after that anyhow."

I was tempted to reach over and kiss him.

"You're a good person, Ford Boone."

"That's due to Momma." Ford frowned fiercely at his steering wheel, shifting uncomfortably. I guess it was one thing to tell him he had a mighty fine penis or a spectacular backside—and it was a whole other thing to opine on his character. "I reckon most of Moonlight Valley looks at us Boone boys and dismisses us as a bunch of rednecks, Darrell Boone's no-account kids who were like to take after his backwoods, broke-ass self.

"We do like our trucks and our barbecue, and we're all about independence and family. And that goes double for our wolves. Nobody messes with a Boone without all of us coming for him. But our momma always encouraged us to be smart and have manners."

"She sounds like she was an amazing woman."

His hand pressed against my knee briefly, as if he needed that connection. I laid my hand on top of his.

"She is—was. She had a whole pack of us to raise, and she did it alone. She got us to church, to school, and to anywhere else she thought we should be. If she knew how to do it, she taught us. Anything we didn't know, we headed over to the library to look it up in a book. Momma believed there was a book for every problem in the world.

"She was real entrepreneurial, too. Even though she came from money, she didn't believe in sitting on your laurels or your bank account. She thought you should be out there, doing things."

I felt an unexpected kinship with Ford's momma. "She was a real smart lady. I have all these ideas and plans, but it feels like the days keep slipping through my fingers, one after another, and I want to *do* things, not merely read about business strategy in yet another book or take another college class."

Ford nodded as if he did get it, but then he surprised me by asking, "So what have you done to get your business up and running?"

This kind of question made me squirm.

"I've got checklists and a business plan. I've got the application for a business license, and I've been researching what I'd want to stock, foot traffic patterns, real estate costs. But it's all stuff in my head, thinking and not doing." I sighed. "I guess I'm not living up to the whole *if not now, then when?* thing."

Ford slowed, signaled, and turned off the main road and onto a gravel offshoot. The baby road was a bumpy, dusty slice of space barely wide enough for a vehicle to pass through all the trees.

He looked thoughtful, but not because he was trying to remember the directions or something equally mundane. He was considering what I'd said.

"You don't have to wait until you've got your storefront leased in Nashville to go into business. There's the internet. And mail order. Farmers' markets, the state fair, and those holiday bazaars they hold at the church."

"Those are small potatoes. I'm not going to get a business loan to run a stall at the local flea market."

"Sure, but it's an opportunity to sell. To test the waters. There are customers here."

"There are like five hundred people here. Plus, I'm betting werewolves would be offended by my selling cute little T-shirts for cats and dogs."

His mouth curled up. "We have dogs. You might be surprised. You should sell us hard."

"Are you volunteering to model for me?"

He squeezed my hand gently. "It would be no hardship at all. I'm happy to model for you any time."

I leaned forward, adopting an ostentatiously meditative look. Rodin's *The Thinker* had nothing on me. "Do you do naked modeling?"

"For you, yes."

"Hot damn."

We both laughed. He was so amazing, funny, and playful. I tried my best to forget that he was mine for only twelve months.

He'd be an incredible partner.

It was impossible not to fall a bit more for him. Falling for him felt safe, because he was a good guy.

* * *

We went on a woodsman date. After hiking in to yet another secret waterfall (if All-Purpose Animal Services ever failed, the Boones could go into the tour guide or mapmaking business), we splashed around in the pool at the base of the cascade.

Then we devoured the four-foot-long hoagie Ford had brought from You're Great In Bread, the only sandwich shop in town. Pimiento cheese—sharp cheddar mixed with spicy pimiento peppers—was slathered on one side of the roll, while cream cheese and mayonnaise covered the other side.

Following that, Ford produced a box of fried chicken and biscuits with hot honey. The meal was delicious, and I ate far too much.

The river raced next to us, the rippling reflection of the evening sky shot through with silvery flashes from the fish hanging out near the bottom.

The cicadas buzzed and then the frogs joined in. They were all calling for a mate, but despite being surrounded by horny insect life, I felt calm.

It was only seven, so we had a good two hours left before it even considered getting dark out, but it was hard to be completely easy knowing the light was going. Lying flat on your back in the woods was supposed to be the ultimate in outdoor relaxation (I'd read that in an Ilona Andrews book so it had to be true), but my muscles were slowly knotting themselves into a boccie ball of tension.

Ford laced his fingers through mine and tugged gently, calling my attention back to the here and now. "You seem tense."

I leaned into his solid frame and frowned up at the sky. I had no cell phone reception this far out, so I couldn't check my weather app to determine exactly when the sun would set tonight. I'd meant to do it before we'd left, but the delicious sight of Ford in his blue jeans had distracted me.

"Did you hear that?" Something rustled in the bushes. It was followed by a spooky hooting that probably came from an owl but that could also have been a deranged serial killer signaling to his serial killer buddy. "It'll be dark before long."

"I won't let anything hurt you."

Ford sounded confident, but no one was invincible.

"There could be wild animals out here. Wolverines, or maybe a fisher cat. There was a confirmed mountain lion sighting two months ago, and we have black bears up in the mountains."

"We do have those." He said it the way you'd admit to having ketchup or hot relish in your fridge. Ho-hum. No big deal!

"So it's dangerous out here."

He snorted. "Honey, you've got me."

And then I felt both a little scared and a little naive. "Because you're a part-time wolf."

It must be nice to stride through life as a scary apex predator. When God had passed out balls and bravado, I had not been in that line. I'd been queued up for logic and reason, thank you very much.

Ford cleared his throat. "I'd like to…"

My mind went wild, imagining what he could possibly want that he wouldn't up and ask for. Demand. Coax. Ford was very, very good at *coaxing*. I sure hoped he wasn't about to try to convert me to a Jesus cult or anal sex.

"…shift," he finished. "I'd like you to meet my wolf."

"Your *wolf?*"

He gave me a crooked grin. "He'd like to say hello."

My frown deepened.

"You talk like you've got someone else living inside you."

"Not exactly." He moved restlessly, his shoulder brushing mine. "He's got some opinions, though."

I bet. If the wolf had a *few* opinions, Ford had even more. I wondered what his wolf could possibly think about me.

"How does it work?" I couldn't help being curious. This was all new to me. "Are you there, inside the wolf? Are you in control? Would it be safe?"

His grin deepened. "As much in control as I ever am around you."

"Is this the lust myth?" Excuse me for sounding suspicious, but I knew bullshit when I heard it. "Because I know you're in control of your penis, just like I'm in control of my vagina. We don't go around ravaging other people without permission because we're *out of control.*"

I made air quotes because this was an important point.

Ford looked offended. "Make no mistake about it. I want you, Alice Aymes. But if you don't want me or aren't in the mood—"

"Or are flat-out mad at you," I added to be helpful.

He gave a little laugh. "Or are flat-out mad at me, what we do or don't do in bed is up to you. I was talking about my feelings."

"I agree." I turned my head so I could look at him. His handsome face made my heart beat fast and then faster. At this rate, I'd have the cardiovascular system of a twenty-year-old Olympian before I turned thirty.

"So may I? Shift?"

I was nervous, to tell the truth. And curious. I was a werewolf newbie, and I couldn't imagine a scenario in which my date turning into a werewolf was a feature and not a bug. But he'd asked, and he was right that the wolf was a part of him. "Okay."

He dropped a kiss on my forehead and disentangled our hands.

"I'll still be me," he offered. "Just with fur."

And teeth and vicious predator claws, but he already knew that and did not need to hear it from me.

"I'm gonna undress," he said. "Because if I shift fully clothed, you'll be driving into town with a naked man."

"Huh," I said, my witty rejoinder drowning in a sea of lust. Now *that* was a feature.

Instead of arguing with him about the benefits (or drawbacks) of shifting, however, I curled up on our picnic blanket and watched him methodically strip down. This was an unexpected bonus, even if he did turn around, presenting me with his backside, when he shucked his boxer briefs.

Ford's big body was a miracle. He had a light dusting of hair on his legs and chest, like frosting for his muscles. He was even more impressive naked than he was fully dressed.

And his butt... Sweet baby Jesus, I wished I had the words to describe it. It was firm and rounded, taut and muscled. I itched to take a photo in case my memory ever went and I needed a reminder.

"Your clothing should be illegal," I blurted out. Missing out on an opportunity to drive to Moonlight Valley next to a big, naked Ford was like being one number off on the Tennessee Daily Jackpot.

The bastard laughed.

Then he shifted.

One minute, I had Ford Boone standing in front of me, naked as a jaybird, hands on his hips, and then Ford became a wolf. It was the strangest thing I'd ever witnessed. His human skin melted away, fur flowing in to take its place. There was a horrible crunching sound, as his insides remade themselves in some kind of supernatural origami.

It took almost no time at all, but there was no doubting the results: I was alone in the Tennessee woods with a wolf who had been a man and was still my date.

"Wow." I reached forward and cautiously touched his shoulder.

His fur was a dark auburn, slightly coarse and shaggier on his shoulders. He looked almost as if he was wearing a darling little fur cape, except that he was preternaturally huge. Naturally, I'd done some googling when I'd discovered werewolves existed outside the pages of a book, and he was at least twice as large as your average *Canis lupus*.

Ford shook himself and padded around our picnic blanket. He was giving me a chance to look at him, I realized.

"And you're really in there?"

Ford yipped. I interpreted that as a yes. I wasn't sure how I'd expected us to communicate once he'd shifted, but it stood to reason that wolf jaws were different from people jaws and he wouldn't have the physical ability to speak English.

It was amazing.

144

He was amazing.

Rationally, I knew there must be a logical explanation for why he had this ability while most of the world did not, but something about the casual power with which he prowled about the clearing was one of the hottest things I'd ever seen. He was all dominant, sexy alpha.

I wasn't entirely sure I was down with the werewolf thing.

In fact, I worried that his transformation might be contagious like a bad virus.

...or at least I thought I should worry.

A thrill shot through me as he loped toward me, muscles bunching as he moved. In this form, his eyes were all amber but shot through with swirls of blue. Was that his human side peeking through?

He fit, I realized. He was an integral part of this place, these mountains, this part of Tennessee. He'd always belong here and therefore he would never leave. He'd found his place.

He butted his head against my hand. I narrowed my eyes. Was he—

"Ford Boone, you had better not be marking me."

I was not a tree or a piece of property, and I got quite enough of that behavior from Aunt Sally's cats. They had decided that as the very last human, I could be of use to them, so there was much head-butting, scratching, and rubbing when I was around them.

This time Ford howled. It was a growl-bark that grew louder, deeper, echoing through the clearing. His wolf sounded like him, or maybe it was the other way round. I was trying to decide which it was when he shifted, grabbing the picnic blanket to cover a very impressive portion of his anatomy.

He nuzzled my neck like his wolf had, dropping a kiss on it. "You okay?"

I was sure my eyes were huge. So was my smile, however, so it evened things out. It was hard to believe that the wolf had come from inside him like that. I had so many questions.

"What happens if someone gets scratched or bitten by your wolf? If you shift with clothes on, do they get ripped apart? Does it hurt?"

"Nothing unless it's a mating bite, public indecency, and not really."

"Fascinating. Can I ask follow-up questions?" Mostly, I wanted to ask him to do it again, but he wasn't a movie at the two-dollar cinema for me to be watching.

Laughing, he wrapped a hand around the back of my neck and leaned in to give me a kiss. Seeing as how my mouth was open—about to ask yet another question—this had our kiss going from zero to sixty in no time at all.

Ford's kiss made me feel seen and appreciated, safe and desired. Or maybe he was tired of talking about science and wanted to do something different.

Either way, I kissed him back.

CHAPTER
THIRTEEN
~FORD

*Contrary to popular myth, werewolves myth, werewolves are born, not made.
No matter how many times they bite someone, that person will not turn, though
they will probably bleed profusely and will definitely be annoyed.*

— MOLLY HARPER

I'd put my clothes on and then Alice and I had hiked out to the truck. It was full-on dark now, and our date was going real well.

This was a safe conclusion because Alice Aymes was kissing me, rimming my ear with her tongue, her fingertips sneaking up my thigh and easing around the thick ridge of my hard-on, all while I drove us on the back roads.

She was marking me.

While I drove and warned my wolf that we were NOT, under any circumstances, going to give her our mating bite, she'd managed to pull open my flannel, get under my T-shirt, and past my belt buckle. She was as ruthless and single-minded as any wolf on the hunt, and I wanted her naked *now*.

This time I didn't put on a Spotify playlist. The only sound was our rapid breathing, the diesel engine, and her seemingly endless questions:

Is this okay? How about this? Can I touch you here? Do you want to pull over and do it in the bed of your truck? You don't shift into your wolf when you're having sex, do you? Because I'd need a heads-up if you do.

Then she'd proceeded to explain other bedroom scenarios in which she'd also want a heads-up (these included my going for her back door and an AWOL condom).

But despite her easy acceptance of my wolfish side and her sexy moans and exploratory touches, the drive gave me time to remember the plan.

Twelve months and then we'd be over. This was a limited-time opportunity, and the first time we made love would not be in the bed of my truck, in the front seat of my truck, or anywhere remotely truck-adjacent.

There would be romance. Nice music, silky sheets. Maybe a fire.

Quality compliments would be paid.

I would *not* rush unwrapping her.

I'd always figured, in the unlikely event Alice agreed to step out with me, that we would hold off on having sex. We'd share our feelings for each other first, confessing our love and mutual appreciation. I'd give her a ring.

After that, maybe I'd rent one of those luxury Airbnb cabins or even a castle (I'd bookmarked several) because our first time would be memorable. She was special, so she deserved a special night. We might even wait until we were married. Or mated.

We do *not* screw this up, my wolf ordered. **She's our queen.**

He was right, but my assumptions hadn't taken into consideration her ambitions and plans.

We would have no anniversaries, romantic getaways, or a wedding night. We had twelve months, and the clock was ticking. Each second, minute, and hour that I spent *not* romancing her or making love to her was time I could never get back.

Regardless, despite Alice's impatience to consummate our relationship, I couldn't abandon my secret dreams. She might be okay with the bed of my truck, but I was not. It was not romantic.

Not at all.

I would stick to my plan. I had a long list of erotic acts to perform with her. She would get all the foreplay, not a five-minute quickie in my truck.

If I could convince her to keep her fingers north of the band on my boxer briefs, I'd be able to implement that plan.

Twilight had fallen on the return drive. I was not going to park with Alice in front of the Little Love Den because I did not ever want her thinking she owed me something or that I expected her gratitude in the form of a blow job.

So tonight's pit stop on my grand twelve-month plan was at the remains of an old covered bridge spanning the river that cut through Moonlight Valley. The bridge had mostly fallen down, and only a fool looking for a swim would drive over it, but we'd all parked there in high school.

There was lots of grass (enjoyed by those of us who did not possess our own vehicles,) and you could see fireflies at certain times of the year. It was also as private as you got in Moonlight Valley without driving two towns over or joining the Witness Protection Program.

I hadn't finished putting my truck into Park and killing the headlights before Alice stopped trying to undo my buckle and focused on her seatbelt instead. A nanosecond later, she was swinging onto my lap.

"Are we *parking*?" Laughter filled her voice. "It's a good thing I really like you."

There being no need to state the obvious, I settled her on top of my hard-on and slid a hand up her leg.

"Get naked," she ordered, tugging on my belt buckle. The blood from my brain rushed south to help her out.

"Alice—" I braceleted her impatient hands with mine.

"Let's have sex." Her teeth nipped my neck. "I can't stop thinking about you."

"Take off your leggings."

She grinned at me in the gathering darkness. Darkness. Right. I did my best to focus.

"Are you okay with this?" I'd come up with another plan if she wasn't. Or wait. She was worth it.

Damn right, she is.

Alice slid her arms around my neck. "I'm already out here with the big, bad wolf."

So she was.

"I like him a lot," she added, her mouth right up against my ear.

"Good. You don't have to worry about anything out here."

This time she laughed. "Why, Ford Boone, are you gonna run off the bogeyman for me?"

Damn straight.

"Always, darling."

Her grin was pure mischief. "That deserves a reward."

She whipped off her crop top, and it hit my windshield. Hot…damn.

I'd drawn some conclusions earlier about what Alice might or might not have been wearing underneath that tiny top, and I'd been right. She had not bothered with a bra. Her breasts were perfect little handfuls, tight and firm and with a freckle on the underside that demanded kissing.

"Let's do it right now, okay? I could ride you like a cowgirl," she panted.

My imagination promptly drew me a picture. Alice, straddling me. Me, sinking deep inside her. It would be fucking amazing. *Remember the plan.*

"We're doing this my way," I growled. "When we make love, it's going to be romantic. Special."

I'd run out of adjectives. And steps in my master plan. Alice had that effect on me.

Alice made a face. "So bossy. This is not some *Fifty Shades of Grey* game, buddy."

My brain short-circuited. I hadn't seen the movie, but Knox had picked up the first book from the library book sale over at the Green Valley Library. He'd insisted we all read it, and it had taken all of us to shout down Ranger, who'd decided to pick it for his book club.

Alice, however, was not waiting on my answer. Not at all. She was wiggling, trying to get her leggings off. The way her breasts bounced…

Jesus H. Christ. She was going to kill me. She shifted off me long enough to pull her leggings off. My truck had not been designed for having sex in the front seat, which was an oversight.

Alice seemed to be of the same mind. On her next awkward wiggle, her knee smacked my dashboard and she muttered something uncomplimentary about my pickup. Not helping matters, she'd tried to take a shortcut and leave her sneakers on, and now her feet were all stuck.

Alice's face was pink. I could tell by the way she bit her lip and huffed that she was frustrated and halfway to pissed off because she was basically trapped in an athletic chastity belt, her leggings hobbling her ankles.

She muttered another curse word.

I couldn't help it. I laughed.

I leaned over, pressed my face against the sweet curve of her belly, and laughed. Hard.

"Ford Boone, are you laughing at me?" she growled, sounding like a wolf herself. She tried to reach down and untie her shoes, but my head was in the way.

"You bet." My shoulders shook.

She looked ridiculously adorable, leggings tangled up around her ankles. It felt more real this way. More honest. We'd have passion, yes, but there would also be laughter.

Alice's laughter sounded a little forced. "How about a little help here?"

I nodded, reaching down to untie her sneakers and slide them off her feet. And then since I was down there and I was a thorough man, I worked my way up again, kissing each sweet inch of my Alice.

There was not enough room to appreciate her fully, so I shoved my seat all the way back and pulled her onto my lap. That was better, but a king-sized bed now topped my fantasy list.

"Ford, don't tease me," she pleaded. "Please let me—"

"I need to feel you." I slid my hands up her thighs to her hips.

Her panties were a scrap of pink that I itched to tear off. They were not my property, though, and I was always respectful of property.

I stroked her over the center of her panties with my finger. Once, then again, and again. Her eyes closed, her fingers digging into my shoulders as she rode my hand.

She was goddamned beautiful. Yeah, we were in my truck and my dick thought we were doing ten miles an hour in a sixty-mile zone, but this was about Alice and making her feel good. Special. Showing her that she was the center of my universe. She danced for me, moved and sighed and demanded more.

I gave it to her.

I'd give her anything she asked me for.

You're mine.

My mate.

My other half.

I kept the words to myself. Even as she shook and came riding my fingers, I didn't speak those words.

She was mine, mine and my wolf's.

But our time would be up soon.

CHAPTER

FOURTEEN

~FORD~

His eyes, more golden than amber now, looked into the distance. He was wandering somewhere inside his head, and antagonizing him right now wasn't wise. Somehow I didn't think that he'd respond with werewolf poetry.

— ILONA ANDREWS

She wanted to go down on me.

My wolf said yes.

I said no.

I invited her for hummingbird cake instead.

I had two reasons for this, possibly three. First, Jennie Dean's hummingbird cake was amazing. Second, I still intended to take things slow, savor our relationship like the last piece of chocolate. Third, and most importantly, that wolf of mine was close to the surface. Not only did he want to come hard, balls deep in Alice, but he wanted to mark her.

And that was a step too far. I was not marking her, no way, no how.

A wolf put that mark on his lover as a mating sign. There was no taking it off—it was an until-death-do-us-part commitment, more binding than anything Alice and I could have said, standing up with each other in Moonlight Valley's church.

Once a wolf mated, he had to be near his chosen partner. He couldn't roam far from her or he'd be unable to shift from his wolf form to his human body.

And then, if you bit your mate a second time, there was a chance—a small one—that you'd change the person you loved so much into a wolf. You put yourself into them with your saliva and what amounted to wolf germs or bacteria—and then you hoped for the best.

Hope was not a strategy.

Momma would have agreed, if she hadn't been trapped in a wolf's body, with the mind of an animal and no human left at all.

My brothers and I, for instance, hoped that Momma's current predicament would improve. She didn't recognize us, roaming around the thousand acres that made up the Boone spread and hiding from us. She was skittish.

We put out food; we put out cameras. We made sure no one came onto our land to hunt, and we brainstormed feverishly, trying to solve the pickle our family had found itself in.

Darrell was banished to Alaska, trapped in his wolf form because he was far away from Momma and he'd lost his tether to her in the botched transformation, but *she* was here, equally trapped because of the distance and the bite. Nevertheless, we loved her, would always love her.

And as long as she was out there, running free and safe, there was a minuscule chance she could come back to us.

I would not take chances with Alice, so therefore there we were, stopping for hummingbird cake. Alice had argued strongly for continuing with our make-out session; she'd listed the things we could be doing to each other in the front seat of my truck.

Alice was an outstanding list maker, and it had taken all my willpower to politely refuse and make a counter-argument for cake.

It was not an argument I wanted to win, even though I *needed* to. My wolf snarled, suggesting we mark her. **We don't have to bring her *over*, blockhead. We can just mate her. One bite, not two.** I wanted that so badly…but I couldn't. Not unless she knew what it meant to me to be mated. Not unless we had more than twelve months.

So instead I thought about the French Revolution and the guillotine. This was a trick Ranger taught me. No boner could withstand the chop-chop-chop of the heavy blade coming down.

We pulled up in front of Easy Eats, and I put the truck into Park. Alice sighed and set her head on my shoulder. Her left hand petted my right thigh.

"I like your body."

"My body likes you."

We like more than her body, my wolf groused. **And you might want to use a strong word there.**

A smile crossed her face, and for a long moment we sat there together, neither of us in any rush to separate. This was a first, and I loved it.

"Talking to you is so easy." She sounded wistful. "Like, firefly easy."

"Do fireflies talk a lot?" I wrapped an arm around her shoulders and hugged her close.

"They talk by flashing. If you're a male Photinus, you flash twice to say 'hey, I'm interested in hooking up and making babies,' and the female flashes back once. If you flash the light on your phone exactly right, they'll talk to you. It's very clear."

I gave a bark of laughter. "That would make the bar scene easier."

"Instead of buying endless shots and making drunken asses of ourselves, we could turn the flashlight on our phones on and off. Like an erotic Morse code. You're the first guy who—"

My possessive urges howled to life. I shifted so I could see her face. "I'm the first guy who what?"

She shrugged. "Didn't think I was too weird? Or too much work or too slow to get into bed? Although you're the sexual slowpoke in this relationship."

I nipped her ear gently, and she squealed. "Remember that later, when I'm showing you how *slow* I can be."

"But I don't have a whole lot of data points," she continued. "Not when it comes to guys."

"Alice, have you ever—" It was none of my business how many people she'd been with, unless she hadn't been with any. Then it seemed like an important thing to know because I'd read books.

There were supposed to be secret sexual tricks to make a woman's first time amazing. Which, since I didn't know them, meant that I'd have to take my time and use my words. Along with my mouth, tongue, fingers, and any other body part I could think of.

I planned to worship Alice in bed, and after that the details didn't matter.

Alice frowned. "What? No! This won't be my first rodeo. I had a boyfriend in college. He wasn't the waiting type, so we had sex in the front seat of his roommate's car in a parking lot. It had a lot less room than your truck, and I hadn't had time to research any amazing sex tips."

It didn't sound as if she'd had a happy ending. Which sucked and wasn't right, although it did mean I didn't have to worry about my competition.

"Just the one guy?"

She nodded, then added thoughtfully, "I think he needed to do some research. First I had to put his penis inside me for him because he couldn't aim it right, then he couldn't finish. It was a disaster. What about you? How many girls have you been with?"

This was not something I liked to talk about. Wolves had reputations, but in my case, it was more chimera than fact. "One."

"One?" She held up a finger, wagging it in front of my face, as if she needed to check that we were using the same mathematical system.

I nipped her finger gently. "One."

Was she disappointed? Should I have practiced? I could point out that I was a big reader and motivated to learn what she liked, but those were mostly my opinions.

"One." She sat up, which was a disappointment. "I guess you really were in love."

Her words surprised me and had me wondering whether she knew about true mates and how wolves bonded for life. Whether she knew that was how I was feeling about her.

"With Deelie Sue. I guess you did love her. I wondered."

"Deelie Sue? In love with Deelie Sue? Oh, *heck* no." I pulled back so fast I about hit my head on the window.

Alice dissected my face with her frown. For all my insistence on intimacy, this was not something I had planned on sharing. I nodded toward Easy Eats. "Let's go inside."

"For the record," she said carefully, "sex can be a great choice. Just like not having sex can be a great choice. This isn't a math problem where there's one right answer."

"There won't be a test later? Or a grade?" I teased.

She smiled slowly. "No, but there could be a participation trophy. A really big one."

I couldn't help grinning at that.

Also, I totally planned on winning her prize.

I walked around the truck and opened the door for Alice. She muttered a thank you, but let me get the door to the café as well.

For me, it was a way of showing the world that I cared for her and was looking out for her. My wolf would have brought her a dead rabbit for supper, but I figured door-holding was preferable to hunting and gathering in Alice's eyes.

The café was packed, especially for late at night. We snagged the last two stools at the counter near the door.

I really like you.

I can't stop thinking about you.

I like your wolf.

Okay, so she hadn't *exactly* said that last one, but she'd admitted to liking the big, bad wolf. Unless that was code for a Red Riding Hood kink—and I'd be down with that, as long as she was willing to tell me what she wanted me to do—she liked me. Us. All of me.

"So...Deelie Sue?" Alice prompted. This stopped the Technicolor Red Riding Hood porn playing in my brain.

I nodded, inhaled, and looked her in the eye. The stools in Easy Eats were set close together, so our knees bumped gently. The expression on her face was full of trust, lust, and admiration. This was better than the porn. I did not deserve her, even for twelve months.

The reminder that ours was a temporary relationship sobered me. In less than 365 days, Alice would walk out of my life for good.

"Why did you date Deelie Sue for five years if you didn't love her? Why not date someone else? Move on?"

She wasn't you, so it didn't matter.

I lifted one shoulder, stalling. "She knew what I expected, that I wasn't ever gonna be serious unless it was for pack reasons." I dropped my voice for that one because I did not need to announce the existence of werewolves to all of Easy Eats. "It was more we didn't want the same things. She has her job, so she's short on time for dating seriously. We were convenient for each other, and certain people had expectations about us."

I did not know how to interpret the expression on Alice's face. Excited? Hopeful? Highly skeptical and far too cynical? "So you've never hooked up with anyone else? Used a dating app? Been interested in someone?"

"You weren't here, so no." This was the truth.

Alice's eyes widened, and she looked surprised. "You were waiting for me?"

I had been.

And we have the blue balls to prove it, you fool.

"There was no point in seeing someone who wasn't you."

Alice looked away at that. I suspected I'd made her uncomfortable. At the very least, she hadn't anticipated my devotion. She'd agreed to give me twelve months, but she hadn't signed up for my feelings.

"That's a tall order." She blurted the words out, breaking the awkward silence that had been growing between us. The happy noise of Easy Eats was not enough to drown out the tension. "I'm not sure I'm—"

She searched for a way to finish her sentence.

Staying, maybe that was the word she needed. Or *settled. Committed. Certain* worked, too. But I wasn't going to ask her to be any of those things. That would be demanding she change her dreams to fit my life, and then they would be my dreams, not hers.

Instead I raised her hand to my mouth and kissed the back of it. "The only order we've got to give is for cake. Or pie, if you're in that kind of mood."

Alice beamed at me. "I'll go get us some slices. Don't go anywhere."

She slid off her stool, and I let her go, following her with my eyes as she rushed down the counter. Despite the late hour, the glass rotating display behind the hostess held plenty of slices of pie and cake. I hated letting go of her for that short jaunt, the need to touch her, to feed our connection, tugging at me.

"Boy," a familiar voice drawled.

My wolf's hackles rose, and I turned slowly on my stool. The growl that escaped me said it all. I did not want anything to do with Lucky Jansen.

"Lucky." The irritation and disinterest I felt leaked into my voice.

He'd brought his wolves with him. Several younger wolves I didn't recognize, plus an older, meaner one who liked to fight. At the back of the pack was Deelie Sue.

Deelie Sue being Deelie Sue, she did not hang around in last place. No sir. She marched up and slid her arm through Lucky's, staking a claim. At the end of the counter, Alice stepped away, disappearing into the restroom.

"Hi, Ford." Deelie Sue flashed me her megawatt smile.

She's traded you in a for a newer model.

Older.

Older, my wolf amended. **Super antique. Definitely richer. More successful. Alphahole.**

"Deelie Sue." I swallowed my frustration with her. I'd texted and called her nonstop for the last week. Atticus had also reached out, floating various times for the three of us to meet up and plan how we were going to catch Lucky shifting on camera.

But Deelie Sue had responded only that we should swing by her work if we wanted to talk. Since I didn't need a new vehicle—and nobody ever left without one—I had dug in my heels and refused.

Lucky glanced at his wolves and then nodded once toward two booths at the back of the café. "Those tables."

Two of his guys sauntered over to the diners, pulled out some cash, and said something inaudible. Charm and pressure, that was how Lucky worked. And then, if that failed, he sent his goons. This was a demonstration of what he expected from me. He ordered; other people made way for him.

Sure enough, the customers in question slid out of their seats, not looking Lucky's way. As they'd agreed to give him what he wanted, they got the carrot; if they'd stayed put, sooner or later he would have shown them the stick.

I did not want to become Lucky's stick.

"Convenient, us meeting up like this," Lucky said as I watched his wolves finish their booth cleanup and spread out at the back of the restaurant. He smiled benevolently, white teeth flashing as the customers filed past him, stammering out their thanks for their "free" to-go meals. "Saves me running out to your place."

I leaned against the counter, hoping Alice took a good long time in the bathroom. I did not want Lucky paying her any attention. "You want to borrow my hedge trimmer?"

Lucky looked offended. "I've got people to handle my yardwork, boy. We both know I've only got one use for you. Three more days, then I'll be expecting your answer."

I was tempted to give him an answer right then, one punctuated by my middle finger, but my own luck had run out. Alice was headed my way, carrying a tray with slices of cake and cups of coffee.

Your plan sucks.

Lucky's gaze followed mine. When he spotted Alice, he stiffened, his shit-eating grin fading, as if the sight of her was unexpected. He did get up from her seat, though.

Alice was beaming, but I knew the exact moment when she realized Lucky had been occupying her spot and was occupying my attention. She inspected him like he was an unexpected bug specimen, the happy smile fading from her face to be replaced by questions and reserve as she approached us warily.

I did not want Alice anywhere near Lucky and his wolves. We needed to go.

"Am I interrupting? I can give you a moment to finish your conversation." Alice's gaze bounced between me and Lucky, her fingers tightening on the tray of cake like she figured that was one thing she could save.

"Not at all, Miss Aymes." Lucky gave her a slick smile. He stood far too close to her. "How is my daughter doing? I hear she gave you job down at Vanity Fur Salon."

"She's good." Alice looked uncertain how much she should divulge, given that Sanye and her daddy had stopped speaking years ago.

Lucky smiled again, a gleaming, shark-toothed smile that did not reach his eyes. No one outside of the Iron Wolves disagreed with Sanye's decision to cut ties with him.

"Would you mind grabbing us some boxes?" I said to Alice. "We'll get this to-go."

Instead of asking the hundred questions I saw in her eyes, Alice nodded and headed to the hostess stand.

Lucky kept his gaze fixed on Alice. "So that's who you're seeing, huh?"

"That's none of your business, old man."

Lucky turned his head, his eyes sheeting amber. "Oh, I think it is."

"How is Alice Aymes any of your goddamned business?"

"Because you're gonna be part of my pack, *boy*."

"Nothing has been settled."

Lucky talked over me. "Wolves and humans shouldn't mix, not like that. Do you think you can work for me and see her on the side? Or you're thinking you'll hide your wolf, pass as human, hoodwink the Wolf Council into thinking that if you're so well behaved, your older brother must be as well? Because the evidence I've got on Maverick is damned serious, son."

"I don't take orders from you," I ground out.

Lucky bared his teeth at me. If he'd been in his wolf form, his ears would have been up, his eyes squinting. "You got until the full moon to accept it."

Let's rip his head off, my wolf suggested. **We can take him and his pack.**

"I put a reminder in my phone," I gritted out. I needed to get Alice and get the hell out of here. Because if we didn't move it, I was going to take my wolf's advice and swing at Lucky's goons. Six against one was not in my favor, and I would likely get my ass kicked.

"There's no future for a wolf and a human. You could take a girl like that to bed, maybe once or twice, but that would be selfish. She's far too good for the likes of you, and you should leave her alone. You can't tell her about us, about what we are, so it would be pure selfish to go after her."

"What Alice and I do or don't do together is none of your business."

"Wolves have tried it. Some of mine think they can handle cross-species dating, but no Iron Wolf has made it work. Hell, your own daddy tried it and look what he did to your momma. He went for the bite and he killed her. You want to do that to your girl?"

"I'm not one of the Iron Wolves."

Lucky cracked a smile. "Not yet. See you on the full moon."

FIFTEEN
~ ALICE ~

How could you? He is only a werewolf, and they can be terribly emotional creatures, you understand? Quite sensitive about these things. You could do permanent damage!

— GAIL CARRIGER

Ford Boone had reneged on our deal.

At least, that was how I interpreted three days of silence on his part.

After parking with me by the covered bridge and letting me buy him cake, he'd gone silent.

Monday had passed with nary a text.

Tuesday? Gone in absolute, unboyfriendly silence.

I'd used my words like an adult and asked him if he wanted to get together, but he'd told me he'd have to pass because he *couldn't*.

He did not elaborate on what, exactly, *couldn't* meant. Perhaps there had been wild animal infestations of biblical proportions, requiring him to work twenty-four-hour days and sacrifice his personal life. Perhaps he had to wash his luscious beard or give a presentation on wolf things to the Wolf Council and was therefore unavailable for dating me.

You did not, however, need to *actually* sacrifice your love life if you were a busy person. Multitasking was something many people successfully managed to do, and I would have understood if he'd brought up a busy schedule when he'd proposed our twelve-month deal.

Since he was a man (or at least a wolf-man), I decided he likely had poor communication skills and possibly inadequate practice communicating, and it was on me to bring his speaking skills up to par. Therefore, I gave up on the texting and developed a new plan.

After work on Wednesday, I stopped by the Piggly Wiggle and picked up peaches so I could make a peach cobbler. I got enough to feed eight lumberjacks.

This was also a key step in my plan.

I asked Sanye to help me with the baking and then to drive me over to the Boone place that evening, with the intention of feeding those boys, but also corralling my wolf alone so we could talk through the current state of our temporary relationship. I figured that if Sanye drove off, stranding me, he'd either invite me in or drive me home, and I intended to use that time to talk. If I was being a drama queen or needy, he should tell me that.

Every day was barely going to be enough to fit in all the things I wanted to do to him. And also with him, for him, and alongside him. I wanted all the prepositions with Ford.

I'd been out to the Boone place before, but not since climbing Ford in the lake and spending the night in their guesthouse, and never as a Boone girl-friend. Driving up the majestic alley of trees that led to their place felt different, although I could not have explained why.

Trucks jammed the big, circular driveway in front of the Southern Gothic mansion they called a farmhouse. At least four of the Boone brothers were home. Ford's beast of a truck was there, as was Ranger's EV truck, a shiny new Ford F-150 Lightning.

He'd been one of the first people to buy one. Ranger believed in preserving the environment and had been heard to argue that it needed any life ring we could toss it, which included making wise decisions in trucks.

Sanye—who was on board with the surprise boyfriend plan and was convinced that there were two ways to a man's heart (one through his stomach and another through a more southern and rigid organ altogether)—barely paused long enough for me and the peach cobbler to hop out before she was speeding away, leaving me choking on a cloud of red dust. We'd strategized that the Boone brothers, being Southern gentlemen, could not turn me away if I had no way of going home.

Plus, I had peach cobbler. No one passed up a free dessert.

I climbed the steps, past some impressive banks of orange daylilies in full bloom, and banged on the front door like I was the electricity meter reader come to turn off the power because the bill had not been paid.

The Boone property was not small, which only proved I was right when I said they were wrong in calling their home a farmhouse. Sanye and I had joked more than once that someone had been compensating by DIY-ing the biggest, most expansive property in Moonlight Valley.

Forty acres, kissing distance from the Great Smoky Mountains National Park, with a hundred-year-old mini mansion that had started life as a tiny farm-house and grown into six thousand square feet of living space with a wrap-around, colonnaded veranda on three sides.

Moonlight Valley gossip said the Boones had not one but seven fireplaces and that the place was a *This Old House* wet dream. For sure, the Boone brothers had spent most of their lives replacing, refinishing, and refurbishing the place by hand themselves, and their work was not done yet.

While I waited for a Boone to acknowledge my existence, I worked on channeling confident, sexy, and controlled. The porch was pretty. Someone had painted the wooden floorboards a deep clay-red and hung a swing from the ceiling.

I could picture myself curled up there doing…what? Reading a book? Canoodling with Ford? Planning a long and happy future with him? Yes! My imagination skipped dessert and rocketed past happily ever after.

Still, there were imperfections in the house.

It was old, it had done its best to fall down at some point, and the Boone brothers had clearly refused to let it. Paint peeled in spots and new boards alternated with the old in the porch. Care and neglect, new and old.

Boone was their daddy's name, but their momma's family had been the kind that wore cashmere on a daily basis and looked like they'd stepped out of the pages of a J.Crew catalog. I'd always imagined them with a garage full of gleaming Land Rovers, a marble kitchen bigger than a graveyard, and more connections than a spider web did strands.

They'd certainly been people who did not talk about money, but had always had it and assumed that their children would always have it. Kate Pemberwell had changed all that by stepping out with Darrell Boone as high school sweethearts and then by marrying him the day after their graduation.

People had whispered that he'd been expecting one heck of a wedding present from the Pemberwell family.

Instead, he'd wound up with seven kids, an anger management problem, and a local reputation that made the Grinch look benevolent.

I banged on the door and waited. When no one answered, I tried again, feeling like the Jehovah's Witness lady come calling.

Eventually, I gave up and wandered around the outside of the house. Animals were everywhere I looked; either the Boone brothers brought their work home on a regular basis, or they were fixing to open a zoo. I spotted multiple dogs, cats, an armadillo, a raccoon family, a fox, and a three-legged deer.

About when I was ready to give up, I spotted a redhead with broad shoulders, standing legs akimbo and hands on hips. *Target acquired.* Either Atticus or Ford was minding a large grill.

"You got my meat?" he asked without turning around.

Ford, my heart yelped.

I had a bad case of the nerves. I shook them off as best I could. I'd come out here, and I'd committed to my assault on the Boone place. I could not retreat now, even if I had to resort to sweet, sweet bribery.

"No." I cleared my throat. "But to be clear, I did bring peach cobbler."

Ford turned around, startled. For one awkward moment I wasn't sure if my plan would fail. If it had been terrible and doomed to crash land. Then Ford smiled, his face lighting up.

He came down the steps to the porch two at a time, wrapping me up in a giant bear hug that paid no never mind to the dessert I was carrying. His mouth found mine, delivering one heck of a kiss, his hands sliding underneath my shirt to stroke my bare skin. This worked so well for me that I moaned and almost bobbled the cobbler.

I'd have liked to have kissed him forever, but after about two minutes, we surfaced and put an inch or so between us. Ford's mouth nuzzled my ear, making me warm all over.

"It's been forever since I saw you," I sighed, cupping his face with my free hand. His beard was deliciously soft beneath my palm, and I desperately needed to divest myself of my dessert burden so I could fully appreciate him.

"I missed you," he growled and gave me another kiss. This one was longer and deeper, spinning out the tension between us and thickening the air. I wanted to do so much more than kiss him. So, so much.

"Don't mind if I do." Someone plucked the baking dish out of my hand mid-kiss. Or rather, end-kiss.

Ford growled some, but didn't let go. Instead, he gave an irritated huff and nipped my neck too gently to leave a mark before lifting his head. I turned in his arms and discovered Ford's twin standing next to us. He shot me a welcoming smile before returning his gaze to the cobbler he'd claimed.

But they weren't *really* identical, I'd come to realize. Sure, on the outside, they looked alike and were monozygotic twins. Mix-ups and mistakes happened all the time in town. I'd mixed them up on that critical, first-kiss night.

Now I knew better.

They were two very different people. Atticus was smoother, less rough. His smiles came easily, and he got along well with people. Ford, however, had all these interesting edges and unexpected spots. He hardly liked anyone, and I treasured being one of those select few.

Atticus waltzed away with the peach cobbler.

"Don't be eating that!" Ford yelled.

Atticus ignored him.

"I brought you all something sweet," I blurted out. I'd forgotten the sophisticated, witty script I'd practiced in Sanye's car. Hopefully, my delicious peach cobbler would compensate.

Ranger came out of the house in time to hear this. "But we're having a sausage party."

"A sausage party?"

Ranger set the platter of sausage he was carrying next to the grill. "Yes. This is my championship-winning sausage. It's hot."

"Range," Knox growled at his brother, dropping down into the Adirondack chair nearest the grill. He dipped his head at me. "Evening, Alice."

Ranger shot an unimpressed glance at his brother. "You don't want to eat my sausage? We also have zucchini."

If Ranger suggested eggplant, I'd lose it.

Ford scowled at Ranger, then wrapped an arm around my waist and drew me against him. His mouth quirked when he realized I was trying not to laugh, but he did not comment on Ranger's menu. Instead, he shifted us to an Adirondack chair, set me on his lap, and resumed scowling at his brother.

His scowl made no impression on Ranger, who pointed over my shoulder. "My garden has produced an overabundance of zucchini. Ergo, it is zucchini and sausage night."

Since in addition to being a champion pitmaster, Ranger usually won a half dozen ribbons for his amazing produce, this seemed plausible.

I squirmed on Ford's lap, trying to get comfortable. His arm banded around my middle; his hard thighs pressed against my own softer backside. By the time I was situated, he was groaning and I could feel his...*zucchini*.

I felt a little dazed. I had a whole new sympathy for Ranger's fascination with large, phallic vegetables.

"I have giant zucchini," Ranger volunteered.

Knox leaned over and smacked the back of Ranger's head. "Keep your zucchini to yourself."

"I can't do that," Ranger said, sounding offended. "First, an overabundance of supersized vegetables is no joking matter. Plus, if Alice is staying to eat with us, it's important to plan ahead. Fortunately, I have plenty of zucchini for her."

"Ranger!" His brothers bellowed his name in unison. They did not appear to appreciate Ranger's sense of humor.

"What? I'm just saying I'll eat her peach if she tries my zucchini."

"You are not getting anywhere near her peach," Ford barked.

"So no zucchini?" I sighed dramatically. "That's very disappointing for me."

"Go show Alice your zucchini," Atticus said to Ford, waving us off. "She's clearly experiencing a vegetable shortage. Go fix that."

I leaned back and looked up at Ford. "It is true that there is a terrible shortage of huge zucchinis in my life. You should rectify that."

Knox choked on his laughter. Atticus snorted.

Ford glanced at me, his face caught between amusement and disapproval. I grinned at him.

"Show her around the garden," Ranger agreed, his tone bland. Then he added, "But come back for my hot zucchini. Because it's the best."

"*RANGER!*"

* * *

Dinner turned out to be amazing, although eating with the Boone brothers was disturbingly like eating with a pack of wolves who had only bothered to shift into human form because paws and forks did not work well together. They growled, they squabbled, and they clearly loved each other. Ranger's sausage hit the spot, and his zucchini was deliciously spicy. There was not a crumb left of my peach cobbler either.

I had an early shift at Vanity Fur Salon on Thursday, so we headed out soon after supper finished up. When Ford put me into his truck, Knox, Ranger, and Atticus stood on their front porch and waved goodbye. They were sweet men and their perpetual bachelorhood was a waste.

As I promised to return tomorrow night (accompanied by a blackberry cobbler), I decided that I should really exert myself to find them each a girl-friend. How hard could it be? Plus, it would make me really popular with the female portion of Moonlight Valley's population.

I was planning my strategy when Ford made an unexpected left onto a road that was little more than a dirt track. We hadn't gone more than a mile from the Boone place.

"Is this where you tell me you know an awesome shortcut?"

"I'd never try to reduce the amount of time I spend with you. I know you've got work in the morning, but I wanted to show you something."

"Something good?" Pine trees shot up into the darkening sky on either side of us.

Ford slid me a glance. "Knox and I built a hunting cabin out here four years ago. It's a private place. Secret."

"Atticus doesn't know about it?" There wasn't much Ford's twin didn't know. I hadn't quite decided how I would feel if, say, Atticus learned our inti-mate details.

"No. Not even Atticus. Knox thought we'd keep it between the two of us. And now you. It's my cooling-off place, where I come when I get angry and need to let my wolf out to run."

The possibilities of a private space ignited my imagination. A place to make new memories for the two of us. We could be just Alice and Ford here, away from all the expectations of family.

Maybe here I'd tell him how I felt about him, how I was starting to think I could put the *love* label on those feelings. Maybe we'd make plans here for the rest of our twelve months.

Ford drove with absolute confidence, steering left, then right, then who knows where. With anyone else, I would have been nervous, but this was Ford. I was safe with him. I let him drive, let go of my worries about where we were going.

The hunting cabin that popped out of the gathering darkness was a surprise. It was made of logs, with a red tin roof, and set back under the trees. It wasn't large at all—just big enough to hold a couple Boone-sized mountain men.

Ford came around to open my door. I waited for him because he liked doing this, and when I got out, his right hand came to rest on the small of my back, a heavy, comforting weight.

His left hand held out a set of keys. "These are for you."

"For me?" I grinned up at him. "I'm pretty sure you already gave me a house. This is becoming a pattern. It'll set the bar high for our paper anniversary."

He laughed lightly and shook his head. "That was your house. This is my place. Now you can come in whenever you want."

I could feel the heat of him at my back, the comfort and security of his arms around me. Time stood still for a brief moment, or at least I sure wished it did.

This felt good. Right and perfect. Like something to hang onto, a hug or an embrace. *Let's stay here. Let's not move* FOREVER.

Not having secret mindreading skills to go with his secret lycanthropy, Ford walked us toward the cabin. I followed, connected to him by his hand at the small of my back and something else far more intangible. I let him unlock and open the front door so we could step inside.

The cabin was small. And perfect. And perfectly, unexpectedly romantic.

I'd anticipated hunting gear and leftover furniture. Maybe some sleeping bags and a primitive kitchen with boxes of cereal and cans of soup. Instead, I found myself in a woodworker's masterpiece.

The kitchen cabinets were fancier than the ones in my tiny house, with wolf heads carved into the doors. Wolves edged the table and featured prominently on the backs of the matching chairs. I could imagine Ford taking his time to create the hardwood floors and the paneling on the walls, head bent over whatever tools he used (okay, so I knew nothing about wood or carving or whatever this was).

Even better, there books were stacked beside an armchair pulled up in front of the fireplace and a lumberjack-sized bed covered with an honest-to-God white comforter. There was nary a big-screen television or video game console in sight. No dirty laundry, no crumpled beer cans, no random piles of gym equipment.

"There's no electricity," he said, as if that had just occurred to him. "Not up here."

"Okay?"

So we were going to cozy up by the fire like a nineteenth-century hero and heroine? I was *so* on board with that.

Ford plucked a lantern off a shelf and fiddled with it. A flame sprang into being. "Are you okay with the dark?"

"I might be," I admitted. I could imagine the two of us spending the night together here, sharing our truths, opening up.

Ford watched me carefully, taking in my reaction to his hideaway. He was likely thinking about us getting naked. About us having sex—no, *making love* —in this tiny, perfect jewel box of a cabin.

"Ford, you are such an overthinker."

"An overthinker?" He raised an eyebrow, crossing thick arms over his broad chest.

"You bet. You see, your hideaway here is romantic. But I feel the need to point out that I'd have sex with you even if you didn't own the perfect sex palace. I don't need romantic fires, candlelight and privacy."

I waved a hand at the lantern he'd lit and set on the table. "I'm not holding out for a perfect moment. I don't want you to be hands-off or planning out our bedroom activities. I just need you.

"I love your wild and reckless side. I'd be happy to jump you in your truck, behind the band gazebo, out in the woods. It's not the setting I need—it's you."

I was so sure of this that it scared me. I was a scientist, and science was not about certainty. Nothing could be established as being one-hundred-percent certifiably true, and we dealt in near certainties based on experimental evidence. My Ford experiences all pointed to one certainty: he was a good man, a committed man...and he was *my* man.

I loved him, and that love meant I didn't need or want romantic gestures. Gestures could be empty, and words could be just words. How and where we made love together didn't matter.

Ford's gaze softened as I spoke, his eyes warming up. He gave me a heated, full-body inspection.

171

I was as happy as a clam at high tide. And hot. I was so, so hot. Perhaps he would take me at my word about not needing perfect moments and go for it now? We could do it hard and fast, up against the wall. Or on the floor. There were many surfaces we could christen with our passion.

Ford moved with slow deliberation toward me. That ruled out the fast—but not the hard—portion of my half plan. He didn't stop coming until he'd backed me up against the wall.

When he set one big hand behind my head and the other on my hip, I considered panting. Or moaning. Possibly grabbing on to him and never letting go.

His eyes flickered with amber and heat. He stared down possessively at my mouth as he said, "Alice, I've put a lot of thought into our first time. I won't rush it. We're not picking up burgers to eat out of a bag in the car. Not when I could take you out somewhere special and we could have all four courses and dessert twice. I have plans for you…"

"I do like a good plan." I sounded breathless. "Although to be fair, I'm also a huge fan of burgers."

Ford leaned into me, capturing me between his big body and the wall. His beard scratched deliciously at my cheek, and a shiver ran through me.

The fingers gripping my hip slipped underneath my shirt, his thumb drawing small circles on my bare skin. He was an inch north of my waistband, and my body urged him to head south, south, south.

"Ford," I said, his name a demand, my hands fisting the sides of his flannel and yanking him closer. "I do not need or want to be on some kind of perfect princess pedestal, especially if you're not gonna join me there."

"You don't know all the steps in my plan, Alice. And it has a *lot* of steps." His mouth found my earlobe, kissed it, and I shivered. "I've got dozens of steps."

"Then let's start now." I tightened my grip on his shirt, pressing my needy body into his bigger, warmer one. This felt good, and other things would feel even better.

We could christen his beautiful bed. Or his wall. The floor. The shaggy rug in front of the fire. There were no bad options.

He shifted his weight off me with a sigh. His face was sober and stern, fierce and restrained. "There's no pedestal. I respect the hell out of you, though. That's nonnegotiable, whether you like it or not."

* * *

As he had after our previous dates, Ford walked me to the pink door of the Little Love Den and pressed a suitably chaste, third cousin twice removed–approved kind of kiss on my mouth while Emperor Meowpatine stared at us through the window. It was sweet and intimate, but no tongue and nothing that was not G-rated.

His parting grin was big, though, and I was tempted to run after him and yell *I'm in love with you, Ford Boone!* Instead, being both intrigued by his alleged plan and not wanting to jinx our blossoming relationship with premature declarations of feelings, I let him go.

I'd planned to spend an hour or so sorting through Aunt Sally's things. When Ford had cleared away the flattened remains of her trailer, he'd boxed up what he could, and I'd been going through the boxes. So far, there hadn't been much to salvage.

The cats had demonstrated in no uncertain terms that they were indoor/outdoor cats and that being forcibly removed from Aunt Sally's property had not been to their liking. They did not care that there had been tree issues and had no problem with accepting Little Love Den as a suitable replacement domain. Ford had made them tiny cat doors, so it seemed fine.

I started with the closest box. An hour later I had a stack of books next to me and an empty box full of cats. Barack Obameow perched on top of the newest Nora Roberts, two years of Aunt Sally's favorite cooking magazine, and several random encyclopedia volumes.

I liked knowing that Aunt Sally had touched these pages. That she'd held these books. Spent her time with them.

I was particularly pleased to find *A Little Princess* halfway through the box; it had been "our" book, and Aunt Sally had read it over and over to me during our summers. I'd liked to imagine that I was the long-lost princess, and I'd wished desperately for a monkey. We'd looked up a recipe for Bath buns, and Aunt Sally had made them every Sunday while I conducted experiments on yeast.

I let the book I was holding fall open, riffling through the pages. I was wasting time and being inefficient, but I missed Aunt Sally. This was the closest I would get to her now.

The truth was that although our relationship had not been as close as it could have been, I wasn't ready to box her up and let go of her.

I hated knowing I couldn't visit her in the summers, that she wouldn't be here. I was furious at the pine tree for taking away the last place where I could feel her—and deeply grateful to Ford for salvaging what he could from the sticky, green mess.

This was when the note fell out of the book, straight into my lap. I could practically hear Aunt Sally chortling up there in heaven. The note was addressed to me in her swoopy, near-illegible handwriting, but like she always had, she'd turned the *I* in my name into the nose of a happy face.

I opened the note, my heart hammering loudly in my ears. It wasn't long; Aunt Sally was not someone who had seen the point in expending a great many words, either in person or in a letter.

Alice,

I did not invest in any diamond mines while I was alive. Pastor Phee was quite certain that as silver and gold were God's metals, they were certain to be a blessing. I therefore purchased silver coins and it has turned out that God has excellent—and lucrative—taste in metal

Pastor Phee also received divine inspiration on several occasions regarding that crypto-money-thingy, and let me admit that God was very fond of Pastor Phee and did not lead her astray.

Taped to the back of this note is a key. Follow the treasure map and use the key. Please try not to think too poorly of me. I hope that inheriting the several million dollars that my investments have yielded will—I have no idea what it will do. But please enjoy it and do not forget to feed my cats.

Love,
   Aunt Sally

In addition to Aunt Sally's short note, there was a page that looked like it had been torn out of a map atlas. She'd scrawled a big X on top of the fine state of Texas, and in the margins she'd added an address. There was another, much shorter note: *Upon further contemplation, I believe leaving you clues and no address would be counterproductive.*

She'd left me directions to a bank in Texas.

She'd left me a treasure.

She might have been addicted to hermitizing and collecting cats, but she'd been there for me the best she could.

CHAPTER
SIXTEEN
~FORD~

Being a werewolf had taught her— among other things—to ignore the past, live in the present, and not think too much about the future. It worked, too, as long as the present was bearable.

— PATRICIA BRIGGS

Alice: Sorry to text you so early in the morning. I'm driving to Texas to do something for Aunt Sally.

    Alice: Shoot. I hope your phone's on do not disturb.

Alice: I'll call you when I get there in nine hours, okay

Alice: I miss you already.

Alice: We should talk when you have a moment.

I could have kicked myself for not leaving my phone on. Alice had tried to reach me, and I'd failed to be there for her.

I didn't see her text messages or the missed call until Thursday afternoon, when we'd wrapped up All-Purpose Animal Services business for the day. Atticus and I were on our way home from routing a raccoon from Mrs. Dillworthy's garage.

I started with *dadgummit* and rapidly worked my way up to less polite words.

Fuck, my wolf prompted. **That's the word you're looking for.**

"What's up?" Atticus slid me a concerned glance from the driver's seat as he stepped on the gas, getting us away from Mrs. Dillworthy. She was a lovely lady, but nosy as hell. Shifting where she could see me would be bad.

"Shut up a second, okay?" I stabbed the button on my phone to play Alice's voice mail.

"Hi, Ford. It's me. Alice. Alice Aymes." I snorted at that. She was the one and only Alice in my life. I would always know who she was.

"I made it to Texas, and I'm headed out to my hotel soon. I don't know what my reception will be like, but it'll take forty minutes to get there. If you have time to talk, call me?" She paused and cleared her throat. Her voice dipped. "I miss you."

The second message was shorter, cutting in and out. "I'm on my way to the hotel. I have time to call now if you do?"

I couldn't believe I had missed an opportunity to talk with Alice. Worse, I'd missed it to crawl around in Mrs. Dillworthy's garage.

I should have kept my phone on me. I should have invested in a special ringtone for her so there would never be any question about my picking up or not.

There was no third message.

I was also well past the window in which Alice had indicated she was waiting for me to call, but I called her anyhow. My wolf and I needed to hear her voice.

Atticus hummed a bar of Dionne Warwick's song about two ships passing in the night. He did not have Ms. Warwick's vocal talent, nor did I appreciate the distraction.

Did Alice need me? Was this a general, vague missing of me, or did she have a specific and pressing need that I was failing to meet?

My heart about leaped out of my chest when she answered. "Hello?"

Missed her.

"It's me. It's Ford. I didn't get your messages until now. I was working and my phone was off and…that's not important. Are you okay? What's happened? Do you need me there with you?"

Yes. **We can shift, run, and be there in five, maybe ten hours.**

This seemed optimistic to me, unless my wolf had recently developed superpowers that included locomotion at the speed of light. But I could get a plane ticket. Drive down there. Violate speed-related laws in multiple states.

Never mind that the Iron Wolves were waiting on me to do their test job and that I had my own plans for them. Those plans could and would wait if Alice needed me.

This was not practical, and I knew Atticus was giving me stink eye, but Alice was my priority. If she needed me, I would go. The Iron Wolves and their threats could go to hell.

Alice didn't say anything for a moment. I wished I could see her face. I was about to suggest we switch to a video call when she spoke up.

"Thanks for calling me. I—I'm glad you did. I'm at a bank right now, so I can't talk for long. We're about to go into the vault, plus it might be really rude."

I paused for a second, then asked, "Your Aunt Sally sent you to a bank in Texas?"

"She had some stuff here in a safety deposit box. She left me a key and everything. It's full of papers. A journal."

I wasn't sure how close Alice had been to her auntie, but I was fiercely glad she had something of her left. I hoped there were good memories in that journal, stories Alice could treasure.

"Do you want to call me back later tonight? When you're free and all?"

"Yes!" Alice's unadorned and enthusiastic response made me smile. "I can totally do that. That's a great idea. I'll call you then."

"I won't turn my phone off again," I promised.

"Thanks?" She sure sounded like she wanted to add something else, but the words didn't seem to come to her.

Atticus helped fill up the long moment of silence by whistling again. Finally, Alice said, "I'll talk to you later."

I didn't think that was what she'd really wanted to share with me, but she was at a bank and in the company of others. I was sure she didn't want them all listening to her personal conversation. Fortunately, I had only Atticus with me, and he already knew I was gone on Alice.

"I miss you, Alice Aymes."

"Me too," she blurted out, like she hadn't been sure I'd feel that way and had been wondering whether her feelings were premature or silly. I hated that she didn't see herself the way I did, as special and worthy.

Tell her I miss her, my wolf demanded.

"My wolf says hello," I added, feeling stupid. "He misses you, too."

She laughed quietly. "It's so weird, but I can't wait to see both of you when I'm back."

"There are too many states between us," I said. "I want to be right there beside you, right now. If you need me to, I can get there by tomorrow."

"No," she said, sounding uncertain. "No, I've got this, and I won't be here for long. This whole situation is a little weird, and it's not a long-term kind of thing. I'll be back soon."

I did not like the sound of *a little weird*, but it was not a veiled plea for help. Or so it seemed. I was willing to be convinced otherwise and go running straight to Texas.

Let's do it.

When we called later tonight, I decided, I would ask more questions, suss out the situation. If things felt off then, I'd fly out to be with her.

"Okay, talk to you tonight."

"Yes. Please. Bye."

There were other words that I almost said, but instead I echoed, "Bye."

Then she was gone.

Atticus cursed quietly beside me. "What's up?"

"Aunt Sally left Alice a to-do that took her to Texas. Something about a secret safety deposit box. She can't come over tonight."

"That's a tragedy."

I nodded, not paying him much mind because I was replaying my conversation with Alice in my head.

You should have tried for phone sex, my wolf growled.

Not with my brother in the car.

I did have some boundaries.

My wolf grumped in my head and snippets of dialogue flashed through my head. My wolf had a surprising talent for dirty talk, but I was certain Alice was not going to let me talk out my erotic plans for her body when she was inside a bank vault with suit-wearing strangers.

Bummer, my wolf snapped.

He wasn't wrong.

"So…no eating her peach tonight?"

I glared at my twin. "First of all, she was bringing blackberry cobbler. And second of all, there will be no peach-eating for you, Atticus Hank."

"No need to get upset with me, Ford Montgomery. It was an important, dessert-related question, that's all. I simply needed to check before making alternative arrangements."

When I did not cease my glaring, he shrugged. "The woman's peach was delicious. You can't be surprised I want more."

"You don't get her peach unless she says so."

I ignored Atticus's muttering and shifted my gaze back to the window. I was debating pulling up a travel website and checking plane ticket availability when I saw flashing police lights in the side-view mirror. A siren chirped, making Atticus tense in his seat.

"What the hell?" Atticus frowned fiercely into the rearview mirror. "Is that Alessandro?"

I nodded, gritting my teeth.

He's ambushing us, my wolf complained. **Coward.**

"Stop the truck." I sighed, massaging my temples. "We'll play his game."

I hated to admit that Alessandro was, in fact, a real law enforcement officer —and that he, therefore, had the ability to do certain things. Getting pulled over by an animal control cop was irritating, particularly since he could ticket us only for animal-related offenses. It was a good thing he didn't know we were wolves, or he'd have locked us up in the animal cages he had in the back of his vehicle.

Cursing with gusto, Atticus pulled over carefully. There was not a whole lot of room on this mountain road, and part of me secretly hoped Alessandro would skid off the edge.

My secret hopes thwarted, Alessandro strode up to the driver's side and shined his industrial-sized flashlight into the truck. Atticus squinted as the beam hit him full-on. It was light out, so the flashlight was another power play from Alessandro.

Let's show him who's the real authority here, my wolf growled.

"Which one of you is Ford?" he asked, bouncing the flashlight beam between our faces as if he was playing ping-pong. I hated him.

"You can't pull us over because you want to say howdy, Alex," Atticus said, keeping his tone friendly and even. "Not unless you've got a hot tip that we've got somebody in our trunk or you've got yourself a warrant."

Personally, I thought giving Alessandro concrete ideas was a bad plan.

"And you would be Atticus," Alessandro said, frowning a little at my twin. He shifted his gaze back to me, turning off his monster flashlight, then braced a shoulder against the truck, his beautiful hair flowing in the wind like he was modeling for a book cover. "Alice is out of town. Were you aware of that, Ford?"

I straightened in my seat, surprised that Alessandro had pulled us over to chat about the location of his third cousin twice removed.

"Yes. Although maybe you should ask her to share her location on her phone. It would be quicker than pulling us over."

"Aunt Sally left her quite a legacy. Alice is cleaning out her safety deposit box in Texas."

Atticus and I shared a look, and I knew exactly what he was thinking. *Why on God's green earth is this man telling us this?* I was thinking the same question in stereo.

"Alice told me this. Like I said, I just spoke with her."

Alessandro nodded, and I realized he was deliberately keeping his features neutral and his voice impassive.

Danger, my wolf piped up. **He's planning something, but we'll kick his ass first.** I liked my wolf's plan, but I couldn't put my finger on what Alessandro was up to.

A sense of certainty came over me. We needed to go. This would not end well.

"I appreciate the heads-up. We'll be going now." I beamed a *start the truck, you jackass* thought at Atticus.

"If you know about the safety box, then I guess you know about what was in it. Yeah?"

Don't flinch. Had there been venomous reptiles in there? Was this an *Indiana Jones* thing where Alice had opened the box and daggers had flown out?

"I know all about it, sure. Let's go, Atticus."

Atticus started the truck, but Alessandro didn't move. He kept himself draped over the window's edge like he was a model on one of those game shows our momma had liked to watch.

"So then you know that Aunt Sally left her a ton of silver, plus a whole drive full of cryptocurrency? That she's now swimming in money and will be leaving Moonlight Valley to start that dream business of hers?"

Atticus's face barely twitched. My twin was good. I mimicked his stoic calm as I stared at Alice's third cousin twice removed. Never mind that my heart was beating fit to burst and cold sweat was trickling down my spine.

Fear.

We don't *do* fear, my wolf whined.

It was scared, too.

Atticus covered for me. "Like he said, Ford just ended a call with Alice. He knows exactly what is going on. And since I'd hate to accidentally run you over, *officer*, it would be great if you could step away from my vehicle."

Alessandro frowned. He looked like he'd asked Santa for a pony for Christmas and awakened to find a juicer underneath the tree.

He stepped back reluctantly, and Atticus meticulously and with great attention to all of Tennessee's traffic safety laws rolled up the window, started the truck, signaled, and got us back on the road at exactly the speed limit.

We drove away sedater than a mourner following the lead car in a funeral procession.

It was not likely that Alessandro had lied to me. Alice had shared the same bare-bones story—Texas, Aunt Sally, safety deposit box—and Alessandro had nothing to gain by making up a financial inheritance other than temporarily tormenting me. All I would have to do, however, was call Alice and his fabrications would be revealed.

So I didn't think he was lying.

Which left the truth.

Alice had been texting and calling me all day, asking to talk.

We should talk when you have a moment.

I miss you.

"Dammit..." I snarled. My wolf howled silently inside me. Something sharp and vicious peeled back my ribs and stabbed my heart. It hurt so much, the pain radiating up, out, and into every inch of me. Was I having a heart attack? Was this what *childbirth* felt like?

"Did you know that Alice was planning on leaving Moonlight Valley?"

"Not yet she wasn't," I said roughly. My voice was thick with emotions I didn't want. "She was saving up money and..."

And we were already running out of time.

We'd had only twelve months to being with.

"Alessandro could have been lying," Atticus said. He must have been turning the new information over in his head, working out how it fit in to what he already knew. "Alessandro hates us, and he's angry that you've got it bad for his cousin."

Alessandro's severe dislike of me was true. He'd have hated on principle anyone who had dated Alice. Honestly, I felt much the same about the men who had come sniffing around after Mack.

"He's not lying about her leaving. If she didn't need a business loan, she'd be out of here tomorrow. She told me that on our first date."

Atticus did not volunteer any more thoughts or opinions after that, for which I was grateful. Neither my wolf nor I wanted Alice to leave.

She had the money that was her ticket out of here. She would go. And I would never hold her back.

* * *

I'd agreed with Alice that we'd call tonight, but I'd had to consider some alterations. I needed to track down Deelie Sue and get her to agree to help my brothers and me with our Lucky Jansen problem, which meant that I should switch my phone off and let Alice go straight to voice mail.

I could not afford to be distracted, and I would not be able to think about anything or anyone but Alice if we talked.

We should fight, my wolf raged. **This is ridiculous. She's *ours*.**

In this my wolf was wrong. Alice belonged to no one but herself, and I would not forcibly keep her here. It was not even my place to be mad at her. I didn't get to be angry, not when I wanted to be her partner, her everything.

I was going to support her, no matter what.

We could *bite* her, my wolf suggested. **Who wouldn't want to be a wolf? Then she'd have to stay. It's perfect!**

And you remember what happened to Momma, I said. *That was not a happy ending.*

If I didn't pick up, she'd text me. Or leave a voice mail. Possibly, I'd get an email.

In all the scenarios in which we communicated tonight, however, I assumed the content would be the same: she'd tell me that she was not returning to Moonlight Valley. It would be easier that way because I would not have a chance to lash out at her.

When the phone rang, however, I answered it.

Knew you couldn't resist, my wolf said. **Go for it. Convince her.**

You make convincing *sound dirty*.

The wolf laughed.

"Ford?"

"Alice."

She happy-sighed when I picked up, as if she hadn't been one-hundred-percent convinced that I would. Maybe we'd developed boyfriend-girlfriend telepathy, like the connection I shared with Atticus? Before, when I'd thought there was every chance she'd come back to Moonlight Valley and to me, I'd have welcomed that change.

"It feels so good to hear your voice! I know it's only been like a day and we talked earlier briefly so it's not even really that, but it feels like an eternity. Or at least a dozen years. I miss you."

She sighed again, followed by a snuffling noise that I told myself was *not* cute. I was such a liar. "Ford, I need to tell you something."

"I'm listening." This was like baring your throat to an alpha who had bested you in a challenge, waiting for his teeth to tear through your skin and end the fight. I knew I'd lost. I knew I didn't *deserve* to win. I wondered whether knowing it was all over would be a relief or a torment.

But then she said, "Ford Boone, I love you."

The teeth sprang away from my throat.

My wolf howled triumphantly.

I opened my mouth to say my line in the script I'd written in my head— that even if we were over and she was going, I would always value our friend-ship and wish her well—and then realized she'd switched plays on me.

I had not seen this coming.

"I love you and I'm in love with you, and I realize that we're probably in the liminal stage of things, but I don't see my feelings changing.

"And I know that this is not the sort of conversation one should have over the phone, but today's been upsetting because I've learned some things about Aunt Sally and my family that came as a shock. And I so I didn't want to make that kind of mistake myself, the waiting-too-long kind of mistake.

"We haven't been seeing each other for all that long, plus there's the whole wolf thing, but we've been circling each other since childhood, and I think you're the electron to my proton.

"All those arguments we had growing up, those were our firefly flashes. We were twinkling at each other, waiting for each other to notice. I might have thought you were grumpy and rude and more than a little mean, but I think I've also always loved you."

Alice sniffed, her voice thickening. She was crying, I realized, my own eyes threatening to well up in response.

Don't you cry too, the wolf growled. **Be strong and bold. Tell her you'll *TAKE* her.** I ignored him.

Fuck, I didn't want Alice to cry over me. I didn't want her to cry at *all*. She deserved only happiness and good things, but there was no way for me to hold her or care for her, not when she was eight hundred miles and several states away.

Alice loved me.

Alice *LOVED* me.

That thought ricocheted around inside my head. I could not respond. I could not say it back, let her know that fuck, yes, I was her man and she was my mate and we belonged together.

Maybe Alessandro had been lying. Maybe Alice intended to stick it out here in Moonlight Valley and with me for the twelve months she'd promised me. But if she did have the money to go now, then I was the reason she was hanging around...

I was the one holding her back, forcing her to stick when she wanted to go.

I was as bad as my daddy, biting Momma and compelling her to be something and someone she had never signed up to be.

"I love you," Alice said again. I think she would have said it all night. I closed my eyes, sucked in a breath, and told myself to do this right.

I could *not* say those words back to her, could not ask her to be my mate in every sense of the word. Could not bite her, claim her, love her any more than I already did.

I swallowed hard. My wolf growled, a softer whine, encouraging. He was starting to understand why I had resisted. I knew what I had to do.

"Alice, this is not the time. We'll talk when you get back, okay?" I kept my voice steady and calm. *I'm not upset at all. You did* not *just rock my world.*

There was a small sniff from the other end, the sound of fabric being dragged over skin, and I almost showed her my throat. I almost caved, gave in, rolled over, and exposed my soft underbelly. I almost told her I loved her and she was my mate.

But all I had to do was consider what had happened to Momma, to imagine how Alice would feel if I forced her to stay in Moonlight Valley. She wouldn't get her shot at being a Nashville businesswoman. I would be the anchor locking her in a place she'd never wanted to be.

She would come to hate me.

Momma had hated our daddy. He'd burst into her life, romanced and love-bombed her, and then become the millstone around her neck. He'd ignored her unless he wanted something from her, and he'd stolen her chance at living a bold, free life.

She'd loved us kids, but she hadn't wanted to be a wolf. The wolf side of our lives had scared her.

Darrell had bitten her anyhow, and he'd all but killed her.

I would never do that to Alice.

"Sure," she said finally. Her voice was a whisper. Sad. *Uns*ure.

"Sure. Bye, Alice."

She hung up without saying anything more.

That was it. We were done.

Sure, she'd come back to Moonlight Valley at some point, possibly in a few days or even a few years, but I had tossed her beautiful words and her heart back in her face.

My twelve-month plan had been stupid.

Alice wasn't going to break my heart when she left town.

I was going to break hers.

CHAPTER
SEVENTEEN
~FORD~

Oh, for goodness' sake, he's a werewolf, and he likes to fight. Is it so wrong to suggest he might, oh I don't know, fight for her?

— GAIL CARRIGER

I was not a happy wolf when Atticus and I pulled up in front of Wheels of Good Fortune at eight o'clock. My conversation with Alice played in my head on a loop and I was in no mood to be around people.

Despite the late hour, the car lot was a beehive of activity. Deelie Sue kept extended hours in the summer to accommodate all her would-be car buyers. I was not one of that number, having had the same truck since I'd first got a driver's license, but Atticus was a car fiend, and he always came here.

The big glass-windowed showroom was full of the newest model trucks and cars. Salesmen and women in matching polo shirts waited by the doors to pounce. I recognized one older couple looking at a fancy truck. Mrs. Dillworthy had apparently decided to fill her garage with something new now that she was raccoon-free.

Best truckin' idea ever!

I ignored my wolf's bad pun, the new car smell, the shiny truck accessories, and even the Corvette that sat in pride of place in front of the floor-to-ceiling windows. I was a wolf on a mission, one that I wanted to finish fast.

My mind kept replaying snapshots of my time with Alice. Our kiss in my truck, the night she fell out of the deer blind and into my arms. Our hike to my secret waterfalls. Cozying up in the Little Love Den.

I could call up her face so easily—the corners of her plush, pink mouth quirking up as she called me on my bullshit, the warm twinkle of her eyes, the trail of freckles on her collarbone.

Once I'd taken care of the Iron Wolves, I was shucking my human skin and shifting into my wolf form. Maybe I'd stay like that for days. At least a week.

I would go up into the Smoky Mountains and run and run. Surely, if I ran long enough, I could outrun my memories of Alice.

"...you have to give her some sugar."

I snapped back into the present. Atticus was staring at me, waiting for my response. "What?"

"With Deelie Sue. You're going to have to show that woman some sugar. Be sweet. Flirt a little. She's not interested in me—she'd sooner run me over with that Corvette out there—but she likes you, always has. She'll do anything for you if you ask nicely."

Deelie Sue was a proud, independent businesswoman. "She would not."

Atticus smirked. "Would, too. Yeah, she'll put her career first, but you're running in second. She likes you as much as she could like anyone—and you need to remind her of that if you want her to help us out."

I swiped a hand down my face. "This is not a good idea. I'm no good at being charming."

"Then don't charm her. Tell her the truth—that you need her help and you can't do this without her. She'll enjoy that. Deelie Sue likes to feel important."

This was because her family had spent her childhood making her feel unimportant. I did not want to use this as leverage. Before I could tell Atticus this, however, Deelie Sue's assistant manager spotted us.

She handed off the older couple to one of her associates and came over to meet us. She was Deelie Sue's gatekeeper, kind of a human moat who kept out Tennesseans who didn't actually intend to buy a vehicle. She beamed cautiously at us.

"Are you boys looking for a new truck?" She shook my hand, then turned and all but clutched at Atticus's big paw when we shook our heads about the truck-buying. "Atticus, do you have a moment to help me with a software issue?"

"You bet." Atticus grinned at her. "I'll be right there, darling."

He steered her toward the giant bank of computers on her desk as she chattered away at him. There wasn't a computer that Atticus couldn't fix or an employee here he couldn't charm.

I, on the other hand, had no smiles left in me at all because I was missing Alice. Nevertheless, I was relieved to have my way made smooth before me, thanks to Atticus's mild flirtation. I strolled right on up to Deelie Sue's office and rapped my knuckles on the door.

As soon as she looked up and saw me, a smile lit up her face. She appeared surprised, but pleased. Atticus wasn't wrong about her feelings for me. I stepped inside, shutting the door behind me.

She stood up and came around her desk, holding out both hands to me. "Ford!"

"Deelie Sue." I took her hands and squeezed, trying to sound like I was as happy to see her as she was to see me. It was hard, though. There was too much baggage between us.

She held onto my hands, searching my face for something. I had no idea what, but she sighed and gave me another squeeze before letting go.

"What can I do for you?"

I studied her for a long moment. She looked real nice, in a pair of expensive jeans that hugged her legs, and a fitted, white T-shirt.

Because she was the owner/operator of Wheels of Good Fortune, she had a khaki blazer with the emporium's name embroidered over her right boob. With her sky-high heels, she was almost on eye level with me. She looked classy, sexy, and confident. This was not a woman I could or should bullshit.

"I need your help," I said, putting my cards on the table.

"And here I thought you were here to buy a truck." Surprise replaced the easy confidence on her face.

"No truck."

Her next look was assessing, but that was Deelie Sue for you. She was always thinking, and she was practical to a fault. She smiled slowly, and I wasn't sure I'd be leaving without a new truck after all. "Is this a wolf thing? Have you finally decided to take a mate?"

I sucked in a breath. "No."

"No?" She blinked, surprised. "You know our mating has come up with the Wolf Council. We'd make an excellent breeding pair."

I was not surprised she had inside intel on what the Wolf Council thought, but it did not change my answer.

"No. I'm not marrying on demand, Deelie Sue. We would not be good together."

Her lips tightened. "We've been plenty good together before, Ford. I heard no complaints from you."

"I am not having sex with you again." This came out balder than it should have, but I needed to be clear.

I might not be getting the future I'd dreamed of with Alice, but I would not betray her with another woman (or wolf). Not now, not ever.

"There aren't so many wolves in the world," she pointed out. "You need to pick a shifter as your mate unless you're planning on being a bachelor the rest of your life."

"Not happening," I said again.

This was not one of those end-of-the-world books Knox left stacked up in the bathroom, where there were just two people in the whole world and breeding was more important than liking.

"Then what do you need from me if you don't want sex or a truck?"

I frowned. "There's more to you than that."

She laughed. "Sure, but those are the only two sides of me you've ever paid attention to."

"Can we sit down and talk? Honestly?" I gestured at the chairs in front of her desk. These were where she reeled in her customers and convinced them they needed a fifty-thousand-dollar truck. I didn't mean to imply that Deelie Sue was a liar or a cheat, but sometimes she did get creative with the truth.

She stood there with her back to the door, thinking about my question. Apparently, it was a hard one, after all. Eventually, the words tumbled out of her in a rush. "Sure we can, Ford. You know you can trust me—we're on the same team, after all."

She meant the werewolf team.

"And we have a history together," she continued. "A good one. It counts for a lot."

I motioned to the chair next to me. "Will you sit with me? Please? I have something I need to say."

Deelie Sue shot me a smile that made me think she might be seeing wolf babies when she looked at me. It was not a comfortable feeling.

She walked over, hips swaying, and perched on the edge of her desk. Her legs bumped my arm playfully. I couldn't play her flirty what-if game or have casual sex with her, no matter how beautiful she was.

I had given my heart away and there were no take-backs.

But I could be honest and direct, and I could definitely admire Deelie Sue for her drive and talent. She was a good person, a good wolf.

I told her that.

And then I explained our situation to Deelie Sue in precise—but not abundant—detail.

I told her the truth.

That was the only decision I could make. My family needed her help, and I would do anything for my family.

CHAPTER
EIGHTEEN
~ALICE~

You're either predator or you're prey, remember? And you sure as shit don't want to be prey.

— ANGELA KNIGHT

T wanted to be angry.

I was determined not to waste a nanosecond more on what Ford Boone thought about me.

Mostly, though, I was hurt and sad and confused by... Well, there had been quite a few shocks and revelations in my life this month.

I had opened Aunt Sally's safety deposit box.

Except she wasn't my aunt. She was my birth mother. I had been stunned by the birth certificate tucked inside the metal box.

Fortunately, the banker who retrieved the box for me had also provided me with a private room in which to sit and go through the things that Aunt Sally had considered important enough to hide in a fireproof, theftproof, fifty-dollar-a-month metal box. *I* had been in that box.

Right on top of everything rested a piece of pink construction paper the size of a paperback novel with two baby footprints inked on it in blue beneath *my* name and birth date. This shocking piece of news had been followed by various pieces of legal paperwork wherein Aunt Sally had transferred custody of me to my parents.

My parents had admitted the truth when I'd called them. They'd adopted me when I'd been two days old.

When I'd asked who my bio dad had been, they hadn't known. Aunt Sally hadn't shared that secret with them. She'd said that he had not been a nice man or a good man and we were all better off without him in our lives.

That hadn't been the full extent of Aunt Sally's secret keeping, however.

Aunt Sally had been a shifter herself. She'd explained this in a handwritten letter addressed to me.

My dear Alice,

If you are reading this, I am dead. That sounds very dramatic, so I suppose I should start over except that it is true.

If you are reading this, I am dead and never got around to telling you that we are a little more related than you believed. I am your birth mother. Your parents adopted you at my request.

At some point, if you spend much time in Moonlight Valley, I expect you will learn that the town has some rather unusual residents. These include werewolves.

At this point, I had to pause in my letter reading to indulge in panic, followed by some scientific deduction. I had a BIRTH mother? Who was Aunt Sally? I had no idea how I felt about that. And then there was the rest of her letter, the part where she mentioned werewolves.

Include implied...what? That there were *other* unusual people living in Moonlight Valley? Did we have vampires? Witches? A summer camp for supernatural beings? Aunt Sally was light on details.

I am a shifter myself, although of the feline rather than the lupine variety. That makes you half shifter, which is likely not enough to change your form, but I have made sure that you can live under the radar by adopting you out.

. . .

My brain threatened to shut down. This was... I was... A CAT? I glared at my hand, willing it to turn into a paw.

Nothing happened.

Of course it didn't.

People did not turn into cats.

Werewolves, yes. Which sort of torpedoed my *shapeshifting is impossible* argument. I didn't know what to think. I needed to make a list. I needed to test this hypothesis that I could maybe, probably not, but maybe shift into a cat. And also: under the radar of *whom*? I had so many questions. In light of the fact that Aunt Sally had waited until after she was dead and buried to volunteer any information, I was nothing *but* questions.

I was also emotional, upset, angry, and full of doubts. She should have told me when she could have answered my questions. When we could have tried to work on a relationship that was more than my crashing at her place during the summers.

My questions did not diminish after I finished emptying the lockbox. Aunt Sally had, indeed, literally left me a ton of silver (which was in a separate bank vault and required an armored car to transport).

She had also not been misled in the matter of cryptocurrency by Pastor Phee. I was, indeed, several million dollars richer.

And angry. Very angry.

All I could do was accept her money. There was no time left to do anything else, to ask questions, to try to get to know the woman who had, apparently, given birth to me. I had never had the chance to get to know her well or to tell her I loved her.

That ship had sailed, crossed the River Styx, and disappeared into the underworld.

Fine.

I'd called Ford after spending the day at the bank right up until it closed. Inheriting a fortune and a secret turned out to be exhausting. I was wrung out and needed to hear his voice, hence the phone call.

In which I had announced point blank that I loved him. My feelings had been brewing for a while, but spending the day thinking about Aunt Sally had clarified them.

She was dead, and I would never get another chance to talk with her. Ford was very much not dead, but I did not want to risk things happening that might end our relationship before I'd had a chance to share my feelings with him. There was no time to waste.

Ergo, I'd called him and told him I was in love with him. He'd responded by saying nothing. Perhaps he would write me a terse love letter in thirty or sixty years, telling me he'd secretly been a monk consecrated to sexual abstinence or afflicted with syphilis or…

Something.

I was looking for a reason why he'd listened to me profess my love for him and then met that confession with *nothing*.

It had been ridiculous to fall in love so fast and so hard. He probably thought I was a deranged stalker. Maybe I was insane. Maybe it was a family trait. After all, we'd all thought that Aunt Sally was a loveable if slightly weird old cat lady. And it turned out that we'd been right, although not in any way I could have anticipated.

She'd turned into a cat, and I was related to her. Maybe I could shift into a cat, or maybe I couldn't. Maybe my biological father had been a lion or a panther or a door-to-door salesman (although clearly he had been a colossal dick). I would never know.

My parents had come out to Texas the next day to devise a plan for a ton of silver and my even weightier emotions. They'd been impressed with Aunt Sally's business acumen, although I had kept the actual source of her investment advice to myself.

My daddy had left on Sunday, off on another business trip. Before he'd headed to the airport, he'd told me I was his daughter and he loved me. He was proud of me for taking charge of my life. Tears were shed. We hugged. He left in a rush because his flight time had been moved up and he did not yet have TSA precheck.

My parents were not perfect. I'd known this for years, and I'd loved them anyhow. After all, they loved me and *I* was decidedly imperfect.

I texted Ford on Sunday. He left my message unread. The crack in my heart split wider than the Grand Canyon.

On Monday I alternated between crying and texting Sanye to thank her for taking care of my cats and covering my shifts at Vanity Fur Salon. I also checked my phone compulsively for some kind of communication from Ford, but there was nothing.

By Tuesday evening, Momma and I were both anxious to get back to our lives. Momma had some serious hustle, and she was in one of those predatory MLMs where you sold cosmetics to your friends, your neighbors, and random Facebook groups. It had been such a good year for her that she was only a few major sales away from landing her second purple Cadillac.

Since I'd come into money, I dutifully bought one of everything she was selling and then drove her to the airport, which was also a convenient opportunity to ask the obvious questions: Do you know who my bio dad is? Why did you all keep it a secret? Did you know that Aunt Sally was a cat?

Momma looked at me weird when I asked this last one. "Like one of those people who identify with animals? A furry or a therian?"

"Not…really?"

Should I tell her I might be a cat shifter? How ridiculous did that sound? Was there a chance that she *already* knew?

I wished I could ask Ford for advice on how to break the news, although he'd also made it clear that he wasn't supposed to run around telling people he was a werewolf.

Just in case I really was a cat shifter and there was a Cat Council (although cats seemed more like they would have a Supreme Dictator), I decided to be careful.

Momma had gone back to her texting. One of her neighbors needed to restock her beauty supplies ASAP because her Pekinese had gotten into them and there was not much left. Momma smelled a massive opportunity.

"Aunt Sally believed she could turn into a cat," I said after Momma had done some more tapping and smirking. Was that vague enough? I waited for some enormous divine cat paw to come down from the sky and smush me.

A mile and a minute later, I decided I was probably free and clear. Momma carefully turned her phone off and tucked it inside her handbag.

"Your Aunt Sally was an interesting lady," she said. "I'm sure she did believe that."

Her tone made it clear that while she did not wish to speak ill of the dead, she also was convinced that Aunt Sally had been nuts.

For the rest of the drive, we stuck with my adoption and not the possibility that Aunt Sally had actually shucked her human skin and run around Moonlight Valley in furry form.

Momma reassured me that adopting me had been one of the best things that had ever happened in her life. She'd wanted a baby girl and she'd got the very best one.

Then she switched to quizzing me about my Nashville business plans and offering unsolicited advice about franchising and growing my nonexistent business into a national conglomerate.

That was a little more pressure than I would have liked, but that was Momma for you. She hadn't earned pink Cadillacs by not pursuing her goals with the ruthless tenacity of the Mongol horde conquering China.

When I finally drove into Moonlight Valley, it was late. So late that I decided not to bother Alessandro by barging into his house—he needed his beauty sleep—and instead kept right on driving until I was at the Little Love Den.

The moon was almost full, and Aunt Sally's yard was lit up like a Walmart parking lot. I staggered inside, dropped my overnight bag by the door, and realized I had no next step. What did I do with myself now?

The cats were nowhere to be seen. Ford had added cat doors to the front and back of the house, so perhaps they were out tomcatting around. *What if* they're *shifters* too?

That was a horrifying thought, so I promptly vanished it. Mostly.

Okay, so I also made a mental note to schedule a quick trip to the vet to make sure I was owned by four perfectly normal cats and not something more supernatural.

I pulled on my favorite sleep shirt—an oversized T-shirt with a silk-screened firefly announcing *I'm LIT* from its butt—and a pair of boho knee socks that normally made me feel like I was living my very own Jane Austen movie, then climbed up into the cute little loft.

Except, now that I was tucked up in bed and should have passed right out after the long, long drive up from Texas, my brain would not shut off. The unexpected money bonanza, the dragon-worthy silver hoard, and my new status as a crypto queen—those weren't what kept me awake.

The truth was, my brain was filled to the brim with Ford thoughts.

During the nine-hour drive, I'd decided somewhere between the Texas border and the middle of Arkansas that I would hunt down Ford. On our first phone call, he'd said he missed me and he'd offered to fly out to support me. And then he'd blown me off on our second phone call despite my big love confession.

Had I misunderstood him? Misinterpreted his interest? My head obligingly replayed a montage of the pivotal moments in our relationship—every touch, every word, every hot look—on a never-ending loop. I thought he'd made me promises.

When we argue, that's me listening to you and you listening right back.

I'd never not pay attention to you.

You're the most interesting person I've ever met.

When we make love...

Did we not speak the same kind of English? Was this a love language mistranslation? I was so confused.

The bed shook underneath the weight of multiple cats. They all must have come home from their midnight sexcapades.

Paws jabbed into my thigh, my kidney, my belly. I had enough time to protect my boobs with my hands before Emperor Meowpatine stood on my chest, his yellow eyes boring into my face.

"Hey, kitty." I reached out to scratch behind his ears.

You should mark him, hooman.

Holy moly... What...

He is a bad dog, Genghis Khat announced, popping up by my shoulder. **We do not need a dog in our territory.**

"He's a wolf," I said weakly.

WHEN HAD MY CATS LEARNED TO TALK?!

We could always talk, Oedipuss announced as he sat on my feet.

I waited for Barack Obameow to chime in, but apparently he had not bothered to come home yet. Or couldn't be bothered. Perhaps he was off dealing with important matters of cat statesmanship in the woods.

You were not worthy, Emperor Meowpatine summed up.

That was the story of my life. But...wait. If I could hear the cats in my head, did that mean that I could shift? Or was it just further proof that I'd end up an eighty-year-old woman with twenty cats?

You could try, Emperor Meowpatine sniffed. **But we are the best at being cats.**

I had no idea how one shifted. Was there a manual? A checklist? WHY had Aunt Sally never written this down? My life had never needed an ordered list more.

You should make breakfast. Genghis Khat butted my face with his head. **Up.**

I gave up trying to figure out my DNA and my life and got up. After I'd fed the cats breakfast (at midnight, but I was not going to arguing with talking cats), I grabbed my car keys and the keys to Ford's mountain love nest. I debated finding pants, but in my opinion, after midnight was a pants-optional time zone.

Driving up the mountain in the dark was more motivational than I'd expected. Despite the important conversations my parents and I had had and the issues we had semi-resolved, I did not like the dark.

Given that I possessed no time machine and could not go back to my childhood and erase that long, dark weekend I'd spent alone, I was quite certain I would *never* like the dark.

The near-full moon, the silver clouds scudding across the sky, the happy twinkle of ancient stars and planets—those I liked just fine. It was the dark, no-light air around me that made me nervous. Once I spotted the turnoff that led to Ford's place, I felt marginally better.

I felt angrier, however, when I pulled up in front of his cabin and realized there were lights on inside. Smoke rose from the chimney, blotting out the starlight as it drifted across the sky.

He did not get to have a romantic fireplace fire without me.

No sirree.

I got out of my car, slammed the door, and stomped toward the cabin. By the time I was face-to-face with Ford's front door, I was livid.

I didn't bother with knocking—he did not deserve my courtesy. The locked handle was not a problem either, since he'd handed over the keys to this particular castle.

"Little wolf! Little wolf! Let me in!" I jammed the key into the lock, twisting it more forcefully than necessary. It did not budge.

It *flew* open.

In fact, the door not only swung open, it took my key (and the hand that was attached to the key) with it.

What the... I growled, head whipping up, ready to give the door a piece of my mind. I had a lot to say, but all the words drained out of me faster than water from a bathtub because standing there in front of me was a sleepy, peeved Ford Boone wearing unbuttoned blue jeans and black boxer briefs.

The man did not need locks or doors. His nearly naked muscled body was so distracting that I stood there, mouth open and about to burn up from the heat flashing through me.

Dear God...I loved his body. It was beautiful. It demanded worshipping. With my mouth, my tongue, my fingers. Numerous other parts of my body volunteered for the job. I needed to wrap myself around him and drink in his presence. He was my safe spot, my reassurance, my anchor.

"Alice?" His forehead puckered in a cute little wrinkle of consternation and disbelief. He had not expected to find me on the other side of his door. Like a sexy burglar fantasy or sexy Santa Claus. Sexy something. Whatever.

It was not my fault I could think about only sex.

I blamed Ford's boxer briefs.

And their contents.

And, oh heck, Ford himself.

"I am not happy!" I bellowed at him.

My words bounced off the trees, echoing loudly all around us. There was some ominous rustling noises from the shadows; I'd scared the local wildlife. Too bad for it, because I needed to defend my mental honor. Showing up pantsless in the middle of the night and trying to break into his cabin seemed like something only a deranged person would do. Or a horny one.

Ford's eyebrows drew together. He looked upset.

"Ford Boone, I..."

I should have planned what I was going to say on the drive up here, but I'd been too busy trying not to run off the road. He needed streetlights. Spotlights. Something. This was all his fault. I poked him in the middle of his rock-hard abs.

"What was that for?" He made a grab for my finger, but maybe I had inherited catlike reflexes after all because my hand was already safely back on my hips.

I tapped my foot and glared at him. "I'm super pissed off at you!"

"You're mad at me?"

"Yes! I needed you and you were here, not there, and then I told you that I loved you and you..." Finishing that sentence felt a bit too much like willing Ford's nonsentiments for me into existence. I stopped and tried to poke him in the stomach again.

Since he had wolflike reflexes, he anticipated this second attack and wrapped his big paw around my finger, tugging me forward and into his cabin-lair. He kicked the door shut and banded a hard arm around my waist before I could sink to the floor in a sad, sorrowing puddle and continue my pity party.

"Listen—"

"I'm beyond mad at you." I thrashed in his arms. Since I'd abandoned all dignity along with my pants, I might as well go all in on the melodrama. Plus, it felt like something a movie heroine might do.

"I thought we were twelve-month partners. That we were in this together, that you wanted me and would be there for me when I needed you. But when I told you that I *loved* you, you wanted to stick a pin in it and revisit it later."

This was not a one-hundred-percent-accurate quote of what Ford had said to me, but it certainly summarized what I had heard.

Ford added a second arm around my middle and held on. My back was pressed against his front, so this meant my butt was cradling his penis. Which was hard.

I couldn't decide whether I was insulted or flattered or concerned that his physiological response to anger and confrontation was a massive hard-on. I flailed some more.

"Alice—"

"You are an asshole!" My plan crystallized: I would hurt Ford Boone. Hurt him as much as he'd hurt me when he'd dismissed my true-love confession.

"Calm down," he growled into my ear.

"Don't you tell me to *CALM DOWN*!"

That was fuel on my fire.

"Now," he growl-snapped, lifting me off my feet and carrying me across the cabin's floor.

I thrashed harder, pushing at his arm and wriggling. "*Never ever*!"

With one firm movement he flipped me around and sent me sailing backward. I had a second to be concerned about my landing, but then my back connected with a firm mattress.

Ford followed, coming down on top of me and caging me between his body and the bed. His hands pinned my wrists over my head, his weight holding me in place.

Not willing to concede the fight, I bucked. Ford muttered roughly, his breathing ragged. I was not exactly put together myself. I glared up at him, willing him to read my mind. I was so pissed off.

As oxygen started to make its way back into my brain cells over the sea of red clogging my vision, I realized Ford appeared to be as mad as I was. His eyes were pure amber, his wolf peering out at me.

Then his gaze shifted lower, his eyes catching on my lips. For a brief second he looked distracted, then his expression changed, crumpling into fury, hunger, and outright lust.

"Alice..." he whispered.

The anger eased up inside me. He looked all confident and predatory, but he sounded as lost and confused as I was. We were equals in that.

"I'm so mad at you," I repeated, as if we were in a fairy tale where saying the phrase three times would turn it into a magical incantation.

I did not want to have happy feelings for Ford; he had bruised my heart badly and I was close to angry-crying. Or sad-crying. Everything was all mixed up inside me.

His eyes shifted up, and he frowned. Then winced. He let go of my wrists and cupped my face, his thumbs swiping away a tear that had not gotten the memo that I was a strong, badass woman who did not cry over a man.

"Don't stay mad, Alice. Don't cry. Please don't do that."

He brushed his lips over my cheek, pressed a kiss against the corner of my eyebrow. A kiss on my forehead. Another, slower kiss between my eyebrows. The corner of my mouth. My jaw. My neck. He nuzzled my neck over and over, kissing it, nipping gently.

This was good, better than talking. Or being sad. Mad. Since he'd ceded control of my wrists, I cradled his face between my palms. I loved the rasp of his stubble-covered jaw, the soft warmth of his skin against mine.

Even better was the feel of his mouth when I kissed him. I was not waiting any longer. I was *doing*. Making my intentions clear.

I was here for Ford Boone.

His hands slid from my cheeks, down my throat to my shoulders, lower still until the hem of my oversized T-shirt was bunched up in his grasp. He tugged and I nodded, answering his unspoken question without breaking our kiss.

Not kissing Ford would have been a crime. I loved his mouth, loved how intently he kissed me back. Instead of being two separate people, we were slowly melting into each other and becoming one.

Force? Alord? The portmanteaus sounded unpoetic, but who needed rational, elegant thought?

Ford's stripping my T-shirt off me did not significantly impact our kissathon. I heard him toss it somewhere, but I did not care.

He pushed his jeans down and sent them off to keep my poor, lonely T-shirt company. Maybe they'd create an entire baby wardrobe, frolicking together on the floor of Ford's cabin.

Excited by our near nudity, I pushed at his chest until he rolled over, taking me with him. I straddled him in my knee socks and panties.

"You," he groaned hoarsely. I decided he was as gobsmacked by our chemistry as I was, and I loved that. His excited gaze bounced between my throat and my breasts.

"Me," I agreed happily. "And you. Together. Now. Or at least now-ish and hopefully in the next five minutes."

Ford's eyes flashed amber. Part of him was clearly thinking about it, probably the part that directed him to run his fingers over my thighs and into the back of my panties.

We should stop kissing for explanations. That would be the mature, adult thing to do.

I knew this. But I wanted kisses—Ford's kisses—because my brain said they were essential.

My heart was already on board with the Kiss Ford plan, fluttering faster than a firefly's flash. Instead of lup-dup, lup-dup, it beat out *this man, this man.* Ford was an amazing kisser.

My hips, however, thought we should discover what else he was good at. I rocked my core against the center of his black boxer briefs.

That felt so good I did it again.

His big, thick penis pressed against me, protesting the layers of cotton trying to keep us apart. Someone (me) made a weird hiccup of need. I slid down him again. Back up. Over and over.

Grind.

Slide.

Multiple times.

It was so much better than riding that ridiculous waterslide he and his brothers had built. But maybe we could do this on the slide?

I spared my new erotic fantasy a millisecond before I lost myself in rocking against Ford. I'd research later. Figure out my hot hypothesis when I wasn't about to—

To—

Ford groaned as I ground against him, a tiny heartbeat springing to life between my legs. His fingers gripped my hips, guiding me, suggesting a sexy rhythm.

My fingers dug into his shoulders, like we were making sure we were good and stuck together. Like maybe, if we could get through this, do *this* together, then we'd be stuck together afterward. Could hold onto this moment forever.

Our shared history suggested that as soon as I'd had my orgasm, Ford would retreat. He would tell me the time wasn't right or he didn't want to rush this. The sex light would go from green to red; he'd put up a big ole *no trespassing* sign.

I wouldn't disrespect his boundaries, but I also couldn't keep on making overtures only to be shot down. It hurt. My heart hurt.

Therefore, despite the heartbeat now thundering between my legs, the orgasm that was so, so close, and the delicious, sexy expanse of Ford spread out beneath me, I pulled away.

I dismounted and settled on the bed beside him. I probably needed to put the entire state of Tennessee between us. Possibly the continent. Or a galaxy.

Because for a hot moment, I stared at him. He was gorgeous, and mostly naked, and very, very into me. His penis tented the front of his boxer briefs, begging for my touch.

"Hold on…hold on a minute," I said to his boxer briefs. I laid the palm of my hand over his beautiful, arrogant mouth.

"Hush," he whispered, the word tickling my skin. "Let me have tonight, Alice. Please. Just tonight."

Only tonight? I knew I should have follow-up questions, but he'd sexed them right out of my brain.

Right now, all that mattered was that I needed him and he needed me right back. We *both* needed this.

With him, I could be myself. I wasn't too strange or too nerdy, too weird or too needy. We fit together, smoothing out each other's rough edges and filling in each other's holes. Which sounded far, far dirtier than anything we'd done yet. There was still time.

So there was only one answer to Ford's not-question. Only one thing, one person, I wanted to be doing right now. "Yes, Ford."

He tucked his fingers into the waistband of my panties and tugged them down. I lifted my butt and then my legs to help him out, shivering from the intensity of what he made me feel. My own fingers got busy, grasping his boxer briefs and shoving them down until he took over, toeing them off.

This was the first time I'd seen Ford fully naked. I'd ogled his arms and his chest, his back and his glorious, amazing butt. I'd spent quality time admiring his hands, his feet, and his face.

I'd never had the full picture though, and I was greedy. Also, amazed. Hot. On *fire*.

I shifted down so I could see all of him. Ford did not disappoint, not in the penis department, not at all. "You are something," I told him.

"Something good?"

"Something," I repeated. "Amazing comes to mind. *Bad*, as well. Like dirty bad, hard bad, deliciously bad."

He laughed roughly, then rolled, switching our positions. It did seem only fair to take turns being on top. I had always wanted an equal relationship.

His muscular thigh pressed up against my center, sending bright sparks of pleasure through me. I arched, seeking more. More was good. More was best.

Ford, that bastard, laughed again and started kissing and biting his way down my body. My big, bad wolf was eating me up, and I loved it.

I loved it so much I was about to be selfish. I should've been touching him and talking dirty. Letting him know how much I appreciated his attentions. It turned out, however, that feeling what he made me feel was a full-time job and I had no bandwidth left to be doing anything else.

He kissed his way down my stomach and over my hip. Along the crease of my thigh, and then…

He went south of the Mason-Dixon line, headed down yonder, and I couldn't stand the tension any longer. I hollered about him not rushing on my account, he laughed, and then he bent his head and kissed me right there, his mouth on my center, his tongue making wicked, wicked forays where I was wet and slick and positively shaking with my need for him.

My head fell back on his pillow, and I exhaled a huge, relieved, pent-up sigh, probably from holding my breath while wondering if he'd put me off again. And then all that released tension built right back up again because Ford was kissing me, paying me every attention, his thumbs opening me up so his mouth could pay me homage. There were no words for what he made me feel.

I lifted my hips, squeezing my butt muscles tight as I chased after the pleasure, rocking against his rough-gentle lips, chasing the sensation of his stubble-roughened jaw right *there*, right where I wanted him most.

When I came, it felt like I was riding the Slingshot, launched out of my body and into the air as pleasure rushed through me. There was heat and bliss, all that delicious tension snapping and setting me freer than free.

Ford lifted off me.

The sound of a condom wrapper tearing open barely penetrated the symphony of joy humming through me.

For a brief moment, I was alone.

Empty.

Waiting (which I did *not* do patiently, not ever).

Then he was back.

I opened my arms for him, wanting to lose myself in his embrace. That did not make a whole lot of sense, but it was his fault I'd come so hard. He did not get logical thinking.

Ford lowered himself over me, his sheathed penis rubbing against my slick, sensitized folds. He was so beautiful that my heart hurt.

"I need you." He kissed me, hard and fast, as he nudged at my entrance. "May I? Can I have you? Just for tonight."

That last was not a question, but I answered it anyhow.

"You can have me forever. Yes." I wrapped my arms around his broad, muscled back. I could explore lower like this, wrap my legs around his lean hips and squeeze his butt. I could make him feel as good as he'd made me feel, show him much he meant to me, and not only in bed.

As soon as he pushed inside me, my plan to not be selfish went up in smoke. He was... Ford was... Oh my *God*. I blasphemed shamelessly, greedy whimpers falling out of my mouth.

Ford moved deliberately, his body driving into mine, pushing deeper, staking a claim. He buried his face in my throat with a groan, his teeth scraping erotically over the tender skin there.

"What are you *doing*?" I demanded. This was not like me, to be so out of control.

"We're making love." Ford's eyes met mine, open, watchful, laid bare, and I knew he meant that *we*. I knew he loved me, even if he wouldn't say the words. He cared about me. He *loved* me.

I was not so stingy with my own words. "I love you. I love you. I love you so much," I chanted, wrapping my legs around his hips and my arms around his neck.

I pulled him as close as I could, hoping my words would penetrate the emotional armor he wore and make their way into his heart. Make him want to say the words back to me. Make him tell me the truth.

Ford didn't say anything. He kissed me instead, driving into my body with hard, sure strokes. I moaned, making sounds I hadn't known a human mouth could make because he undid me so.

His eyes went over amber, holding mine, and the intensity of his gaze almost pushed me over the edge.

"Alice, I..." he whispered my name. Stopped. Tried again.

I would have sworn his teeth lengthened, but it felt right. Looked right. Ford wasn't soft, wasn't completely human, and I loved all of him.

He didn't say anything else, just continued his erotic domination of my body, pushing into me, making space for himself. There was a Ford-shaped space between my legs, up north in my heart, and always in my head. He fit into me, and I loved it.

"I love you," I whispered again because I could never say it enough. "Your wolf, too."

He cursed, tensing and growling in rougher, deeper tones than I'd ever heard before. I was certain his wolf had heard me and that the wolf loved me back. He buried his face against my neck, his teeth nipping, biting the tender skin there. An erotic pleasure stabbed through me and I yelled his name, coming even harder than before. This time, he came with me.

I wrapped myself around him, holding onto him, and he held me back, like we'd both finally come home and knew it.

CHAPTER
NINETEEN
~ALICE~

The white wolf—a male—locks his gaze with mine, his eyes a startling shade of dark ruby. Then a voice reaches my ears, deep and gravelly. "It seems I have saved you."

— *TESSONJA ODETTE*

"Can I ask you something?"

Ford and I had spent the last hour touching and petting, cuddling and kissing. It was the best, most romantic night of my life, and it made me think there was something to be said about angry sex.

"You bet..." he said, sounding drowsy and unsure.

I was the little spoon in our bed, my back pressed up against his bare front. The flames danced in the fireplace, and I fought the urge to drift off.

I wasn't ready to let go of this amazing moment and fall asleep. Once I did, it would be over and I wasn't willing to concede yet.

"Do you ever shift when you're making love?"

His big hand stilled on my hip. He'd been stroking me possessively, his hand brushing out a *mine mine mine* rhythm that my heart had silently echoed right back.

"No," he said curtly. "No, I do not."

"Not that I want to have sex with a wolf," I rushed on because since I'd made things awkward between us, I might as well go whole hog. "I don't think bestiality is my thing. But for a moment there, near the end, I thought…"

I'd thought that maybe he was thinking about biting me.

I brushed my fingertips over the side of my neck, where the skin felt sensitive and ever so slightly, just barely, abraded. Touching that almost-mark sent a shock of pleasure through me, so my words were not intended as a complaint. I was, in fact, already making a mental list of other places Ford could bite me.

"It's a wolf thing," he said finally.

I waited, the logs popping in the fireplace, but apparently Ford was under the impression that those four words explained everything. *I love you* too might have done the job, but *it's a wolf thing* most definitely did not.

"And?" I prompted.

"Wolves mate for life," he said reluctantly.

Secrets ahoy. The fire was burning low now, the room growing darker and darker. Ford's arms around me reminded me I had my very own super hero. "And the biting?"

"We mark our true mates."

"So it's like the wolf version of a wedding ring?"

He shrugged. "Sure, if by *wedding ring* you mean irremovable ball and chain."

Huh. There went the romantic atmosphere, up in smoke. "Did you think about biting me, Ford?"

"I would never do that without your permission," he said stiffly. "You do not have to worry about that."

"And if I gave you permission?" I asked, curious.

"I won't bite you." He sounded so certain that the urge to interject and argue with him was strong. "It's not right, and it does not end well."

"Have you bitten someone before?"

I was suddenly, insanely jealous.

"No!" Now he sounded horrified. "That is not how a claiming works. Once you mark your mate, there is no one else for you. You are bound together. *Forever.*"

"So there's no wolf divorce court."

"No." His tone made it clear he was done discussing this, but I had questions.

"So you're not mated currently." I twisted in his arms so I could see his face.

"No."

"And you've never been mated?"

"No."

"Not to Deelie Sue?"

He hesitated. "No, but she did make it clear that she would be…amenable. There aren't all that many wolves here, and other wolves have suggested that we would make a good pair."

I choked on nothing, certain I'd heard wrong. "Like, they want you to hook up and run Moonlight Valley?"

"It was suggested that we could be Moonlight Valley's breeding pair." He tensed. "Which sounds like a sperm donor plan and awful, and I was never inclined to agree. I told them no."

"Are they pressuring you?" I set my palm against his cheek. "Should I go kick some wolf butt?"

"No. The Wolf Council thinks wolves should go only with wolves. It sure makes keeping the secret easier."

Was this when I should mention Aunt Sally's unexpected revelation that I was, apparently, part cat shifter? I hesitated. It felt like I was keeping secrets, or at least taking the easy way out. And yet, now didn't feel like the right moment to share that particular secret. Even if I was part cat (and I still didn't understand how that worked), I was not a wolf. I was not mate material in the eyes of this council of his. They were illogical. And bigoted. And I didn't like it at all.

"So both your parents were wolves?"

"No. Just one."

If his body got any tenser, he'd snap like a plant in a cold freeze.

"Which one?"

His eyes narrowed. "Does it matter?"

"Yeah, it does." I frowned at him.

"Yeah." He stared at me steadily. He definitely wasn't telling me everything.

"And your daddy?"

He closed his eyes briefly. "Darrell is a werewolf."

Huh. He'd used the present tense, but I'd thought…

I re-ran what I knew, looking for mistakes in my conclusions. Darrell had disappeared. The gossip (aka "unverifiable, unscientific, and absolutely not a proven fact") was that he'd run afoul of the biker gang he'd hung out with, and they'd done him in. Other people thought someone had come for him for something he'd done to a loved one.

Absolutely no one believed, not for one instant, that Darrell Boone was a fine, upstanding, ethical man. He'd been a lying, abusive, often violent piece of shit, and that was a fact. He'd certainly shown that side of himself often enough in public.

"So your momma…"

"Is also a werewolf." His gaze dipped to my chest, and he reached out a hand to cup my breast, his thumb rubbing gently over my nipple.

"But you said only one of your parents was a werewolf?" Perhaps the amazing sex had adversely affected my ears.

"Our daddy did not tell Momma about his being a werewolf. She found out when Maverick was a baby and shifted in her arms. It was a shock." He moved, easing me back onto the mattress and swinging over me. I was surrounded by a hot, hard cage of Ford.

"Ford." I struggled to remember what I had been asking. "Ford, how did she become a werewolf then? Did someone do something to her?"

"He bit her," Ford growled. "He marked her and then he tried to change her over by biting her some more. He went ahead and did it without asking her. She would never have agreed, and it didn't take. It mostly doesn't. His bite transformed her, but she couldn't shift back."

I stared at him, speechless. That was awful. That was wasn't just crossing a boundary. That was blowing it up with dynamite and then bringing a mountain down on top of it for good measure.

"She's out there in the woods. Sometimes we see her. The Wolf Council banished Darrell to Alaska."

"He—"

"When a wolf is too far from his marked mate, he can't shift back," Ford said. "He loses his human side and goes over to wolf. Darrell is up there, running around with the polar bears, and none of us ever want to see him again. That's why I would never bite you."

"Okay…" I didn't want to be changed into a werewolf, unable to shift back. Plus, who knew what would happen since I was half cat shifter.

Should I tell him that now? More importantly, did his momma know what had happened to her? How much human was left in her? And could we get married like humans did, get each other rings, stand up in front of the preacher?

It was early days, but I could imagine that future for us. Not to make light of what had happened to Mrs. Boone, but thinking about Ford and me together forever felt right. "We should probably talk about your ignoring my call on Thursday, though. I'm still mad about that."

"I should not have ignored you." His mouth traced the curve of my breast.

I leaned into his touch, my eyes closing. "Promise me that you won't ever do that again. I need to know that I can call and you will always, always pick up."

Ford hesitated, stopped his delicious ministrations to my breast. The silence stretched out between us, growing colder and more tense. I did not think he was plotting how best to have his wicked way with my willing body.

I opened my eyes and met his gaze. He braced himself over me, his arms braced on either side of me. His lips parted, paused. He was thinking on what to say—or how best to say it. I did not think it would be a compliment on my bedroom skills.

Finally, he said, "For as long as we're seeing each other, I'll pick up when you call. I promise."

"No." I narrowed my eyes at him. He was splitting hairs. "No, no caveats. No asterisks, no fine print, no disclaimers. I just want a promise. You promise me that you will never ignore me again. For the rest of our lives. *Forever.* If I call you up in heaven after we're dead and buried, you will answer. You will not cut yourself off from me."

Ford swung off me, and then climbed off the bed for good measure. This was not a promising direction for our conversation.

He prowled toward the fireplace, pacing back and forth. Since the cabin was cozy and he was large, he had to make multiple circuits while he worked out what was troubling him. I enjoyed my view of his fine butt and his muscled shoulders, but I could see the storm coming. We were about to shipwreck.

"Ford?"

He turned around abruptly, swiping his boxer briefs from the floor. He sat down on the edge of the bed to pull them on, careful not to brush against me.

What. The. Hell?

He reached for his jeans, then got up and retrieved a T-shirt from somewhere.

"Are you leaving me?"

Ford's stormy blue eyes met mine. "I can't promise you what you asked."

215

I had to take a moment to process what he'd said. It made no sense. We'd done things, said things, *meant* things.

At least, I had.

I scrambled off his bed, dragging his sheet with me. Naked fighting felt too vulnerable right now.

"Why not?"

"You know why not."

"I have no clue!" I clutched my sheet tighter than an embarrassed virgin confronting a Regency rake in her bedroom. It was righteous outrage or bodily assault, so I was taking the high road here. "Sometimes you talk to me and sometimes you don't.

"Apparently, you've been pining after me for years, waiting for me to come back to Moonlight Valley. You announce that you're courting me, but then you spurn my sexual intimacies! Shutting me down! We make a deal to date for twelve months and then you're *still* not all in. You're more than half out! Why am I the only one committing here?"

Ford buttoned his jeans with short, jerky movements. I glared up at him. He was too tall, too big, too massively, mountainously unreachable.

"You are going to leave, Alice. Your *all in* has a time limit. You just want a playmate until your time is up and you go."

He stabbed me ruthlessly with his words. Punch, punch, punch.

I couldn't breathe, couldn't think. "That is crap, Ford, and you know it. Have I done anything to make you question my commitment?"

"When you go, you go for good. Don't expect me to call, to text, or to be your friend. I won't do it. I can't do it."

This time his word-dagger sliced through my ribs and hit my heart. I'd given him everything, opened up in every way possible in that bed. This cabin. This night. I'd been completely, one-hundred-percent honest.

Ford gave me a look and then returned to his pacing. "Tonight was a bad idea."

I could not... What did he *mean*? "Like...a mistake?"

"Yeah." He frowned fiercely at the fire. "A mistake. A giant, colossal mistake."

If I was in, he was out. This seemed to be the unfortunate pattern in our relationship.

"I don't get it." I tried to think of a tactful, diplomatic way to ask my question and then gave up and blurted it out. "Why would you ask me to be in a twelve-month relationship with you if you didn't plan on giving us twelve months?"

"Alice…" he started, then exhaled, frowning even more fiercely. "Alice, I know all about your plans."

"My what?"

"Alessandro told me about your aunt. About your inheritance. About your plans to head straight to Nashville."

"What?"

"To leave. To get on with your life. To follow your dreams right now since you no longer need to wait on a business loan."

"I have no idea what you're talking about."

Ford swung around, swiping a hand down his beard. His eyes narrowed. "Your cousin, Alessandro. He pulled Atticus and me over on Thursday afternoon, and he told me you'd inherited a fortune, more than you needed to launch your pet emporium. He said you were planning on getting started right away."

I shook my head. "He lied to you."

Ford straightened, swinging around to face me. His sapphire eyes looked downright incredulous.

"I mean—" I hurried to clarify. This was not the moment to be inaccurate. "My…*aunt* left me a ton of silver. And cryptocurrency. There's enough money there for me to get my business up and running. In fact, if I'm careful, I have an enormous safety net. I might not have to work, ever.

"But I wasn't planning on moving to Nashville tomorrow or this week. Nor anytime soon."

His beautiful mouth tightened. "Why not?"

I stared at him. He held himself aloof, his body tight, rejecting me. I'd told him a mere handful of minutes ago—perhaps not even an hour—that I loved him. He had to have been thinking, even then, that I would up and leave, would never come back.

"Hold on." I held onto that thread. "You thought I was…and so when I showed up here, you… We made…" I stabbed an angry finger at the mussed-up bed.

"So Alessandro tells you I've got some money and you decide that everything is finished between us but there's time for one night of sex? You had no problem letting me walk out of your life? Because I meant so little to you? Did you ever want *me*, or was it just convenient sex for you?"

Ford glared at me, balling his hands into fists. His eyes were amber, but that was fine with me. I was mad at his wolf, too. I was mad at the *world*.

So I kept right on going. It felt good to clear the air between us. "Or do you not trust me? Is it because I'm not a wolf? Am I not good enough for you because I can't shift?

"Or do you not trust my ability to honor a commitment that I made voluntarily and with my eyes wide open? Are you that sure that I'll leave? *Let me have tonight, Alice. Just tonight.* That's what you said to me."

Ford stood there. Silent. Reserved. Judging me.

"Tell me right now! The only reason we had sex tonight is because you believed I was leaving town tomorrow. Soon. Now that I have the ability to leave, you don't trust me to stay. You *never* trusted me."

"I trust you," he said quickly.

I spoke over him, saying, "We are not done, Ford Boone!"

"Alice." He growled my name, almost reluctantly. "We have always known we would be done. We said twelve months and no more. Now we're just done sooner.

"We don't have a future together. You know you'll be making your plans for Nashville. We were always marking off the time together, and now I'm saying we'll call it now. We're over."

"You don't get to call time on us!" I yelled.

"I do too," he bellowed. "I'm doing it because I won't hold you back. I will not keep you here when there are things you need to do elsewhere. I am not Darrell!"

"Did you not hear me when I said that I love you? Ask me to stay." I strode up to him, putting myself into his space. I would not allow him to ignore me. He did not get to put me in this weird, Darrell-shaped box. He was no more his father than I was his mother.

"If you love someone, you set them free. You don't trap her!"

I staggered back, my butt planting on the bed. Was that... Had he said... Was I the someone he loved?

"God forbid that you take a chance, that you don't know what the outcome of a decision will be, right? You're one-hundred-percent in control. You won't even say 'I love you' outright, will you?"

Ford's gaze went from heated to ticked off in a heartbeat. I'd struck a nerve. "You win. *I LOVE YOU.* I love you. Of course I love you. Why else would I be here with you?"

"Great!" I hollered at him. "We've finally found something we both agree about, because *I LOVE YOU* TOO. I've only been saying it over and over. So why can't we be together?"

Ford inhaled sharply, pulling himself back together. "This is not a movie, Alice. As much as I love the future I see in my head when I think about us together, you see something different. I don't—I *won't*—take that future away from you."

"So you'll march off and live alone, a cranky hermit wolf?"

"I'll be fine."

I glared at him. "Fine? Fine is not happy or satisfied or a billion other good things. It's mediocre. Fine, Ford. No. You should want better for yourself."

"I'll be fine," he ground out. "I'll be even more fine knowing that you're ruling the Nashville business community."

I grabbed his arm. He did not get to push me away.

"Is this about the wolf bite? Why do you have to be so noble? Can't you trust that we'll be good together, that we can navigate all the bumps life puts in our way? I don't need a fairy tale, Ford. I need you."

"Life is not a fairy tale. I know that. Let me tell you about the *hell* of living with a selfish wolf. My daddy was a mean sonofabitch. He took what he wanted, and he didn't care what all the rest of us needed, let alone wanted.

"The way he saw it, Momma lived for him, and us kids were merely his future legacy, little mini-me mirrors that were mostly annoying. He marked her so that she could never, ever walk away from him, no matter what he did or said.

"I vowed I would never, ever be like him. I will not mark the woman I love. I will not tie her to my side, unable to go more than ten, maybe twenty miles from me without enduring pain and discomfort. I will always make sure that the people I love have options."

There was nothing I could say to that. He was a good man, and his decision was honorable. Nearsighted and wrong in a way I could not articulate, but well-intentioned and loving. He thought he would hold me back, that he would force me to give up my dreams. He was afraid he would diminish and imprison me.

Ford gently disentangled my fingers from his arm, then brought my fingers to his mouth. "You have dreams, Alice. They're good dreams. But more importantly, they're yours. Not mine. I will not stand in your way. I will not tie you down here. We're over."

Ford clenched his jaw, released my hand, and stepped away. He pulled on his socks and his boots, found his keys.

I watched him.

I did not have any more words.

I did not have a plan for this heartbreak.

I did not know how to fix it.

I could not hurt him by demanding he stay, that he let *me* stay. He refused to let me in or to trust me with the part of himself that had been so badly hurt by what his daddy had done. Because I knew he wasn't Darrell. After all, no one was Darrell but Darrell.

And Ford was Ford.

He refused to let me in, he had closed the door on our relationship, and I had to respect *his* choice.

I gave it one last shot, though. He was worth trying for, worth sacrificing my dignity for.

"I would like to renegotiate the terms of our relationship. Instead of twelve months, give me forever. Stay with me now, stay with me tomorrow. Stay with me every day. And I will do the same for you. I promise you that. Let me be enough for you; let me be your mate."

He winced and opened his mouth.

I stopped him. I opened my heart. I let him see that vulnerable, loving, Ford-shaped space I'd made inside me for him.

"Come with me, Ford."

He blinked, surprised. "What?"

"Come with me to Nashville. Come with me wherever I go tomorrow and the day after that. We'll go together."

Ford looked at me.

He did not say anything.

Instead, he walked over to the door and opened it. Paused for a moment with his hand braced against the doorframe. And then that bastard shifted, his human form cracking and reforming, thick auburn fur boiling over his skin as the wolf took the place of the man.

The wolf took one look at me and bolted out the door.

CHAPTER
TWENTY
~FORD~

"I know you better than the few hours we've been together suggest I should. I truly feel like...I know you down to your core." She laughed a little. *"Well, except for the whole werewolf thing."*

— J.R. WARD

I ran down the mountain as a wolf, my tail between my legs.

I left Alice naked in bed.

I left Alice.

And I left my heart behind. I ripped it out and tossed it on that bed because it belonged to her, and even though I hadn't bitten her, I could not bear to leave her.

Worst mistake *ever*! my wolf roared. He'd achieved the acme of pissed off while I'd been descending to the nadir of depression.

Alice's newest plan, the one in which she'd suggested I leave Moonlight Valley with her, move to Nashville (again, with her), and then proceed to conquer the world *with her* sounded like one of those supernatural romances Ranger read voraciously. He liked the happy endings for the beast men, and for the first time I understood his fixation. It was tempting.

I'd been so, so tempted to say *yes*.

Go back, my wolf ordered. **Grovel. Say yes.**

Cannot. Happy endings were for books and for other people. I had All-Purpose Animal Services, my brothers, my responsibilities, the mess with the Iron Wolves, and Momma stuck in her wolf form and running around in the woods.

Darrell's example could not have been any clearer. He had taken what he wanted without once thinking about how his desires would affect his family. We'd been a prop, a convenience, an inconvenience, and a means to his own ends. He did what he wanted, when he wanted.

I was not that man, not that wolf.

Fucking ethics.

Running away *with* Alice was a fun fantasy. Exciting, romantic, and a bucket list trip. In reality, however, it was completely impractical.

Atticus and Ranger needed me here in Moonlight Valley. All-Purpose Animal Services was a demanding mistress, and my brothers could not work double- or triple-time to compensate for my absence. Plus, my life's savings were invested in our business, and I wasn't going to live off Alice and her inheritance.

What's that human saying? The Sunday one?

Pride goeth before destruction, I supplied. Was I proud?

Hell. Yes.

I was too proud to be a useless hanger-on in my mate's life. I would pull my own weight. Contribute. Take care of her.

Love her, my wolf finished. **And bang her six ways to Sunday.**

That was a lot of Sunday happening, but my point stood.

I was too proud to take from her.

So I'd shifted and rushed out of the cabin before I'd given in to a moment of weakness and either chained her to me here in Moonlight Valley or chained her to me in Nashville.

There are possibilities there.

It was a long hike down the mountain to our place, but I'd shifted and run it, taking satisfaction in the slap of the branches against my side, the solid feel of the ground beneath my paws in a world where everything else had gone topsy-turvy. By the time I arrived at the house, I was itching for a fight. I did not know how to let go of what had happened up there at my cabin. Hitting something seemed like a plan.

Being raised by Darrell had convinced me I would not be a drinking man. And Momma would have had plenty to say if she'd found me drunk. Besides, getting shit-faced meant being out of control, and then I'd likely run back *up* the mountain and undo the good (and bad) that I'd done.

I therefore decided it was a good time to start demolishing the ancient greenhouse behind the main house. It was listing hard enough to kiss the ground, and we'd voted to take it down in our last family meeting. I'd get a head start on the chore and work off my temper.

But as I prowled around the side of the house in the predawn gloom, I stopped short. Maverick, my oldest brother, was unexpectedly poking around the porch steps, a large army-green duffel bag dropped on the ground by his feet. He'd apparently come home at the ass crack of dawn and was now doing... I didn't care what he was doing, only what he *had* done.

Get him, my wolf demanded.

For once, we were in total agreement. I shifted back to human and tore across the lawn at him, buck naked and out of fucks to give. I needed to talk to him, let him know what had happened in his absence. I also needed to share my feelings on the subject with him, preferably through some wrestling and minor punching.

He heard me coming, turned, took in my bare-assed state—his eyes lit up, an amused grin curling his mouth—and he said, "Did you lose your pants, Ford? Did you miss me?"

I socked him in the jaw.

Again. Once is *not* enough.

I hadn't hit him anywhere near as hard as I could have. Partly this was because knocking him out would have defeated the purpose of talking to him (or flat-out yelling until I felt better). Mostly, though, it was because I was already ashamed of myself for using my fists. I'd wanted to hurt him and be hurt back by him, and I'd acted on impulse.

Mav staggered, shaking his head. "What the hell is wrong with you?"

Fight, fight, fight!

I weighed being a mature, sensible adult who used his words against the relief of fighting it out physically, and I gave in to my wolf. This time, Maverick saw me coming.

We'd all learned to fight and fight well. We were wolves and boys, semi-feral and uncivilized. Maverick, having spent too much time under Darrell's and the Iron Wolves' tutelage, fought better and dirtier than all of us.

After I'd knocked him off the deck, however, we rolled around the yard, flattening the orange daylilies surrounding the porch and sending dust everywhere. Fists flew, kicks were delivered, punches landed.

My cheek felt swollen and Maverick's lip had split when we were interrupted by an angry whisper. "What are y'all doing?"

We rolled apart, reluctantly on my part. Ranger's angry face was more effective than a bucket of cold water. He stood there on the porch, arms and legs akimbo, wearing a T-shirt that announced *Cos, I said so*.

"You all are making a mess," he groused. "Fighting. Carrying on. You'll be waking everyone else up next. You're interrupting my ponderings."

Maverick grimaced, shooting me a dirty look—which I repaid with interest—and whispered a loud "So sorry" at our brother.

Ranger propped his hands on his hips and glared at us both. It was not an equal glaring, more of a sixty/forty split. I was the recipient of the bulk of Ranger's disapproval. "Not on Momma's flowers."

I pulled myself unsteadily to my feet, nodding contritely. "Sorry."

"And now you owe me biscuits and gravy, Ford Montgomery Boone," Ranger admonished. "There must be consequences. And hash browns." Then he turned and marched back inside.

I had no idea what Ranger pondered, but Atticus maintained it was world domination.

I did my own pivot and started marching toward the barn. I kept extra pants there.

Maverick followed me, working his jaw back and forth. "What the hell did I do to you?"

"YouTube," I growled, picking up my pace. "TikTok. Starred in a film. You went for our daddy where Lucky Jansen could catch you with his phone camera, and then you went one further and shifted."

Maverick's eyes widened even as he frowned. "You weren't there. So how do you—"

"Because of the *phone camera*, you fool. Lucky filmed the whole thing and now he's blackmailing us. He wants Atticus and me to join his pack as his new enforcers and beat people up on his command. Otherwise, he's torn between outing you to the Wolf Council—who will banish you to Alaska or possibly the Outer Hebrides—or to local law enforcement. And they will send you to West Tennessee State Penitentiary."

I pulled open the barn door and strode inside.

"Damn it." Maverick sounded shocked and disbelieving. That was fine. I gave him sixty seconds to process the bad news while I found and pulled on a pair of jeans. When I'd finished doing up my buttons, he'd sunk down onto a bale of hay and was holding his head in his hands.

"Did you join? Are you working for Lucky now?" He did not look up from his close examination of the floor.

"Nope. We've been stalling him."

Maverick exhaled roughly. I assumed he was remembering his time as a wolf gang member and all the reasons he'd put that life behind him. "That's good. Really good." He examined a crack in the floor, inhaled, exhaled. "And Ranger hasn't got a plan?"

"Ranger doesn't know."

This made Maverick lift his head up. "What do you mean Ranger doesn't know? You kept this a secret from him?"

"Of course I did," I said impatiently. "He won't get pulled into this mess, not if I can help it."

Maverick's head snapped up. "Are you a fool?"

I gave him a look. This was not the time for insults.

"When I realized that the Iron Wolves were bad news and joining them had been a mistake, I tried to walk away. They wouldn't let me. Said I had to buy my way out, pay a price.

"It didn't seem too bad—Lucky demanded I get blackmail material on the other gang members that he could use to squash any future dissent. He was already fighting with Piston back then because Piston was never gonna be happy being second in the pack—he was jonesing for a big promotion.

"I decided I didn't care who was in charge as long as I was out, so I asked Ranger to show me how to use drones. I figured it was a good way to get video of the gang members doing illegal things." He shrugged. "It worked. I recorded a bonanza of illegal, stupid, sometimes downright embarrassing stuff. After I gave Lucky the footage, he ordered the Iron Wolves to let me go, and I washed my hands of them. Ranger, however—"

Ranger had a librarian streak in him. He liked order and cataloging stuff. We'd got him a label maker one year for Christmas, and you'd have thought we'd given him a Porsche. It had been love at first sight.

"You think Ranger stored backup copies somewhere."

Maverick nodded. "That boy archives everything, and he's nosy. I bet he kept the footage. And if he hasn't, he's still flying those drones all over Moonlight Valley. He'll have picked up new things. All we have to do is ask him if he has something we can use to blackmail Lucky to get him off our backs."

* * *

We took turns cleaning up after our bout of fisticuffs by plunging our heads into the horse trough behind the barn.

We'd flattened a couple daylilies, but they would come back next year. I did what I could on the garden front before taking myself off to the kitchen to pay the breakfast penalty Ranger had demanded. Maverick took over biscuit duty while I whisked up the gravy and shredded potatoes for the hash browns.

Breakfast was almost ready when we heard footsteps in the hallway and Maverick went to investigate.

"You've been back twenty minutes and you've already been in a fight? What happened?"

Recognizing Knox's voice, I returned my attention to my biscuit gravy. Ranger would not put up with lumps.

Maverick came back into the kitchen without answering Knox. He pulled the biscuits out of the oven and set them on the table.

Knox followed him into the kitchen a few seconds later, his eyes examining Maverick's face. Not only had I cut his lip, but I'd left him a purple mark on his cheek that was a twin to the one on mine. "Were you attacked on the trail?"

"I had a bondage session with a daddy bear." Maverick grabbed the coffeepot and poured himself a cup.

Knox was in the process of swiping the few remaining dregs for himself when he caught sight of my face. I had a matching set of bruises, but no daddy bear action. With a shake of his head, he wandered off.

The delicious lure of freshly baked biscuits had Atticus shuffling into the kitchen. I should have made bacon. Nothing got us all together faster than bacon or a wolf run under the full moon.

"Do I smell gravy?"

I smacked his hand away from the cooling biscuits. "Yes. You also smell stupidity."

I tipped my head in Maverick's direction.

Atticus looked in the direction I'd indicated. He was smart enough to know that if he didn't look, he didn't eat. Still, when he spotted our oldest brother, he frowned, the corners of his mouth pulling down. From the look on his face, he was debating using his words versus shifting into his wolf and biting some answers out of Maverick.

When Maverick had been an Iron Wolf, beaten up had pretty much been his default state, and we'd gotten used to it as best we could. But since he'd quit the gang and turned over a new leaf, he'd been shinier and safer.

"What happened to you?" Atticus finally asked.

"Your twin happened."

Atticus nodded thoughtfully, then set about making fresh coffee. "We're helping each other out on this. Ford, do we have a plan?"

"We're waiting for Ranger to get his butt out of bed." Or wherever he'd parked it to "ponder," but I did not need those details.

Atticus spilled coffee grounds on the counter. "I thought we were not inviting Ranger to this summit."

"Mav says Ranger might have a solution."

Ranger picked this moment to reappear in the kitchen, clearly in a snit. "Nobody talk to me until I've had my biscuits and gravy. I'm mad as a wet hen at both y'all."

Ranger fixed himself a plate.

We stared.

He took a bite.

We stared some more.

Ranger set the plate down and groaned. "Okay. New plan. Y'all are scaring my appetite. Tell me what's going on."

CHAPTER
TWENTY-ONE
~FORD~

It takes a lot more than an alpha werewolf with an overblown sense of impor-
tance to scare me.

— KRISTEN PAINTER

I laid it all out for Ranger: Lucky Jansen's unexpected visit, his demand that Atticus and I work for him, the leverage he had, our half-baked plan to convince Deelie Sue to secretly film Lucky doing something he wouldn't want the world to see, and Maverick's conviction that Ranger would have something up his sleeve that would fix the whole mess.

As I talked, Ranger worked his way through six biscuits and a corresponding amount of gravy, nodding at some points and frowning at others. When I mentioned calling on Deelie Sue for help, he glowered.

"Are you done?" he asked when I lapsed into silence, eyeing my untouched biscuits.

"With the situation or my breakfast?" There was no way I could eat now. "Yes."

I passed over my untouched food and scrubbed a hand down my face. It had been a long morning, and not just because I'd run down a mountain and into a fistfight with Maverick.

Ranger methodically cut up a biscuit, swiped it through the gravy, and chewed. It was agony. After he'd swallowed, he asked, "So why not come to me as soon as Lucky started making threats?"

Atticus spoke up for both of us. "We didn't want you implicated if we had to give in to Lucky's demands."

"Your regard for my well-being is duly noted and appreciated," he said, sounding like a nineteenth-century gentleman. "But I thought you were smarter than that. Plus, Maverick's correct. I can be of assistance in this situation you find yourselves in."

"Go ahead and tell us what to do, Ranger." Maverick flashed his trademark charming smile at our brother, the effect only slightly dented by his split lip and the shiner now forming on his eye.

"There's nothing to do." Ranger drained his coffee mug and set it down.

Does he mean we have to go with the Deelie Sue plan? Atticus thought-beamed at me. I thought-answered back. *It's probably not too late for me to propose a wolf-mating of convenience with her.* Atticus winced-thought, *And barter off your virginity to the highest bidder.*

We're doomed, my wolf whined. **Totally screwed in a non-erotic, highly disappointing way. I miss Alice.**

I missed her too. A giant, Alice-sized, heart-shaped hole had opened in my life.

Ranger either intercepted our mental telepathy or spotted the despair on our faces because he leaned forward in his seat and added, "To be precise, there is nothing *to* do. It's already been done as Maverick suspected. I have footage of our daddy driving away and ditching Moonlight Valley after his fight with Maverick.

"I wanted to be sure he'd really gone, so I followed him with a drone for a few miles. Tennessee law enforcement will have no reason to step in since Darrell obviously did not suffer an untimely and felonious demise."

Ranger pulled out his phone and frowned, tapping away at the screen. Our phones all vibrated, buzzed, or made the sound of a lightsaber igniting as Ranger's text reached out.

After a moment, Maverick looked up. "While I appreciate not being at risk of being charged with a Class C Felony and spending fifteen years in Tennessee state prison for voluntary manslaughter, I'm not looking forward to a lifetime in exile in Alaska for outing the werewolves, either."

"I'm taking a class over at the local community college," Ranger responded, as if Maverick had asked him about his summer plans or something equally unrelated to Maverick's not-unfounded if newfound fear of going to prison.

"Great?" Maverick sounded almost sincere.

"It's a film-making class," Ranger continued. He tapped his phone. A swooshing sound followed a chime. "And you would not believe what I've learned about computer-generated imagery. It's amazing what you can do with a laptop and some software these days. I've allocated part of our family budget to purchasing one of these fine tools so that I can enhance Mr. Jansen's video."

"Could we skip to the end? Or sum up?" Maverick inserted. "Because I'm about to pee myself from anxiety."

"I'm going to make a second, deep-fake video of the alleged wolf fight where it looks like two humans fighting and post it alongside the first one that has a human and a wolf. We post them to TikTok—maybe to YouTube too—and then we invite everyone to look at our really cool special effects where we turned a human into a wolf.

"And if the Iron Wolves aren't convinced after that, I have plenty of drone footage of *them* doing things their mommas would not approve of. The Iron Wolves will be in no position to harass you, me, Atticus, Ford, or any wolf, Boone or otherwise. If you felt so inclined, we could blackmail them back."

Jesus H. Christ on a popsicle stick, Atticus thought at me.

Right? I sent back. Conversation with Ranger had more unexpected twists than a corn maze. I was speechless.

And in awe.

"That's brilliant," Atticus announced.

"No," Ranger correct. "*I* am brilliant. Also, you all will have to take over the house chores and the cooking while I make the deep fake. My creative process does not like to be rushed."

"Thank you, Jesus." Atticus leaned back in his chair. His face went from relieved to ecstatic to downright giddy. I knew exactly how he felt.

"Insofar as further action is required from us, the Boones, we should perhaps consider a visit to Mr. Jansen's associates. Perhaps Piston would take a meeting with us, wherein we can explain that the Boone family is off-limits and cannot be recruited to join their pack, either by fair means or foul."

"You want all of us to troop down there and confront Piston?" Maverick eyed Ranger as if he'd suggested we pay a visit to hell and take Satan some sweet tea.

Piston was Lucky's second in his pack of wolfish misfits, although no one

231

would have been surprised by a change in management. If I hadn't known Piston was a wolf, I would have bet he turned into a piranha. Or a megalodon.

"Not all of us, no." Ranger knighted me on the shoulder with his knife. "Ford here could go."

I was not a fan of this plan and said so. Adamantly.

"Plus, we already have his 'invitation' to join him for his full moon party," I pointed out.

"That makes you an excellent choice," Atticus said cheerfully. "Seeing as how he'd invited you to drop by."

I was not cheered.

Messengers get shot, my wolf declared.

He wasn't wrong.

Ranger frowned at me. "Why are you looking as if someone pissed in your Cheerios, Ford?"

"I am fine," I said. I had nothing more to contribute to this conversation, and I certainly wasn't going to complain that I'd foolishly walked out on the woman I loved because there was no way both me and my pride could stand by her side.

I would get over her. Move on. Discover new joys in living. In another decade or so.

Unfortunately, Atticus gossiped worse than a church lady. "He's upset because Ms. Sally Aymes left her niece, Alice, a fortune in silver and crypto-currency. So Alice is now a wealthy woman and doesn't need a business loan to start her pet T-shirt business in Nashville. She's good to go, and Ford here has decided he shouldn't be the one to hold her back."

I glared at my twin, mentally threatening him with bodily harm.

"Miss Aymes is headed out of town?" Ranger looked genuinely upset.

I lifted a shoulder. "I don't have a clue."

Atticus looked incredulous. "How can you not? Alessandro the Ass pulled us over, shared all the dirty details with us last week. We were both there."

"Alice Aymes…" Maverick looked like he was rummaging through his mental image gallery. "Didn't she work at that pet store two towns over one summer? You've been pining for her since we were kids."

"That's not a happy memory, Mav." I glared at him.

"Is she going or not?" Ranger pressed.

"I don't know!" I shoved my hands into my pockets. All the better to resist the urge to throttle my brothers. "She said she wasn't fixing to leave, but she has no reason to stay."

"After all you've meant to each other? She is a heartless wench!" Ranger threw up his hands.

"She is not," I snarled. "She asked me to go with her. She wants to chase her dreams, and I am being supportive. I refuse to drag her down, so I broke it off."

Because you're a fool.

Atticus and Ranger exchanged glances, then Atticus said, "Why not go with her? How is that a problem?"

Shocked, I stared first at my twin, then at my older brother. They looked back as if their questions were supremely logical. Which they weren't. The reasons why Alice and I could never be together were perfectly, horribly clear. When I looked at Maverick, he looked like he didn't get it either.

I was certainly related to fools. Growling, I turned away, planning on stomping to the exit. I needed to get out of here. Run in my wolf skin. Chop wood like a deranged serial killer. Something.

Live a long, sad, lonely life. All alone.

Did I mention alone?

Ranger blocked the exit. "Wait a second. Atticus asks a good question. You've been longing from afar for Miss Aymes for years, and it seemed as if things were going well. What went wrong? I can find a way to fix it."

No. He couldn't. "I'm part owner of All-Purpose Animal Services."

Ranger shrugged. "And?"

"And you all need me to help out. I can't do that from Nashville, and you can't keep the business running when you're down a wolf."

Another shrug. "We could work eighty-hour weeks because we're bachelors. Alternatively and more attractively, we could post on Craigslist for your replacement. Or find an intern."

I had no idea what to say to that.

See? You're replaceable, my wolf said smugly. **Knowing that, you should hurry up and have make-up sex with our Alice before she figures that out.**

"My savings are all tied up in the business. All my income comes from working here. What would I live on?"

"We could buy your share," Atticus suggested. "Or you could get work in Nashville—plenty of animal problems there."

"Or you could swallow your pride and be the best househusband-slash-boyfriend ever. Let her support you. Help out with her business." Maverick gave me a shit-eating grin.

The urge to resume our fistfight was strong.

"You don't have to stay here." Ranger's voice was soothing and pedantic and supremely irritating. He was such a know-it-all.

"I'm not Darrell," I gritted out. "I have honor. I do not abandon my responsibilities."

"To whom? Me? Atticus? Momma?" Ranger shook his head. "You have a chance at a woman like Miss Aymes, you take it. There's nothing you can do for Momma that we can't do. You stay here, you'll grow grumpier by the day."

Ranger finished his biscuit, wiped his mouth neatly on the cloth napkins he insisted we use, and then pointed at Maverick.

"You're on dish duty. Consider it reparations for messing up the front yard.

"And you," he said to me, "you call Deelie Sue and make it clear that we do not need her trying to record Lucky in a compromising position. We've got it covered, and her machinations will only make things more complicated."

Reluctantly, I nodded.

Ranger was right about the Lucky Jansen plan.

And the Alice plan? My wolf asked eagerly.

I didn't know, but Ranger had made me think. Was there a way to keep Alice in my life without demanding she give up hers?

CHAPTER
TWENTY-TWO
~ALICE~

There was something about him in that moment that made me feel like I was a part of something. Maybe it was a pack thing. Like he was always trying to bond, but at the same time keeping me under his heel. Perhaps I was a Werewolf after all...

— *CAROLINE PECKHAM AND SUSANNE VALENTI*

ord's absence left me feeling more scooped out and hollow than a Halloween pumpkin. There was no easy fix for the way I felt.

Therefore, I moped.

I dragged myself around Moonlight Valley in a sad, distracted funk. I doubted myself and my powers of attraction while my brain unhelpfully replayed the highlights of my relationship with Ford, pausing for in-depth failure analysis far too often.

My parents chalked up my depression to the death of my *mother*. I still called her Aunt Sally; that was who she'd been to me, while Momma had been my mother.

After several dejection-filled phone calls, my parents had taken to texting me links to business jobs in Nashville that I *might want to follow up on* and the names of a half dozen financial advisers from their personal network.

Then my momma would tag me in a cute Instagram post about *Busy hands, happy heart* (or a similar emotional soundbite) and ask how my pet boutique business plan was coming along and had I checked out the four possible store-fronts she'd sent me information on.

She was of the opinion that keeping busy would not only help me adjust to Aunt Sally's passing, but would catapult me ahead in life. It was a win-win in her eyes.

I appreciated her attempts to help, but I wasn't fixated on the loss of Sally. I was sorry she had died, but we had not been as emotionally close as could have been, more friendly roommates and acquaintances than family.

I did not understand why she'd maintained that emotional distance. Had she believed it was a necessary part of giving me up for adoption, that she could never, ever extend an emotional olive branch? Had she not been good at expressing her feelings? Why had she not told me about my cat shifter DNA?

In reality, the focus of my sad obsession and the cause of the apocalyptic state of my heart was of the lumberjack-bearded man-mountain ilk.

I'd worried that Ford would get back together with Deelie Sue. She was easy to get along with, as opposed to my more high-maintenance self (which the Internet assured me was a grave character flaw and one I should fix ASAP). She was beautiful, and she had deep roots here in Moonlight Valley, so he would not have to ever think about moving elsewhere, even temporarily, which he was so against doing with me apparently.

When we'd met up for a mentor-and-mentee coffee earlier this week, however, she'd assured me they were not a couple despite his recent visit to Wheels of Good Fortune specifically to see her and the numerous calls and texts he'd sent her.

She also insisted—more than once, which caused *methinks the lady doth protest* too *much* to loop through my head—that during said used car empo-rium visit, Ford had indicated no interest in resuming their friends-with-bene-fits relationship. They were not dating even if he "sure did call her a lot." She was trying to be nice, although it backfired because it made me imagine Ford dating someone other than me.

Spoiler alert: I was not in a cheerful mood.

And also: I was jealous. As I was hiding in the loft of the Little Love Den, eating ice cream and shopping online, I did not want to hear that Ford was living his best life in Moonlight Valley. Hanging out with old friends. Possibly buying an overly accessorized new truck or spending time with gorgeous female werewolves.

The thought of him and her together made me madder than a hornet. It was not rational—we had broken up—but it was honest.

Maybe Ford had wanted to live out the rest of his life here in Moonlight Valley because he had werewolf-appropriate dating options. Maybe I wasn't enough for him.

Maybe he was looking for a shifter mate, someone who could run around in furry form with him. I hadn't told him about Aunt Sally's bombshell revelation, but I was pretty sure that even if I had been able to turn into a cat on demand, that would not have been the right kind of shifter.

I would never be a wolf, and I would never be part of their world—just someone who had accidentally discovered their secret in yet another temporary summer.

* * *

Dear Ford,

According to the American Heart Association, broken hearts are actually a thing. A person can come down with takotsubo cardiomyopathy, which is a polysyllabic way of saying that that unfortunate person has a stricken heart that's pot-shaped like an octopus trap.

Having an octopus trap for a heart was not part of my life plan and it is painful. It is, apparently, that organ's response to our breakup and the resultant emotional stress. I do feel that it is also highly symbolic. In this instance, I was the trap and you were the octopus, except you got away and left me all alone in your cabin wearing a sheet. I kept trying to hold onto you and convince you to stay, and you kept withholding yourself and fleeing in consternation.

I did not intend to trap you. Or turn you into delicious sushi or an aquarium pet. I just wanted to be with you.

I meant it when I told you that I had no immediate plans to leave Moonlight Valley, and I certainly was not going to rush out of here like a cartoon character with its hair on fire. I have my obligations at Vanity Fur Salon to finish, Aunt Sally's things to sort, and sundry other promises that I made and will keep. I may have a business plan and life goals, but that doesn't mean I can't stop to appreciate today. That doesn't mean I won't honor my obligations. Integrity is important.

Deelie Sue and I met up as we're both businesswomen, albeit she's far more experienced than me and therefore has many words of wisdom with which to bless me. After we'd finished the professional portion of our conversation, she mentioned that you've been calling and texting her nonstop for the last couple of weeks. This was hurtful to me, although I recognize that since you broke us up, you are, in fact, free to see someone else. Or several someone elses. If you have decided to see someone else, I will attempt to wish you the best.

I want to try explaining what I tried to say that night at your cabin because I don't think it came out right at all and I keep imagining what I should have said. So please consider this letter my do-over, and also feel free to ignore it and/or walk away from it as you did me that night. This is something I need to say for myself.

So here goes:

I do love you and want us to share a future, so I asked you to come with me to Nashville when I'm ready to launch my small business there. It was a big ask. It is not an easy thing to upend your life for someone else and walk away from your job, your people, your home. But I thought that perhaps we were each other's happy place and that would be corny but enough.

I cannot help but notice that at no point did you ask me to stay—or attempt to find a compromise that would work for both of us. I believe it is okay to compromise. World history bears me out on this point. It is also okay and not at all dishonorable, controlling, or otherwise wrong to ask me to stay. I would love it if you did.

Love,

Alice

This was not my first draft; my first draft had, in fact, been a list of bullet points. It turned out that I had far more to say than could be summed up in a concise list of items. The more I wrote, the more I remembered about that night he'd left the cabin.

It made me sad—and very, very mad.

The bullet points for the mad portion of events went something like this:

- Left alone
- In the dark
- Naked but for a sheet
- After sex
- DICK

That last was an executive summary of my thoughts on the matter. Remembering about how Ford had sauntered away from me, red-bearded, overly large, and definitely overly confident, made me see red (and not in the delicious, bearded way, either).

My anger remained, although I recognized that putting my more irate feelings into a love letter would be counterproductive. I wanted him to come back —whereupon I would alternate between yelling at and loving on him—not decide that his mistake had been in not walking away from me sooner.

DICK was not an affectionate and loving nickname.

It was a scientifically accurate description.

As my ten-minute break was up, I tucked my phone away and marched proudly out of Vanity Fur Salon's employee breakroom. I would be a model employee if it killed me.

Sanye gave me a sympathetic look as I returned to the pet-washing station next to hers. Some of her sympathy was engendered by my next client—a French bulldog that had been skunked—but most of it was due to the Ford situation.

"Are you doing okay?" she asked. "You've seemed really down since you got back from Texas. I'm so sorry about your Aunt Sally. I'm not sure if I said that before, but now that you've been all over kingdom come to settle her estate, I feel like I should say it now. You spent summers with her, so the two of you must have been close."

I warmed up the water while I considered how to answer her. "We weren't," I said finally. "Close, that is. I guess you could say we were more like roommates those summers. Or more accurately, I was her lodger and she was always considering kicking me out."

Sanye's forehead wrinkled in confusion. "But you were family."

I forbore from pointing out that Sanye's family was hardly the stuff of reading hour at the local library. Her dad, Mr. Jansen, was horrible and undoubtedly a major contributor to her family's extreme dysfunctionality.

"She'd leave me notes. Put a key under the mat for me. We didn't talk. I figured she was either not comfortable interacting with people or she'd decided we didn't have much in common and so she wasn't going to make the effort."

I busied myself with the dog, shaking off my hurt. I'd accepted Aunt Sally's peculiarities years ago, but learning that she was actually my birth mother made the sting feel fresh. It also made me notice all the ways in which she'd deliberately kept me at arm's length.

Of course, she'd also been a part-time cat, and cats by definition kept the world at arm's length.

I was so confused.

I wasn't ready to tell Sanye about the details of my inheritance, financial or shifter. I was equally unready to talk about Aunt Sally turning out to be my birth mother.

My feelings were more mixed up than one of those tins of Christmas popcorn with the thin cardboard inserts that kept nothing in its proper place, so the cheese popcorn bled into the caramel corn and butter popcorn and you had no idea what you'd end up with.

"Is that why you look so sad? Do *not* feel guilty about inheriting her stuff," Sanye ordered.

I shook my head obediently. Because I didn't think I felt guilty about it. Stuff was just stuff, and while Aunt Sally had turned out to own valuable and life-changing stuff, I was conflicted.

I'd tried to stay open to the possibility of finding love, but what I'd really found was an emotional disaster that would takes year—if not forever—to recover from. I'd been abandoned naked in the middle of the wilderness.

Sanye's eyes narrowed. Ostensibly, she came over to help me lather up the French bulldog, but really, she was about to pry.

"You're hiding something."

I shook my head and concentrated on building up a mountain of lather on my client's fur. The soap and water got all mixed up with the tears pouring from my eyes. And damn it, I was a sobbing, snotty mess and a bad, bad employee.

The French bulldog barked and disappeared along with Sanye. I stood there, trying to pull myself together but only crying harder. Footsteps announced Sanye's return, and then she pulled me into a bear hug. I cried more and harder, hanging onto her.

"What happened? Are you okay?"

My response was more tears and some snot. I did not have any words left to explain how I was feeling. Eventually, I pulled myself together enough to show her the letter I'd drafted on my phone.

She flipped the Open sign to Closed, read the letter while I paced and tried to pull myself together, and then frowned angrily on my behalf. "Ford Boone is a first-class dick."

She would get no argument from me.

"He abandoned you in *bed*?"

I got my crying under control enough to bring her up to speed on the details of that unfortunate night: my sad phone calls and texts from Texas, his radio silence after my first love confession, and my ill-advised midnight pursuit of him at his hunting cabin.

Our lovemaking, my second heartfelt confession of feelings for him and even more ill-advised use of the l-word, and his subsequent abandonment of me under the guise of honorably respecting and protecting my choices about my future also poured out. By the time I'd finished, Sanye looked horrified.

I shrugged, because pretending like this was no big deal and something I could recover from seemed like my only option. "It's good. I'm good."

Sanye frowned ferociously. "That is total bullcrap!"

I nodded.

"Do we...want him back? Or are we plotting murder?" Sanye's eyes glowed with fierce intensity. "FYI, I'm down with either."

"I don't know!" I sobbed.

Sanye squeezed me. "You stay at my place tonight. We'll buy all the ice cream we can carry and then we'll trash-talk Ford and make you a plan. For right now, it can be a Choose Your Own Adventure-type plan with a Ford option and a hurt-on-sight option."

Sanye was officially the world's best friend. I laid my head on her shoulder. "Yes, please."

Sanye's frowned deepened. "Bless his heart. He's something else. Come on. Let's quit early and raid the Piggly Wiggly for ice cream."

* * *

By the time we pulled out of the Piggly Wiggly parking lot, the back seat of the car was colder than an empty igloo in Siberia thanks to the four bags of ice cream sitting there. We'd loaded up on all the chocolate flavors, plus a peach, a mint chip, and a bourbon pecan.

When my phone buzzed in my hand, I answered it automatically. I had only one bar of service, and being in a moving vehicle was not doing my reception any favors.

"Hello?"

"Alice? Are you there? It's Deelie Sue. Can you...help. Come out...big problem..."

"Wait. Say that again? You're cutting out on me."

We rounded a bend, the road rose some, the trees thinned out, and I heard Deelie Sue say, "...Jansen place and please get a move on. I'm in big trouble and..."

"Are you at Mr. Jansen's house? Do you need a ride?"

Sanye frowned, her gaze bouncing between my face and the road.

"Please. I'll—"

The call dropped. I tried calling back, but it went straight to voice mail.

"I think we need to go get Deelie Sue," I said, trying to sound calm and in control. "She's at your dad's place."

"At my *dad's*? She wants you to go there? Like you're a Lyft or an Uber?"

"Actually, more like the cavalry or a rescue party. She sounded like she needed help."

I sat there, hoping a plan would come to me. Fall out of the sky and land at my feet. *Something.* Since this was definitely a case of *do the next thing*, I pulled up Alessandro's contact on my phone.

"I'm going to call Alessandro," I told Sanye. "And ask him to meet us at your dad's place."

"You really want to go out to my dad's? It's full moon tonight, and there's always a big party. It'll be full of Iron Wolves." An unmistakable note of panic rang in Sanye's voice and I felt like I was missing something. Perhaps it was that she and her dad were estranged and she hadn't stepped foot in his house since her marriage to Evan?

"Take me back to Vanity Fur Salon so I can get my car. I'll go out there on my own."

"Absolutely not." Sanye pressed her lips together. "We'll go together."

Alessandro didn't pick up, and my call went straight to voice mail. Shoot. I left him a message and then texted it too for good measure.

"You don't have to come," I tried again.

"Oh, I do," she said grimly. "I really, really do. You have no idea."

CHAPTER

TWENTY-THREE

~ALICE~

"Damn, that werewolf melts my butter... He's so miserable," she added delightedly.

— KRESLEY COLE

S anye looked increasingly tense as she turned her truck up the mountain. I tried Alessandro again. I wanted someone to know where we were headed. I was not going to be that person in a horror movie who didn't tell someone where she was going and so no one knew where to look when she didn't come back.

"Should we call 9-1-1? Or get more people to go with us?"

Lucky Jansen, Sanye's daddy, was a bully, and I had my doubts about his business ethics, but I'd never heard that he dismembered bodies or buried nosy people in his backyard. On the other hand, Deelie Sue had sounded downright scared.

Sanye tightened her grip on the steering wheel until she was all but strangling it. "I don't think that would be a good idea. Maybe it's a miscommunication or she's got a flat tire or something."

I wasn't sure what to make of that, but I was glad I wasn't doing this alone. I was even more glad when we drove up to the Jansen house.

It was clouding over fast, the sky turning the dark purple that promised a thunderstorm. When we got out of the truck, thick, humid heat hit us. We were in for one heck of a storm.

A bunch of sports cars and trucks had been parked in the circular drive in front of the house, and a ton of motorcycles ranged across the grass. Mr. Jansen was indeed hosting that full moon get-together Sanye had mentioned.

She backed in, parking pointed out, and left the keys in the ignition. She was clearly planning for a quick getaway, and I wasn't sure whether her foresight impressed or scared me.

We walked toward the front door together, holding hands. That connection felt good, as did having someone by my side. I'd never come up here, although everyone knew where the Jansens lived, halfway up the mountain in a custom-built house.

From the looks of the bikes and trucks, what I'd heard about Jansen was true: he ran with a rough crowd. I'd also heard that wise people avoided the Jansen place at all costs. It was not the kind of place you popped over to with a loaf of banana bread or to sell your Girl Scout cookies.

My plan had been to knock on the door and then, if Deelie Sue wasn't the one who answered, ask for her. After that, my plan had involved driving back down the mountain as fast as possible.

Sanye surprised me by detouring before we reached the front door. She tugged me along the side of the house and out back. From the racket coming from behind the house, Jansen was hosting a barbecue or something. There was music—of the bone-jarringly, teeth-rattlingly loud ilk—and woodsmoke.

Sanye hesitated when we got to the back of the house. I spotted two lumberjack-sized men pacing back and forth. They were enormous. Like, the kind of tall where they could have painted a ceiling without a ladder or grabbed that last carton of milk from the back of the top shelf of the dairy case at the Piggly Wiggly.

The men were apparently deep in discussion about something and also apparently not in a good mood. The air was full of a lot of curses and threats of violence. Sanye stiffened and came to an abrupt halt.

"This will do," she said, even though we were still outside and nowhere near the party Jansen was hosting in his backyard. Also, Deelie Sue was nowhere in sight.

I pulled out my phone to try calling Deelie Sue, but Sanye shook her head.

"Reception's all but nonexistent up here." She sucked in a breath and called out to the two lumberjacks. "Brute. Big Bass. You all got a moment?"

The two lumberjacks—who I had serious doubts had been christened Brute and Big Bass by their mommas or in any church hereabouts—swung their massive heads our way. This was when I got my second surprise of the night. Amber rolled over their eyes.

"Are you here to visit with your daddy?" the stockier of the two asked. His hair was shaved close to the scalp, and he was dressed all in leather: black leather pants, black leather jacket, black motorcycle boots, and a black T-shirt with IRON WOLVES and a white wolf skull on the front.

The wolf skull had fangs.

Holy crap. Were Lucky Jansen's biker buddies *wolves*?

"You can stop right there." Sanye pointed to a spot a good twelve feet away from us. It was closer than I would have liked. "I'm not visiting. This is Alice Aymes. Her cousin is Alessandro Aymes, the animal control officer, and her friend, Deelie Sue, called us earlier tonight to come and get her. She needs a ride, so here we are."

The two wolfmen exchanged a look, then the same one who'd inquired about our purpose up here on the mountain took a step forward and held out his hand to me. "I'm Big Bass. This here is Brute."

I stepped forward on autopilot to shake his hand, but Sanye yanked me back. "We're not here to make friends."

"You should have a beer. Come on out back by the bonfire. I'm sure your daddy'll—"

"What's the problem?"

Whatever invitation Big Bass had been about to make was cut off by a third man who appeared around the side of the house. He was slightly shorter than Big Bass and Brute and maybe a decade older, but they immediately tipped their heads, hunching their shoulders in on themselves.

His hard, mean gaze snagged on my face, and he looked briefly surprised. I was almost certain he recognized me, which did not make me particularly happy.

"Sanye has come back, and she's brought a new acquaintance." Big Bass jerked a thumb in my direction.

"I'm here to pick up Deelie Sue, Snake." I couldn't see Sanye's eyes, but suddenly I wanted to. She sounded tense and angry, and I could have sworn I heard her growl at the new arrival.

If Brute was a wolf, and Big Bass was a wolf, was she one as well? Was I the *only* fully human person up here tonight?

Wait. I wasn't one-hundred-percent human either.

And what kind of a name was Snake?

"What are you doing here?" The man I really hoped did not turn into a massive reptile stared at me. Disapproval and anger shaded his voice.

"I came for Deelie Sue, Mr. Snake. I let my cousin and a few other people in town know that we were coming up here to pick her up."

Snake considered that. Shrugged. He nodded to Big Bass. "Go get Deelie Sue and bring her here."

Big Bass turned on his booted heel and took off at a rapid clip. His biker buddy, Brute, followed silently.

This left Sanye, Snake, and me standing around in the gathering dark. The moon was up already, full and bright in the evening sky. I spared a moment to hope that what Ford had told me was true and that the Moonlight Valley were-wolves did nothing more scary than get a bad case of the hives during the full moon when they didn't shift.

Sanye and Snake glared at each other, silently communicating their dislike of each other. Sanye had not brought up her family much, although once or twice she'd briefly mentioned her childhood had not been a good one. She did not spend time with either of her parents, and I'd gathered their distance was both her choice and a boundary she'd drawn because she did not condone their behavior.

To my surprise Snake decided to strike up a conversation with me. "I was sorry to hear your...uh, your aunt had passed."

I nodded. "She did."

He studied me hard enough to pick me out of a police lineup. "I knew her when we were in high school."

"My Aunt Sally?" Given that she had been a people-hating hermit and Snake was a werewolf biker, that was a surprising bit of news.

"Yeah." He tipped his head at me. "Sure did."

"Huh." That was one heck of a coincidence. "It's a small world."

"Not as small as you thought," he muttered, but I heard him.

He knew something. A cold shiver went down my back. "Were you good friends?"

"Hard to say." He seemed to think on it. "She was funny and smart. Told a great story and could talk your ear off. Real gorgeous lady. She was a cat person, if you know what I mean, though, and that made our friendship a challenge."

His gaze held mine. Crap. He definitely knew about the shifter in my family tree. Was that good? Bad? Did the Iron Wolves have an anti-cat policy?

Sanye nudged me gently in the side. "She was like you then."

I opened my mouth to deny it, but—

Maybe?

I wasn't sure I wanted to have anything in common with Aunt Sally. She'd had a whole bunch of traits that weren't something to boast about: her disliking people, for one, and her insistence on keeping her family in the dark, for another. She'd hugged her secrets tighter than a miser hoarding gold and then she'd gone and died, leaving me with questions but no answers.

"She changed," I said. There was a flash of lightning followed a few seconds later by the rumble of thunder. Instinctively, I counted. *One one-thousand, two one-thousand, three one-thousand. Four...* "She was not a talker. She kept to herself."

Snake looked like he was about to say something, but Big Bass and Brute reappeared. They had four other guys with them, all big, shaggy-haired, and muscled. I was willing to bet my new inheritance they were wolves. Sanye stiffened by my side but held her ground.

Unfortunately, I was right. There was another flash of lightning, but the sounds that followed were raw and familiar, wet and loud. Where there had been two men a moment before there were now two large, rangy wolves glaring at me with hungry eyes.

"What the hell?" Snake turned to glare at the newcomers, putting his body between us and them. "What are you all doing?"

The men and the wolves kept moving toward us, and I didn't know which was worse—the ugly determination on the human faces or the animalistic hunger on the wolves'.

"We've got to go." Sanye took a step backward, her fingers curling around my wrist and pulling. "Run!"

It was too late. Sanye and I whirled, aiming for the driveway and our truck, but we were no match for either the bikers or the wolves.

I got three steps before someone lifted me off my feet, hard arms banding around my middle and tossing me over his shoulder.

I heard Sanye curse, realized she was shifting. Her wolf, pale and beautiful, darted off into the shadows pursued by one of the other wolves.

Snake strode forward, raging. "What the fuck is this? You do not shift in front of humans. Put her down right now!"

"Sorry, Snake," Big Bass said as I bucked against his hold; I made zero headway. "Piston wants to see the girl."

CHAPTER
TWENTY-FOUR
~FORD~

Hmph. A big, bad werewolf just blew me a kiss. That was the sexiest and cutest thing I'd ever seen.

— JULIETTE CROSS

Call our girl.
  I ignored my wolf.
  Chase her. Go right on over there and make our case.
There's no case. And no.
We could be making sweet, sweet love.

I shook my head. Even if I'd wanted to take bad advice from my lovesick wolf (**am not!**), I had a not-so-hot date with Lucky Jansen and his werewolf gang. My brothers and I were a bearded surprise party on our way up the mountain to his place.

I had parked in front of the gas station because Ranger had declared an immediate and pressing need for duct tape. Maverick had gone into the store with him to ensure there was no dillydallying. I was tonight's designated driver and in charge of our hypothetical quick getaway.

Bet you'd break a few traffic laws if we were on our way to Alice's.

"You should do it," Atticus said. He was slouched in the front passenger seat, tapping his fingers on the armrest. "Call your girl. Don't be such a fool."

251

"You flatterer, you." Not for the first time, I cursed our evil twin connection. Of course he knew I was thinking about Alice.

To be fair, I hardly thought about anything else.

"Not yet," I told man and wolf. "The time is not right."

Definitely a fool.

"What are you waiting for?"

"A plan, blockhead. I'm working on a plan. I can't go to a woman like Alice Aymes without having thought it through."

Atticus snorted. "It's not rocket science. You call her—don't text—and tell her you were wrong. Then you grovel and ask if you can see her. When she says yes, you have make-up sex. Then your dumb ass can get on with living happily ever after and stop being such a grouch."

"Have you met Alice?" Atticus, not being gullible, ignored this purely rhetorical question. "She's not going to make this easy. I dumped her. I made her feel bad."

At least, that was what she'd said, and I was clinging to it. Because if she *didn't* feel bad, then there was no hope for me even if hoping for Alice's emotional misery felt six kinds of wrong.

Atticus shrugged. "Call. Grovel. Make-up sex. Trust me. It works."

"I need to sort this situation with the Iron Wolves first. I do not want her drawn into it, and they've been a distraction."

Atticus rolled his eyes. "How about you stop waiting for the stars to align and everything to be one-hundred-percent perfect before you act?"

"I am not half-assing this." *Like you.* My brother was not one to give one hundred percent to his relationships. Or even ten percent. Surprisingly, he kept getting dates.

Because he looks exactly like us, my wolf said smugly.

Good point.

My phone buzzed with a text from Deelie Sue.

Nice of her to finally get back to us.

I'd let her know yesterday that I no longer needed her.

She hadn't bothered to respond to that text, which had not particularly surprised me, seeing as how she ignored most of my previous messages. Deelie Sue preferred to do her talking face to face, all the better to charm you.

. . .

Deelie Sue: Deelie Sue is unavailable for consultation. Call your Uncle Piston. He's got your toys.

This was both vaguer and much more clear than I would have liked. I decided to assume the sender was Piston, although I would not have pegged him for a user of allusion.

I showed Atticus my phone screen, and he cursed.

"She did something and got caught," he said, stating the obvious.

Fortunately Maverick and Ranger finally came out of the gas station and beelined for my truck.

"You would not believe how many kinds of duct tape there are. And Ranger stocked up on paper clips." Maverick threw himself into the back seat behind me.

"These are life-altering decisions." In my rearview mirror I saw Ranger slide into the truck, his reusable Baggu bag clutched to chest. "Ask MacGyver."

Atticus threw my phone into the back seat with our brothers. "Heads up. There's a monkey wrench in our plans."

"Or a Deelie Sue," I muttered.

Ranger frowned at my phone. "The allusion to Deelie Sue is insulting. He is objectifying her unnecessarily and reducing her to something you could possess."

"What would be a necessary objectification?" Atticus asked.

Maverick leaned over the seat and smacked him on the back of his head. "Do not feed the beast."

"I also object to being objectified," Ranger protested.

My oldest brother threw up his hands. "You *are* an animal! You shift into a wolf!"

Ordinarily I would have waded into their argument, but I was a) driving and b) impatient to get this whole situation with the Iron Wolves sorted. And also c) impatient to go after Alice and employ The Grovel, which could not happen until the first two points were resolved.

In deference to my anxiety, I drove as fast as I could up the mountain to Lucky Jansen's place. Between the thunderstorm rolling in and the full moon, I was itchy and restless.

I kept that anxiety under control until the unhappy moment I spotted Alice

Aymes and Sanye Jansen-Webster being forcibly carted behind Lucky's house. Snake raged alongside them, shouting and issuing threats that were ignored.

I inferred the ladies' unwillingness from their positions: Alice was decorating the shoulder of an enormous werewolf and doing her best to pummel the daylights out of him while Sanye must have shifted because she was similarly decorating the shoulder of Alice's werewolf's companion, mostly but not entirely wrapped up in someone's <u>flannel</u> shirt.

"What the hell?" Maverick's voice was tight. It was clear as day that the redhead almost but not quite wearing a borrowed shirt was Evan Webster's widow. I'd long suspected that Evan's death all those years ago had been the catalyst for Maverick's sudden and inexplicable resolve to clean up his act and get out of Jansen's gang of wolves.

"Park this thing, now!" Maverick already had the door open, which was not safe as I was moving.

"Do not distract the man while he is parking," Ranger reprimanded. "We are here to retrieve the lady performing an inside job for us and to make a few points clear to the Iron Wolves, not to scratch up their paint jobs with our bad parking."

"We're *retrieving* three ladies," I growled, aiming to get us as close to the house as I could.

Go, my wolf barked. **Go go *go!***

I came in hot, killed the engine, and sprinted out of the truck. My brothers would have to fend for themselves. I ran around the big house at a speed that would have impressed my high school track coach, scanning the crowd of shifters standing out back around an enormous bonfire and paying no never mind to the combative glares directed my way.

I could hear Piston, but he was nowhere to be seen, so I locked onto the sound of his angry voice and charged through the crowd. Or tried. My passage was stopped by a wall of wolves, some in human form, some in furry form.

Let's kick their asses.

Simple. Direct. Deeply satisfying. My wolf's plan worked for me.

"Move it!" I bellowed, fisting my hands and easing into an active stance. Someone was yelling *hold on a moment* behind me, but fuck that noise. I needed to get to Alice.

"We're here to see Piston. He said he's got something I want, and I know for a fact he'll want what I have. Either tell him to get out here or take us to him."

Jansen's cookout-slash-wolf fest fell strangely silent. Someone had killed the music, although the bonfire made a heck of a noise. Every face was turned toward us, watching. Waiting for their signal.

A biker wolf I thought I recognized—Buffalo? Crow?—made his way toward us. "Let's settle down, son. Mr. Jansen invited *you* and your twin. These other Boones are party-crashers."

I did not drop my fists. "Think of it as a free gift with purchase. We're one of those package deals."

We should fight.

Biker wolf thought it over, then shrugged. "Come on, then."

The crowd of wolves and men parted like the Red Sea before Moses. Hostile eyeballs bored into us. Behind me I heard Ranger say, "Good evening."

When we got to the far side of the yard, where the outbuildings began, our conductor stopped. "Hands on the wall, feet apart."

Fists clenching, I did as I was told. My three brothers followed suit, all four of us boring holes into the wall with our angry glaring. It did not sit well, taking orders and letting Jansen's wolves call the shots.

We'd come unarmed (at least in terms of firearms), so it should have been straightforward, but then about forty seconds after I'd been roughly patted down, I heard Ranger say, "Those would be my paper clips, ma'am."

I shoved away from the wall, looking to regain my dignity and self-control. Ranger was engaged in a spirited conversation with the lady Iron Wolf patting him down.

"Why do you need a thousand paper clips?" she asked.

"You should never run out of office supplies," Ranger responded. "Plus, you might need to fasten two pieces of paper together."

The Iron Wolf frowned. "You expecting to do some office work here?"

"No, ma'am."

"Then why bring them?"

Ranger shrugged. "You can fix anything with a paper clip. Pick a lock. Jerry rig a pulley. Miniature catapult."

Her eyes narrowed. "That definitely does not sound like office work. You planning on doing any of those things?"

Ranger actually thought about it. "If the opportunity arises."

She took the box of paper clips away from him.

After we'd been frisked and de-paper-clipped, we were led inside what must have once been a barn but was now an expensive man cave full of leather recliners and a massive wet bar. The woodwork had been painted black, the doors were black, and the floors were black. Jansen must have told his interior decorator to imitate a black hole.

I eyed the room, needing to do something, anything, to keep the fear at bay. Fear and I were not close acquaintances. We were not friendly or even on speaking or head-tip terms. But panic threatened to send me rampaging through the room.

Let's rip some throats out!

Reluctantly, I reminded myself that unfocused rage would not be helpful in this situation.

Agree to disagree.

A big barn door slid open, and Alice and Sanye stumbled in. They both looked angry, but I spotted no visible injuries or tears as Lucky's wolves pushed them down onto a sofa.

Something tight in my chest eased up. My girl was okay. I hadn't failed her. Not yet. I shifted my gaze to the man behind them, a shifter I recognized as Piston Jennings, the second-in-command of the Iron Wolves pack. He was followed by Lucky Jansen.

Lucky flashed us his trademark reptilian smile. If I didn't have Alice by my side in seconds, he'd need to invest in veneers because I was going to knock his teeth out.

Ignoring my obvious anger, he said, "In case you were fixing to decline my invitation to join my pack, I thought Alice might help me convince you."

Alice's eyes met mine. She didn't look surprised to see me, although she did look hopeful. And scared. And concerned. I shared some of that concern. We were outnumbered more than I was comfortable with.

Lucky finally tore his gaze away from his daughter's face and redirected his attention to me. His eyes sheeted amber, his wolf real close to the surface.

I'd seen him shift, although not to fight, and there was a reason he led the Iron Wolves. In his wolf form, he was ruthless and fought dirty. I was more concerned about Piston, his second-in-command, however.

Piston had a reputation. He was a big, scary motherfucker and rumor had it he was nigh unstoppable in a fight. He always went for his opponent's throat, although he also liked inflicting damage first. His amber eyes met mine. "Boys. Are the two of you in or out?"

"Out." I didn't hesitate. Piston was scary as hell, but dragging this out would only rile him up further.

"You sure?"

"We're not joining the Iron Wolves. We won't be your enforcers or do your dirty work. Is that clear enough?"

"Crystal," Piston said dryly.

Snake scrubbed his hand over his face. He obviously thought that I was a fool.

"Then your brother is either headed to state prison for voluntary manslaughter or, if the Wolf Council gets him first, to Alaska to spend the rest of his life freezing his balls off with the polar bears.

"As for the rest of you all, my wolves are gonna beat the ever-loving shit out of you."

"Not happening," I said. "Not on my watch. Not with what I've got to tell you."

"Do tell," Piston drawled.

"First of all, we have proof that Darrell Boone was alive after that alleged confrontation between him and Maverick."

Lucky's eyes narrowed, and he bared his teeth. "Oh, really?"

"Yes, sir. We have drone footage of him hauling ass out of Moonlight Valley in his truck, alive and well. Ranger is texting you a link now." The odds were high that the Iron Wolves were recording us, so I did not want to say anything incriminating.

Behind me, Ranger fussed with his phone, texting Lucky a link to the video we'd uploaded to YouTube prior to arriving. We'd figured that the more public the video, the safer it would be for all of us as Lucky would not be able to kill the messenger.

"But you see, in my video, your brother shifts into a wolf. The person recording did *not* expect that," Lucky added, almost thoughtfully. "He about peed himself, discovering that werewolves exist.

"Once *I* upload *that* to YouTube, the Wolf Council will be extending Maverick here his own invitation to join your old man. They do not look kindly on wolves who expose their little secret."

We all paused while we considered that. Lucky must have been certain that he could anonymously upload his video because he flashed his gleaming teeth at us. Those teeth were looking pointier and sharper as the night wore on.

"Cat got your tongue?" Piston's smile grew.

To my great relief, Ranger stepped forward and took over. "There are no feline obstacles at this time, no. The Wolf Council will not be taking an interest in your video, should you choose to upload it. As a matter of fact, it has *already* been uploaded."

"You posted it online?"

"With some modifications." Ranger ducked his head, looking modest. "In addition to being a drone aficionado, I am also taking a computer-generated imagery class at the local community college. The video I posted online looks at that fight between Maverick and our old man both before and after CGI was applied to make Mav here look like a werewolf. It was extremely well done and already has two thousand likes. People are very impressed with my fake werewolf."

"You did what?" Piston took a step forward, his eyes sheeting amber.

"I explained how footage of an unfortunate but perfectly unsupernatural fight between an estranged father and son could be altered to make it look like one of them was a werewolf. I'm thinking about starting my own YouTube channel," Ranger said thoughtfully.

"Or a TikTok. A wolftok. Which reminds me. As you all know, I like to fly my drones and capture aerial shots of our beautiful town and state for the Tennessee Department of Tourist Development. Just one of the ways I give back to my community and my fellow citizens of Tennessee.

"Sometimes, people make a guest appearance in my footage. And sometimes, those people are doing unfortunate and highly illegal things. Take, for example, what the Iron Wolves were doing on the fourteenth of May last year. You should consider this before making an ill-informed decision to take us out."

"Excuse me?" Snake asked. He'd positioned himself at Lucky's right shoulder.

"Take us out," Ranger repeated, sounding as if he was delivering a TED talk rather than explaining an ultimatum. "If you take us out, then all of my drone footage will be uploaded to the internet. In addition to the May fourteenth footage, I have excellent coverage of the Iron Wolves'…activities."

Piston looked murderous. "Is that a threat, boy?"

Ranger looked thoughtful. "It's more in the nature of—"

Danger, my wolf yelped.

On it. Ranger could be annoyingly, dangerously pedantic, although he preferred to call it linguistic purity or some such. He'd nitpick every word Piston said until everyone in Lucky Jansen's man cave wanted to kill him.

"We're not here to make threats," I said firmly because Piston clearly favored plain speaking. "If you insist on us RSVPing in the affirmative to your invitation to work for the Iron Wolves as your enforcers, we'll upload all the video that we have.

"I'd like to think, however, that the world's big enough for you all to go your way and never come near my family and Miss Aymes and Mrs. Jansen-Webster again. If we don't meet up again, there's no reason for us to be over-sharing anything we might know."

Although I would be taking a look at the footage and discussing with my brothers how we could best use it to rescue the Iron Wolves' victims.

Piston's eyes went amber, his fists curling into claws. He was pissed, and I braced myself for whatever came next. All that mattered was getting Alice and my brothers out of here. Sanye, too, as she was important to Alice and an inno-cent bystander in this. It was not her fault that her daddy was an asshole.

"You don't think you all can walk on out of here without paying me some respect, do you?"

I kept my head up and met his gaze square-on. I did not let him see my relief that we would be walking out of here. Not dead, not grievously injured. On our own two—or four—feet.

"My boys deserve some entertainment," Piston continued. I couldn't help but notice he did not bother looking to Lucky for backup. Changes were coming soon to the Iron Wolves pack. "You want me to turn over your ladies to you, you owe me a fight."

I'd heard stories about the pit fights, that the new recruits had to fight whomever Piston decided needed to be taught a lesson or taken down a peg. Or sometimes it was the other way round and Piston used the fights to clean up the pack. It was bloody, it was brutal, and even the winner walked away with scars.

I was good with my fists and my teeth, but I sure hoped Alice liked that *Beauty and the Beast* movie because I was not going to come out of this without some souvenirs.

Ranger stiffened up next to me, clearly about to resume his negotiations, but I raised a hand to stay his objections and nodded. "I understand you need to save face. Fair enough. I'll do it."

Alice made an outraged sound, but I ignored it, fighting the urge to look at her. I did not want the Iron Wolves figuring out exactly how much she meant to me and holding her hostage.

Keep her safe, no matter what.

Always, I promised my wolf. *We're hers.*

Like knights and shit. My wolf sounded satisfied.

"We did *not* negotiate for that," Ranger objected through clenched teeth. "This is not a fair arrangement."

"No," Sanye growled, leaping to her feet. Since she and Alice were holding hands, Alice came with her.

"Not your decision," Lucky told her. "And you're staying here with me regardless. This is your pack, and it's time you took your place in it."

Let's fight him first!

Sanye looked at Alice. "You know how to do this. You just have to believe you can, all right?"

"No one's doing anything," Piston growled. "We're gonna head down to the pits, your boy's gonna fight, and then if he wins, you all can head out."

"That was *not* what we agreed upon," Ranger snapped. "This is highly irregular."

"Channel Thelma and Louise," Sanye told Alice. She raised their clasped hands. "You've got this."

Piston turned toward them, snarling. I started forward too, but Sanye shifted. One minute she was standing there in her human skin, and the next, she was changing, bones crunching, her human skin replaced with the lupine one.

My gaze darted to Alice, and despite looking scared at holding a wolf's paw, she didn't look surprised. She looked downright determined. She dropped Sanye's paw, took a deep breath, and—

Shifted into a tabby cat.

Holy. *SHIT*.

Atticus cursed and Ranger laughed.

The girls darted for the door, and I took that as our cue to leave.

CHAPTER
TWENTY-FIVE
~ALICE~

Like she wanted a Wolf breathing down her neck while she was driving—or doing anything else.

— ANNE BISHOP

O MG I was a freaking CAT.

Thoughts pelted through my brain faster than a firefly signaling for sex.

I could shift.

I'd shifted in front of Ford.

I'd shifted in front of Lucky Jansen and his goons. Sanye. Various Boone brothers.

I mean, they were werewolves, so they likely wouldn't spill my big secret, but this was the kind of news that had government agencies knocking on your door in the movies.

Was there an Area 51 for shapeshifters?

Would I disappear into some weird, illegal, and highly subterranean government laboratory?

Or a pet farm?

An illegal breeding operation like I'd read about in a paranormal romance that now seemed less sexy and more ominous?

After what felt like an eternity of running past giant-sized humans, out the barn (which smelled strongly of cow poop despite Lucky's man-cave redeco-rating), and then over the gravel to the truck, I'd spotted the trucks. Could Sanye drive as a wolf? How fast could she shift?

These were questions for later. Right now, there was an ever-growing commotion, the ground vibrating beneath booted feet behind us. I zoomed toward Sanye's truck. The gravel was rough and uncomfortable beneath my paws, but fear was an awesome motivator. I sprinted even faster than Emperor Meowpatine toward a bowl of tuna fish water. Ranger bolted past me, popped the truck door, and climbed in. Sanye leaped over him and into the front seat.

Ranger turned the key and looked down at me. "Come on, kitty."

The engine roared, the humans behind me were yelling, and for a second I considered bolting underneath the truck. It looked dark and safe, a spot where I could peer out at this whacked-out world and plot world domination. NO. I was still me, wasn't I? My perception of the world was simply shifted.

Literally.

Ranger reached down, patting the side of the seat. "Here, kitty, kitty. We got to get going."

I turned my head. He wasn't wrong. Ford and Atticus spilled out into the driveway, running hard. It was too bad I was mad at Ford because he looked spectacular, all grim and focused, his muscles bunching as he ran. Really, he should have shifted into a lion and not a wolf. God had missed an opportunity there. Behind him was a crowd of people, all hooting and hollering, with a generous amount of cursing thrown in. A gun might have been brandished.

I hissed; Sanye growled; Ranger cursed.

Convinced, I leapt for the truck and had to scramble, digging my claws into whatever I could grab. I landed on Ranger's thigh and he did some cursing of his own as I bolted across his lap to sit beside Sanye.

Ranger shut the truck door quickly, snapped his seat belt on, and then accelerated like a rocket headed for the moon.

I could not sit still.

I bounced around the truck cab, poking my nose under the seat, beneath Ranger's legs, into the deliciously dark and pungent space between the seats and the back wall of the cab. Sanye had tossed her trash here! I batted a wadded-up receipt, gave an old paper cup a quick lick. Not bad!

"I believe we may have a scientific conundrum on our hands," Ranger said, as if Sanye was in any condition to be answering him back. "And I imagine that since Alice hasn't shifted before—she hasn't, has she?—she might need more guidance than I can provide."

Sanye yipped and poked her nose over the seat to look at me. I had no idea what she was trying to communicate.

"Perhaps you could convince your friend to come out here and buckle up," Ranger suggested.

Another yip from Sanye, higher pitched as the truck took a switchback at high speed. I knew it was time for me to come out.

Possibly, to assume the crash position.

The truck rocked ominously, as Ranger picked up speed.

I popped out, only semi-voluntarily, and dug in next to Sanye. Ranger leveled a glare at me. "Do not scratch my upholstery."

As if that mattered. I narrowed my eyes at him.

He muttered something and then gave the road his full attention. Good boy. My nose twitched. Ranger's soap was stinky.

To distract myself, I worked my way around Sanye—solid, a silvery gray, and fluffy—until I could set my paws on the windowsill and look out.

I'd thought cats were color-blind, but that turned out to be untrue. Sure, there was a whole lot of grey, but I saw blues and greens, as well. Up close, I might have been looking through a microscope, so clear were the details of the fuzz caught in the window track, the small fly hanging on for dear life to the side mirror, the leaf stuck to the glass. The rest of the world, however, was unexpectedly fuzzy. Trees whipped by in a blur, the road spooling away in a soft, dark river.

The next ten minutes were a blur as I tried to anchor myself—Ranger would have to get over himself and his precious upholstery—as we flew down the mountain roads at a speed that violated several traffic safety laws. We flew through Moonlight Valley at record speed only to brake hard.

When I'd untangled myself from Sanye, I spotted my house through the window. I was home.

Ranger killed the engine and looked at us. "Shift."

As if I took orders from him.

I sniffed.

Apparently wolves were fools. They were related to dogs after all.

Maybe. I'd have to Google that later when I had opposable thumbs and a computer.

Sanye shifted. One minute a wolf rode shotgun next to me, and the next minute Ranger had slapped his hands over his face because Sanye was human, naked, and pissed off in the front seat of her truck.

"Ranger Boone," she snapped.

"Yes?" he mumbled.

"You fix this."

There was an awkward pause, while Ranger gave serious thought to his options. He had a naked woman in the front seat of the motor vehicle he was operating; it was not as if he could just drive to Walmart.

"I will be removing my hands," he announced. "But my eyes will remain closed. I give you my word."

Sanye growled something. She still sounded distinctly wolfy.

Still, Ranger was a gentleman. I'd give him that. He dropped his hands, got his flannel off, and handed it to Sanye. She sniffed, but took it.

I curled up on the seat beside her. Two equally unpleasant thoughts had just suggested themselves to me.

Firstly, I was apparently going to be naked as a jaybird when I shifted. It was typical that I'd been plunged into a situation where I would not look good. This was a bad situation, made worse because Alessandro's truck was parked outside my house. He would not take kindly to my being naked in a motor vehicle belonging to a Boone.

I suspected Ranger had come to the same conclusion.

"Is it safe?" he asked.

"Your eyeballs are safe," Sanye said dryly. "No boobs, no ass, and nothing you wouldn't see at the beach."

"Well, now. Let's just say that one can see quite a lot at the beach. There are topless beaches. Brazilian thongs. White swimsuits with insufficient linings. Perhaps you could be more specific about the sanctity of my eyeballs?"

"Open your eyes," Sanye snapped. "We have a bigger problem."

Ranger cautiously unscrewed his eyes. Really, he was overreacting. Mostly. It would have helped if Ranger had been the sort of man who went in for oversized, lumberjack wear. Instead, his flannel was size-appropriate for him, neatly pressed, and barely skimmed the tops of Sanye's thighs. Barely summed the situation up rather nicely.

I moved on to my second unpleasant thought. Which was that there was only one of Ranger, it was not particularly cold out, and he had not been wearing much in terms of layers.

I eyed his T-shirt. It was a white Hanes made of sturdy cotton and smelling of starch.

It would have to do. I laid a paw on his abdomen and poked.

Ranger looked down at me. "Ford is going to have words with me."

"He'll have to take a number." Sanye clapped her hands. "Shift, Alice. Make it quick because Alessandro will be out any minute now."

This brought us to a third, unexpected, and extremely unpleasant thought.

No one had given me a copy of the secret shifter training manual.

I had no idea how to shift back.

Ranger wrapped one big hand around my middle and lifted me to eye level. I flailed. What on earth was he thinking? This was NOT acceptable. I was not on board with the manhandling. I expressed my displeasure as best I could. I might, in fact, have left some lovely, parallel red lines on Ranger's forearm, but what else could he expect?

"Shift," he ordered.

I wanted to tell him that shifting wasn't like unlocking a car. You couldn't just push the magic button on your key fob. There was no happy beep, no automatic opening in my brain. Or my biology.

I was stuck as a cat.

Sanye peered down at me. "Oh boy."

That was not helpful.

Neither were her subsequent suggestions about opening myself to the universe and inviting it in. She followed this with a nugget about thanking my cat for its service and now would be really great.

I agreed, but how did I shift? But it wasn't like I'd taken notes or practiced. Nothing in Aunt Sally's brief letter had prepared me for this. My shift had just kind of happened back there in Lucky's barn. Perhaps it took mortal peril and fear to make me transform?

"Let's think about this logically." Ranger indicated my furry self. "You can figure it out. And we'll help."

Said the man who wasn't stuck inside a cat body.

"Let's go back to the beginning. You remember what you did at Lucky's. What you were thinking about right before you shifted. I always hold an image of my wolf in my head. Maybe you did something real similar."

I let his words roll over me, smooth and calm. He wasn't wrong, either. I had been thinking about what my cat might look like. I'd built a picture in my head—as much as you could in a handful of seconds when you were being threatened with death and other violent acts—and then somehow I'd become that cat I saw.

"So now you remember your human self," Ranger said. "You hold that picture in your head and you walk toward it."

"She might need to run," Sanye volunteered. "We don't have all night, Ranger."

I hissed at her.

Ranger ignored her. "Take a breath. Hold it."

Sanye groaned. "This is not the time for yoga. We need to move it."

"And let it out," Ranger continued. "See your human side. Embrace it. Love it."

"SHIFT," Sanye bellowed. "RIGHT GODDAMNED NOW."

I startled. The images in my brain got all mixed up, flying every which way like popcorn kernels in my popcorn maker. One moment I was my cat me, and then the next I was falling forward, sliding into my human form. It felt horribly like pulling off that latex bodysuit Sanye had talked me into last Halloween. The bodysuit had been comfortable until I'd tried to remove it and then it had clung and clung until...

POP. I expanded, shooting out of my cat skin. The change didn't hurt but it sure felt weird. And then it got weirder still because I was sprawled on top of Ranger Boone.

And I was naked.

I scrambled off him. "Sorry, sorry!"

Eyes screwed shut, he whipped his T-shirt over his head and held it out. I yanked it on.

The front door banged.

Alessandro stood on my front porch, hands braced on his hips, legs apart. He did not look happy.

"Maybe we should keep driving?" Sanye suggested.

It wasn't the worst suggestion.

"I promised my brothers that I would see you ladies home," Ranger argued.

"Do we tell Alessandro about the shifting?" I whispered frantically. "Does he know?"

Ranger shook his head slowly. "He catches dogs for a living. He is not Team Wolf."

I was pretty sure Alessandro had trapped more than a few feral cats, too.

Oh, God. I was not prepared to end up in a cage in the back of a truck belonging to my third cousin twice removed.

It was time to face the music.

And to lie like I'd never lied before.

"Get out," I told Sanye. "I'll be right behind you. Ranger, you might want to head on back to your place."

"I will see you to your door," he said stubbornly.

Ugh. Whatever. Sanye got out and I dismounted from the truck as gracefully as I could. Being pantsless was a challenge I was not prepared to face.

Alessandro looked at us. His mouth worked.

"So," I said. "Funny story."

"Where are your pants?" he roared. "And why is there a half-naked Boone with you?"

I decided right then that he did not need to know that this was not my first naked Boone, not by a long shot.

CHAPTER
TWENTY-SIX
~FORD~

You're in my every breath and every thought, intertwined so deep inside me that love's not a strong enough word—you have my devotion, your name branded on my soul, my wolf yours to command. A hundred years? It'll never be enough. I want eternity.

— ANGELA KNIGHT

Sanye had lit out of her daddy's barn as if her tail was on fire, Alice right behind her. The ladies had had an advantage, being on four paws and low to the ground.

We'd followed almost as fast, tearing through the barn, the backyard, and around the house. The thunderstorm that had been promising all evening had been pelting down rain.

I kept replaying our escape—because that was what it had been—in my head. The moment Alice had shifted.

The tabby cat bolting away from me.

The way Cat Alice—*my* Alice—had paused in the driveway. Maybe she hadn't like the rain. Maybe she couldn't remember where Sanye had parked. Maybe—

Maybe she was waiting for us, blockhead.

Had Alice always been able to shift? Why hadn't I known this? Did she

269

like being a part-time cat? My brain twisted itself into more knots than a macramé project. I did not know what to think.

Snooze, you lose. My wolf sounded grumpy.

Or maybe he was just carsick because I was not giving the switchbacks anywhere near the sort of respect they merited. No, I was attempting to throw myself—along with my truck and its occupants—straight down the side of the mountain.

Ranger peeled off after a bit, taking the road that led to Alice's place. Ours was in the other direction. I should follow her, shouldn't I?

But what if Lucky followed me?

Should I decoy him? Stop and make a stand? What was the right thing to do here?

"Ford, let her go. There's no time for shilly-shallying, and Alice has Sanye and Ranger to keep her safe. We gotta split up in case we're being followed."

I was not convinced. Not because I didn't have a healthy respect for Sanye's claws and her badass abilities, but because it should be me rescuing Alice. *I* needed to be her knight, keep her safe, hold her in the peace and quiet of our home. But Ranger was hauling ass, almost out of sight.

Muttering a curse, I nodded reluctantly. Atticus was right, and I hated it.

I sped away, vowing never to visit Lucky Jansen's place again.

Twenty minutes later, it was silent as the grave inside my truck, and we were alone on the road.

I kept glancing in my rearview mirror, mostly expecting to see a posse of trucks, bikes, or wolves chasing our asses down the mountain. All I spotted was dust and mud.

By the time we'd hit the main road and were outside Moonlight Valley, I couldn't take it any longer.

"Mav, call Sanye. Confirm they made it back safely."

Maverick held up his phone. "Already did. Alessandro's with them, pissed as heck because they went up that mountain and busted in on the Iron Wolves. Apparently, he thinks that should have been a job for law enforcement and not for pet groomers. He and Alice are arguing 'job description' versus 'girl code' right now."

I blew out a breath. "So she shifted back okay?"

"She must have since she's giving him hell." Atticus frowned at his phone. "Apparently she's mad as a wet hen that she did not get to help Deelie Sue or give her a ride."

"Crap." I met Atticus's eyes in my rearview mirror. "We left Deelie Sue there."

Abandoning Deelie Sue did not sit well with me. Not because I had feelings for her, but because I'd asked her to help me and then hadn't followed up with her. The last message from her phone suggested the Iron Wolves knew she'd been planning on betraying their pack and someone had taken steps. I was not okay with leaving her unprotected and at risk. That was shades of our momma all over again.

Maverick cursed and thumbed his phone. "I'll call in a few favors. Get someone to go up there and get her out. If she's actually there."

"You think she double-crossed us? Sold us out?"

Maverick hesitated. "Maybe?"

"Don't think that." But the thought was out there.

Despite Deelie Sue's unabashed love of making money and looking out for number one, she was not—and would never be—a liar. Or deeply unethical (although very minor, ever so slight crossings of ethical boundaries might occur when she did her taxes or talked up a car she was selling). I decided I believed this whole-heartedly.

So leaving her behind, instead of fighting to bring her with us, was on me, although I had been out of options back at Lucky's.

I turned possible scenarios over in my head for the next few miles and finally decided I could live with outsourcing this particular rescue.

I gave Maverick a nod in the rearview mirror. "Okay then. Please let me know when she's safe."

Atticus groaned. "Do we want to know what Ranger saw on May fourteenth?"

That one was easier to answer. "No. No, we do not."

No one had anything else to say for a while after that. My thoughts turned back to Alice like a compass pointing true north.

I needed to go to her. Explain what I was feeling and why I'd done what I'd done. My instincts urged me to wrap my arms around her and carry her away.

We could go to my cabin, and I could lock her up there until we'd sorted out everything between us. That worked in books and in the movies, right? I wanted Alice to look at me with love again. Not anger and pain.

God help me, I needed a plan before I showed up in her life.

"You want to drop us off so you can head over to Alice's?"

271

I glanced back at Maverick and shook my head. "No."

"Why the hell not?"

I had no answer for this.

I've got nothing.

"I agree with Maverick," Atticus said, then added, "Which is a miracle."

When I didn't say anything, Maverick groaned. "Look. That woman loves you. I saw the expression on her face when she spotted you, the fear in her eyes when you volunteered to fight for her."

"I need to come up with a plan. I've got nothing. I cannot go to her empty-handed." This was the truth. "I need—"

Maverick cut me off. "Those last two words right there are your problem. It's not about what you need. It's about what *she* needs. What *the two of you* need. You can't wait until you have a plan for every single moment of your life. You'll spend all your time planning and none of it living. If you love her, you go after her. You go *right now*. Not tomorrow."

"If not now, then when?" Atticus sang out from the backseat.

He makes a good point, my wolf chimed in.

I shot Maverick a glance. He was doing some waiting on his own woman.

He flipped me the bird and then turned in his seat so he could see my face. "Alice is all in on loving you. You don't want to lose that, believe me. You can figure out the freaky cat and wolf shit later. You go now."

* * *

I considered standing outside Alice's bedroom window and singing some soulful ballad until she came out (I was tone deaf).

Writing a message in carnations (Moonlight Valley did not have a flower shop).

Tossing pebbles at her window.

Buying a carrier pigeon farm and sending birds with love letters every day until I was forgiven.

Truth was, I had no plan. I didn't even have an idea of what I was doing, other than showing up and hoping Alice would give me a chance to explain what I felt for her.

This kind of reckless, impulsive behavior was out of character. I might fail or make her ten times madder than she was already, true. But Atticus's words had resonated when he'd said *if not now, then when?*

My brother was not wrong.

The last time I'd made a spur-of-the-moment, impulsive decision, I'd kissed Alice Aymes after she'd literally fallen into my arms.

Maybe we should be asking the Universe for a sign.

I jogged down the road from our house to Alice's tiny house—with no plan, no forethought, no practice run in front of the bathroom mirror—certain of one thing and one thing only. It had been a horrible, awful day, and I needed to see her.

I needed to fix our relationship before another day had passed and she'd had yet more time to consider the angry words we'd exchanged and decide that living a Ford-free, wolf-free life was in her best interest.

The Little Love Den was lit up like a pink cupcake by the moon. All the lights were off inside, but her car and one of the cats were out front. The cat bristled angrily at me as I came to a halt.

About time, it said.

The words were slightly tinny and fuzzy around the edges, like the voice was coming from far, far away except that it was inside my head.

This was…

Unnatural, my wolf suggested. **Could be you're bonkers. Everyone knows cats are unstable, evil dictators. We should make a strategic retreat.**

The cat sniffed. *Genghis Khat. My name is Genghis Khat. I have illustrious ancestors.*

My wolf was silent. Neither of us wanted to find out what talents Genghis Khat might have inherited from his ancestor.

You may feed me, Genghis Khat announced. He stalked away, tail flicking, and disappeared through the cat door.

I walked around the house, collecting a few pebbles—and doubts—and stopping underneath her window. I was going with the pebble plan as the cats might interpret the carrier pigeons as a DoorDash dinner delivery.

The first pebble made a clinking sound, and I winced a little. If I damaged her window, she'd be upset. It took three more tries though before the window opened.

Alice stuck her head out, her lopsided bun catching on the frame and listing to the side. She frowned, inspecting the glass.

Now would be good, my wolf said.

He was right. I cupped my hands to my mouth and whisper-shouted, "Alice!"

There was a silent pause that I should have filled up with words. I wondered whether it was too late to whip out my phone and google something by Shakespeare.

There was that famous balcony scene, right? Although I seemed to recall it had not ended happily. And had involved prepubescent teenagers with no emotional maturity. Surely the Bard had written something happy and age appropriate?

"Ford?" Alice sounded confused. She looked around, but I'd apparently managed to park myself in her blind spot. My romantic gesture was off to a great start.

"It's me. I'm here."

She looked for me in a couple hardwood trees, then twisted to look up. I resisted the urge to tell her that, as I was not Santa Claus, I would not be lurking on her roof.

But we could ask her if she wants to be on our naughty list.

I ignored my wolf because I'd realized a flaw in my approach. I'd figured I'd wake her up and we'd talk. Maybe I'd romantically climb up a tree so we could talk face to face. I'd sit on a branch and she'd lean out the window. There would be moonbeams and shit. Possibly poetry, if I could surreptitiously search for it on my phone.

Except that when I'd removed that enormous, dead pine tree from on top of her Aunt Sally's trailer, I'd been a responsible arborist and had cut back the trees all around her new cottage. If I wanted to sit in a tree outside her window, I'd have to wait fifty, maybe a hundred years.

Real smart.

"Can I come up? Or can you come down?"

I should have brought my ladder.

"What makes you think that I ever want to see you again?" She glared down at me. "You are something else. After tonight, I would be justified in never, ever wanting to see another Boone again."

I didn't answer because a plan had suddenly popped into my mind. I'd built a little sloping roof that covered the wraparound porch like a peplum on a shirt. If I jumped, I could...

I did and snagged the edge of the roof, pulling myself upward.

"Are you scaling my *house*? Are you delusional? You are not Spiderman,

Ford Boone! You are going to kill yourself, and you've already used up all your luck for the day."

"Hush, I'm coming for you." I pulled myself up onto the porch roof. My boots rang on the tin, and three inquisitive, furry faces popped into view at the bottom of the porch.

Alice carried on haranguing me as I got myself across the roof. She was still grousing when I reached her window.

"...are you an adrenaline junkie? Do you have a death wish? You are not going to need to save for retirement if you keep this up. Have you updated your beneficiaries? You need to think about your safety..."

I climbed in.

She shut up.

For a millisecond.

Then she started in again, hypothesizing that I must have high-deductible medical insurance and had already met my deductive for the year.

This was not what I wanted to be discussing with her, not at all.

"Can I kiss you?" I blurted out.

Maybe I did have a death wish, because Alice stared at me for a long moment. It got horribly silent, and I found that I missed hearing her every thought (even if some of them did *not* paint me in a good light).

I didn't know what to say, except the truth.

"I would really, really like to kiss you right now."

And later, tomorrow, and forever, but I was starting small and working my way up.

"Why?" she asked finally.

And I...well, I gave her my second piece of truth.

"Because I desperately want to. And because I would like to verify for myself that every amazing, aggravating, independent, fierce inch of you is unharmed."

"So, a safety check?"

That only covered a small fraction of what I was feeling, but Alice didn't wait for my answer.

She kissed me. A small smack of a kiss against the corner of my mouth. Another kiss on my lips. A veritable hail of kisses on my cheek, my ear, and anywhere else she could reach.

It was only fair to reciprocate.

"Did you miss me?" My words were muted because my mouth was pressed against her throat, and talking through kisses was a muffled business.

Rather than using her words, Alice wrapped herself around me and kissed me back firmly. My fingers stroked up underneath her citizen science T-shirt and hers fisted in my flannel.

I loved her soft skin, the curves and the lines of her, the delicious heat and warmth beneath my hands. She did not hold back: she went up in *flames* everywhere I touched. My thoughts shifted from groveling to touching her everywhere.

I loved how she welcomed me so openly, how she arched into my touch, making small, greedy sounds, as if being with me was all-consuming.

But then she stiffened and slapped my hand away. Twisting in my arms, she popped herself out like a cork from a bottle and landed across the room from me. On the bright side, the room was the size of a closet (because *tiny* house). On the downside, she'd put the bed between us. She stared at me, accusation in her eyes,

"Why are you here?" She propped her hands on her hips.

"We didn't finish talking earlier."

"When?"

"Before now."

Her eyes narrowed. "Be specific, Ford. Do you mean when you abandoned me in the middle of the night at your cabin? Or earlier today when we were held hostage by a pack of hostile wolves?"

I had done her wrong at my cabin, but the danger I'd put her in at Jansen's compound was ten times worse.

"Yes," I managed through my self-hatred. "I want to apologize for leaving you in the cabin and running off. I'm sorry. It was wrong and it was shitty."

"And you want to discuss it right now? After midnight? I have Mace. And a baseball bat."

"Good." I never wanted her to be in danger again.

She chewed on that, then blurted out, "Deelie Sue showed me her phone. She claimed you were calling her because you had realized that you were in love with her. That you wanted a second chance."

"Deelie Sue and I have never been in love. We were…friends with bene-fits." Right now, no benefits were coming to mind. "I called things off when you came back to town because I wanted you and me to be together."

"All right." Alice wrapped her arms around her middle. "All righty. I told her that I was not worried about the two of you taking back up together again.

"But I don't understand. Why did you go to Wheels of Good Fortune? Were you really going to ask her to make a secret video of Lucky shifting into his wolf form in public?"

I tensed. This was not public knowledge. "Who told you that?"

"The wolves—those *were* wolves, right?—at Lucky's place were talking about it. They knew you were going to use her to get at Piston. She called me earlier tonight and pretended to be in trouble."

"Deelie Sue lied to you tonight?"

"Yes. Well, she said she needed a ride home, to get away from the Iron Wolves. She acted like she was in a whole mess of trouble, and then she wasn't even there when I showed up. Sanye's daddy said it was a setup, a way to get you to come out to his place."

"That was not okay, and I apologize," I said, when her explanation finally petered out.

We should go back up there. Crack some heads. Make our point.

"Why are you sorry?"

"For sucking you into my mess with the Iron Wolves. For endangering you."

She frowned. "None of that is on you. In fact, it's mostly a Deelie Sue thing. But I am missing some pieces. Most of that conversation went right over my head, but I want to understand. Can you fill in the gaps for me?"

I sucked in a deep breath, returning her frown with my own. I owed her the truth, but there were parts I was not allowed to tell. There were wolf secrets here.

"You won't." She sounded disappointed. "You don't trust me."

"I can't. No," I corrected. "I shouldn't. Some of it isn't my story to tell, and there are rules I'm supposed to abide by. Shifter rules, although I guess you're a shifter, too."

"Part," she said. And I thought I heard her mutter something about it being *a long story* and *not speaking ill of the dead.*

"I do trust you. The Iron Wolves have been blackmailing Atticus and me, demanding we join their pack and be their enforcers. We've been running out the clock, and I thought that pulling Deelie Sue in might help.

"She wasn't picking up my calls, though, so Atticus and I went to see her at Wheels of Good Fortune. She agreed to help. As a favor."

"What did the Iron Wolves have on you?" Alice chewed on her bottom lip.

I scrubbed a hand over my head, knowing this was not going to come out right. "That's not something I can share. It was about Maverick. Not me, not Atticus. Just Maverick. We can ask him if he'll tell you."

Her face lightened. She'd lived in Moonlight Valley long enough to have heard the stories about my oldest brother and his wild child days when he'd run with the Iron Wolves. I was sure she was attributing all sorts of felonies to him. It was his problem.

"So we went out there tonight," I continued, "to tell the Iron Wolves that we would not be acquiescing to their demands."

"And Deelie Sue double-crossed you."

I shrugged. "I honestly don't think so. I think she's sure interested in dating Lucky, which is not who I would choose to step out with, but I don't know how the Iron Wolves found out we were planning to spit in their face, so to speak. We had a couple of aces up our sleeve that they did not see coming, and now there's some bad blood between us all."

"Do you think she's okay?"

I nodded. "I do. Plus, Maverick's checking on her."

"Good," Alice said softly. "No one should get left behind."

"I would never lie to you, Alice. Not about this, not about how I...feel."

"You are honest to a fault, Ford Boone."

My heart ached fit to break. She was almost close enough to touch, to wrap myself around, and yet she felt distant.

That was my fault.

She'd offered me her heart once, and I'd refused it.

"Well." She looked down at her feet. "I appreciate the explanation. You can use the front door to let yourself out."

Leaving was the last thing I wanted to do. The first thing I wanted to do was close the distance between us. There were likely words or explanations, acts or deeds, that would have done the trick. I did not know what they were.

I'd come here without a plan, so all I could go with were my instinct and the words that were bubbling up in my throat, coming from deep inside my heart and—I suspected—my soul.

"I believe in being responsible. I look out for my family; I keep my word. I don't ever take what I haven't earned. No handouts or free rides, and absolutely nothing without permission."

Her eyes shot up to mine. "Consent's important, although that doesn't sound like a bedroom question. But I have a question for you."

"Shoot," I said.

"If you had all the money and I had none and we were together, would you think I was taking a handout from you? Getting a free ride? And not a gift?"

This felt like a trick question. "Whatever I have is yours."

"And vice versa. Plus, I'm the one who wants to live in Nashville, so how I ask you to pay for—"

"Hush a minute?"

Alice frowned at me but nodded—I figured I had sixty seconds and no more.

"I want to…" No. That word—*want*—wasn't correct. "I *need* to be with you. To go with you. And that's what I'm fixing to do, if you'll have me.

"You've been my one and only ever since our first stupid prank. I thought that I should be courting you, taking things slow. I had a whole plan worked out in my head, one that guaranteed that every step in our relationship would be successful. I hadn't thought about your dreams. Or that you might have a different vision for our future."

"Ford—"

"So I went back to the drawing board. I thought up something new. I figured that if I set a twelve-month limit on our being together, then my heart would be safe. I wouldn't, *couldn't*, lose it in a year. I could control the outcome, make sure it was what I expected even if it wasn't what I wanted it to be.

"You were right about me. I held back. I was not all in. *I* was the one who was looking to leave the whole time we were dating, looking for an excuse to end things sooner because I already knew that I would never be able to walk away *later*."

Alice wrapped her arms around herself, as if she were holding herself back, making herself wait. I hated that I'd made her second-guess her feelings, made her feel less than safe putting her heart into my hands.

"We don't have to be over," she said. "Not now, not in twelve months. I feel selfish, though, asking you to leave Moonlight Valley when your family is here."

I needed to touch her so badly. I fisted my hands by my side.

If not now, then when, you fool?

The wolf was right. I crossed to Alice, holding out my hands, opening

279

my arms because I needed the sweet warmth of her against me. "You did ask. And I'm saying yes, thank you. I couldn't have asked you to stay here, and I sure as hell wouldn't have invited myself along. But since you're asking…"

Alice's eyes widened, and her lips tightened as if she was holding in words. I closed my hands around hers, pulling her gently toward me, erasing all the awful, unwanted space between us. I was never letting go of her again.

"Since you asked, and since I love you, and if your feelings haven't changed—"

"Come with me!"

I folded my girl into my arms, brushing a kiss over the top of her head, and —even though we did need a plan for this, and I had no idea how to do this other than to let go and trust Alice to catch me—I said, "I will. I'm all yours."

"But what about your family business? And your brothers?"

"We'll work something out. Atticus and Ranger said I should go for it, that I was a fool to turn you down."

"I could try an internet business. Or opening a place here."

"That," I whispered against her hair, "was not your dream, Alice Aymes. I am not compromising your dreams. Or your heart."

Just your body.

"But what about what you want?"

"You. I want you. You're my everything. When I think about my future, I see you."

I wasn't entirely reformed, though. I wanted her so badly, so I kissed her. I put everything I hadn't said yet into that kiss, sliding my hands under her T-shirt and along her back to hold her closer. I pulled her body tight against mine, my hips pressed against her belly, my hands moving lower because my newest plan called for me to strip her panties right off her body.

She moaned a song into my mouth when my hand came back, cupping her core and parting her with my fingers. She was hot and sweet and I wanted her underneath me, me inside her, marking her as mine.

"I won't give you my mating bite," I promised her when we broke apart, panting. "Not yet. Maybe in a year. Maybe two. Someday when we're both ready. But for tonight—"

She exhaled. Maybe I heard my name.

I cupped my free hand around her breast, teasing and shaping the delicate weight. My other hand got busy loving her, stroking her center.

"I want you," I growled. No more poetry, no grand declarations, were left in me. It was me and the woman I loved with all my heart.

She rocked against my hand. "Was this your master plan all along?"

"My only plan is to love you," I promised, bending down to kiss her.

Her gorgeous mouth slanted up in a naughty smile. "Good idea. Let me make some suggestions."

She ran her hand down my shoulder, over my chest, and straight to the front of my jeans. And then she cupped me, rubbing my hard length through my jeans with her palm.

This was fun, but I wanted more. I wanted to be balls deep inside her, making her mine. I backed us up until her knees hit the bed and then I took us both down. She stared up at me with excited, hopeful eyes as I braced my arms on either side of her pretty face.

"Get naked," I suggested, parting her legs. "And make some room for me."

I rolled off her long enough to strip off my shirts, toe off my boots, and unbutton my jeans. I shoved them down my legs and left them on her floor while she watched me. She made me feel like a million dollars and more.

With Alice, I felt like I was *enough*.

Alice pulled her T-shirt over her head and tossed it on top of my pants. Then she opened her arms for me, and she whispered, "Ford, you come and court me now."

I climbed on top of her, opening her up and making room for myself, stroking her until her need matched mine, and then I whispered back, "With your permission, I'd like to court you hard all night long."

* * *

"Penny for your thoughts?"

I stared up at Alice's ceiling, through the skylight I'd put in for her, and out at the moon in the night sky. We'd been curled up together, lying here in happy silence for long enough that we should have been asleep. I'd spent the last three hours courting her hard, and both my wolf and I were finally satisfied.

Alice was, too, but she couldn't or wouldn't keep her hands to herself. She kept reaching out to touch me, to run her hands down my arms and along my back, petting and kissing, memorizing every inch of me.

I was not complaining. She could have whatever she wanted, and until she wanted to sleep, I would hold her and love on her.

281

"My Aunt Sally wasn't my aunt," she whispered. "She was my mother."

Before I could process this, she buried her face in my shoulder and started crying. I wrapped her up in my arms. *Listen*, I reminded myself. *Don't fix.*

"She was your mother?"

Alice nodded, pressing her damp face against my throat.

"And she was a shifter?"

Another nod.

"How long have you known?"

"A few days. I found out when I was in Texas," she mumbled.

I muttered a curse, holding her tighter. I should have been there, by her side. I'd been a proud ass.

"I'm sorry you found out alone. I wish I'd been there with you."

Alice shook her head. "In all those years, when I was right here with her, why didn't she say something? She gave me to her sister, kept me at arm's length during the summer, never told me that I was hers and a shifter until it was too late.

"I love my momma and my daddy, but I never felt that close to Aunt Sally. And now I never will. She's gone, and it seems silly to feel so sad."

I kissed her firmly before I answered. "It's not silly. Or wrong. You had two parents who loved you, and your auntie tried to do right by you, even if she got it wrong.

"My father mostly saw us kids as an inconvenience, except for the rare occasions when we could do something for him or reflect well on him. I only wish Momma had been able to get away from him sooner."

Alice wiped her tears on the back of her hand and frowned fiercely. "He was awful, biting her, forcing her to be something she hadn't asked to be. I'd like to hunt him down and make him see how much he missed out on by ignoring you and your brothers."

"It's okay." I combed my fingers through her hair, tucking her against my chest. "But you get to decide for yourself what you want to do about your Aunt Sally. There's no right or wrong—there are only choices."

Alice was my choice. She always would be.

Damn straight, my wolf said sleepily. **Alice is ours.**

As though reading my thoughts—perhaps we were developing a bond like the one I shared with Atticus—she pressed a kiss against my shoulder and said gently, "You know I've decided that I want you, right? You're all mine, Ford Boone."

"I accept."

I felt her smile against my shoulder. "Do you promise? Do you promise that you'll always pick up when I call? That you'll never ignore me and always be here for me?"

"Yes," I responded straightaway. "For forever. Including and up to when you're up there in heaven, although you may have to pull a few strings to get me in."

"No matter what happens?"

"Always. I promise, because I love you, Alice Aymes."

"And I love you, Ford Boone. So very, very much."

THE END

ABOUT THE AUTHOR

New York Times bestselling author Anne Marsh lives in rural North Carolina full of neighbors who will pull you out of a ditch, bring you a truck of mulch, or fix your car just because they can. Who said heroes don't exist in real life?

* * *

Find Anne Marsh online:
Website: https://anne-marsh.com/
Newsletter: https://anne-marsh.com/newsletter/
Twitter: https://twitter.com/anne_marsh
Instagram: https://www.instagram.com/author_anne_marsh/
Facebook: https://www.facebook.com/annemarshauthor/
Pinterest: https://www.pinterest.com/annemarshauthor/

Find Smartypants Romance online:
Website: www.smartypantsromance.com
Facebook: www.facebook.com/smartypantsromance/
Goodreads: www.goodreads.com/smartypantsromance
Twitter: @smartypantsrom
Instagram: @smartypantsromance

Also by Anne Marsh

The Awesome Agency

Bet Me, Mr. Billionaire

Cute Guys with Cuter Dogs (Angel Cay)

The Player

The Beach Baby

The Heartbreaker

Really Funny Harlequins

Have Me

Hold Me

Her Intern

Hot Boss

Hookup

Inked

Royally Hung

Ruled

The Inheritance Test

The True Love Experiment

Lumberjack Men with Hoses (Mister Hotshot)

Hung

The Big One

Swagger

Wolves on Bikes! (The Breed MC)

Wolf's Heart

Wolf's Property

Wolf's Claim
Lone Wolf
Bad Wolf

ALSO BY SMARTYPANTS ROMANCE

Green Valley Chronicles
The Love at First Sight Series

Baking Me Crazy by Karla Sorensen (#1)

Batter of Wits by Karla Sorensen (#2)

Steal My Magnolia by Karla Sorensen (#3)

Worth the Wait by Karla Sorensen (#4)

Fighting For Love Series

Stud Muffin by Jiffy Kate (#1)

Beef Cake by Jiffy Kate (#2)

Eye Candy by Jiffy Kate (#3)

Knock Out by Jiffy Kate (#4)

The Donner Bakery Series

No Whisk, No Reward by Ellie Kay (#1)

Dough You Love Me? By Stacy Travis (#2)

Tough Cookie by Talia Hunter (#3)

Muffin But Trouble by Talia Hunter (#4)

Oh Brother! Series

Crime and Periodicals by Nora Everly (#1)

Carpentry and Cocktails by Nora Everly (#2)

Hotshot and Hospitality by Nora Everly (#3)

Architecture and Artistry by Nora Everly (#4)

Green Valley Heroes Series

Forrest for the Trees by Kilby Blades (#1)

Parks and Provocation by Juliette Cross (#2)

Letter Late Than Never by Lauren Connolly (#3)

Peaches and Dreams by Juliette Cross (#4)

Young Buck by Kilby Blades (#5)

Package Makes Perfect by Lauren Connolly (#6)

The Teachers' Lounge Series

Passing Notes by Nora Everly (#1)

Band Together by Piper Sheldon (#2)

Story of Us Collection

My Story of Us: Zach by Chris Brinkley (#1)

My Story of Us: Thomas by Chris Brinkley (#2)

My Story of Us: Grayson by Chris Brinkley (#3)

Seduction in the City
Cipher Security Series

Code of Conduct by April White (#1)

Code of Honor by April White (#2)

Code of Matrimony by April White (#2.5)

Code of Ethics by April White (#3)

Cipher Office Series

Weight Expectations by M.E. Carter (#1)

Sticking to the Script by Stella Weaver (#2)

Cutie and the Beast by M.E. Carter (#3)

Weights of Wrath by M.E. Carter (#4)

Common Threads Series

Mad About Ewe by Susannah Nix (#1)

Give Love a Chai by Nanxi Wen (#2)

Key Change by Heidi Hutchinson (#3)

Not Since Ewe by Susannah Nix (#4)

Lost Track by Heidi Hutchinson (#5)

Ewe Complete Me by Susannah Nix (#6)

Meet Your Matcha by Nanxi Wen (#7)

All Mixed Up by Heidi Hutchinson (#8)

Bad Habit Book Club Series

Nun Too Soon by Lissa Sharpe (#1)

Educated Romance
Work For It Series

Street Smart by Aly Stiles (#1)

Heart Smart by Emma Lee Jayne (#2)

Book Smart by Amanda Pennington (#3)

Smart Mouth by Emma Lee Jayne (#4)

Play Smart by Aly Stiles (#5)

Look Smart by Aly Stiles (#6)

Smart Move by Amanda Pennington (#7)

Stage Smart by Aly Stiles (#8)

Lessons Learned Series

Under Pressure by Allie Winters (#1)

Not Fooling Anyone by Allie Winters (#2)

Can't Fight It by Allie Winters (#3)

The Vinyl Frontier by Lola West (#4)

Out of this World

Made in the USA
Coppell, TX
26 June 2024

33983793R00177